MW00528603

MUNICHS

by the same author

NINETEEN SEVENTY-FOUR
NINETEEN SEVENTY-SEVEN
NINETEEN EIGHTY
NINETEEN EIGHTY-THREE
GB84
THE DAMNED UTD
TOKYO YEAR ZERO
OCCUPIED CITY
RED OR DEAD
PATIENT X
TOKYO REDUX

MUNICHS

A Novel

DAVID PEACE

W. W. NORTON & COMPANY

Independent Publishers Since 1923

As is typical of historically inspired works of fiction, *Munichs* was written against the background of events that were widely reported in the news at the time of their occurrence. While the names of real people appear, however, the actions and dialogues concerning those persons are products solely of the author's imagination and are not intended to depict actual scenes or to change the fictional nature of the book.

First published in Great Britain in 2024 by Faber & Faber Limited.

For information about permission to reproduce selections from this book, write to Permissions, W. W. Norton & Company, Inc., 500 Fifth Avenue, New York, NY 10110

For information about special discounts for bulk purchases, please contact W. W. Norton Special Sales at specialsales@wwnorton.com or 800-233-4830

Manufacturing by Lake Book Manufacturing

ISBN 978-1-324-08626-0

W. W. Norton & Company, Inc.
500 Fifth Avenue, New York, NY 10110
www.wwnorton.com

W. W. Norton & Company Ltd.
15 Carlisle Street, London W1D 3BS

1 2 3 4 5 6 7 8 9 0

In memory of my father,
Basil Dunford Peace

One by one they were all becoming shades.
Better pass boldly into that other world,
in the full glory of some passion,
than fade and wither dismally with age.

'The Dead', James Joyce

A Premonition

They came out of the tunnel like a ghost train, all in white, into the Highbury afternoon gloom, first Byrne, next Gregg, then Foulkes and Jones, Colman and Edwards, Charlton and Morgans, Taylor, Viollet and Scanlon, with black armbands for the dead, the already dead, on the sleeves of their shirts and off they set, across the field, under the heavy skies and watchful eyes of gods and men, sixty-four thousand men or more, filling the stadium, up to where it touched the sky, that menace of a winter sky that threatened more than rain, more than snow, these men and boys, from all points north and south, east and west, in their Saturday-afternoon best, from West Ham, Chelsea and even Spurs, reluctant fathers with their eager sons who'd said all week, had nagged then pleaded, Dad, Dad, can we go, can we go, please, Dad, please? To see football taught by Matt Busby, his bunch of bouncing Busby Babes, the famous Manchester, Manchester United, those Red Devils at last, in the flesh at last –

Saturday, February 1, 1958:

But not in red, in white today, samite and mystic, across the dark and open ground they ran, on pitch of soil, of grass and paint, to set about their art –

From the start, Tommy Taylor was the mobile hub and Eddie Colman the link. Albert Scanlon, Dennis Viollet, Bobby Charlton and Kenny Morgans flew down the lines of longitude, switching the ball with a swift, flowing precision that left the Arsenal spinning.

First, Morgans cut inside and passed to Duncan Edwards, the man-boy all the London boys had come to see. Duncan

1

cruised forward, with strength and with poise, and from twenty-five yards out – CRACK! – he shot under Jack Kelsey, the Highbury legend, and all those London boys, they turned to their dads and said, Did you see that, Dad? Did you see what he just did?

That was after ten minutes. Twenty minutes later, from a quick clearance by Harry Gregg, Scanlon showed a clean pair of heels to everyone in sight and sprinted seventy yards down the left. Over flashed the centre and tubby Bobby Charlton, his shinpads already pitched away, stockings around his ankles, breath coming in great gasps, somehow crashed the ball home.

But United were not finished. Just on half-time, Scanlon crossed from one wing, Morgans returned the ball from the other and Taylor nipped in to tuck the ball home after the luckless Kelsey could only parry away his first effort. Three–nil.

But no lead is ever big enough, no victory ever certain, and with sixty minutes gone, in three blinks of an eye, Arsenal had wiped out the lead of a coasting, dozing Manchester United with one goal from Herd, then two from Bloomfield to make it three-all.

The wall of noise that now thundered over the stadium summoned up the Arsenal atmosphere of old, when Jack, Hulme, Bastin, James and Lambert were sweeping all before them. But rudely awakened from their European dreams, this young United team did not wilt where others surely would, but showed their mettle and simply said, All right. If you score three, four or five, then we will score four, five or six. And so they set about their work anew.

First Charlton fed Scanlon, who raced away again to cross for Viollet to head United back into the lead again. Next, another quick clearance from Gregg found Colman, who then sent Morgans away. He beat his man, then switched the ball to Taylor. He took the last pass and beat Jack Kelsey from an acute angle. Five–three.

To their credit, Arsenal did not surrender yet. Bowen and Groves continued to push United. They opened the way for Herd, and away went Tapscott to steer a shot inside the far post. But that was the finish.

Breathless in the lengthening shadows, the encroaching night, arm in arm the victors and the vanquished left the field of play. Each knew he had helped to fashion a thing of which to be proud, a match that would live forever, in memory and imagination.

I

STOP ALL THE CLOCKS

1

Bobby's mum was filled with a black worry, ever since she got up, all morning long. More worried than she had ever been in the whole of her life. She knew something was wrong, she just didn't know what, but she could not settle, not settle at all. And so after lunch, when she still didn't feel right, just couldn't shake it off, Cissie put on her coat, her hat and her gloves, and went out into the snow, the thick, heavy snow, and trudged down the backs, round to her friend's, and she knocked on her door –

I thought it'd be you, said her friend, I just knew. So come on, get yourself in, pet, out of the cold.

Cissie stamped the snow off her boots on the step, went into the warm and said, But how did you know?

I just knew, said her friend. Can you not sense there's something in the air, something not right?

Aye, you're right, you're right, said Cissie, but what is it, what's wrong, do you know? Can you tell us? Because it's driving us mad. I just want to know.

Her friend helped Cissie out of her coat, brushed the snow off its collar, then guided Cissie into the back and the kitchen, sat her down in a chair at the table, and said, Well, the one thing I know is that fretting won't help. But a nice cup of tea, of hot, strong, sweet tea, well, that just might. Then we'll put our two silly old wooden heads together and see if we can't think what it is . . .

*

This is it, thought Bill, his head jammed into his chest, crouched right down in his seat and strapped in so tight he could barely breathe, the snow racing past, the engines surging, but not enough, he knew, not surging enough, one, two, three sickening bumps where there should have been none as Bill closed his eyes and thought again, This is it, thrown up, around and into darkness, darkness –

Get the bloody hell out of there, man . . .

Bill could hear a voice, someone knocking on the window. He opened his eyes. Albert Scanlon had been in the seat in front of Bill, but Albert was gone, he'd disappeared, the whole of the right side of the aircraft with him, Roger and the lads who'd been sitting with him all gone, disappeared. There was just sky now, only sky. But Bill was untouched, still strapped into his seat –

What the hell are you doing in there?

Bill turned to the window, saw a man with a tiny fire extinguisher in his hand banging on the window, yelling at Bill, Get out, man, get out!

*

Harry thought he was dead. They all must be dead. That this was the end. He'd never see his wife, his daughter, his mother and his father, his brothers and his sister again. That this was death: one second light and noise, the next dark and still. In a country from which he could never return, a language he would never learn. The only sound the sound of hissing, like snakes hissing, hissing in the dark. His mouth full of salt, the taste of salt. He did not dare to raise his hand, to touch the crack across his head. The top of his head taken clean off, like a hard-boiled egg, sheared straight off, and left for dead, without his head. That this was death, his end. But just above him, to the right of him, then he saw the light, a shaft of light, streaming down on him, calling out to him, Harry, Harry, come on, Harry, and he realised he was lying on his side, still buckled in his seat. He reached down, unfastened the belt, and he started to crawl up, up towards the light, the light coming from a hole. He reached the hole, his head out of the hole, he looked down on the ground below and he froze: Bert Whalley, the youth-team coach, was lying in the dirty black slush in his bright blue cardigan, his eyes open, looking up at Harry, staring back up at Harry. There was not a scratch on Bert, but Harry knew he was dead, that Bert was dead. Harry took a step back. He kicked at the hole, made the hole bigger, then he dropped down through the hole, onto the ground. The engine to his left was burning, the rest of the wing gone. Maybe everyone was dead, everyone but him. No, that couldn't be right. He could hear voices, in the distance, could see five people running away, away through the snow. They were shouting, shouting at him, Run, man, run!

*

Bill didn't need telling twice, but when he tried to get up to get out, he couldn't get up to get out. He was trapped in his seat, still wearing his strap. He unbuckled the belt as fast as he could, then clambered out through a serrated hole in the side of the plane, careering past shards of twisted, burning metal, certain the plane was going to blow, its engines explode at any moment, in any second, blown to kingdom come, running as fast as he could through the thick, wet snow, but never touching the snow, his feet never touching the ground, just sprinting as fast as he could, away from the plane, from kingdom come, running for dear life, dear life.

*

Run, you stupid bastard, run! It's going to explode!

The captain had appeared from around the side of the cockpit. He had a small fire extinguisher in one hand, waving at Harry with the other, yelling at Harry, telling him, ordering him to run, man, run. Then he disappeared again, back around to the front of the cockpit, and Harry would have run, was about to run, but then amid the crackle of the fire, the hissing in the air, the shouting in the distance, Harry heard a cry, a kiddie crying, and Harry shouted at the people running away through the snow, the figures disappearing in the distance, Come back, you bastards, come back! There's people still alive in here!

But they didn't come back, they kept going, and in anger and in rage, Harry cursed them. He cursed them as he climbed and he crawled his way back inside the aircraft, scrabbling through the darkness, thinking of his daughter, his own daughter, that someone would do the same for his daughter, go back for his daughter –

He felt a coat, a tiny coat in his hand, in the darkness, afraid of what he would find as he lifted the child's coat, but there was nothing there, under the coat. He heard another cry, coming from further back. He crawled, he clambered deeper into the wreckage, towards the cries, towards the child, and he found the child, the tiny child, pinned under a pile of debris. He cleared away the debris, he freed the child, lifted up the baby and held it in his arms. Then Harry began to crawl again, back over the debris, through the wreckage and out of the aircraft, with the child in his arms, and when Harry came out of the darkness, back into the light again, the kiddie in his arms, pinned to his chest, he headed in the direction of the people in the distance, tried to catch them up, calling for them to stop, to wait, to take the child from him –

The radio operator stopped running, turned and came back towards him. Harry handed the kiddie to him and said, There's people still alive in there.

The radio operator nodded, took the child from Harry, then he turned and began to walk away again, the baby in his arms, pressed to his chest.

But Harry didn't stand and watch him go. Harry went back to the aircraft, back inside again he went, found a woman under another pile of wreckage, in a terrible state, an awful gaping wound to her face, the mother of the child, and Harry had to push her out of the wreckage with his own legs, her legs both twisted and broken, then to drag her clear of what was left of the aircraft –

He still could not understand what had happened to the aircraft, how it could be so utterly destroyed, whole sections disappeared. But back again, inside he went, through the tangled, twisted hell, searching for survivors, calling out to his pals, his best pal –

Blanchy! Blanchy?

Harry came across Ray Wood in his big orange sweater, but Harry couldn't shift him, couldn't get him to move an inch. He found Albert Scanlon nearby and he was almost sick was Harry, the injuries Albert had, he struggled not to throw up did Harry as he tried to budge him, but Scanny wouldn't budge either, and Harry was sure he was dead, both of them dead, Albert and Ray, and Bobby Charlton and Dennis Viollet, too. They were still strapped in their seats, hanging half in, half out of what was left of the plane, not a mark on Bobby and not much wrong with Dennis, but Harry couldn't rouse them, he was sure they were dead, but he grabbed them by the waistbands of their trousers and dragged them through the slush and the snow, still in their seats, away from the aircraft, away from the flames, and then back again went Harry, back around the aircraft, searching, calling out for Blanchy! Blanchy . . . ?

*

Frank lay trapped in a tangle of metal, watching flakes of ice fall through a gap where only seconds, less than a minute before, had been the tail of the plane. He didn't know why, but Frank was thinking about the crash at Ringway the year before, in March it was, when a British European Airways flight from Amsterdam had crashed as it came in to land. It was a Viscount aircraft, and about a mile from the runway, it made a sudden right turn, at such a steep downward angle that its right wingtip had touched the ground. The plane broke up, burst into flames and crashed into a house on Shadow Moss Road, killing a mother and her baby inside the house and all on board, fifteen passengers and five crew. The chap whose house it was in Wythenshawe, who had lost his wife and son, he was a former fireman at Ringway Airport, and only the year before, he had launched a petition to highlight the dangers of low-flying aircraft. But when it happened, Frank remembered wondering what flashed through folk's minds in those last fatal few seconds before injury or death struck them down. Well, now he knew, he thought, watching the ice flakes fall down from the dull grey sky onto the twisted tangle of carnage and chaos around him, this was what it was like, and it was a bloody silly way to die, and Frank closed his eyes, a very silly way to die, and stepped into the darkness.

*

When Bobby opened his eyes, the first thing he saw was the sky, the big, grey, dirty sky looking down on him, big black and white flakes of snow falling down on him. The taste of smoke, of dirt, of blood in his mouth. He closed his mouth, tried to turn his head, but Christ, it hurt. His whole body, from his head down to his toes. It bloody ached, but most of all his head, staring back up at the sky, flat on his back in the snow, still strapped to his seat, his seat from the plane. He closed his eyes. He'd been looking out of the window, watching the world bounce by, then there'd been that almighty thump, the harsh grind of metal on metal, then the lights went out, everything black.

*

Bill stopped, stopped running. He was out of breath, bent double and panting. He caught his breath, then turned to look around, look back, and Bill could not believe his eyes, the sight that met his eyes. The aircraft had been sheared in half, was now just two great, jagged, twisted masses of smouldering, steaming metal, burning bushes and fuel drums scattered here and there. The back end of the plane looked to have speared a house and some trucks, looming over them the Union Jack, blazing away on the tail, the pitch of the fire in the air, piercing the air. But worse, worse yet were the bodies strewn in a neat and ordered line, amid the carnage and disorder, all present and correct in pools of slush, of dirty slush. Bill started back towards them, walking back towards them, the bodies in the slush, the bodies in a line, in the dirty slush, their neat line, unable to understand, to comprehend how he'd survived, unmarked, unscathed, looking down at his hands, raising his hands, holding them up to his face, his eyes, looking for marks, looking for wounds, wondering how, wondering why, not knowing how, not knowing why. He couldn't understand, just couldn't comprehend, in a daze, an absolute daze, he hadn't a clue, he didn't know why, just couldn't think why.

*

Harry was shocked, he was stunned when he got around to the other side of the aircraft. There was a house with half of its roof torn off, and then further on was another building, in a sort of compound, behind a big wire fence, with the rest of the aircraft sticking up out of the ground of the compound, surrounded by fuel drums, the drums exploding, sending huge plumes of smoke up into the sky. But here, between the burning building and the remains of the plane, Harry found the Boss. He was propped up on his elbows, his hands across chest, rubbing his chest, but his left foot was pointing the wrong way, in the wrong direction, and he was moaning, My legs, my legs.

Hang on, Boss, hang on, said Harry. He found a piece of wreckage, brought it back and propped the Boss up, talking to him, telling him, You're doing all right, Boss. You just hang on now. It's going to be okay –

But Harry could see some bodies further on, about thirty yards off, thought he could hear voices, someone crying out. He stood up, left the Boss, went towards the bodies and found Jackie, Blanchy lying on his back in a pool of melted snow, pinned down by the body of Roger Byrne, Roger draped across Blanchy's waist, not a blemish on him, nor hardly a stitch, in just his vest and underpants, without a mark, a single scratch, just looking up at Harry, staring up at Harry –

I can't move, Harry, cried Blanchy. I can't move. I've broken my back, I know I have. I'm paralysed, I know I am. I can't feel my legs . . .

Harry said, You're okay, you're okay, you're going to be okay. But Harry knew he didn't sound as though he thought Blanchy was going to be okay, that anything was going to be okay, because Harry was looking down at Roger, Roger looking back up at Harry, and later Harry would always regret that he didn't bend down then to close Roger's eyes. But Harry had just noticed Jackie's arm, the lower part of his right arm looked almost severed. He had to try to stop the bleeding, had to try to save his arm. Harry took off his tie to make a tourniquet, but he pulled too tight and the tie tore in two. Frantically, looking here, there, standing up, kneeling down again, Harry searched

14

for something, anything, in the mud and the slush that would do and felt, then saw someone standing over him. He looked up, saw one of the stewardesses from the plane, just standing there, barefoot in the mud and slush, looking down at him, staring down at Roger and at Jackie –

Don't just stand there, screamed Harry. Get me something to tie his arm. But the poor girl didn't move, never moved, she just stood there, barefoot in the snow, staring down, down at the ground, the abysmal ground.

*

Bobby opened his eyes again. He could feel the damp, the wet of the slush soaking through his clothes into his skin, but it didn't bother him, he didn't care. He tried to turn, to move his head again, to look, to see, and saw a house on fire. Men in helmets, running around, screaming words he did not understand, a din of bells and whistles, sirens coming closer from afar. He could see flames flickering under and around the front half of the plane, great plumes of black smoke rising up into the dirty grey sky. He must be about forty yards or so from the plane, Dennis lying next to him, not in his seat but out of his seat, laid out in the slush and the snow and covered in blood. Dennis was not moving, not speaking, but then from somewhere, behind him or to the side of him, Bobby could hear someone groaning, calling out in pain. He thought it was the Boss, sounded like the Boss. Bobby tried to turn, to look, to see, but there was a body, saw a body, a body he knew instantly was dead, knew instantly was a teammate, a beloved mate he'd never name, the injuries he wished he'd never seen, and beside him other bodies, some of the other lads, his mates all in a line, stretched out in the slush and the snow, in a line from the plane. Still and stricken, nobody moved. Bobby felt he was in the middle of a painting, a terrible painting of a terrible landscape, and he turned away, he looked away, heard the sirens coming closer and closed his eyes again. He hadn't seen his best mates, his firmest friends Eddie and David, nor Duncan. He didn't want to see them stretched out in the snow, not moving, wanted to see them alive, hear them say –

Bobby? Bobby? Can you hear me?

Bobby opened his eyes, turned his head again. Dennis was sat upright in the snow –

What's the matter, Bobby, said Dennis. What's gone on? Have we crashed?

It's dreadful, said Bobby, then wished he'd not.

*

Bill took off his jacket, knelt down in the slush beside the Boss, wrapped him in his jacket, took his hand in his own, held it in his own, and said, It's going to be all right.

My side, it's my side, moaned Matt.

Bill looked up, around. He could see Harry close by, blood all over his face. He was running here, running there, like a man possessed: one minute on his knees in prayer, in tears, the next haring here, tearing there, now Harry was kneeling down again, tending to Jackie, Bill thought it was Jackie, could hear him groaning, calling out in pain, in fear. Bill thought it must be only Harry and him who were up and about, walking about, but then, just then, quite suddenly Bill saw Bobby and Dennis get up from their seats as though from a nap, they'd just been having a nap. They walked over towards him and the Boss, looked down at him and the Boss. They didn't speak, didn't say anything, and Bill wasn't sure they knew where they were, who they were.

Bobby began to unbutton his jacket. He took off the jacket, bent down, placed it under the Boss, then stood back up just as a man came running up with a stretcher.

The man dropped the stretcher on the ground beside the Boss and said, Someone's coming for you soon.

And not a minute too bloody soon, thought Bill, and he and Bobby and Dennis began to gently, gently lift the Boss up out of the slush, the dirty black water, and onto the stretcher, ready for the ambulance or whatever help was on its way, Bill wondering what was taking it so long, wishing they would hurry up, just bloody hurry up.

*

Quick! There's someone else here, Pete. Give us a hand.

It looks like Frank Taylor. Yes, it's Frank –

Frank felt himself being raised up, pulled along, taken out of the wreckage. He opened his eyes and saw Ted Ellyard and Pete Howard carrying him, putting him down on the ground, onto a stretcher –

Hold on now, Frank, they were saying. Hold on, help's on its way, just hang on . . .

Frank wanted to speak, but he could not speak, he could hardly breathe, it hurt so much when he did. He just looked up at them, stared up at them, but then they were gone, and he tried to sit up, to see where they had gone, but Harry Gregg was there now, his big hand on his chest, gently pushing him down –

Don't worry, Frank, you're going to be all right, you just lie still now . . .

Frank had a cigarette in his mouth, and he couldn't think how or why he had a cigarette in his mouth. His wife had advised him to stop smoking, and he had stopped, so God only knows what Peggy would say if she saw him like this, thought he'd started up smoking again. She was going to be mad enough as it was about the state of his suit, the mess he'd made of his suit, a new suit, all covered in mud and slush, all soaked in blood. Frank looked down at his feet, saw his right foot, almost severed it was, with blood oozing out, his blood it was, and Frank passed out.

*

The *Daily Mail* had sent three men to Belgrade to cover the game against Red Star: Eric Thompson to write the words; Peter Howard to take the pictures; and Ted Ellyard to wire the pictures back to London. After the crash, after going back to the wreckage, and having done what they could, the best that they could, Pete and Ted were led back to the airport building, where Pete asked to use a telephone. He dialled the *Mail's* offices in London and said, I am phoning the terrible news, the Manchester United plane has crashed at Munich. We were just taking off. We had only just got off the ground. Can you hear me? I am all right. I feel a bit wobbly. Tell my wife I'm okay. Please let her know. We had a pleasant trip from Belgrade. Everyone was happy and laughing and joking because we were coming home and United were in the semi-final. It was snowing when we landed at Munich. Then we went back to the aircraft to continue the flight. I was sitting in the second row of seats on the starboard side with Ted Ellyard. When the pilot tried to take off, there seemed to be some kind of slight fault with the engines. He stopped. Then he tried a second take-off. That didn't seem satisfactory, so he taxied back to the apron to get things checked up. It was on the third take-off that we crashed. I think we were about at the end of the runway. Only a bit above the ground. The plane suddenly appeared to be breaking. Seats started to crumble up. Everything seemed to be falling to pieces. There was a rolling sensation. All sorts of stuff started coming down on top of us. There wasn't time to think. Everybody seemed to be struck dumb. No one cried out. No one spoke. Just a deadly silence for what could only have been seconds. But it seemed a long time.

I can't remember whether there was a bang or not. Everything stopped all at once. I was so dazed that I just scrambled about. Then I found Ted Ellyard and I was still together. We found a hole in the wreckage. We crawled out on our hands and knees. As soon as I got clear, my first instinct, quite frankly, was to run away. I was terrified. But I managed somehow to stay put. I turned around, and there was big Harry Gregg the goalkeeper, who managed to get out. He seemed to be unhurt, too. Anyway, his voice was in working order, for he was shouting, Come on, lads. Let's get stuck in. That got us going. Gregg, Ted Ellyard, the two stewardesses, the radio operator and myself went back into the wreckage. It was a terrible mess. It made me want to shut my eyes. I was conscious of the same deadly silence that was there just before the crash happened. We turned to and did what we could. I saw Captain Thain get hold of a fire extinguisher. He started putting out small fires. I looked around to see if there was anyone I knew. I saw Captain Rayment trapped in the cockpit, but he was got out. A Yugoslav woman passenger and her small baby were pulled clear by the radio operator, Mister Rodgers. I remember getting Frank Taylor, sports writer of the *News Chronicle*, out. He was badly hurt. We also got Ray Wood out and one or two others. Bodies were strewn in the snow for a hundred and fifty yards. I went to look for Eric Thompson. I could see no sign of him. I am just realising what an awful thing that is. It looked as though all those who had been sitting in the forward part of the plane were the lucky ones who got out, those in backwards-facing seats, sitting with their backs to the crew's cabin. Just before it happened, I'd been moaning about our seats being too near the cabin, because it was noisy and there was a bit of vibration. Good job we chose them. It was the part of the plane which got least damage. Everybody had done all they could. Just before I left the wreckage, it suddenly came to me that I had had a camera and that I had taken some pictures before taking off. I looked for my camera but I couldn't find it, there was wreckage all over the place. Part of the engines of the airliner had gone forward a hundred and fifty yards and hit a small house, which burst into flames. But the fuselage did not catch fire. I wish I could say what has happened to the rest of the party other than those I have mentioned. I didn't see Matt Busby after the crash. Now I am thinking about my wife, Pam. She is bound to be worried. Please tell her I'm safe. I think I'm perfectly all right, but they are insisting I go to hospital. I'll have to go now, but the sooner I can get back to Manchester, the better. My mind seems stunned. I wish I could tell you it was not too bad. I'm afraid some have gone for good. But it was all over very quickly. There was no panic. It makes me feel proud of United. These lads are my friends. I have been everywhere with them. I shall never forget this. I'll have to pack up now. They want to drag me off to hospital. See you soon.

*

Slow down, shouted Bill. You're going too bloody fast.

The Volkswagen minibus was bouncing and skidding over the snow, going as fast as it could, away from the plane, Dennis and Bobby sat up front with the driver, Harry and Bill in the middle seats, Jackie and Johnny lying in the back, with the Boss beside them, all on makeshift stretchers, the Boss wrapped in Bill's jacket, holding his chest, mumbling, It's my side, my legs . . .

Bill and Harry reached back over their seats, trying to hold the Boss and the stretcher steady –

I said slow down, will you, shouted Bill again.

But the driver wasn't listening. He just shook his head, repeating, *Krankenhaus, Krankenhaus* . . .

Suddenly, he braked hard and the minibus skidded to a stop, everyone thrown forwards –

What the bloody hell are you doing, shouted Bill.

But the driver ignored him again, opening his door and jumping out into the snow. He went round to the back to open the doors of the minibus. Two men loaded a lady into the back, next to the Boss. She appeared very badly burnt, but Bill and Harry recognised her: it was Missus Miklos, the wife of the travel agent.

The driver got back behind the wheel and set off again, even faster now, swerving this way and that, lurching through the slush and the snow –

Bloody slow down, will you, shouted Bill again. You're going to fucking kill us . . .

Nein, nein, said the driver. *Krankenhaus, nein* . . .

Bill turned back from the Boss in the back. His hand in a fist, he began to punch the back of the head of the driver as hard as he could. Slow. Fucking. Down.

But still the driver didn't stop.

Bill grabbed the driver from behind, his hands around his neck. But still the driver did not stop, did not slow down, swerving one way, skidding another, driving on, faster and faster, into Munich, Dennis and Bobby beside him, staring straight ahead, their eyes blank, their faces blank, the slush on the roads, the spray on the windscreen, Jackie and Johnny and the Boss in the back, on their stretchers, mumbling and whispering, Eleanor Miklos passed out from the pain, a police car ahead of them now, leading the way, police on the streets now, clearing a path, more ambulances behind them, the driver up front, Bill's hands round his throat, going faster, still faster, shouting louder and louder, over and over –

Krankenhaus, Krankenhaus . . .

*

21

It had been another cold, wet day in Manchester, but another busy, expectant day at the Old Trafford ticket office, what with all the applications for the League match against Wolves the day after tomorrow, then for the Cup tie against Sheffield Wednesday the following Saturday, the familiar, steady stream of fans coming to the office to get their tickets, as well as the usual sackfuls of post arriving for the players, so young Les Olive, the assistant club secretary, was short-handed, what with his boss, Walter Crickmer, having gone with the team to Belgrade, and with the telephone ringing off the hook, every second minute it seemed to Les, picking it up again for the umpteenth time that day and saying, Ticket office –

Les, is that you, said Joe Armstrong, the chief scout. I've just heard some terrible news . . .

Les listened to Joe, the news he was telling him, the words he was saying, then Les put down the telephone, then Les picked it back up again and he dialled the house of the Chairman, the home of Harold Hardman, who had not gone to Belgrade, had not flown with the team because he was ill, he was home sick in bed, and Les said, I'm very sorry to call you at home, Mister Hardman, sir, but I've just had some bad news . . .

And after Les had told Harold Hardman what Joe had told him, Les put down the telephone again, then he got up from his desk, closed the ticket office, went down the corridor and up the stairs to the office of the Boss, where he knew Alma George, the Boss's secretary, was still working, making the most of the peace and the quiet while the Boss was away.

*

Manchester, Manchester, back again, in Manchester, stout and hearty Jimmy Murphy came flying out of London Road, bearing a box of oranges from the Promised Land, no less, and before flakes of snow from skies above had had time to melt on hat or collar, he crashed down into the back of a cab with his bag, the box and a, Hello there, son, how are you then?

Back to barracks, is it, Mister Murphy, sir, asked the driver. Or home, straight to the wife and kids?

Jimmy laughed. You know me, son. Old Trafford first, please, if you will. And here you go . . .

He leant forward to put four oranges on the seat beside the driver. Fresh from the gardens of Zion.

Thank you very much, said the driver. The taxi spluttered into life and pulled away from the station. That's very kind of you. And congratulations.

Jimmy laughed again. Thank you, son. I'm in a more generous mood with you than we were with them, I'll tell you that. Afraid we've sent them back to Israel empty-handed. Though I'll tell you this, they showed some fight, they really did. And their keeper, their captain, Chodoroff, now he's some player, he really is, and brave, too, up against Big John. Dislocated shoulder. Broken nose. Concussion, and still on he played. Then straight off the pitch at the whistle he goes, into an ambulance and off to hospital. Best player on the pitch he was.

But Wales in the finals, said the driver, and for the first time. Now that's some achievement, Mister Murphy, that really is. England, Scotland, Wales and Northern Ireland, too, all off to Sweden now.

Jimmy glanced out of the window of the cab, glimpsed folk gathering in groups, standing on street corners, under the lamps, all coming on now, in a late afternoon that was already half night, just standing there in the falling, open-mouthed silence, an evening paper shared in their red, raw hands. Bit cold and wet for that, thought Jimmy, but he smiled and said, Well, we were not at our best, son, and we'll need to be better. But the best thing for me, the best news of all, is the boys won in Belgrade.

23

See you do a good job, I'd said, the last thing I'd said, and they did, they have. But I didn't like not being there, so that's a great weight off my mind, son.

Well, we can't have everything, laughed the driver. You'll probably go on and win the bloody thing now, and then we'll never hear the end of it. But I've told you before and I'll tell you again, you should get yourself over to Maine Road, Mister Murphy. You're wasted, hiding your lamp under Matt Busby's bushel.

Jimmy laughed. No, no, second fiddle's the fiddle for me, son. And you're doing well enough without me.

Maybe, but we'd be doing even better with some of the old Jimmy Murphy black magic, I know that.

Jimmy looked out through the sleet, the streets of Stretford running down the window, Old Trafford somewhere out there in the late-afternoon gloom, the League Championship flag already at half-mast. Well, we'll need to work our magic on Saturday, he said, if we're to keep the Wolves from our door . . .

Two of the oranges rolled off the seat beside the driver and onto the floor of the cab, the vehicle creaking along, something on the wind, the air –

Something, some thing . . .

They've brought the weather back with them, said the driver. Typical of you lot. As if we haven't got enough bad weather of our own.

*

It was freezing, fucking freezing, deep in the guts of Old Trafford, but the lads on the ground staff had done their jobs for the day and were just mucking about in the dressing rooms, joking and pissing around, keeping the cold from their bones, waiting for little old Arthur Powell to come waddle in and decide whether to make them wait until five on the nail or to let them off early, all depended on his mood, the miserable old bugger, but young Nobby Stiles, he thought there was a chance today, like what with the weather and because they'd have all the boots from Belgrade to clean and do tomorrow. But when Arthur came in, Bill Inglis, who looked after the reserves, was with him, and they both had faces on them like the grave, and Bill said, Sit down, lads, settle down, I've got some bad news for you, and all the lads dropped silent and was sat down in a second, wondering what could be up, or who had done what, even if one of them was for the chop, the chop or not, but then Bill said, The plane has crashed, but we don't have many details yet, so let's just hope it's not too serious. And old Arthur nodded, and said, Aye, we'll let you know later, boys. Then Arthur and Bill went back out, left the lads to their silence, sat in the reserve-team dressing room, no one not saying anything, until someone said, Be something and nothing. Few broken arms. Or maybe a leg. And someone else said, Aye, and if it's enough of them, then we might get bumped up, get a game in the A team. Then someone else laughed, Some of us might, but not you, pal. They'd all have to be dead and gone 'fore anyone picked you.

*

Into the ground and up the stairs, two at a time, went Jimmy, up to the offices, up at the top, the ground, the building, all quiet he thought, no one about, most strange is this, no one around, no one at all, the Boss not back, his office dark, only Alma at her desk, their secretary she was, sitting in the black, her lamp not even on. Jimmy set down the box of oranges and his bag, switched on the office lights and said, You'll strain your eyes, you will, Alma, love, you really will, sitting in the dark like that.

The plane's crashed, she said.

Well, let's have a drink then, just to warm us up. Just a little one, you know, while the cat's away.

25

Haven't you heard, Jimmy?

Jimmy walked over to the tray of bottles which stood on top of the cabinet. Heard what, love?

About the plane?

Jimmy poured two drinks. What about it?

It's crashed. The plane's crashed.

Jimmy handed Alma a glass. Cheers.

You don't understand. Listen to me, Jimmy, please, she said. Please. The plane has crashed. A lot of people have died. And she put down the glass on her desk, sat back down in her chair, and she started to cry.

The bottle of Scotch and the glass in his hands, Jimmy stood there, just stood there, frozen, in the middle of the office, Matt's office, staring down at Alma, her shoulders, her body shaking, her words in his ears, in his head, inside his skull, going round and round inside his brain: *The plane has crashed. A lot of people have died. The plane has crashed, a lot of people have died, a lot of people have died, have died, have died . . .*

Jimmy tried to shake his head, to silence the sound, the echo of her words, to feel his legs, to lift his feet, his legs of ash and feet of stone, to leave the room and walk away, but then back in again, back in again to start this all again, that this then might not have been –

A lot of people have died . . .

Jimmy looked up. He saw the clock on the wall, its hands pointed to four. He stared at those hands, stared and stared at those hands, trying and trying to get them to stop, to make them go back, back, back to before, but they would not go back, would not stop –

A lot of people . . .

He turned away from the clock on the wall, its every cut a deeper wound, closed his mouth as tight as he could, his lips, his teeth as tight as he could to swallow a scream, a terrible, howling scream, and then on legs of ash and feet of stone he walked into his own little office. He put down the bottle and the glass on his desk, closed and locked the door behind him, then poured himself a drink. He drank it down, then filled his glass again, and then again, once more, and then, and only then, did he begin to cry, to cry himself at last. But then he stopped, rubbed dry his face, took another drink and got back up again, on his feet and to the door again –

Alma, love . . .

*

It was between half past four and a quarter to five and already dark outside, and Mrs Dale, the doctor's wife, was sharing the daily happenings in the life of her family on the Light Programme, when suddenly a sombre voice cut her off and said, The reason we are interrupting *Mrs Dale's Diary* is that we have to report a serious air crash at Munich Airport. We haven't the full details yet, but the aircraft was on charter from British European Airways and was travelling from Belgrade to Manchester. On board was the Manchester United football team, returning from a match in Yugoslavia with sports writers of Fleet Street newspapers and team officials. As far as we know, twenty-five of the passengers and crew are believed to have died.

*

Bobby's mum had not been back an hour when she felt a shadow fall across the yard. She looked up from the sink, out of the window, and through the snow, the falling snow, she saw Ted Cockburn, the man who had the paper shop, coming into their yard, up to her door, but Cissie had got to the door before he'd knocked, even raised his glove, and Cissie said, It's our Bobby, isn't it?

27

Yes, said Ted Cockburn. I'm sorry, I'm so sorry, but I wanted you to know before it went up on the placards, because I was afraid you didn't know, you'd not been told, but the *Chronicle* has made up bills saying your Bobby's been in a crash, a plane crash, but I wanted to make sure you knew, before they went up.

Thank you, Ted, thank you, said Cissie, looking up at the snow, watching it fall. But I knew, I just knew.

I'm sorry, said Ted Cockburn again. I'm sorry.

Cisse looked at Ted. What are they saying?

I'm sorry, love, said Ted again, but they're saying there are no survivors. That everyone's dead.

Cissie didn't believe that. She knew something was wrong, had sensed it coming all day. But she couldn't believe Bobby was dead, not deep down, she didn't feel it within her, not in the place from which Bobby had come. But she needed to know, know he was safe. She turned back to the kitchen, grabbed her purse and her coat, but not her hat and her gloves, not this time, running out of the yard, down the backs, through the snow, down to the call box on the corner, trying to ring Old Trafford, trying to find out the truth, the coins cold in her hands, her fingers red as she dialled. But the snow and the wind had brought down the lines, the telephone lines all dead, so maybe she was wrong, she began to think she was wrong, that Bobby was dead, lying in the snow, alone in the snow, the German snow, his eyes open to the sky, looking up at the sky, searching for her, seeing her now, in the call box on the corner, the receiver dead in her hand, crying, No, Bobby, no. Wake up, Bobby, please, wake up.

*

Frank was in and out of the light, thought he'd been in some kind of minibus at one point, bouncing and bumping over fields, then speeding along, faster than the devil, Billy Foulkes holding

28

him down, telling him, You're going to be all right, Frank. Just lie still. Don't worry, but he was worried because he couldn't breathe properly, still only with difficulty, terrible difficulty, and the pain in his leg, Jesus Christ, the pain shooting up his right leg, why was that, he didn't know, in and out of the light, trying to think of Peggy and the boys, his two little sons, Andrew and Alastair, back home in Manchester, running around, he could hear them running around, pestering Peggy as she prepared the tea, How long before Dad comes home? How long is it now? But he was going to be late, very late now, and he was sorry, thinking how sorry he was, for the worry he'd caused as someone, a doctor, he thought, hoped was a doctor, tore off the sleeve of his jacket, the jacket of his new bloody suit, ripped up his shirt, then plunged the needle of a hypodermic syringe into his arm, deep into his arm, and said, Ssh now, ssh, this will put you to sleep, and Frank nodded, Frank smiled and closed his eyes again, Frank already weary, so very, very tired, out of the light again, but happy now, happy now that sleep was here, was here at last.

*

Elizabeth Wood was changing her daughter's nappy, wondering what to cook Ray for his tea, thinking he might like a nice piece of gammon, English gammon, after having been abroad and away, when Elizabeth heard a tapping at her window and looked up and saw her neighbour beckoning her over, and Elizabeth picked up their Denise, carried her over, and opened the window –

Have you heard the news, Missus Wood?

No. What news, asked Elizabeth.

The neighbour shook her head and said, It's awful. It was on the radio. They interrupted *Mrs Dale's Diary*.

Why? What's happened, said Elizabeth.

There's been an accident at Munich, a plane crash with the boys. But your Ray's all right, isn't he?

In Munich, asked Elizabeth.

But your Ray's at home, isn't he, said the neighbour again. He didn't go, did he?

*

Wilf McGuinness was having a bad week. He'd twisted his knee playing for the reserves on Saturday against Arsenal. The knee had locked, and when he went into the ground on Sunday, Ted Dalton, the physiotherapist, told him he'd probably torn a cartilage. Ted had sent him to see a specialist on the Tuesday, who told Wilf he'd need to operate, and so he was supposed to be going into hospital tomorrow, Friday. This then being his last day of freedom, Wilf had called up his pal Joey, who worked on the sales side for the *News Chronicle*, and arranged to meet him in town for a last hurrah, and it was when they were walking down Princess Street together that he saw the placard: 'UNITED IN CRASH ON RUNWAY' –

Be just a bump, said Wilf.

Aye, said his pal Joey.

Your lot will write anything to flog a few extra copies, laughed Wilf. But all the same, he bought a first edition, and they stood there, in Princess Street, on the corner with Bloom Street, reading the paper. But it was all a bit vague, so –

Tell you what, said Joey, let's go up the office, find out what's going on. Just to put your mind at ease.

They set off walking up Bloom Street to Sackville Street, then turned up Portland Street, cut through Piccadilly Gardens, and were jogging by the time they were going down Shudehill, Wilf not worried about his cartilage or the weather any more, worried about his mates now, the sudden, awful silence that seemed to have fallen from the sky, blanketing the city centre, until they came to the *Chronicle* buildings and went inside, and that was when it hit them, the noise of the news, the news of –

'Heavy loss of life feared . . .'

*

The telephones were going mad, ringing off their hooks, and Joe and Les were in the main office with Alma now, trying to help her and Jimmy, calling the police again, calling the BBC, the *Chronicle*, the *Evening News*, the *Guardian*, every paper they could think of, every journalist they knew, to find out details, to pass information along to the families, the relatives, trying to reach the families, the relatives, those that had a phone or a contact number with a neighbour or a local shop, but the minute they put down the phone, the phone would ring again, someone asking them for details, asking them for information, and then they'd have to wait again for an outgoing line, minutes passing, and when they did get an outside line, manage to ring the families, the relatives, half of them weren't answering, weren't home –

They'll be at the airport, said Alma, suddenly. They'll have gone to meet the plane . . .

*

British European Airways Flight 609 had been scheduled to land at Manchester Ringway Airport at 5 p.m. that afternoon. Many of the wives and girlfriends, along with some fans, the ones who never missed the chance to welcome home the team, had come out to the airport. The fans were particularly pleased because Jean Busby had come out to meet her husband. But Jean had come because she was worried. It was less than a month since Matt had had the operation on his legs for his varicose veins.

31

He'd been told to take time off, to go to the south of France to sit in the sun and its warmth and recuperate. But that was never very likely, not in the middle of the season, with the League, the FA Cup and the European Cup all still to play for, no. Matt wouldn't even hear of missing this trip to Belgrade. But Jean knew he'd be shattered, it would have taken its toll, so that was why she was here, though she'd never let on, not to the fans. They were all sitting in the lounge, laughing and joking, the mood jubilant after the result last night, light and expectant until –

People waiting for BEA Flight 609 from Belgrade should call at the reception desk in the main hall, came the voice of a BEA hostess, in almost a whisper, over the public address system, into the air.

Unsure and reluctant, but standing, uncertain yet slowly now walking, the wives and the girlfriends went through to the BEA desk, some of the fans, the fans whom they knew, following behind, hoping it was just a delay, an overnight stay at worst, not wanting to intrude, but wanting to know why the BEA airport manager was leading the wives and the girlfriends off to another lounge, a private lounge, where he was very sorry to have to tell them, But there's been a serious accident, and we don't yet have the full details, but it seems the plane has crashed on take-off at Munich Airport . . .

But they weren't flying from Munich, someone said. They are flying from Belgrade. It must be a mistake.

The BEA airport manager said he was sorry but, It's not a mistake. The plane had stopped to refuel.

You say serious. How serious?

The BEA manager said he was sorry again, But I don't have the full details yet, but –

But you know it's serious. You said it was serious, said one of the girlfriends. What do you mean, serious? You mean people are dead, is that what you mean?

The BEA airport manager nodded, was sorry to say, But yes, we believe there are fatalities, yes.

Oh, God, screamed someone. No –

And the wives and the girlfriends, they turned to each other, they reached for each other, holding each other, some crying, one screaming, They're all wiped out, I know it! I just know it. All wiped out –

Jean Busby felt her legs go from beneath her, then a BEA hostess was holding her up, guiding her to a chair, raising a glass of brandy to her lips, putting a cup of tea in her hands, telling her there were survivors, some survivors, and that taxis were being ordered to take them back home, and that BEA were making all the necessary arrangements, and that they would be the first to know any news as it came through, but to remember there were survivors, some survivors –

Only ten left, said a woman in the main hall as Jean Busby was being half led, half carried out to her taxi, and Jean stopped and she turned and she looked at the woman, the woman in a thick, white winter coat, standing in the main hall of Ringway Airport, and Jean said, What did you say?

I've just heard it on the radio, whispered the woman. There are only ten survivors.

*

There was no more news, or no news that they were saying, so Arthur Powell came back to let the ground-staff lads go, but when they came out of the ground, they found loads of folk just standing around, in groups or pairs or just on their own, just stood around, people who had come for tickets who'd then heard the news and stayed on, others who must have just heard the news and then come along, straight from the factory, the office or home, journalists, too, knocking on the doors, trying to get in, policemen with whistles, trying to hold people back, to move people on, but more folk were arriving, from factories, their offices, not knowing what was true and what not, what else they could do. Nobby had never seen or felt anything like it, heard a silence like this silence, and he couldn't stand it, couldn't bear it, none of the lads could, and so he wasn't going to hang around here, no chance, none of them were. Nobby got the bus into Piccadilly, gnawed by a rising sense of dread. He got off the bus in Piccadilly. There were people standing around here, too, loads of folk, in groups, in the shadows, in the sleet, just standing around, not speaking, not saying nothing. Nobby waited in a line for a paper, a paper that said, 'MANY DEAD'. In a trance, his feet walked him through the silent crowds to his stop, took him onto the 112 bus and sat him down inside. He could hear a woman weeping as the bus went up the Rochdale Road through Angel Meadow. In a trance still, his feet stood him up and got him off at Cassidy's pub, then walked him round the corner to Saint Pat's on Livesey Street and through its doors and put him down in a pew, then onto his knees, where Nobby prayed and he cried. He idolised United, this team. United were his life. He was United from the start: his earliest memory was when he must have been a six-year-old, sitting on his dad's shoulders at Old Trafford, watching the '48 team of Carey, Mitten, Rowley. Then he'd gone with his brother Charlie. They'd be there two hours before kick-off, stood at the scoreboard end. Eddie Colman was his idol. He used to try to copy him, coming side-on and shimmying, but he was nothing like Eddie, he knew. Not fit to clean his boots, though he did, now he was on the books at Old Trafford. But that changed nothing, except to make him even more in awe of how good they really were, when you saw them in training and games and you'd think, I'm never going to get this. But Jimmy Murphy, he'd put fire in his belly, had given him a red shirt and said, See this red shirt? It's the best in the world.

When you put on that red shirt, nothing can beat you. Nobby had put on that red shirt, and he'd never take it off. He would go through a brick wall for Jimmy, for these lads. For United. He was a punter, a supporter; first, last and always a punter, a supporter. They were his life, he lived for them. Nobby lived for them, and he would die for them, rather him than them, please, God, just take me, please, he prayed. Just let them live, he cried, just please, please, God, let them live.

*

In its theatres, on its wards, in all its rooms and corridors, the Rechts der Isar Hospital, on the right bank of the River Isar, had enacted its emergency plan. All off-duty staff had been called in, all shifts extended. Doctors and surgeons were scrubbed up and ready, nurses and porters running backwards and forwards as stretcher after stretcher was carried into the hospital and taken up to theatre, past Harry, sat in the corridor beside Bill, staring down at the floor.

What's happened to your shoe, asked Harry.

Bill looked down at his shoes, but one was gone. His foot in just his sock, sopping wet in a puddle. He looked back up, turned to Harry and said, We should find a telephone. Let Teresa and Mavis know we're alive.

There must be someone here from the embassy, said Harry, getting to his feet. Come on, let's –

Gentlemen, please come with me, said a nurse in halting, nervous English, beckoning Harry and Bill to follow her, another nurse holding Bobby by his arm.

Harry and Bill followed the two nurses and Bobby down the corridor and onto one of the wards. They led them to a bed, where a little man was being stripped of his United club blazer, the rest of his clothes.

Who is this, please, asked the nurse. His name?

Bobby turned his head away towards a window, but Harry and Bill, they looked at the little man on the bed, his leg broken, his pelvis broken, his elbow broken and his jaw broken. His bottom teeth had cut through his upper mouth into his nose, many of the teeth now missing. His skull was fractured, his face bruised and his hair matted with blood. He was almost unrecognisable, but Bill said, It's Johnny. His name is Johnny, John Berry.

His wife's name is Hilda, said Harry.

Please write here, said the nurse, and she handed Bill a label and a pen. His name, please.

Bill took the label and the pen from the nurse. He tried to steady his hand, to write down, to print as carefully as he could the names of Johnny and his wife.

Thank you, said the nurse. This way now –

The nurse led them to a second bed, a second man being stripped of his clothes, a big orange sweater, one you'd never forget. Harry said, It's Ray Wood, it must be Ray Wood. But I could have sworn he was dead.

Ray Wood looked up from the bed at Harry and Bill, but he could not see Harry or Bill. His eye was half out of its socket, his face gashed, and he had concussion.

His wife's name is Elizabeth, said Bill.

Please write for me, said the nurse again, and she handed Harry a label and a pen. Now follow, please –

The two nurses led Harry and Bill and Bobby off the ward, down a long corridor and into a small private room, where Peter Howard and Ted Ellyard were sitting side by side on the one bed in the room. There was another man from the plane there, too, a giant of a man whom they did not know but thought was a diplomat or journalist from Yugoslavia, leaning against the wall.

You know what's going on, asked Pete Howard.

Harry shook his head. No idea, have you?

Have you seen anyone from the British Embassy or from the airline, asked Bill. I need to call my wife.

Suddenly, the giant of a man from Yugoslavia began to slide slowly down the wall, one of his legs dangling, pointing in an odd direction, obviously broken.

The nurses cried out, calling for help. More nurses and some nuns came running, some carrying needles, porters following them into the room, trolleys at the ready. They hoisted the big Yugoslav onto one of the trolleys, injected him with something and then carted him off.

Gentlemen, give me your arms, please, said the nurse in her halting, nervous English, but Harry and Bill were having none of that. Not on your nelly –

They ran out of the room and down the corridor, Bill in only one shoe, hopping along, his one wet sock flapping, slapping the floor, back to the doors of the hospital, to the top of the steps, the night and the cold hitting them there, full in the face, at the tops of them steps, everything night and everything cold, and Harry stopped, suddenly stopped and said, Bill, Bill, wait, will you, wait! Where the fuck are we going?

*

Sandy Busby had never had an apprenticeship at Old Trafford. His father had not wanted that for him, didn't think it would be good for him. Instead, Sandy was on the books at Blackburn Rovers, under Johnny Carey, the former United captain. They were having a good season, had just beaten Derby away, and were pushing for promotion. But Sandy wasn't in the first team, Sandy was in the reserves. Not that bad, but just not that good. But Sandy knew all the boys at United, was mates with all the lads, the ones who liked a flutter on the dogs or a night on the town, the Ritz or the Plaza, the Continental or the Queens.

And Sandy still lived at home with his father and his mother on Kings Road, in Chorlton-cum-Hardy, the house he'd grown up in. So every day, Sandy had to get the bus into town, the train from Victoria to Blackburn, changing and then training, then showering and changing back again, then back again, on the train from Blackburn to Victoria, the bus from town back out to Chorlton, more often than not the bus stuck in traffic on the Palatine Road, crawling its way back out to Chorlton as he wondered what was for tea tonight and who fancied who. But not that day: late that afternoon, he got off the train at Victoria Station with a friend of his, and suddenly this pal of his said, Have you seen the placards, San? 'MAN UTD IN PLANE CRASH'. But Sandy just walked on, about fifty yards on, because he knew the tricks the papers played, a slight delay becomes a disaster, engine trouble is a tragedy, probably something and nothing, a mountain out of a molehill, another bit of tittle-tattle to sell some more papers, walking on before it struck him cold: Crash? That's serious. It didn't say 'fright', it said 'crash', and the look on the face of his pal said the same, said, You'd better call home. Sandy dashed to the telephone box. An aunty and uncle were staying with them, down from Scotland, from Bellshill, and it was his uncle who first picked up the phone and said, Is that you, San? Thank God. We called Blackburn, but you'd left. Where are –

His aunty grabbed the phone from his uncle, started screaming, kept on screaming, Get home, Sandy, get home! Just get yourself home, as fast as you can!

Sandy hung up. He ran over to the taxis, told the driver he needed to get to Chorlton as quick as he could, then sat back in the cab and closed his eyes, thinking, still thinking, She's prone to panic is my aunty, thinking again, It'll be something and nothing, mountains out of molehills, but when they got to Kings Road, pulled up in front of the house, saw the cars all parked up, and he got out of the cab, the lights all on in the house, the front door standing open, wide open, Sandy knew he was wrong, that something was wrong, really, properly wrong –

The house was pandemonium, but his mother was just sat in a trance, in the front room, on the sofa, staring into the fire, not blinking, not speaking –

Mam, Mam, said Sandy. It's me, Sandy?

She's been like this since the airport, said his big sister Sheena. We can't get a word out of her.

Mam? Can you hear us, Mam?

I don't think she can, said Sheena.

Sandy turned his head, put his hand to his mouth, whispered, But what about Dad?

Nothing yet, said Sheena as quietly as she could, her head turned, her hand raised. Only rumours.

The whole house, the whole city was filled with rumours, rumours of the dead, the whispers of the dead, the news of the dead, the names of the dead, the name of Frank, some said, not Frank, but yes, Frank Swift was dead, surely not, not Big Frank, I know, but yes, I just heard, they just said, Swifty was gone, Frank Swift was dead, these rumours, these whispers, under breath, behind hands, just as Frank's wife Doris arrived at the door, she only lived round the corner, her daughter and son-in-law, they were with her, too, her daughter named Jean, after Sandy's own mam, as they stepped into the hall, a sudden circle of silence surrounding Doris and Jean –

Does Monsignor Sewell know, asked Sandy.

Sheena nodded and said, Uncle Paddy went to pick him up, to bring him over.

Hear that, Mam, said Sandy. Do you hear that? Monsignor Sewell is on his way. He'll soon be here.

But his mum was not listening, not hearing, not hearing him or hearing Sheena, the friends and the relatives, the crowds

39

of friends and relatives who were filling the house, the hall, the kitchen, more people arriving every minute, on the stairs now, as Sandy pushed his way up, up to his room, where he fell to his knees –

Beside his bed, head bowed and hands together, Sandy began to pray, to say aloud, Please, God, let my dad be okay, let my dad be alive, please, God, please –

Sandy, Sandy, shouted his Uncle John, running up the stairs, straight into his room. It's your dad, your dad, we've just heard he's alive. He's alive!

*

The doctor smiled at Bobby, told Bobby that he was lucky to be alive, that he was just suffering from a mild concussion. Bobby touched, could feel the small bruise on his head. It didn't seem much, it didn't seem fair. The doctor turned from Bobby, said something to an orderly in German. The orderly nodded, looked and smiled at Bobby, as if to say, it seemed to Bobby, that all this was just routine, that the world was still turning, that you're one of the lucky ones, that you're alive and well, and you'll soon be on your way again, see your family soon again. But Bobby knew that wasn't true, that he'd not be on his way because the world had stopped turning, and Bobby started to scream, to scream and to rage at the orderly and his smile, raging and screaming, howling in pain, Don't you smile at me! Don't you dare smile at me! There's nothing to smile about, nothing to smile –

The orderly grabbed Bobby, held him by his shoulders, and the doctor stuck a needle into the back of his neck, then they sat him back down and left him to stare, to stare at the wall, the corridor, the hospital, the world drifting in and out, out and in, then out, just out.

The lady from British European Airways found Bill and Harry sat outside on the steps to the hospital. Bill had no shoe on one foot and Harry had no tie around his neck. They were not wearing coats or even jackets. The lady from BEA said, You'll catch your deaths sat out here like this in the cold. Come on, get back inside with me.

The lady led them back inside the hospital, sat them back down in the corridor. She introduced them to a man from the British Consulate in Munich. He told them that the names of all the survivors had been forwarded to the relevant authorities in London and Manchester. He told them not to worry, their families would know they were safe. Then he gestured at Bill's feet and he said, Now let's see what we can do about some dry socks, shall we?

Will you bloody shut up for one minute, said Harry. Can't you hear what they're saying . . .?

What are they saying, asked Bill.

Harry pointed up at the tannoy speaker on the wall. I could swear they just said Frank Swift is dead, but I couldn't bloody hear for this fellow wittering on.

That can't be right, said Bill, looking up at the lady from BEA. Not Big Frank? Not Swifty?

The lady from BEA glanced at the man from the British Consulate, then she nodded at Bill and at Harry, and she said, I'm sorry. I'm very sorry.

I'll just go and see about those socks, shall I, said the man from the British Consulate, with a quick smile, then a brisk stride, off and away, down the corridor.

Not Big Frank, said Bill again. Not Swifty.

I don't think it's a good idea to stay here, said the lady from BEA. We've arranged a hotel for you, and I can take you there

41

now, if you'd like? If you're both feeling well enough. It's not far, less than ten minutes by car.

Neither Bill nor Harry said anything.

I'll find you some shoes and clean clothes, too, said the lady from BEA. Warm clothes.

Bill looked up from his hands. He turned to the lady and asked, Ten minutes by car, did you say?

Yes, said the lady from BEA. It's very near.

Do you speak German, do you, said Bill.

Yes, she said. I speak German.

Will you ask the driver, then, not to go fast. I can't stand it. The way people drive. The speeds that they go.

*

It was around about six o'clock by the time his pal Joey had driven Wilf McGuinness back home. Wilf had just sat there, all the way home, in a state of shock, knowing that Bobby, and that Dennis, and that Bill Foulkes and Harry Gregg had survived, they were probably all right, but he'd not heard anything yet about Eddie Colman, or Billy Whelan, or David Pegg, or so many of the other lads, the rest of the team, his mates. But then when he got back, went in through the door, everybody already knew what he didn't want to know, that it wasn't a dream, was a nightmare, and all of it true when his mother and his father told him to keep his coat on, that there had been deaths. Many deaths. And Wilf followed them straight back out the door and round to Our Lady of Mount Carmel to say a novena: Lord of Mercy, hear our prayer, may our brothers, whom you called sons on earth, enter into the kingdom of peace and light, where your saints live in glory. We ask this through our Lord, Jesus Christ, who lives and reigns with you and the Holy Spirit, one God forever and ever. Amen. But Wilf didn't want to think of Eddie and Billy and David being dead, or any of them dead, and he prayed instead, he prayed and cried and said to God, he said, I'll do anything, anything if they're all right, anything you ask, just please let them be all right, let them be alive.

*

Everyone alive that day would have a tale to tell of death, of who and when and where they were upon that cold, unwanted day, and for some alive that blackest day of all, that tale would have a twist, a twist that paused the pulse, that made one stop and think that but for fate or grace or economic considerations, that could have been me upon my back upon the snow, the hands of my watch, the words in my throat stopped, silent in the slush, the ice –

It was the manager of *The Times* whom Geoffrey Green had to thank for keeping him from the snow, the slush and ice that day, the manager of *The Times* who, almost at the eleventh hour, and on purely monetary grounds, had ordered Geoffrey to cancel his tickets to Belgrade and to go instead to Cardiff, to report on the World Cup qualifying match between Wales and Israel.

You must be bloody joking, Geoffrey had said.

I'm not, he'd said, and he wasn't, and so Geoffrey had gone to Cardiff, watched Wales 'dismally complete the second leg', written and filed his report – 'WALES QUALIFY FOR WORLD CUP / But No Glory in Win Over Israel' – then returned to London overnight from Cardiff, read the reports from Belgrade – 'MANCHESTER REACH SEMI-FINAL / Red Star Rally in European Cup' – and gone off to sulk in the warmth of a cinema all that afternoon: *Chase a Crooked Shadow*, followed by *Witness for the Prosecution*, and he'd even toyed with seeing *The Man Who Wouldn't Talk* but decided on a drink instead, and that

43

was when he saw the evening-paper placard, under a streetlight surely switched on by the devil himself, screaming out the most dreadful news in the heaviest of types – 'MANCHESTER UNITED IN AIR CRASH' – and unlike some, and unlike him on any other day of the week, he didn't think this time this was a stunt, a newspaper screamer to catch out the gullible, no, he somehow knew, deep down he knew, knew this was true, so he didn't stop to buy a paper, to ask the stranger standing beside him, a copy in his hand, reading the news, a crowd around, to ask him what it said, no, Geoffrey knew, he somehow knew, and so off he set for home, like a hare from a trap, just in time to hear the telephone ringing –

Where the hell have you been, said the office. We've been trying to reach you for the past two hours.

It's true then, said Geoffrey. Christ.

Precise information is still scarce and confused, but yes, the stark fact is that United's aeroplane crashed on take-off at Munich Airport, with heavy loss of life.

I'll be in then as quick as I can, said Geoffrey, and he replaced the receiver, poured himself a drink, then glanced at his watch, switched on the wireless to hear the announcer on the BBC Home Service say, Here is the news. An airliner carrying the Manchester United team crashed in Germany this afternoon . . .

*

Bobby's mum was back in the house, in the parlour with the radio on, then off again, the news always bad, never good, but needing to know, desperate to know, the radio on again when Cissie heard the knock at the door. It was a copper's knock, she knew, a policeman's knock, she just knew, bringing bad news, always bad news, never anything good, any good news. She got up from her chair, hollowed and emptied, she went out of the parlour and into the hall, her heart already broken, her life already over, and she opened the door –

Telegram for you, Missus Charlton, from the Foreign Office, said their local copper on her step, head to boot in snow, waving a brown envelope in his glove.

Cissie took the envelope from his glove, took the paper from the envelope, and read the words on the paper:

Alive and well, see you later, Bobby.

I knew it, said Cissie, stepping, falling back into the hall, to the floor, the paper in her hand. I just knew.

*

He was alive, alive. Her husband, her light, the very light of her life, he was alive, Mattie was alive. But others were not, she knew they were not, and her thoughts were for them and their families now and what could be done –

Sheena, Sandy, will you go round to Tom Curry's house, to see Betty, will you, please, said Jean.

Jean turned to comfort Doris and Jean, her Jean and her husband, to say how all they could do was to pray for Frank, to hope for the best, that good news would come, holding them, hugging them close, praying the rumours weren't true, that none of it was true.

Bill Ridding, who had played with Matt at City, who had then gone to United, who was now the manager of Bolton, he came over to Jean with Paddy McGrath and Paddy's son-in-law. They took Jean to one side, told her the news that Big Frank was dead, that the rumours were true, then Paddy's son-in-law said he'd walk Doris and her Jean and her husband back round the corner to theirs, to see them home, to break the news to them there, in their own home, then help them with the arrangements, if there was anything they could do, but then

45

their heads all turned to the door because Elsie Nichols, the girlfriend of Henry Rose of the *Daily Express*, the best-known, most-read writer of the day, she'd just arrived at the door and was saying, repeating, I know my Henry's been killed. I know my Henry's been killed, and Jean took her in her arms, held her in her arms, tried to comfort, to quieten her, while Paddy went to fetch a doctor and Bill Ridding kept on answering the phone, the questions from the press.

*

The manager of the Stachus Hotel put Harry and Bill on the top floor, where it was quiet, away from the other guests and the press, who were already sniffing about, back at the hospital and around the hotels. The manager walked with Harry and Bill to the elevator, but Harry and Bill said they would rather walk and so they'd meet him upstairs. Bill hadn't known what his shoe size was in German, and had given his one shoe to the lady from BEA, so he followed Harry up the stairs in his stocking feet, his stocking feet both still wet, but the carpet soft beneath his feet, soft and warm, not cold, not snow, not slush.

At the top of the stairs, the manager was waiting for Harry and Bill. He had two large, warm coats on his arm. He walked them down the corridor to the door to their room and showed them inside. The manager laid the coats on one of the beds, gave Harry the key for the room and said he'd be back again with more clean clothes, and the lady from BEA would also be back soon, but they must call down if they needed anything, anything at all, and he pointed to a bottle of whisky sat on the table between the two beds, a present from someone, and suggested they had a drink and a rest, a good rest, and he'd be back again, he said again, and then left them alone, alone in a room on the top floor of the Stachus Hotel.

Harry walked over to the window and drew back the curtains. Bill followed him over to the window. It was night outside, snow still falling. Bill turned away and walked over to the bathroom. Harry followed him. Bill switched on the bathroom light. Harry and Bill saw themselves in the bathroom mirror. They were black with dirt and they were stained with grease, blood on the cuffs of their shirts, under the nails of their fingers. They did not recognise themselves. Bill turned away from the mirror, the man he did not know. He took a piss, then Harry had a piss. Then Harry walked back out of the bathroom. He picked up the bottle of whisky and he opened it. Bill brought two glasses from the bathroom and held them out to Harry. Harry filled their glasses, then Harry and Bill took their glasses back over to the window, looking down and out on the world, a world of snow and slush, staring down at the cars, the people, the city: going home, slant against the sleet, coats up, hats down, never looking up, up into the sky, those two figures at a window up above, so far, so very far from home.

*

Jimmy kept calling the police, the BBC, the *Chronicle*, the *Evening News*, the *Guardian*, everybody he knew, but the news was always the same. Or worse –

The *Chronicle* had already had confirmation that Geoff Bent, Roger Byrne, Eddie Colman, Mark Jones, David Pegg, Tommy Taylor and Liam Whelan were dead, and the list of the journalists confirmed as dead, men he had known well, men who were his friends, was long, almost all of them gone: Alf Clarke of the *Evening Chronicle*, Tom Jackson of the *Evening News*, Donny Davies of the *Manchester Guardian*, George Follows of the *Herald*, Archie Ledbrooke of the *Mirror*, Eric Thompson of the *Mail*, Henry Rose of the *Express* and poor Frank Swift, who

Jimmy never thought of as pressman for the *News of the World*, but always, simply as one of the greatest, bravest keepers he had ever known. Now the *Chronicle* told Jimmy that Matt's pal Willie Satinoff and Walter Crickmer were also dead. So, too, were Tom Curry and Bert Whalley, Jimmy's oldest, closest pals, especially Bert, poor Bert –

Poor old Bert, whispered Jimmy into his glass, he had my seat, and he went. Because of Wales and the bloody World Cup. He only went because I didn't.

Alma tapped on the door. She had a long, long list of names and telephone numbers in her hand, of organisations and of individuals, some known, some not, with expressions of sympathy, with offers of support: a telegram from the Queen to the Lord Mayor of Manchester, expressing her shock and sympathy; the offer of the use of his car from the father of Nobby Stiles . . .

And the Boss, she said, they called from Munich to say he'd been given another blood transfusion, and that everything is being done that can be done.

Jimmy said, Is he conscious, do you know?

Yes, said Alma, but he cannot speak.

They tell you anything else?

She nodded. They think he'll survive the night. But his condition is the most serious of all. Duncan and Johnny Berry are in very bad shape, too, and the journalist Frank Taylor, all of them are listed as critical.

Is there any good news?

Well, Ray Wood seems to have been just badly bruised and cut, while Kenny Morgans and Bobby Charlton have maybe only slight concussions. And they're letting Bill Foulkes and Harry Gregg leave the hospital, letting them go and stay at a hotel . . .

Jimmy said, Which hotel?

BEA are taking care of it, said Alma. They'll be looked after, don't worry.

48

Jimmy said, I need to go, to be there, in Munich. I can't be here, I should be there, should have been there all along. Never should have not have gone.

BEA are organising a special plane, said Alma, for those families who want to go out there. I know Jean and Sheena and Sandy are going. Tomorrow, first thing.

Jimmy said, I am going, too. I have to go.

Yes, said Alma. I'll call BEA, make sure they have your name for the flight and the hotel.

Jimmy said, Thank you, love.

But, Jimmy, she said.

Jimmy said, Yes?

There's still this, said Alma, handing him another list, the list of the dead, their names and the telephone numbers of their families, or their neighbours, or a shop or pub on their street, round the corner, if they had no telephone, the ones they still couldn't reach, who might not yet know.

Jimmy nodded. Of course, love. Of course. And he took the list from her hand, her hand shaking, his hand shaking, and he set down the list on the top of his desk, looked down at the list on the top of his desk, picked up the glass again, drank from his glass again, set down his glass again, and then picked up the telephone.

*

Harry held out the phone to Bill. He said, Will you speak to her, Bill? Will you tell her not to come . . .?

Hello, Mavis, said Bill. It's Bill here. Bill Foulkes . . . Yes, I'm fine, thank you . . . No, really, and Harry's fine, too, so there's really no need for you to be coming out here . . . No, no, Teresa's not coming, no. I've asked her not to come . . . Well, we don't know exactly, but as soon as we can . . . Yes, yes, hang on. Bye –

49

Harry took the phone back from Bill and said, You see, love? We're fine, I promise you . . .

And then, when Harry and Bill had finished convincing Mavis not to come out to Munich with the other wives and girlfriends, Harry and Bill set about convincing Teresa not to come out –

You see, the thing is, said Harry, there's really no need, so you'll just be making Bill worried, the thought of you flying out here on a plane after what's happened . . . Well, I don't know, but as soon as we can . . . No, don't you worry. There's no fear of that, love. Don't think you'll ever get your Bill on another plane for as long as he lives . . . Well, we'll walk if we have to, love, all the way home, all the way back to bloody Manchester . . .

*

There was still the constant ringing of the telephones, but worst of all was the hammering on the main doors downstairs, the banging and the knocking echoing up the stairs as Jimmy, Alma, Les and Joe tried to keep their heads as best they could, to take and make the calls, then decide who would go where to break the news, the worst news of all, and end all hope, as the hammering, the banging and the knocking went on, on and on –

I'm off down, said Joe. I can't stand it any more, and Joe got up from the telephone, the desk, walked out of the office and down the stairs to the main doors. He opened the door, saw the crowd outside, in their cloth caps and floral scarves, their raincoats and brollies, men and women, old and young, some silent, some sobbing, all waiting under the shadow of the giant stand, and Joe held up his hand, his face grey and voice tired as he said, Please go away, please. We can't tell you any more than what's on the news on the wireless. So please just go home, please, and let us get on with what has to be done.

Joe went to shut the door, but a hand touched and caught his own, the hand of a man whose face he knew, a journalist on the *Mail*, a man he knew well, and the man said, Joe, please, is there really no hope?

*

Later, but Bill and Harry didn't know how much later, time scrambled, stretching, then suddenly snapping, the lady from BEA returned with some shoes for Bill. Not shoes, but a pair of tall, fur-lined boots –

I just hope they fit, said the lady from BEA.

Bill nodded. Yes, at least they fit.

And there's two of them, said Harry.

Have you two eaten, asked the lady from BEA.

Bill and Harry looked at each other. They shook their heads. Bill said, I'm not hungry.

Me neither, said Harry.

But it must be ages since you had anything to eat, said the lady from BEA. You really should eat something. Why don't you both come down and join Captain Thain and the others in the dining room? Be better than just staying up here drinking on your own . . .

Harry and Bill looked at each other. They nodded, and Harry said, Be good to see the others.

Great, said the lady from BEA. Great. So why don't you have a wash and get changed maybe, then join us downstairs whenever you're ready.

Bill and Harry nodded. They thanked the lady from BEA, the lady from BEA who looked absolutely shattered herself. Then they walked back from the door over to the beds. They stared at the new clothes which the manager had laid out for them. The dark suits, the dark ties and white shirts. The clean white

51

underwear, the thick woollen socks. Bill put down his drink, put out his cigarette. He picked up one of the sets of new clothes from the bed and he turned to Harry. She did say 'others', didn't she?

*

June Jones had been in a shop in Chorlton buying cream cakes to welcome Mark back that night. She was standing in the queue at the counter when she heard the ladies behind her talking about United, about a plane crash –

They're saying many are dead.

What can I get you, love?

In the bright shop, before the white cakes, June just stood there, staring at the woman behind the counter.

Whatever is the matter, love?

My husband was on that plane, said June, and she walked out of the shop, back down the street, with their son in his pram, back to their house in Kings Road to wait, to wait six hours, six long, long hours until Joe Armstrong knocked on the door and told her the worst, his words falling on her with the weight of a stone that she could never roll away, but she sprang up then from her chair, ran up the stairs, grabbed her son from his cot, rushed back down the stairs and out of the house, into the street, clutching their son, into the cold, fleeing from death, into the night, running to Mark.

*

In their new sets of clothes, on legs suddenly old, old and tired, Harry and Bill walked down the stairs of the Stachus Hotel and into the dining room. It must have been late, very late, the hotel deserted, silent and shadowed. Just one large table, off to the side, lit up under low lights –

52

Here they are, said the lady from BEA.

Bill and Harry sat down at the table. They looked around the table, saw Pete Howard and Ted Ellyard from the *Daily Mail* again, saw Captain Thain and his radio officer Bill Rodgers, and the two stewardesses, Margaret Bellis and Rosemary Cheverton, but they did not see anybody else, any others. They didn't see Ken Rayment, the co-pilot, or Tommy Cable, the BEA steward, who they knew well because he was a mad United fan. They didn't see any of the other journalists or photographers either. And they didn't see any of their teammates, their friends.

What would you both like to eat, asked the lady from BEA, beckoning a waiter from out of the shadows.

Pete Howard said, The steak's good.

Harry and Bill looked down at the plates on the table, the plates of untouched food, the untouched steak on the plate before Pete Howard, and they nodded and they said, We'll have the steak then, please.

I hope you don't mind us talking about it, said Captain Thain, but I've just been asking Pete and Ted here what they remember about it, while it's fresh in their minds. Trying to get straight what happened, find out why it happened. Obviously we'll know a lot more when Ken comes round, but I just can't understand it because, you see, we'd reached Velocity One –

Slow down, Captain, said Harry. What's Velocity One when it's at home?

Captain Thain smiled. He said, Sorry, and call me Jim, please. But Velocity One, or V1 as we usually call it, is the point of no return. Once you've reach that point on the runway, you can't abandon take-off safely. Now you'll remember, we'd had to abandon two attempts earlier. But this time we reached 117 knots, so I called out 'V1' and waited for a positive indication of more speed so I could call out 'V2' –

V2, asked Harry.

The point when you've reached the necessary speed for take-off, which in our case was 119 knots.

But, said Harry.

But suddenly the needle began to drop, said Captain Thain. First to about 112 knots, then to 105, but I didn't actually feel we'd stopped accelerating, so I did wonder, in a flash, if perhaps there was something wrong with the air-speed indicator, because that had happened to me once before. But it was then that I heard Ken shout, Christ! We're not going to make it!

Two waiters came out of the shadows. They put two plates of steak and fried potatoes down in front of Bill and Harry. They filled their glasses with red wine, then they retreated into the shadows.

Bill looked down at the steak on his plate. He thought he could hear one of the stewardesses crying. He looked up at Captain Thain, saw the scabs upon his knuckle, remembered him . . .

I remember, said Harry, that I saw the wheels lock and unlock twice, Jim.

Captain Thain shook his head. He said, You can't have done, Harry –

I'm telling you, I did, said Harry. I was sat under the wing, looking out of the window, and them first two attempts, I watched them lock and unlock twice.

Captain Thain shook his again. No –

I'm only saying what I saw . . .

Bill pushed away his plate, pushed back his chair, stood up and said, I'm sorry. I'm going to go back up.

*

It was gone ten when the telephone rang yet again at the two-up, two-down house in Archie Street, in Ordsall, down by the docks, just a mile or so from Old Trafford. Dick Colman picked up the telephone. He listened as Jimmy Murphy told him how very, very sorry he was, but it was true, his son was among the dead, Eddie was dead.

Dick Colman thanked Mister Murphy for calling, for confirming the news, their worst fears. Thank you. Dick Colman put down the telephone and told the rest of the family what they had already guessed, what they already knew, then Dick Colman walked out of the house, still in his slippers, his carpet slippers, and he walked down the street, in the sleet and in the rain, into the night, the hours of the night, he walked and he walked.

At three o'clock in the morning, a policeman in Piccadilly Gardens approached Dick Colman, standing in the rain, in his slippers, his carpet slippers, soaked to the skin, and asked him if he was okay.

I'm just looking for my son, is all, said Dick Colman. It's late and I'm worried that he's lost, he can't find his way home.

*

Bill would never know whether this happened or not, though he thought it did, could have sworn it did –

But he couldn't sleep, not that first night at the Stachus Hotel. He waited until Harry had gone to sleep, could hear him snoring. Then, as quietly as he could, he left the room, went down the corridor and the stairs and out of the hotel and back to the hospital. Just to see the lads they'd kept in, how they were getting on.

But the nurses, the doctors, they wouldn't let Bill onto the wards. They kept him waiting outside, in the corridor, pacing up and down, not telling him anything. Bill was at a loss what to do, whether to just wait or what he should do. Then, at the end of the corridor, he saw Captain Thain and one of the stewardesses from the plane. They had a list of names, the names of all the people who were in the hospital: the Boss and Ray Wood, Bobby and Dennis, Johnny and Jackie, Bill knew about them, knew they were here, but Duncan and Albert and Kenny Morgans were also on the list, along with Frank Taylor from the *News Chronicle* and Ken Rayment, the co-pilot.

But where's everyone else then, asked Bill. What about Roger and Geoff? Mark and Tommy? Billy, David and Eddie? What hospital are they in then? And what about Tom Curry, Bert Whalley and Walter Crickmer? They were all on the plane, so where are they? And all the journalists? There were loads of journalists, not just Frank Taylor. So where is everyone, where are they all?

But the nurses, the doctors, every nurse and every doctor Bill asked, they bowed their heads, shook their heads and whispered, *Alle tot, alle tot . . .*

But Harry always said that this never happened, could never have happened. Because it was Harry who could not sleep that night, that first night at the Stachus Hotel, the longest night of his life, he said. Because Bill was tossing and turning all night in his bed, shouting out in his sleep, calling out names, the names of the dead. So Harry had got up out of bed, gone to the window, pulled back the curtains and stared out of the window, out at the snow, watching it fall, falling on the street, falling on the city, every part of the city, falling on the Rechts der Isar Hospital, their friends, their mates, the Boss in their beds on the wards, broken and bleeding, fighting for life, struggling to live. It was falling on the airport, the runway, falling softly on the ruins of the house at the end of the runway, softly falling on the wreckage of the plane, burying the scattered seats, the open suitcases, drifting against the twisted propellers, the broken wings. It was falling, too, upon the mortuary where the bodies of the dead, the twenty dead, lay waiting, wanting to go home.

Twelve hours later, twelve hours since he'd first heard the news, gone into his office, picked up that telephone, the bottle empty now, the whisky gone, everything empty now, everything gone, and Jimmy was back at home, at home in Whalley Range, at four o'clock in the morning, and England was asleep. But Jimmy could not sleep, he could not wake, could not sleep, could not forget –

Never should have not have gone . . .

The voices of the families, the faces of their sons, their husbands, their brothers, these boys, these men he'd known so long, brought up and lived with for so very long, these boys, these men he'd loved, he'd loved –

Never should have not have . . .

Oh, Bert, oh, Bert, repeated Jimmy in the room, the dark front room, into a glass, another glass. You only went because I didn't, you're only dead because I'm not. That seat was mine, not yours . . .

2

It came and went, the world, like this: fleeting glimpses, tangled moments, some that left Frank euphoric, others in despair, a floating, disembodied spirit, drifting in then out of the light, those glimpses, these moments, the pieces of a puzzle he just could not put back together again. He was sure that was Matt Busby in the next bed, but what would Matt be doing in the next bed, why was he there? And that looked like Ken Rayment, the co-pilot, like he was here, too, but why, for what reason? Frank was sure, could have sworn he'd checked out of the room in Belgrade, so why would he be back in Belgrade, in a room with Matt and with Ken? Didn't make any sense, no sense at all. And then, hello? Who's this then at the foot of my bed? Frank could swear it was his good friend Peter Lorenzo, the chief football writer of the *Daily Herald*, and with him the familiar face of another old friend, good old Tony Stratton-Smith of the *Daily Sketch*. Frank had no idea why they would be here, in his room, at the foot of his bed, with not a smile between them, their faces so serious. Frank wanted to say, to ask, Why the long bloody faces? Has someone died? The Queen, is she dead? But Frank couldn't quite get his mouth to work, his lips to part and tongue to move because, by heck, was he parched, he could murder a pint, but before he could speak, get his mouth to open and the words bloody out, Pete and Tony were fading away, just fading away, and were gone, but Frank was still parched, could still murder a pint, someone leaning over him now, kindly sticking the spout of a teapot into his mouth, tipping some sort of liquid onto his tongue, down into his throat, the worst cup of tea he'd ever bloody had, and Frank opened his eyes,

58

saw a pretty young thing, an angel in white, and he spat out the spout and the tea and said, Give us some beer, will you, darling?

Nein, nein, she said.

I'll be up and out of this bed to you, if you don't get us some bloody beer and be quick about it.

You shouldn't speak to me like that, Mister Taylor, said the young lady in white, wagging her finger, pushing the spout of the pot back into Frank's mouth.

Frank spat it out again and shouted, Come on, darling, stop messing about will you and get us me beer.

It's all right, Sister, said a tall, broad-shouldered man in a white coat, turning from the next bed, where it seemed Matt Busby was fast asleep. Let him have some beer, if he really wants it. He's a strong man.

And the young lady in white, this angel in white, she put a few drops of beer to Frank's lips, in his mouth, on his tongue, and they tasted so good, and Frank smiled, so bloody good, the world but a monstrous hangover, this sweet hair of the dog, and Frank closed his eyes again.

*

Bill wasn't sure if it was day or night, what day it was, what night it was, didn't know if he'd slept or not, and if he had, then how long he'd slept. Not that it mattered, that anything mattered now, not in this strange new world he did not know but knew was not his own, moving through it like a stranger far from home, from the bed to the bathroom, to the sink and the mirror and the face that stared back at him, that wore his name –

Bill! Bill, called out Harry from the bedroom. Where are you, Bill, are you there?

Bill turned away from the face in the mirror, walked back into the bedroom and said, I'm here.

Thought you'd buggered off and left me on my own, said Harry. I can barely fucking move.

Bill looked down at Harry on the bed, unable to raise himself up, his face and his pillow smeared in blood, in blood again, and Bill said, You should have had your nose stitched, that nick in your nostril. It's bled in the night again. Let's get you back to the hospital, get you seen to and see how the Boss and the lads are all doing.

You'll have to help me up then, said Harry. I'm that fucking stiff, I'll never make it on my own –

Bill helped Harry roll onto his side, helped him sit up, into his borrowed overcoat, his shoes that didn't match, then up off the bed, out of the room and slowly, slowly down the stairs to the front desk, where the manager found them a car, helped them into the car that then took them slowly back to the Rechts der Isar Hospital.

Bill helped Harry out of the car and in through a side door, away from the press, the gathering press, then down a corridor to get Harry seen. The doctors and the nurses so kind, so very kind, who said they'd send Harry off to have his head and face X-rayed, then to have his back and legs massaged, and so Bill said, I'll see you later then, Harry. I'll be back in a bit for you –

Make sure you do, called out Harry as they wheeled him away. Don't leave me here. Promise me that.

Bill laughed and said, I won't, I promise you that. I'm just off to find the lads, see how they're doing, how they're all getting on . . .

And Bill wandered off down the corridor of the Rechts der Isar Hospital, down one corridor then up another, round one corner then another, not sure again if this was day or this was night, but day or night this world was strange, still so very, very strange, alien yet familiar, this world a dream, a dream of scenes he'd seen, had lived before, terrible scenes now seen and lived

60

again, at the end of this corridor where Captain Thain and one of the stewardesses stood, talking with a doctor and a nurse, compiling a list of the names of all the people from their party who were in the Rechts der Isar Hospital: the Boss and Ray Wood, Bobby and Dennis, Johnny and Jackie, Bill knew about them, knew they were here, but Duncan and Albert and Kenny Morgans were also on the list, were also here, along with Frank Taylor from the *News Chronicle* and Ken Rayment, the co-pilot.

So where's everyone else then, asked Bill. Which hospital are they in? I'd like to go, is it far? I'd like to take Harry, go see Bert Whalley and Tommy Curry, Walter Crickmer and all the lads, of course . . .

But the stewardess, she bowed her head, a tear, then another tear falling from her face to the floor as Captain Thain shook his head, and the doctor and the nurse, they said, We are sorry, so very, very sorry.

*

Bobby's mum couldn't stand to stay at home, getting up, sitting down, then back up, back down, up and down, unable to rest, to settle, no chance of sleep. Last night, late last night, when they had got the lines back up at last, when she had finally got through to Old Trafford and spoken with Mister Murphy, when she had asked about the flights out to Munich, Mister Murphy he had said, Well, of course there's a seat on the flight for you tomorrow, Cissie, love, and for your husband Bob or your Jackie, if they want, but it does leave at nine in the morning, as far as I've heard, though there'd be a seat on another flight, whenever you wanted, but Bobby has said, as far as I've heard, from what Billy Foulkes and Harry Gregg have said, that he doesn't want anyone to come out, love, he doesn't want the bother or the worry, because he's saying he'll be home, he'll be back very soon.

Perhaps even Monday, so there's really no point, especially when you've not been well yourself, love, I mean, you have to think of yourself, Cissie, love, have to keep well and keep strong for your Bobby, to help him to get well and get strong. Because I'll tell you one thing, one thing for sure, we're going to need him more than ever, once he's fit and well enough, that is, only when he's ready, of course.

But what can I do, should I do, Mister Murphy, Cissie had said. I can't just sit around here all day, waiting and worrying, doing nothing all day. I need to be doing something, something to help, if I can. Anything.

Mister Murphy had sighed and said, Well, love, if you can get yourself over here to Old Trafford, then you'd be very welcome to give us a hand with the telephones and all the letters, more than welcome, love.

Are you sure, Mister Murphy, Cissie had said, sure I wouldn't just be in the way and a bother?

Jimmy had laughed. You could never be a bother, Cissie, love, and we need all the help we can get.

Well then, I'll be over just as soon as I can, Cissie had said, and thank you, Mister Murphy –

And Cissie had gone straight back down the street and home in the snow, straight up the stairs to the bedroom, to the wardrobe and the drawers, put a few things in a bag, then gone back down the stairs and said to her husband Bob and her elder son Jack, I'm off over to Manchester, to Old Trafford, to do what I can. Mister Murphy said they need all the help they can get.

But how the hell will you get there, Mam, Jackie had said. We haven't a car, and if we had, it wouldn't make no odds because of the snow, because there's no bloody buses because of the snow, and it took us forever to get up here on the train from Leeds because of the snow, and it's not five bloody minutes since you were in bloody hospital yourself, Mam –

62

Don't you worry about me, lad, she'd said. You worry about our Little One. I'll find a way –

And she did, as Cissie always did, hitching a ride first thing with the newspaper delivery van from Ted Cockburn's paper shop on the corner into Newcastle, then catching the train to Manchester, not looking at the newspapers in the van, not looking at the placards at the station, not looking at the headlines of the papers of the passengers on the train, the names of the dead, the photographs of the dead, just looking out of the window, at the cities and towns, the vales and the moors, all covered in snow, silent and white, or closing her eyes, to the words in the papers, the weather and the world, just thinking of Bobby, always thinking of Bobby, getting closer and closer, nearer to Bobby, her Bobby.

*

When Bobby opened his eyes again, it was morning, and he was in a bed on a ward in the hospital. His head had been stitched and was wrapped in bandages and ached, still ached, but not as bad. He turned to look at the bed next to his, hoping to see a friendly, familiar face, the face of a mate. But the face in the bed next to his was not the face of one of his friends, his mates, but a young German face, a German newspaper spread out on the bed before him. Bobby heaved himself, propped himself up. He could see big, dark photographs in the paper, big, dark photographs of the plane, what was left of the plane, and smaller, smudged and indistinct photographs of faces, faces of men, of friends and of mates. The young German patient felt Bobby's eyes on him, on his paper, its photographs, and the young German patient turned to Bobby, to say to Bobby, in English, he said, I am sorry, and he began to fold then hide away the German newspaper, its dark, smudged photographs.

But Bobby said, No, wait. Please, wait. I want to know, I need to know. Please, tell me –

The young German lad, he opened the paper back up, looked down at the print and slowly, sadly, he began to read, to say, Roger Byrne, dead. David Pegg, dead. Eddie Colman, dead. Tommy Taylor, dead. Billy Whelan, dead. Mark Jones, dead. Geoff Bent, dead. Tom Curry, dead. Bert Whalley, dead. Walter Crickmer, dead . . .

On and on, through the names of the journalists and the other passengers and crew he went. Alf Clarke, dead. Don Davies, dead. George Follows, dead. Tom Jackson, dead. Archie Ledbrooke, dead. Henry Rose, dead. Frank Swift, dead. Eric Thompson, dead. Tom Cable, dead. Bela Miklos, dead. Willie Satinoff, dead . . .

But Bobby wasn't hearing him, hearing these names, wasn't taking them in. He was thinking of David, he was thinking of Eddie. The times he had had with David at New Year, when Bobby had invited him home to Ashington. The times they had had round at Eddie's house in Salford, the many, many times, with his mam and his dad. He was thinking of Billy Whelan, he was thinking of Tommy Taylor. The digs he had shared with Billy, the pints he had shared with Tommy. He was thinking of Mark Jones, the toughest Yorkshireman you'd ever meet, but the kindest, most thoughtful of teammates, who'd take a new lad under his wing, touch the sleeve of your jersey during a game, saying, Lovely ball that, son, well done, then after the game, seeking you out, lifting you up, saying, Well done, son. Well played, lad.

The young German lad in the next bed had stopped reading. He folded up the newspaper, turned to Bobby and said again, I'm very sorry.

But Bobby didn't hear him, just couldn't take it in, it wasn't possible, couldn't be, it just couldn't be, not David, not David Pegg, not Eddie, not Eddie Colman; you'd never meet a lad more

64

full of life than Eddie, swaggering into every room he entered, humming every Frank Sinatra tune he'd ever heard . . .

*

The relatives, the loved ones of the injured, the dying, but not the dead, they gathered early that morning at Ringway Airport for the two Viscount 'Mercy Flights to Munich'.

Jimmy joined Jean, Sheena, her husband Don and Sandy, along with Molly Leech, who was Duncan's fiancée, and his best mate Jimmy Payne, and the wife and brother of Frank Taylor, and some others on the BEA flight, which would go via Paris, while the wives of Ray Wood, Johnny Berry, Dennis Viollet, Jackie Blanchflower and Albert Scanlon boarded an Aer Lingus flight which would go via Amsterdam. But the airlines were already talking about delays to the flights, the terrible weather en route, the danger, the risks that didn't need to be said, of repetition, repetition. But pacing up and down, chain-smoking, Jimmy didn't care. Jimmy just wanted to get there, to be there, and as quick as he could. And so if the weather was bad and the plane was to crash, then so what? That would be that.

*

The fucking massage was worse than the bloody pain, so after the fourth go around, Harry stuck up a thumb and said, Great, that's great. I'm cured, thank you, goodbye, and Harry got himself up off the treatment table and hobbled out of the room, looking for Bill, down corridors, round corners, until he saw the bastard moping about –

I thought you'd gone and bloody left me, you big fucker, said Harry. What are you doing skulking around here? Haven't you seen the lads yet or what?

Bill shook his head. No, I haven't. Not yet.

So what you been doing, chasing nurses?

Bill shook his head again. I don't know.

Never mind me, laughed Harry. Think you need them to take a look at *your* bloody head, lad.

Bill nodded and said, You're right.

I know I am, laughed Harry. I always am. So let's go find the lads, cheer them up a bit.

Bill nodded again. They're upstairs.

Come on then, said Harry, and he grabbed Bill by his arm, linked their arms together and marched them both off down to the corridor towards the hospital lifts –

I'd rather walk up, said Bill –

And so up they walked to the floors with the wards, the wards all small, off a main corridor, with six beds at the most, but in the first bed they came to was the Boss. He was lying in an oxygen tent, breathing through a tube, as pale as the walls, the colour of death.

In the bed next to the Boss was Frank Taylor, his leg strung up high in plaster. He looked fast asleep.

Suddenly, Harry and Bill heard a familiar voice from across the ward, that Black Country accent shouting, Let's have some bloody attention here!

It was Duncan Edwards, and Harry and Bill started to walk over to see him, but a doctor, she stopped them with a gentle hand and the words, He's a very strong boy. But he needs to rest.

Harry and Bill could see he was in bad shape, and as quiet as he could, Harry whispered, What are his chances, Doc?

He's very strong, she said again. Fifty–fifty.

In the bed next to Duncan lay Johnny Berry, Digger looking much worse than before, the day before, now wired up from every finger and toe. The doctor shook her head and said,

Twenty-five to seventy-five, maybe better, we'll have to see. But I am not God.

Next to Digger Berry lay Ken Rayment, the co-pilot, with a huge scar across his shaven head, his eyes closed, but seemingly stable at least.

Hey, Foulkesy! Don't you talk to the poor?

Harry and Bill turned to see Frank Taylor, his eyes open now, waving them over.

Bill went over, sat down at the end of Frank's bed and said, How are you, Frank? How are you feeling?

Me? I'm having a smashing time, said Frank. But I don't think I'll be playing Saturday. Not with this leg.

Bill laughed. You weren't playing anyway.

That's what you think, said Frank. But you just watch. One of these days I'll have your place.

Bill smiled. I know you will, Frank.

You fancy a bottle of beer, do you, Foulkesy, said Frank. There's a young girl here who'll get us one . . .

Harry had come over, stood behind Bill. They watched Frank drift, drifting off again. Then Bill got up from the foot of Frank's bed, followed Harry out of the room, across the main corridor into another small ward.

None of the lads in here looked as bad, but they still didn't look great: Jackie's arm was a mess, Dennis had a broken jaw and gash on his head, and Albert had a fractured skull and had still yet to come round, while Ray Wood also had a bad gash over his eye and concussion.

Harry and Bill went from bed to bed, sitting down beside their mates, trying to think of what to say, what not to say, but there was nothing to say, no words, no comfort, except to touch, to hold, to squeeze a hand, to say, maybe to say, You're going to be all right, your wife is on her way, she'll soon be here and have you home.

67

Here, Harry, shouted Ray Wood from his bed. Will you get them to switch off that bloody radio, will you, it's driving me mad, the noise of it all . . .

Harry looked at Bill, Bill looked at Harry; there was no radio, there was no noise, just the sudden sound now of cameras, of their flashes, of the press, the English press on the wards, going now from bed to bed, taking pictures, popping flashes, blinding the injured –

Ray Wood with his hands over his ears, Bill with his hands over his own ears now –

You bastards, screamed Harry, grabbing one bloke by his coat, spinning him round, yanking his camera from his hands, kicking it across the ward, towards the door. Get the hell out of here, the fucking lot of you!

*

Despite the weather, the van, the train, the cab ride from the station, Cissie was still at Old Trafford by ten, but the ground still seemed to be sleeping, not wanting to wake, some folk stood about in a trance, journalists nodding off on their feet. There were a couple of players she thought she recognised, was certain she knew, Freddie Godwin and Ian Greaves among them, they were coming out of the ground but they did not want to stop, to chat, not sure they knew who she was, even what day it was, they just muttered hello, that training was cancelled till Monday, then mumbled goodbye. But then some members of the ground staff, some ladies from the canteen, they turned up at the ground and headed inside, and Cissie followed them inside, went down the corridor, up the stairs, to the offices upstairs where Alma, Les and Joe were answering the telephones, still answering the telephones, the endless enquiries and offers of assistance, of help and support, still trying to make outgoing calls, the calls they

68

needed to make, to answer the telegrams and the letters, the avalanche that was already here, that would never stop coming, and Cissie saw Alma, Les and Joe flattened thin, so thin by their grief and this work and their lack of sleep, of any real sleep, their eyes red raw with the strain of it all, looking up blindly, numbly as Cissie smiled and said, I'm not here to be a nuisance, to get in the way or under your feet, I'm here to help and only to help, and in any way I can, in any way you want, you must say, just say, but the first thing I'll do is to make us all a cup of tea, one of my Cissie Charlton very special cups of tea.

*

When Bobby opened his eyes again, he was in a different bed on a different ward. His head still wrapped in bandages, his head still ached, but less, a lot less. And this time, when Bobby turned to look at the bed next to his, hoping to see a friendly, familiar face, the face of a mate, he saw Albert, then he saw Kenny, Kenny Morgans and Ray Wood, and Jackie Blanchflower and Johnny Berry, he was sure that was them in the beds over there, and the co-pilot, Ken Rayment, he was here, too, and though no one looked too good, some not so very well at all, at least they were here, and Bobby wanted to jump out of bed, to jump up and down, to hug them and shout, At least we're okay. At least we're alive! But then he thought of Dennis and Duncan and the Boss, wondered where they were, why they weren't here on this ward, and then he remembered, remembered the dead, and Bobby knew there was nothing to jump up and down about, nothing to shout about, knew there would never be anything to jump up and down about, shout about. Never again, for as long as he lived, and Bobby turned and looked away and closed his eyes again.

There were those that woke that morning after with heads heavy and hung over, those who had not wept last night but had had an extra drink or two, or three, or four instead, a drink on them, on United and their dead, and thought, Good. Not good they're dead, them lads, not that, but good they've had a setback, a bit of a setback, if you like.

But when the House of Commons met that morning, Samuel Storey, the Conservative member for Stretford, asked the Minister of Transport and Civil Aviation, Harold Watkinson, whether he would make a statement about the accident to a British European Airways aircraft, chartered by Manchester United Football Club, on Thursday, February 6, and the Minister of Transport and Civil Aviation rose to his feet and said, Yes, sir. As the House will know, an Elizabethan airliner of British European Airways Corporation crashed during take-off at Munich Airport yesterday afternoon. It was on a charter flight with a crew of six and thirty-eight passengers, amongst whom were the Manchester United Football Club team. I regret to inform the House that, as far as can be ascertained at present, more than twenty of those on board lost their lives and a number of the survivors are confined to hospital. Under international agreement, responsibility for the investigating of this accident rests with the German federal government; I have appointed a senior inspector, who has already left for Munich, to take part in the German investigation as the accredited representative of the United Kingdom. I am sure, Mister Speaker, the House will wish to join with me in expressing sympathy with the bereaved and with those who have suffered injury.

*

Bill and Harry sipped their bowls of hospital soup in the hospital corridor. The soup tasted of disinfectant, hospital disinfectant. Bill and Harry couldn't stand the taste, the smell of it, that hospital smell. They couldn't stand the hospital any more. The bloody press everywhere, they just couldn't keep away, wouldn't let them alone, Harry fighting with fellas one minute, chatting with them the next, not knowing what to do for the best, if they should stay, if they should go, but then what would they do, if they left here, where would they go. But Bill knew this wasn't the place, thought Harry would get himself arrested if they stayed any longer.

Let's go back to the hotel, said Bill.

Harry turned, he looked at Bill and said, But we still haven't been up to see the other lads.

They're not here, Harry.

What? None of them?

No, said Bill.

*

Because of the weather, there had been delays getting to Paris, then because of problems with some of their passports, there were further delays in Paris, then because of the weather in Munich, there were yet further delays leaving Paris, then because the weather turned even worse, they closed Munich Airport and so they had to fly first to Frankfurt, where there was talk of a train, which some of them took, because of the weather, the fear that it caused, but then because of a break in the weather, the BEA flight finally, finally left Frankfurt for Munich.

The heavy weather, the strong winds, the shaking and the rattling, the rolling and then the sudden drops, none of it bothered Jimmy. He just closed his eyes and opened his heart, its doors to the past, those better places, better times, humming

71

to himself that old Johnny Mercer tune, Dream, when you're feeling blue –

But as the aircraft shook, as it rattled and it rolled, up and then down, suddenly down, dropping down, those memories, they shook and they rattled and they rolled, up and down, dropping down, too, turning to regrets, the things he wished he'd done and not done, said and not said, searching the past for signs, for signs he should have seen, have read and then heeded. Jimmy wondered how he could have been so blind, so very blind to the signs, to the omens, how he'd missed those signs, those omens. Just last Friday night, or maybe it was even very early Saturday morning, but before the match against Arsenal, at the Lancaster Gate Hotel, where the team always stayed in London, Jimmy had got up for the toilet and heard voices in the corridor, thought maybe a couple of lads were sneaking back in from a night out in the smoke. But when Jimmy opened the door, he saw two policemen, stood like wraiths in the corridor they were, a doctor and then a stretcher going in and out of one of the rooms. Their oldest director, George Whittaker, had had a heart attack and been found dead in his room. It looked like old Mister Whittaker had also got up for a piss in the night, then collapsed and had died. But when Jimmy thought of the boys, that last game they'd played in England, the last time he had sat on the bench, he saw them in white, in ghostly white in the Highbury gloom, the black armbands on their sleeves for old Mister Whittaker, black armbands for the dead, and Jimmy could not help but think it had been a sign, an omen, a sign and an omen he should have seen, he should have read and heeded, that the boys were in danger, mortal danger, and so he should have gone, he should have fucking gone and not been so blind,

so blind, so very fucking blind –

Jimmy felt the wheels touch the ground, straining, skidding, then steadying as the aircraft braked hard, slowed and taxied, and Jimmy opened his eyes, turned to the window to look out and see the place, this place where all hope had come to die, and Jimmy saw the Elizabethan, twisted and torn apart, its wreck lying in the drifting snow, open to the weather and the falling night, glimpsed as they passed, heard the sudden gasps, the cries and sobs of the loved ones and relatives aboard who had also looked out upon that lifeless thing, and Jimmy shook his head and tried to smile, to think of the others, to be strong for the others, the relatives and the loved ones of the injured and the dead, to help them, support them, but to keep his eyes open, to not be so blind, but to try to find hope, to find hope again, humming in his head, only his head, Dream, and they might come true . . .

Over and over in his head, Jimmy humming, praying, Things never are as bad as they seem.

*

Back down on the ground, in a posh house out in Bowdon in Cheshire, things were very much up in the air. Harold Hardman, the Chairman of Manchester United, who was himself not a well man, that morning had attended the funeral of George Whittaker, along with fellow director William Petherbridge, and so the very first item on the agenda of the emergency board meeting of the directors of Manchester United Football Club at the home of Alan Gibson, who himself had a broken leg and, though a younger man, was never a well man either, was to express the condolences of the board to the widow and family of George Whittaker. After which the board heard the latest reports on the situation in Munich and noted that the families of the injured, along with Mister Murphy, were on their way to Munich. The board extended their sympathy and condolences to the families of the deceased and injured. Next, because Walter

Crickmer, the club secretary, was one of those who had lost his life at Munich, his assistant Les Olive was appointed as acting secretary, and the board sent authorisation to the bank for Les Olive to sign cheques on behalf of Manchester United Football Club. Willie Satinoff had also lost his life at Munich. He had been a successful local businessman and a passionate supporter of Manchester United; Willie had named one of his racehorses Red Alligator in tribute to his clothing company, Alligator Rainwear, and his favourite team. Over the years, supporting United home and away, he had become a close and popular friend of Matt Busby, 'almost an honorary member of the team', and there were those that said, given the health of many of the directors, that it was only a matter of time before Willie Satinoff was elected to the board of Manchester United Football Club, some who even said Willie Satinoff was the obvious and perfect successor to Harold Hardman as chairman of Manchester United Football Club, though what was not said, and could never now be known, was whether George Whittaker would have approved the appointment of Willie Satinoff to the board of Manchester United, because, only three weeks before, old George with his Edwardian ways and his walrus moustache had vetoed the appointment of Louis Edwards, another mate of Matt Busby's and a butcher of sorts. But Willie Satinoff was dead, and so too was George Whittaker, and so the board of Manchester United proposed, seconded and carried unanimously that Mister Louis Charles Edwards of Alderley Edge, Cheshire, be and is hereby duly appointed and co-opted as an additional director of the Company of Manchester United Football Club.

*

The world was back again, Frank back again, not sure if he was back again, if this could be right, lying on his back on a bed somewhere, with his right leg up in plaster, his left arm up in plaster, dressed in a short white nightshirt, no memory of breaking his leg or his arm, not sure if he really had broken his leg and his arm, that maybe it was a prank, all a bit of a joke that someone had played, and Frank started to laugh, but then came a cough and the pain, the pain when he breathed, the pain back again, and Frank wanted to call out to someone for help, trying to see if there was someone who'd help, that someone standing at the end of his bed, was that Bill, no, how could that be, his brother Bill at the foot of his bed, and Frank opened his mouth, tried to speak, wanted to say, Is that you, Bill? Are you really here? Because if you are, Bill, if you're really here, that's Matt Busby in the next bed –

Take it easy, Frank, a voice faintly whispered, a voice that could have been his brother Bill but seemed so far away, so very far away, coming from another world, his own world on the way out again as that voice, ever fainter, said, You've got to rest . . .

*

From the airport, the scene of the crime, the relatives, the loved ones of the injured, the dying, but not the dead, went straight to the Rechts der Isar Hospital. They had to push their way through the press at the airport, they were followed into the city by the press, and then had to fight their way again through the press and the photographers on arrival at the hospital. But once inside the Rechts der Isar Hospital, they were met by Professor Maurer and an interpreter. Professor Maurer wanted to prepare the families for what they would face when they went upstairs onto the wards and were reunited with their husbands, their fathers, their brothers and loved ones. Professor Maurer did not want them to be shocked by what they would find, did not want the shock on their faces to cause the injured men any further distress. He also asked the families, their friends not to speak of the dead, of who had lived and had not, because the patients upstairs had been spared the truth so far and were unaware of the dead, the names of the dead. Then Professor Maurer spoke to each family individually about the injuries and condition of their loved ones, and when he came to speak of Matt, Professor Maurer shook his head, and when he shook his head, Jean feared he meant Matt was dead, already dead, they were too late, and she almost fainted there and then on the spot, but then the Professor shook his head again and said, Bad, bad. He is very bad. His chest was badly crushed. He has massive internal and external injuries. His left lung has collapsed. We have him in an oxygen tent, with his breathing being assisted by a tracheotomy.

What are his chances then, asked Sandy.

Professor Maurer said, Fifty–fifty.

Jean, Sheena, Don, Sandy and a nurse then took the lift up to the intensive care unit on the fourth floor. But Jean was still feeling unsteady, so when they got up to the floor, Sheena and Don sat her down for a while, just to gather herself before she saw Mattie, while Sandy went on ahead. He'd have a quick look and a word with his dad, see how he was doing, then pop back to get his mam, his sister and Don, let them know how things were, help prepare his mam. Sandy was also keen to see which of his mates were on this ward, too, see how they were doing, say a quick hello. But the first bed he came to, the first fella he saw, was some old bloke in a tent, and so Sandy thought he must have got the wrong ward and was about to turn back when he suddenly realised that old bloke was his dad, in that tent, that plastic tent, his hair grey, suddenly now grey, his whole body a strange and sickly greenish grey, his dad looked eighty-four, not forty-eight.

Sandy stepped back from the bed, walked back down the corridor to his mam, Sheena and Don, and said, Dad's not looking too good, it'll be a bit of a shock, Mam, you'll need to be strong, we'll all have to be strong.

But they were, they all were, as best as they could. They gathered by Matt's bed, Jean sat by the bed, none of them sure if he knew they were there, but they thought that he did, that he even smiled once or twice when they spoke. But Matt needed to rest, and so they couldn't stay long, though Jean would stay all night if she could, never leave if she could, but when she got to her feet, she struggled again, and the nurses, the nuns in their white gowns, they helped Jean from the ward and into a room, a small room off the ward, where she suddenly said, I must go back, I must go back. I cannot leave him.

But Mam, Mam, he needs to rest, said Sheena, Sandy and Don. The doctor says he needs all the rest he can get, and so do you, Mam, so do you.

But Jean was shaking her head, thinking this might be the end, what if this is the end, and she turned to one of the nuns and said, He should have the last rites . . .

Missus Busby, said the nurse, reaching out, taking and holding Jean's hand in her own, your husband has already had the last rites. Twice, he has had them twice.

*

Harold Hardman told the press, the many press who continued to gather at Old Trafford, Even if it means being heavily defeated, we will carry on with the season's programme. League, FA Cup and European Cup. We have a duty to the public and a duty to football to carry on.

But that afternoon, the Football League confirmed what everyone already knew, that Manchester United's match against Wolverhampton Wanderers tomorrow afternoon was to be postponed. However, the Football League had rejected calls for all the other scheduled fixtures to be cancelled out of respect for those who had lost their lives at Munich Airport. But all players were to wear black armbands and observe a period of silence before kick-off. All flags at football stadiums were also to be flown at half-mast. But Raich Carter and Bert Tann, the managers of Leeds United and Bristol Rovers, bitterly criticised the Football League for deciding to allow Saturday's programme to carry on, just forty-eight hours after the tragedy. Many players did not feel like playing, they said, and critics will say the need to make money transcends all other feelings, because it smacks of a complete disregard for the feelings of those who wish to mourn. No games should be played until all the dead have been laid to rest.

But Mister Hardaker, the Football League secretary, answered these criticisms, saying, The Chairman of Manchester United, Mister Harold Hardman, has authorised me to say that, on behalf of the club, he wholeheartedly agreed with the management committee's decision to carry on with tomorrow's League programme. Mister Hardman asked that players should turn out and play the game in the normal way, which would be their best way of paying tribute to the players concerned in the tragedy. He was confident that Mister Busby and all connected with the United club who lost their lives or were injured would wish it so.

The city of Manchester has been strengthened by the countless messages we have received, said the Lord Mayor of Manchester, Alderman Leslie Lever, particularly from the Queen and the Duke of Edinburgh. Cables had also been received from the Prime Minister, Mister Macmillan, who was in Australia, and messages from the West German Chancellor, Doctor Adenauer, and from Marshal Tito, the President of Yugoslavia, had been forwarded to Mister Macmillan. The Lord Mayor had also opened a relief fund in Manchester to aid the dependants of the crash victims. The first donations were of one thousand guineas from Great Universal Stores and one thousand pounds from the *Manchester Evening Chronicle*. Mister Jack Solomons, the London boxing promoter, had also offered to arrange an open-air tournament in Manchester in aid of the dependants of crash victims.

That night, Manchester's own orchestra, the Hallé Orchestra, were in Sheffield, at City Hall, where it was their unanimous desire that they pay tribute to those fine sportsmen who had lost their lives in a disaster which had shocked them all, and where the thousand in the audience then stood as the orchestra played Elgar's 'Nimrod' as an *in memoriam*, followed by a minute's silence.

*

Jimmy had gone straight from the airport to the hospital, too, but he had not wanted to intrude upon the relatives and the loved ones at the bedsides of the injured. Jimmy had just very briefly been up to the wards, made sure the families had what they needed, knew where the hotel was and how they would get there, smiling and waving to the lads in their beds, telling them, Just rest and get well, boys, don't worry about anything, but keep your chins up, lads, keep those chins up. He'd caught a brief glimpse of the Boss, too, seen Johnny Berry and Duncan, Frank Taylor in that ward, too, but they needed their families, their loved ones, not Jimmy and his jokes. He stepped back into the lift, pressed the button back down, thinking what he should say to the press, the bloody press all over the place, but it was worse than he'd thought, than he'd feared. He'd still half hoped it wasn't true, that none of it was true, somehow all but a dream, a very bad dream, but when he took this lift up, stepped onto the wards, seen the boys in their beds, in their bandages and

79

plaster, seen the Boss upstairs in an oxygen tent, Johnny Berry in the state that he was, Duncan's thigh crushed surely beyond any repair, then where was the hope, what could he say except –

Manchester United will live on, declared Jimmy as he stepped out of the elevator into the thick of questions and flashes. The Red Devils will survive this . . .

I want all United supporters to know that everything possible is being done for the lads. This is one of the greatest hospitals I've ever been in. I've heard it's the greatest in Europe, and it is certainly true.

Matt told me he was feeling a little better, but I had to put my head under the oxygen tent to speak to him. He smiled slightly, his voice was faint, but he said, Take care of things for me, Jimmy. It's all in your hands now. Look after the lads. Go to it and don't worry . . .

No, I cannot say what will happen about the team. We must take first things first. But as soon as I return to Manchester, I shall confer with our Chairman, Harold Hardman, and the directors to decide our future action. But just sketching through the players we have left, it is obvious that we shall need more to help us fulfil the commitments this season. But where are the Manchester United-type players?

What of the future, you ask. It will be a long, hard struggle. It took Matt Busby, Bert Whalley and myself twelve years to produce the 1958 Red Devils. It was long, tiring, hard work, but we succeeded. We reached a perfect system. We had the best set-up in football. But the game must go on in tribute to all the members of our staff who have left us and who did their job so nobly and proudly.

At the moment, I am so confused, so tired, so sad I cannot think clearly, but what I do know and what I can say is that the Red Devils will rise again.

Harry didn't know how long he and Bill had been back at the hotel, been stood at that window, it was all they ever seemed to bloody do, was stand at this window, looking out on the snow, wondering what to do and where they should go, but then came a sudden knock upon the door, and who should come in but Jimmy Murphy, with the bravest face, the biggest smile you'd ever seen, and Jimmy shook their hands and gripped their arms and said, Hello, Billy, hello, Harry, it's good to see you, boys, and up and about and on your feet, looking so well. But how are you feeling, boys, how are you doing?

Well, we're doing okay, we're fine, said Bill. Nothing wrong with us, compared to the others, in fact it just doesn't seem right, to be honest, it doesn't seem fair.

Jimmy nodded. I know, son, I know, but just be glad that you are okay, thankful you are doing fine, for your wives, your parents, your family and your friends, the things they've been spared as well as you, boys.

We want to go home, Jimmy, said Harry.

Jimmy nodded again. I know you do, son, I know you do, and I'll get you home just as soon as we can.

But when, Jimmy, asked Harry. When? I'll go bloody mad if I have to stay here in this room another day longer or go back to that bloody hospital, all the fucking press everywhere, with their questions and their cameras, they never leave us alone, Jimmy.

I know, son, I know. But I think it would do the lads in hospital good to see you both again tomorrow, you know? To see that you're okay, that you've survived, just in case they start asking for you and you'd already left, in case then they started thinking you'd not survived.

But what about the press, asked Bill. If we go back to the hospital, the press'll be there again.

Jimmy nodded. I know, son, I know, but I have an idea or two, how to get them to calm down a bit.

Like what, Jimmy, asked Harry.

But then there was another knock on their door as Sandy stopped by with his brother-in-law Don Gibson to see how everyone was doing, how they were all holding up, and to say his mam was doing her best, but the doctors had had to give her a sedative, just to get her to rest, to help her to sleep. And then there was another knock on the door, then another, and one by one, or in pairs or in groups, all the wives of their mates came to gather in Harry and Bill's room. There was Blanchy's wife Jean, who knew Harry well, and Dennis's wife Barbara, and Ray Wood's wife Betty, and Albert's wife Josephine, who was expecting again, and Johnny Berry's wife Hilda, who was doing her best, she really was, and Duncan's girl Molly and his good pal Jimmy Payne, both doing their best, too, all of them doing their best, putting on the very bravest of faces but complaining about the press, the way they carried on.

But after an hour or so, Bill took Harry to one side and he said, Where's Jimmy? I didn't see him go.

Harry glanced around the room, saw the open door to the empty bathroom, and shook his head and said, I never saw him go. I wonder where he's gone.

I'm going to go have a look, said Bill. I need to get some air myself, all the smoke in here.

Harry nodded. Me, too.

Half of this smoke is yours, laughed Bill. But come on then, let's go and see where Jimmy's gone.

Harry laughed. Let's try the bar first.

Bill and Harry told the others they were just popping out, that they'd be back in a bit, then they left their room, went down the corridor towards the corner to the stairs, turned the corner and found Jimmy there, in the dark, sat upon the stairs, hunched and crumpled, crushed into a tiny, tiny ball of enormous, overwhelming grief, his head in his hands, Jimmy shook, wrenched and wretched, Jimmy sobbed, he cried.

3

But while some men sat on stairs and wept, and women stared at walls, and children took to their beds, asking where the ruddy hell was God in all of this, doubting the purpose, the point, the very existence of the Lord, others pried and probed and poked about; the diggers of the press, yes, but there were others still, tasked to find a cause, a scapegoat to blame, to shame and then to ruin.

The moment that news of the crash in Munich reached the headquarters of the Luftfahrt-Bundesamt in Braunschweig, Lower Saxony, the Chief Inspector of Accidents for the Federal Aviation Office, Captain Hans J. Reichel, and his investigating team immediately began their preparations to fly down to Bavaria.

Captain Reichel had flown a million miles or more, had been a supply pilot for the Legion Condor during the Spanish Civil War, and as he flew a few miles more to Munich now, he stared out of the window of the plane, watched the snow streak and swirl past, already sure that this would prove to be an English disaster of English making, that there would no German hand to blame and shame and ruin here, already certain of what he would find and then prove.

Back down on the ground in Munich, in the hours after the crash no attempt was made by the airport authorities to preserve the scene or to secure any evidence. Instead, as snow continued to fall from the sky, heavy snow in driving wind, firemen and airport officials, reporters and cameramen, gawkers and ghouls had tramped and traipsed back and forth at the end of the runway, through the ruins of the house and the wreck of the plane, back and forth all over the site.

Nor had there been any attempt to illuminate the scene, so six hours after the crash, after Captain Hans J. Reichel and his team had finally touched down in Munich, after Captain Reichel had asked the airport officials to drive him and his team straight out to the scene, Captain Reichel and his team found the site in pitch darkness, the whole scene pitch black but for the snow –

Reichel marched up to a BBC cameraman. Sir, give me your battery lamps, please.

The man from the BBC did as he was ordered, then with a curt nod Reichel turned and marched straight to the right starboard wing of the Elizabethan, which was still attached to the fuselage, with only slight damage and untouched by fire, covered in an even layer of snow about eight centimetres deep. His hand in leather glove, Reichel reached out and touched the snow on the wing of the aircraft, the snow powdery and easily brushed aside to reveal a layer of ice. Reichel took off one of his leather gloves, ran his fingers over the upper surface of the ice, the ice coarse like a kitchen grater, very rough and firmly frozen to the skin of the wing. Reichel put on his glove again, nodded to himself and moved on. He examined all the points of the wing, each time taking off his glove, running his fingers across the skin of the wing, putting on his glove again, but everywhere he looked, at all the different points on the wing, he found the same condition, the same very loose and powdery snow, always easily blown off to reveal the same layer of ice, firmly frozen to the skin of the wing, and each time Reichel nodded to himself.

But after carefully examining the wing, all the points on the wing, with his mind made up, his conclusions already reached, Reichel made a cursory inspection of the rest of the wreckage. He saw the propeller blades set at the take-off pitch angle, saw the throttle levers in the fully open position, saw the main undercarriage was down, and again he nodded to himself, then he marched back over to the starboard wing of the Elizabethan, and having found what he had come to find, had known he would find, he pointed a finger of his right leather glove at the skin of the wing and declared, I can find nothing which might be the cause of the accident, or even considered to have contributed to the accident, apart from ice on the wing.

Naturally, you will wish to examine the site again in the morning, will you not, Captain Reichel, asked the airport officials. In daylight?

Why, asked Captain Hans J. Reichel, the Chief Inspector of Accidents for the Luftfahrt-Bundesamt. The cause of this accident is very clear: the cause is ice upon the wings. You can dispose of the wreckage tomorrow.

But the British European Airways accident investigation team has only just arrived, said the airport officials. The British government are also sending someone from their air investigation branch, who will act as their representative in the inquiry. They will all wish to inspect the scene, will they not?

Of course, said Reichel. It's their crash, not ours.

*

Early that Saturday morning, a very angry Professor Maurer was forced to issue the following statement: Rumours that Mister Busby has died are entirely false and they do not come from us. Mister Busby remains seriously ill, but he asked me to save him from the photographers. He said, Doctor, please, the flashes are blinding my eyes.

Jimmy was appalled by the press, the way the English press were behaving, particularly the cameramen. Jimmy had friends in the press, some of his closest pals, some of whom had died on Thursday, and he knew they would have been appalled, too,

86

would have gone mad, some of them, bloody berserk. But Jimmy had a plan to deal with the press, just to calm things down a bit, so first thing that morning, at the crack of dawn, it seemed to Harry and Bill, Jimmy knocked on their door, with another big smile, another brave face, and said, Morning, boys, morning. Now let's get you up and downstairs, quick as you can, boys.

Why, Jimmy? Are we going home, asked Harry. Are you taking us home, Jimmy, are you?

Jimmy shook his head. Not today, no. But maybe tomorrow, or Monday at the latest.

I can't fly, said Bill. I'm never flying again.

Jimmy shook his head again. No one's flying, Billy. We'll get the train, then the boat, but come on . . .

But if we're not going home, Jimmy, said Harry, where are we going then, Jimmy?

Jimmy winked. Into the lion's den –

Under duress, but hoping for the best, Jimmy took Harry and Bill to the hotel where most of the English press were staying, when they were not hanging around the hospital wards, taking photographs of the injured in their beds, when they were not asking the wives and the relatives if they thought their loved ones would pull through: Do you? But can you be sure, really so sure?

Jimmy sat Harry and Bill down in the lobby, made them promise not to bugger off and leave him in the lurch, then Jimmy went upstairs, banging on doors, shouting, Morning, gents, morning! I've got Harry Gregg and Billy Foulkes downstairs, waiting to tell you their stories, so come on, gents, get yourselves up and downstairs.

Bleary, weary-eyed and foul of breath, the gentlemen of the press toppled out of their pits, dragged their bellies to the doors, then tumbled down the stairs to ask, So how are Matt and the boys? What's the latest?

Jimmy looked at Harry, and Harry looked at Bill, and Bill said, Well, Matt is in an oxygen tent, and Duncan Edwards seems to be quite badly hurt, too, and Bobby Charlton has a bandaged head, and Jackie Blanchflower's arm is badly gashed. Harry had had to strap it up.

But they're saying Duncan will never play again, said the press. Do you think he'll play again?

Bill looked at Harry, and Harry looked at Jimmy, and Jimmy said, They broke the mould when they made Duncan, you all know that. So if anyone can beat the odds, it's Duncan Edwards.

But what are your odds against Sheffield Wednesday, said the press, in the Cup next week?

If the FA Cup tie against Sheffield Wednesday is played next Saturday, I still haven't the faintest idea what our team will be. At the moment, I would say that only Harry Gregg here has a real chance. Him and Billy Foulkes have been examined by a German specialist, but we shall have our club doctor look over them again.

*

Dennis Viollet opened his eyes again. Barbara was still sat by his bed, holding his hand. She smiled and she said, How are you, love? Can I get you anything?

A new pair of feet would be a start, said Dennis. They hurt like bloody hell.

Barbara nodded, she said, It's because you lost your shoes, love, and then you were walking around barefoot in the snow. But the doctor says they'll be okay.

My shoes or my feet, asked Dennis.

Barbara smiled. Your feet, love, but we'll get you some new shoes, don't worry, love.

Dennis tried to smile, but then the pictures started to come back, in his head, his mind, the pictures of things he had seen in the snow, walking around barefoot in the snow, the faces of his mates in the snow, their eyes open or eyes closed, but not moving, never moving, these pictures, these faces he'd seen, or had he? No, he couldn't have done, it was all in his head, his mind, they couldn't be real, couldn't be true, and Dennis smiled again at Barbara and asked, You seen any of the other lads yet? You know how they're doing?

They're doing fine, love, said Barbara, turning and smiling at Josephine Scanlon, sat beside the bed of her Albert, her Albert with his eyes still closed, his eyes still yet to open, holding his hand, smiling back.

But what about Eddie, asked Dennis. How's he doing, love? Is he okay? Are his mam and dad here, were they on the plane with you?

They weren't on our plane, love, no, said Barbara, trying to smile but getting up from her chair by the bed, looking about her, then turning back to Dennis and saying, How about I go and get us both a nice cup of tea?

*

The moment that news of the crash in Munich had reached the headquarters of British European Airways in Ruislip, Middlesex, an accident investigation team immediately began to be assembled. The team consisted of Anthony Milward, the Chief Executive of British European Airways, Captain Baillie, the Chief Pilot, J. W. Gibbs, the chief accident investigator, Captain James, the director of flight operations, and two British European Airways doctors. This team left London for Munich late in the afternoon, early in the evening, and though they were delayed by the treacherous weather en route, the team landed in Munich shortly after ten o'clock on Thursday night, some seven hours after the crash.

Because of the lateness of the hour and the severity of the weather, the team did not attempt to inspect the site of the crash that night, but instead focused on the survivors and the injured. Captains Baillie and James and Mister Gibbs went to speak with Captain Thain, Bill Rodgers and the two stewardesses, while Anthony Milward and the two BEA doctors went straight to the Rechts der Isar Hospital to visit Ken Rayment and the other survivors and to offer any assistance they could.

Anthony Milward and the BEA doctors found Ken Rayment in a critical condition. He had had to be cut from the wreckage and had been admitted to the hospital severely injured and struggling to breathe. He had been given a tracheotomy and placed inside an oxygen tent, but he had lost consciousness and fallen into a coma.

There was nothing that Anthony Milward or the two doctors from British European Airways could do for their pilot. Helpless, Anthony Milward stepped back from the bed of Ken Rayment, turned to see the other injured men in the other beds. There was another man on the ward inside another oxygen tent. Anthony Milward had been told it was Matt Busby, the manager of Manchester United, who had also been given an emergency tracheotomy, but Anthony Milward would not have recognised the poor man now, lying on his back inside that oxygen tent. There was a third man on the ward, a journalist, he'd heard, who, though not inside an oxygen tent, was also struggling to breathe, lapsing in and out of consciousness, his legs and arms raised up in plaster, calling out a name, then falling into silence.

But, with horror, Anthony Milward heard different noises now, the noise of boots and shoes hard down the corridor onto the ward, a horde of cameramen, six or seven, even eight men swarming around the bed of Matt Busby, flashes popping, blinding the man, then six or seven, even eight more following on behind, then another six, seven, eight, nine or ten more, blinding the injured man with their sudden bright white flashes in his eyes as he fought for his life, battling death –

Doctor, Sister, protested Anthony Milward to a German doctor and nurse, one of the many German doctors and nurses working with devotion to save the lives of these foreign men. Can you not do something, say something, and get these cameramen out of here?

Believe me, sir, we have tried, said the doctor, but they will not listen, not heed what we say. But with respect, sir, these are your countrymen, not mine.

*

Bobby opened his eyes again, looked about him, saw the faces in the beds, the wives and families by the beds, closed his eyes again, then opened them again. It was like musical beds on this ward. He could have sworn that when he first came down to this ward – or was it up, or across? – he was sure he had seen Johnny Berry in a bed on this ward, and the co-pilot, Ken Rayment, he had been in a bed on here, too. Now Johnny was gone, Ken Rayment, too, but at least Dennis was here, in the bed next to his, his wife at his side, holding his hand. Ray Wood's wife Betty was by Ray's bed, too. Bobby watched her get up from her chair by the bed, saw her smile and wave at him, and Bobby smiled and waved back, then Betty walked off the ward, down the corridor, looking for a nurse –

Here, Bobby, said Ray Wood, sitting up in his bed. Do you know what happened to everyone? Who made it, who didn't? They keep telling me some of the other lads are in other hospitals, that's why they're not here, why we can't see them. Is that right, Bob?

Bobby could see that German lad in his head, the paper in his hand, up on that other ward, could see his mouth opening

91

and closing, reading out the names of the dead, but Bobby could not hear that German lad in his head, the names he had said, just whispers of names going round in his head, in his brain, half heard or not heard, round and round, so Bobby wasn't sure what names that lad had read out and which he had not, and Bobby shook his head and said, I'm sorry, Ray, I just don't know.

I wish I knew, said Ray, wish someone would tell us. It's driving me bloody mad.

But Betty was coming back down the ward to Ray's bed, with a nurse and some pills. The nurse put two pills in her hand, held out her hand for Ray to take the pills from her hand, but Ray could not take the pills from her hand. Bobby watched Ray try once, twice, three times to take the pills from her hand, but each time he tried, Ray missed, and Ray cursed, What the hell's wrong with me? I'm seeing double here! I'm a bloody keeper, I can't be seeing bloody double.

*

Harry and Bill had been asked by the Chief Executive of BEA, Mister Milward, if they wouldn't mind coming back out to the airport, to the scene of the accident, to help BEA to identify luggage and personal effects. Harry and Bill didn't want to go, they really didn't want to go, but Jimmy Murphy said it would be better if they did, that the sooner they did, the sooner then they could set off back home. But Jimmy knew it would be hard on them, so Jimmy asked Duncan's best pal, Jimmy Payne, if he'd go out there with them, just to lend some support, and Jimmy Payne said, Yes, of course I'll go, yeah.

But after they'd been driven back out to the airport, staring out of the car windows at the city as it passed, the people with their shopping, their Saturday shopping in their bulging bags, watching life go on, going on without them, staring in silence, except for Bill, who kept saying, Slow down, will you, pal, will you slow down, please, then the first thing that happened was Bill and Harry were taken off into two rooms, separate rooms, sat down in two chairs at two tables and asked by a German, two Germans, to tell them all that they could, all they remembered about what had happened on Thursday, about what had gone on, one German questioning Harry about this, the other German quizzing Bill about that.

Then, when the Germans were done, Harry and Bill, and Jimmy Payne and Mister Milward from BEA, and the two Germans, they drove out to the scene of the accident, in silence again, slowly again, Bill and Harry not saying anything, anything now as they got closer and closer, nearer and nearer, stopping now, parked up by the wreck of the plane. The two Germans, Mister Milward and Jimmy Payne got out, then Harry, then Bill, reluctantly Bill, stepping out of the minibus into pools of water, puddles of mud, and into the slush, the slush and the snow, the slush and the snow again, everyone else in their thick winter coats, Bill and Harry in their borrowed, thin suits, but this place was not borrowed, this scene was not borrowed, this place, this scene was theirs, all theirs, the mud and the slush, the twisted, tangled metal parts still scattered and strewn across the snow, the charred black ruins of a house, a shed, the scorched, odd, solitary tree, and the plane, of course, the plane, what was left of the plane, more, much more than Bill had remembered, had thought, one wing, its propeller, the cockpit and much of the front of the aircraft, the front where Harry and Bill had been sat, into which Harry and Bill now peered, where Harry and Bill saw their seats, the very seats where they'd sat and into which Bill and Harry were drawn, bewildered, bewitched, in a daze, a dream, back inside the plane, the wreckage of the plane, Bill finding his briefcase and overcoat still jammed in the rack above his seat, the bottle of gin he'd been given in Belgrade, a present from the

British Embassy, in the pocket of his coat, taking it out, turning it over in his hands, amazed it was still intact and unbroken, his briefcase and coat undamaged, too, and Bill smiled and shook his head, but then just as fast that smile so brief was gone again as Bill saw a hat and scarf in the jumble on the floor, picked up the hat, the scarf from the floor, knew the name in the hat before he even looked. Eddie Colman had loved that hat, that scarf, the red and white scarf, the presentation cap from the Continental Club on Oxford Road, Eddie's name stitched inside and given to Eddie on his hundredth or something visit to the Conti, and Bill could see Eddie now, that cap on his head, that scarf round his neck, that smile, that grin, that cheeky fucking little grin on his face, and Bill thought he heard a laugh, a tiny, hollow laugh, then a voice shouting, *What are you laughing at? We're all going to fucking die here*, then another voice, an Irish whisper of a voice, *If this is the end, then I'm ready for it*, the whispers, the voices from the back of the plane no longer here, and Bill could not stand it no more, turning to Harry to say, Let's get out of here, but someone had Harry by the arm, saying, You were very brave, Harry, to do the things you did, but Harry shook his head and turned away, Harry wishing someone had been brave, been truly, really brave and had had the courage on this plane that day to stand up and to say, to shout, This is crazy, this is madness, stop the plane!

Come on, Foulkesy, let's get the hell out of here, I can't stand it no more, said Harry, taking, gripping Bill by the arm. But as they clambered back out again, Bill with the bottle of gin in his hand, the cameras flashed, the press out here, even here, and Harry cursed the press again, about to swing for one of them again, but then –

Bloody hell. Look at this, shouted Jimmy Payne. He was holding up a diamond ring, a pile of jewellery in the puddle at his feet. Will you look at all this?

And the German police, who as far as Harry could tell had been doing sweet bugger all until then, blew their whistles and sent for armed policemen to come and guard what was left of the scene, while Mister Milward and the two Germans took Harry, Bill and Jimmy Payne back to the airport building, where they sat them down, gave them a drink, a stiff drink of brandy to warm them up, to calm them down, to steady their nerves, and then Mister Milward said, If you could please follow me . . .

Harry, Bill and Jimmy Payne followed Mister Milward and the Germans out of the airport building and into a cold, wide hangar, where laid out on the ground were suitcases and briefcases, some open, some closed, coats and jackets and shoes, some in piles, some in pairs, but some all alone on their own, and Harry and Bill walked up and down the lines of cases and clothes, in and out of the piles, bending down and reaching out, taking labels and tags in their hands, reading the names on the labels and tags, helping Mister Milward and the Germans to identify the luggage and possessions which had been salvaged from the wreckage of the aircraft, but it seemed to Bill that every label, every tag they touched, every name they read was the label, the tag, the name of the dead, and only the dead, and when Bill came to one briefcase, off to one side, alone and forsaken, stuffed with foreign currency and traveller's cheques and a familiar silver hip flask, Bill didn't need to read the name on the tag, Bill knew this briefcase belonged to Walter Crickmer, who had been at United for years, for decades, whose life was United, and Bill could stand it no more, this hangar, this airport, this place, this whole bloody city, every bloody thing about it, every fucking thing on earth, and he wanted to run, to run again, away from this place, this city, this thing that had happened, and Bill dropped Walter's briefcase onto the floor, turning to look for the door, but Jimmy Payne was there, walking towards him, coming up to him, smiling at Bill, putting

95

an arm round Bill, saying to Bill, Come on, Foulkesy, let's get you out of here.

*

Duncan was ill, seriously ill, but he was also upset, very upset, constantly touching his left wrist, patting the sheets and the blankets of his hospital bed, fretting and worrying.

You must lie still, said Sister Solemnis, who was trying to care for Duncan. It's important you rest.

But Duncan could not rest, would not lie still. My watch has gone. Someone's thieved my watch.

Be calm, please, pleaded Sister Solemnis. There was no watch on your wrist when you were brought in, so no one here has taken your watch.

You don't understand, it's my Real Madrid watch. It's gold. I must have it back. Please can you find it?

I'll do my best, said Sister Solemnis.

Do you promise us, Sister?

Yes, I promise, promised Sister Solemnis, but you must promise me you will be calm and will rest.

That Saturday, when Jimmy returned to the wards, Sister Solemnis stopped him. From out of the pocket of her white gown, she took a watch, broken beyond repair, and said, Mister Murphy, do you know if this is the watch that Duncan says he has lost? It was found by one of the rescuers but put to one side. Is it Duncan's watch?

Jimmy took the watch from her hand, turned the watch over in his hand, the watch mangled and smashed, broken beyond repair, and Jimmy nodded. Yes.

Sister Solemnis smiled. Would you . . .?

Jimmy nodded again. He walked onto the ward, where Duncan was lying in bed, his eyes closed. Jimmy stood before the bed again, staring at this shattered boy. He had a broken pelvis, multiple leg fractures, his right thigh particularly damaged, he had fractured ribs, a collapsed lung and, worst of all, severely damaged kidneys. The doctors were hopeful an artificial kidney would help to keep Duncan alive, but they were very doubtful he would ever walk again, let alone ever kick a ball again. Jimmy bent down beside Duncan's bed. He gently strapped the watch to Duncan's wrist.

Duncan's eyelids flickered, then his eyes opened. He looked at Jimmy and he smiled. Hello, Jimmy.

Hello, son, said Jimmy with a smile, the best smile he could. They found your watch. I put it on your wrist.

Duncan smiled again. That's great, Jimmy, thank you, Jimmy. So what time's kick-off Saturday?

Usual time, Dunc, three o'clock.

Duncan closed his eyes again. It's Wolves, isn't it? I must be right for that, Jim. I can't miss that.

Well, we're resting you, son, said Jimmy, trying to keep his voice steady, for his words not to choke or to drown, to say, We don't need you to beat that lot.

Duncan nodded, his eyes closed, then smiled again and whispered, Just get stuck in for me then.

*

In Manchester that afternoon, United should have been playing Wolverhampton Wanderers at Old Trafford. Wolves were top of the table, but United were Champions, Champions two seasons running, and United wanted to be Champions again, to have a hat-trick of titles to match the records of Huddersfield and Arsenal, and so this should have been the biggest game of the season, the chance for United to peg back the Wolves. But the game was off, postponed until who knew when, if it would be ever played. But in Manchester that afternoon, folk still put on their scarves, their red and white scarves, still damp, still wet with tears, gathered in pubs, not to joke or sing, not today, not even to drink, to really drink, but just like they did, they always did, and then they went for the train, not pushing to get on, not today, the train silent today, and then got off at Warwick Road, like they did, they always did, not shoving to get off, no one pushing, no one shoving, not today, no one even hardly speaking, trudging towards the ground, heads bowed down, not daring to look up, hands deep in pockets, walking in silence towards the ground, no vendors, no hawkers, not today, nothing but silence today, silence and cold, so bloody cold, the ground coming closer, folk removing their caps, their hats, then stopping, standing there still, before the ground, outside the gates, some looking up, up at the walls of the stands, others at the floor, their feet, some muttering prayers, whispering words, fighting losing battles against tears, wiping their faces in their scarves again, lighting cigarette after cigarette, one in the mouth and one in each hand, shuffling around the ground, a silent lap of the silent ground, then stopping again, heads bowed again, before turning to leave, back to the station, the train, the pub and then home, homes where their hearts no longer were, their hearts here, forever here, broken in pieces, here on the floor, on the ground, here at Old Trafford on Saturday.

*

Albert could hear Billy Whelan whispering to him, telling him, If this is the end, Scanny, then I'm ready for it . . .

Albert opened his eyes. He was in a hospital bed, his head in plaster, holding his wife's hand in one hand, a telephone in his other. He was shouting into the phone, Hello, hello? Is there anybody there? I'm looking for my friends. I need to get out of here, but I can't find my friends. A nurse gently prised the telephone out of his hand, while his wife softly patted his shoulder, his arm and said, You're all right, love, it's going to be all right. Look, there's Dennis and Ray here, and Bobby and Kenny over there. Why not give Bobby a wave, dear? Albert tried to raise his hand, his arm, but his hand, his arm were made of stone and would not budge, and Albert closed his eyes again, into the dark again, all dark again, until he heard someone walking past, that someone say, Albert Scanlon will never play football again, and Albert opened his eyes. He looked about him, saw the lads in their beds, still in their beds, but then here came Jimmy Murphy, walking onto the ward, up to him now, and Jimmy said, Hello, son, hello. Good to see you, son, and with your eyes open for a change. That's good. So how are you feeling, son?

But Albert shook his head, tried not to cry but started to cry, and Jimmy took and held his hand and said, What's the matter, son? What's wrong?

I just heard someone say I'll never play again.

Well, that's bollocks is that, son, said Jimmy. Utter fucking bollocks. Whoever was it told you that?

Albert shook his head again. I don't know, Jimmy. Just someone walking past. I didn't see.

Well, that's because it was no one, said Jimmy. That's who it was, son. Because you're all right. The doctors say you'll be playing again in no time.

And Albert looked and smiled at Jimmy and said, Is that right, Jimmy? Are you really sure?

Take my word for it, said Jimmy. I promise you, son, you'll be playing again in no time at all.

*

At three o'clock that Saturday afternoon, Stan Cullis, the manager of Wolverhampton Wanderers, and his staff and players gathered on the pitch at Molineux and stood in silence, in honour of the men they should have played that afternoon, and in every ground across the country, and in other countries, too, thousands upon thousands stood in silence, heads hatless, bowed in prayer and thought, or sang together, in their thousands, 'Abide with Me', black armbands on the sleeves of every player, snow, poignant snow across many of the pitches, club flags hanging at half-mast in the winter gloom, or the heavy rain which lashed across White Hart Lane, where Geoffrey Green sat in the press box, here to report on Tottenham's match against Manchester City, knowing as the referee blew his whistle, as the teams kicked off again, that to move onwards, even if sorrowfully, was the only course, striving to achieve what was admired so deeply in the stricken Champions, watching Tottenham and City do their best to that end in appalling, farmyard mud, but still the shadows of those familiar figures, now suddenly and tragically lost, flickered and danced, darting here and there, across the pitch, in mind, yes, in mind, but also sometimes, it seemed to Geoff, even in sight, in plain sight before his eyes, his very eyes, watching Danny Blanchflower playing his usual insistent game, while his brother Jackie lay among the injured in the German hospital, Danny maybe glad of the peace of the pitch, away from the noise of the tragedy, but as Brooks left Barnes and Warhurst slithering in the sludge, all Geoff could see, could really see was that flowing passage of play last week, just one week ago, so very near to here, when Colman and Morgans combined for Tommy Taylor to score United's fifth and his second of that day, the last goal of his life, and as the mud-caked players trudged off the field at White Hart Lane all Geoffrey Green could see, anyone could see, were those Manchester United players, walking from that Highbury field last week, arm in arm in white, prophetic, ghostly white.

*

When Bobby opened his eyes again, Jimmy Murphy was sat by his bed. Jimmy smiled and said, Hello, Bobby, son.

Hello, Jimmy, said Bobby. How are you?

Jimmy laughed. Well, I'm as right as rain, I am, but how about you, son? How are you feeling?

Not too bad, said Bobby. He reached up, gently touched the bandages wrapped around his head and said, I'm fine, in fact. Must look worse than it is.

Jimmy smiled. You've had a right old knock to your noggin, son, but you'll be fine, just need to take it easy, son. Not be going heading no balls just yet.

Not that I do very often, smiled Bobby.

Jimmy smiled again. The Lord put your skills in your feet and your brother's in his head.

Have you heard from us mam, asked Bobby, how me dad and me brothers are doing?

Jimmy nodded. They're all fine, don't you worry, son, Just pleased you're on the mend, of course. But you should maybe give your mam a ring, if you're up to it. She's at Old Trafford, son, so I can see about calling?

Is she, said Bobby. What's she doing there?

Jimmy laughed. Making herself useful, no doubt running the shop by now, if I know your mam.

I bet she is, said Bobby, and he tried to smile at Jimmy, let him know he was okay, that everything was okay, was going to be okay, but the whispers of names that German lad had said, had read out from the paper, up on that other ward, they were still going round in his head, in his brain, round and round, still half heard, or not heard, Bobby still not sure what names that lad had read out and which he had not, and Bobby closed his eyes.

*

Later that Saturday afternoon, Captain James Thain, wireless operator Bill Rodgers, stewardesses Margaret Bellis and Rosemary Cheverton, along with Peter Howard and Ted Ellyard of the *Daily Mail* would be flying home to England. But before leaving Munich for London, out at the airport, at yet another press conference, Captain Thain was questioned about reports that the aircraft had returned twice before the third and fatal take-off, and how that was surely a bit peculiar, very peculiar wasn't it, Captain?

There was nothing peculiar about it, said Captain Thain. I was just not satisfied and returned to consult the engineer. The engine was giving full power, but varying the note. That was all. It was nothing peculiar.

Let us be very clear about this, snapped Anthony Milward, Chief Executive, British European Airways, who had had enough, more than enough of the English press to last him a lifetime. Captain Thain had been quite satisfied before the aircraft taxied for the take-off, and this is the first time our airline has had casualties with the Elizabethan in the eight years of the life of the aircraft.

But is it true BEA are considering withdrawing the Elizabethan from service, asked the press.

We will test every nut, bolt, strut and spar in the wreckage, said Captain Baillie, the Chief Pilot, and if an early solution is not evident, then yes, we may consider withdrawing our fleet of twelve Elizabethan aircraft until the riddle is solved. But I would also like to add that I am certain that Captain Thain here was satisfied with the performance of his engines before the third attempted take-off. Otherwise he would never have attempted it.

What about compensation, asked the press.

Of course, British European Airways will be paying compensation to the families of all those killed and injured, subject to proof of loss, said Anthony Milward.

But how much will that be, asked the press.

An international convention limits the amount that can be claimed for any one passenger to three thousand pounds, said Anthony Milward. But BEA are also providing accommodation and assistance to the families here in Munich and will, of course, be flying all the survivors home as soon as they are fit and able to travel.

But what about the dead, asked the press. Are British European Airways bringing back the dead?

Yes, said Anthony Milward, one of our freighter aircraft is scheduled to leave London for Munich today.

And how about Captain Rayment, said the press.

He remains dangerously ill, said Anthony Milward, with severe head injuries and a broken leg.

Do you think he'll pull through, asked the press.

The German doctors and nurses are working with the utmost devotion in their beautiful modern hospital to care for all the critically injured and ill, said Anthony Milward. But now, if you'll please excuse me . . .

But later that evening, when Captain Thain, wireless operator Bill Rodgers, stewardesses Margaret Bellis and Rosemary Cheverton, Peter Howard and Ted Ellyard of the *Daily Mail* and Anthony Milward of BEA arrived back at London Airport, after the press had insisted on photographs of Captain James Thain, wireless operator Bill Rodgers and stewardesses Margaret Bellis and Rosemary Cheverton on the steps of the aircraft, disembarking at London Airport, in their coats and their gloves, with their forced smiles and furrowed brows, and stares that said, *You have not seen the things that we have seen*, the press then turned their attention back to Anthony Milward and told the Chief Executive of British European Airways what Captain Reichel, Chief Inspector of Accidents in West Germany, had told their colleagues in Munich while Anthony Milward had been up in the air. That there was ice on the wings, that the fact the aircraft did not leave the ground was probably the result of ice on the wings, and so what do Mister Milward and BEA have to say about that, do you think ice on the wings was the cause of the disaster?

Of course, I cannot give the cause of the accident yet, snapped Anthony Milward again. But what I can say is that what would have been a simple mishap, in which people might have climbed out of the aircraft with ankle injuries, was turned into a major disaster by the house situated three hundred yards from the end of the two-thousand-yard runway at Munich Airport.

So you're saying it would've been just an ordinary overshoot, asked the press, if it wasn't for that house?

No, it wasn't an ordinary overshoot by the Elizabethan, said Anthony Milward. Let us call it an extraordinary overshoot, a failure to take off, but also let us say the house should not have been there.

But what about the effect of the weather, said the press, are you saying that wasn't a cause?

Of course, the effect of the weather as a cause of the disaster is a distinct possibility, said Anthony Milward. We shall have to investigate it very carefully.

But why was there no de-icing?

There was no de-icing spraying at Munich, said Anthony Milward, for the umpteenth blasted time already, because the aircraft was in transit and soft, unfreezing snow was falling.

*

Soft, unfreezing snow was still falling in Munich that night, and back in their hotel room, on what Harry and Bill really, really hoped would be their last night in this hotel room, Harry and Bill were back at the window again, watching the snow again, but drinking gin not whisky, and maybe it was the gin, or more

104

likely the snow, just the sight of the snow, but Bill felt cold again, bloody freezing again. He walked over to his bed, picked his coat up off the bed, his own overcoat, undamaged and saved, and put it back on, walked back to the window, his hands in his pockets, the pockets of his coat, where he found, he felt his pack of cards. Bill remembered, vaguely remembered slipping them into the pocket of his coat, but he was not sure when, exactly when, but when he took them out now, held them in his hand, held them up to show Harry, he was amazed and said, Look at that? That's unbelievable.

Bill himself had not the slightest bruise and his overcoat, too, had been blessed with not one single mark or tear, the pocket, all the pockets of the coat intact, without one rip, one missing stitch, but the top quarter-inch of his pack of cards had been sliced clean off and had disappeared, the cut razor-blade, guillotine clean –

I told you, said Harry, if you'd not pulled that big head of yours down at the last minute, I thought you were going to be decapitated, that or your brains crushed to mush, but you'd be heading balls in heaven now, or hell.

Bill shook his head, turning the pack of cards over in his hands, running his finger along the cut at the top, then searching again in the pocket, all the pockets in vain for the quarter-inch that was lost. He shook his head again and said, I just don't understand it, any of it.

The Miracle of Munich, said Harry, his back to Bill, at the window again, the dark and the snow.

The pack of cards in his hand, clutched tight, tight in his hand, Bill turned, looked to Harry, to the window, the dark and the snow, and said, gently, softly, softly, gently said, They're not out there, you know that? They're not coming back, you do know that, don't you?

I'm not daft, said Harry. Course I know that.

So why do we keep on standing here, said Bill. What are we looking for, what are we waiting for?

I don't know, said Harry. Hope?

*

Jean prayed. From the first moment she had heard the news, through that evening, that night, the flight to Paris, to Frankfurt, then to Munich, the first night at the Rechts der Isar Hospital, then that first night at the hotel, that first morning back at the hospital, through the afternoon into the evening, back at the hotel, then back at the hospital the next day, on and on, Jean prayed. Not only for Mattie, but for all the boys, those boys she'd known as well as her own, for all the men, those men who were their friends, the best of friends, the ones who had died, the ones who'd survived, the living and the dead, the injured and wounded, their families, their friends, Jean prayed for them all. On and on, one day gone, one night gone, another day gone, another night gone, certain of one thing and one thing alone, that God heard Jean pray, God heard her prayers, and on the third day, Jean slipped her hand beneath the plastic of the oxygen tent and held Mattie's hand, softly, gently, gently, softly she squeezed his hand and saw him smile, a tiny smile, and heard him say, Hello, dear. Don't worry, dear, I'm going to be all right.

4

Jean took Jimmy's hand, she squeezed his hand and said, God heard our prayers, Jimmy, as we knew He would, our prayers have been answered, Jimmy. Mattie recognised me, I know he did, he recognised me. Go to him, please –

No longer wishful thinking, a white lie for the press, a bit of hope for all those back home, now Jimmy walked onto the ward for real, saw Matt up ahead, still inside the oxygen tent, and Jimmy went up to Matt's bed, leant in close to his bed, the plastic tent, and Jimmy smiled and said, Hello, Matt. Hello, Boss.

Beneath the plastic, inside the tent, Matt slowly, slowly raised his hand to beckon Jimmy closer, closer still, so carefully, carefully Jimmy raised the plastic, ducked inside the tent, where Matt firmly, tightly gripped Jimmy's hand and in a whisper said, Keep the flag flying, Jimmy. Keep things going until I get back.

*

Bill and Harry had gone back to the hospital with Jimmy to say their goodbyes, goodbyes and a hello: at last, long last, after pints and pints of blood, Kenny Morgans had opened his eyes at last, already talking with the other lads on the ward, with Ray and Dennis and Albert and Bobby, and with the wives of Ray and Dennis and Albert. The doctors had even thought at first that Ken might have been well enough to go back with Harry and Bill and Jimmy, but they said Bobby definitely could go, if he wanted –

Why don't you, said Bill. Come on, Bob.

Bobby slightly, slightly shook his head. How are you getting back, are you flying?

Are we hell as like, said Bill. One of them fellas from the bloody airline, he said they'd fly us back to Manchester at their expense, but I told him, You'll never get me in a fucking plane again. Harry said the same.

Bobby tried to smile. He said, I bet he did, or worse. So you're going by train, are you then?

Yeah, said Bill, so why don't you come with us, get yourself home? Be better than staying on here.

But Bobby slightly, slightly shook his head again. But what will you do when you get back?

Well, I don't know about Foulkesy, said Harry, coming onto the ward, up to Bobby's bed, having just been up to say goodbye to Jackie, teasing Blanchy about the state of his arm, the fate of his golf swing, telling Bobby and the rest of the ward, but I just want to get back training and bloody playing as soon as I fucking can.

But there'll be all the funerals, whispered Bobby. They'd want us to go, we'd have to go.

*

It went and came the world, came and went, until that Sunday, when the world came back to Frank and stayed, back with the smell, the feel of soft, cool sheets, so soft and cool that for one moment, one brief, brief moment, Frank thought he'd died and gone to heaven, that someone would be along with his wings in a bit, to strap them to his back, least he hoped they'd strap them to his back, not stitch them to his skin, but as he had a squint about, searching for a sight of those Gates of Pearl, listening for the jangle of Peter and his keys, through the blur of his visions Frank could swear he could spy the face of his wife, his Peggy by his bed, saw her smiling, felt her take and hold his one good hand, and in the best, most normal voice he could muster, Frank said, Where am I, love?

You're in Munich, dear, said Peggy.

Frank nodded, nodded to himself, then smiled and said, That must have been quite a walk, dear?

I flew, she said.

Frank shook his head. You never did?

I did, she said. I did for you, love.

Frank said, Oh dear, I'm sorry, love. I really am. What happened to my kite? Did it turn over?

You had a slight accident, said Peggy, but don't worry about what happened now. All that matters now is you are safe and sound in Munich.

How are the boys? Are they okay?

They're fine, love, and they send their love. They're at home, and everything is fine at home, everything is all right. The doctors have told us you are going to be fine, you are going to be all right, as long as you obey instructions and keep quiet and rest. So you don't need to worry about anything, you just need rest, a great deal of rest. But your Bill is here, so I'll just go fetch him, let him say hello, then we'll let you sleep again –

And Peggy let go of Frank's hand, got up from his bedside, went out into the corridor then came back in with Bill, his eldest brother Bill, whom Frank had last seen four weeks ago, must be more than four weeks ago now, in Workington, in Cumberland, at the Borough Park ground, when United had played Workington in the third round of the Cup, when Workington had given United a right old scare, scoring in the fifth or sixth minute, a chap called Colbridge it was, but whatever words Matt Busby had said, whatever spells he had cast at half-time must have been well-chosen ones because eight minutes of second-half magic and a hat-trick from Dennis Viollet put Workington out of the Cup and a smile on Bill's face.

How are you feeling, Trouble, said Bill.

Frank smiled. Pretty good, but I can't work out why I feel so tired, why I keep falling asleep all the time.

It's natural, nothing to worry about, said Bill. You're going to be fine, so just lie back and take it easy.

But Frank was looking about him, trying to peer through the dim light of the room, to see the face of the man in the plastic tent in the next bed to him, and Frank said, That's Matt, isn't it? I thought I'd been dreaming, but that is Matt Busby. How's he doing, do you know?

He's doing fine, dear, said Peggy. You're both going to be moved out of here tomorrow, to a different room, because you're both going to get well. So stop worrying, stop fretting. Everything's going to be all right.

But Frank was still looking about him, still trying to peer through the dim light, to find other faces, see the faces of his friends, his colleagues from the press, and Frank said, But where's George? George Follows and Henry Rose and Eric Thompson and the rest of the lads?

I'm afraid they couldn't take them all here, dear, said Peggy. There wasn't room for them all here, so they're in another place, safe in another place.

So you just rest now, said Bill. Don't be fretting and worrying, you just rest and get well, all right?

And we'll be back again to see you tomorrow, said Peggy, gently smiling at Frank, softly squeezing his hand, tucking Frank up in his bed, smoothing down Frank's blankets, his covers. But don't forget you're being moved into a proper room in the morning, so don't get a shock when you wake up. Just remember, the doctors say you're going to get better, that you are off the danger list now.

Thank you, thank you, love, thank you, both, said Frank, closing his eyes, Frank pretending to sleep, hearing them leave,

Peggy and Bill, Frank thinking, Danger list! Off the danger list? What on earth did she mean? Frank still pretending to sleep, to sleep, to sleep again, and maybe Frank did sleep, just for a bit, or maybe a lot, he didn't know, Frank couldn't tell, still couldn't tell the nights from the days, the days from the nights, not really, but he knew that voice, would know it anywhere, the voice of Jimmy Murphy. Yes, Frank was sure he could hear Jimmy talking to Duncan, Duncan Edwards, thought he heard Jimmy saying, I'll see you later, son, I'll be back to see you again soon, but Frank couldn't hear Duncan, Big Duncan's reply, his voice, and Frank opened his eyes, his mouth and called out to Jimmy, calling him over, Jimmy? Is that you, Jimmy?

Hello, Frank, said Jimmy. How are you, son?

Frank smiled. I'm fine, Jimmy. I'm fine. But how's everyone else doing, how's Big Dunc?

Oh, fine, son, fine, said Jimmy. You know Duncan. Always raring to go, up for the scrap.

That's the big fellow, said Frank, but Frank knew Jimmy was a good mate of George Follows, too, that Jimmy would know where George was, how George was doing, and so Frank said, Do you know where George is, how George is doing? And Henry and Eric and all the rest of the lads, how they're all doing? My brother Bill is here, and when they're well enough, it would be great if you could take him to meet them, Jimmy, if you had time? But where are they, Jimmy, are they near?

Well, they're all up there, son, said Jimmy quickly, his finger pointing up at the floor above. All upstairs, quite safe and sound, and in good hands, the best of hands, don't you worry about that. But you're a careless fellow, are you not, said Jimmy quickly again, his finger pointing now at Frank's right leg in plaster. Fancy giving yourself a knock like that. How does it feel?

Frank shrugged, he laughed. It's fine, Jimmy. I'll be fit enough to play on Saturday, if you need me.

I know you will be, son, said Jimmy. But you just rest, Frank, and take it easy now, son.

*

They'd said Sunday was a better day, had the press, a better day for the womenfolk, said the press, the families of the injured, the living, the lucky ones, most of them at least. Matt Busby and Frank Taylor had been taken off the critical list, Matt and Frank were going to be moved out of intensive care, and so when brave Jean Busby had faced the press, had had to face the press again, this time Jean had better news at least and said, Matt was delighted to see us, and I really believe that our presence here is giving him new strength in his fight for life. He still can't talk much, but his first questions were about the others here in hospital with him, how they were all doing. The news that most were doing well cheered and helped him.

Even pretty young Molly Leech, Duncan Edwards's sweetheart, was smiling for the first time as she left the hospital that night and said, Duncan is coming along fine. I'm sure he will pull through. Just you watch. In no time at all now he'll be down on the second floor, just you watch. That will be the day.

But it wasn't a better day for everyone, not for Hilda Berry, as her husband Johnny was operated on again and still had not recovered consciousness, and not for Captain Ken Rayment, who was also operated on that day, but at least they had hope, some hope of better days.

*

The Dead set off for home, before the dawn, before the light, in the dripping wet of a sudden thaw, through the dirty, puddled streets of Munich they came in their coffins, twenty-one flag-draped coffins in a procession of cars, out to the airport, back out to a plane, a British European Airways Viscount 800 freighter, a carrier of cargo, a transporter of goods, sat on the ground where they had lost their lives, waiting in the place where they had found death, the doors to its hold open, waiting to take them, to take them inside, to carry them home. The procession of cars came to a stop, parked up beside the plane, and one by one the living began to unload the Dead, then one by one the living carried the Dead in their coffins, their twenty-one flag-draped coffins on board the plane and into its hold. But the plane did not leave, the plane did not go, it just sat there waiting, waiting with the Dead, the Dead wanting to go home, just to get back home. But the blue-coated, white-gloved Munich City Police formed a guard of honour on the tarmac. Then, in a long, solemn line, government and civic officials, representatives of West German football clubs and the British Consul walked through the guard of honour to the foot of the black-shrouded gangway with fifty-eight wreaths of red carnations and white tulips. One after another, they handed over the wreaths and, one after another, the wreaths were taken up the steps onto the plane, the wreaths then placed with the Dead. Then a short service was said, said for the Dead, the departing Dead. Then the one hundred and sixty members of the blue-coated guard of honour raised their white-gloved hands to salute, and all the civilians present stood to attention as the British European Airways Viscount 800 freighter began to taxi away. Then finally that afternoon, for it was afternoon now, almost the very hour of the crash, the British European Airways Viscount 800 freighter took off from Munich Airport, finally leaving the ground where they had lost their lives, the very place where they had found death, lifting, climbing, flying, moaning over the wreck of the Elizabethan, carrying the Dead, taking the Dead in their twenty-one, flag-draped coffins home, the Dead finally, finally on their way home.

We have said goodbye to the boys, said Jimmy to the press, before the open door of the waiting train, on the platform at the station in Munich. But we shall see them again, back in Manchester soon. Limbs and hearts may be broken, but the spirit remains. Their message is that the club is not dead. Manchester United lives on. And my boss and my greatest friend, Matt Busby, would want me to tell you that the Red Devils will survive this. We have a motto at Old Trafford which means 'Work and Wisdom'. The work of the country's finest players and the wisdom of its finest manager have made the club what we are today. We have the greatest club spirit in the world. We had a unique, happy, holiday-camp atmosphere at Old Trafford. We were all friends. We insisted on one hundred per cent, and we got it. Our wonderful system was organised and led by my dear friend Matt, and I'm not forgetting my very good friend Bert Whalley or dear old Tom Curry. Or our very energetic back-room boy Walter Crickmer, who carried out his office duties as smoothly as we carried out our soccer duties. Matt, thank God, is improving at the moment. Slowly, but he is improving. So we will have his spirit with us. Mercifully, too, we have assistant secretary Les Olive. There is none better than him. But it is going to be a long, long, long struggle, but together we hope to be 'back there again', and Matt, I pray, will soon be back, too. Soon the world-famous partnership of Busby and Murphy will be reunited. Soon we will be working together again for the greatest club in the world, and so soon, I promise you: the Red Devils will be back!

And with a wave goodbye to the press, the ones who were not following him onto the train, Jimmy climbed aboard the *Rheingold Express*, made his way along the narrow corridor, into the tiny compartment, and sat down in a seat by the door.

He looked at Harry and Bill, at the poor woman whose job it was as travel courier to see them safely back to England, and Jimmy smiled, tried to think of a joke to crack, a word at least to lighten the mood, but Jimmy felt too tired. He still had not really slept since Thursday afternoon, not properly slept, even got into a bed, laid down on a bed. Cigarettes had kept him going, cigarettes and whisky. But even last night, when things had seemed brighter, just that little bit better, his mind could not rest, going back over the past, the friends he had lost, thinking especially of Bert, of Bert and of Tom, then turning to the future, and what on earth would they do, the plight of the club worse, much worse than Jimmy had thought. Even Billy and Harry, as fit as they looked, Jimmy knew a reaction was bound to hit them, as it surely would Bobby and Dennis, Kenny and Albert, if it hadn't already, and though he knew it was a stupid, pointless thing to think or wish, that no thought or wish could change the past, undo what was done, still Jimmy wished and wished they'd never taken so many players to Belgrade. Geoff Bent, Johnny Berry, Jackie Blanchflower, David Pegg, Billy Whelan and Ray Wood, they were never all going to play, so why had they taken so many of the lads, let so many lose their lives for nothing? But Jimmy knew this way, these thoughts led to nowhere or, worse, to despair, and Jimmy tried to think again of the future, of what could be done, the players they had, the ones who had lived, but try as he might, as hard as he could, Jimmy couldn't see how he could pick a team for any sort of football, who could line up against Wednesday, who could kick off on Saturday –

Jimmy heard whistles blowing, in his head, on the platform, heard doors slamming, felt the wheels lurch forward, begin to move and turn, saw both Billy and Harry jump and stiffen, their faces brave yet tense and set, their fists clenched and knuckles white as the train began its journey, and Jimmy knew it was going to be a long, long journey, Jimmy wishing it was otherwise, would it were not so, but knowing, What a bloody mess we're in.

*

But in Manchester, early that Monday morning, from deep inside the stadium, from out of the ground, came members of the ground staff, the ladies from the canteen, and in the pouring, endless, melancholy rain, they stood and watched the assistant trainer Bill Inglis lead out a group of twenty-two young players in maroon training tops and studs, some with bibs and balls in their hands, and they waved, they clapped them off, up the Warwick Road, on to Chester Road, then the members of the ground staff, the ladies from the canteen, they went back into the ground, back about their work, while Bill Inglis and these twenty-two young players made their way to the White City Stadium to set about their own work.

First, Bill had them warm and limber up with a lap or ten around the dog track, then Bill split these twenty-two young players into two teams, one team in green bibs, the other in white, their maroon training tops now the goal posts. But before Bill Inglis blew his whistle, before they'd kicked a ball, Bill looked at these lads, these twenty-two young lads in their eyes, and said, I know some of you may not want to train or play today, may feel like you never want to train or play again, the way you feel today. But remember, you are all United players, every one of you United. And while this is a practice game, remember this and all: any one of you could be playing in the Cup come Saturday. But most of all, you remember what the Boss and Mister Murphy have always told you, have told every lad who has ever pulled on a red shirt, a United shirt: keep on playing football all the time.

*

Frank knew he was playing a game with himself, a game he had learnt in the war. Frank knew that the man who fretted, who worried, the man who succumbed to depression and became morose, that man slowed down his own recovery, sometimes to a standstill, a permanent stop. So Frank knew he must not think about the accident, the crash, Frank knew he must just think a few broken bones and some bruises were the worst of it, the worst that anyone had suffered, that he must believe his mates, the lads from the Press Gang, and the rest of the boys in the team, the United team and their staff, Tom Curry, Bert Whalley and Walter Crickmer, that they were all just upstairs, all safe in good hands, just as Jimmy had said.

*

Upstairs at Old Trafford, that wet and freezing Monday afternoon, Harold Hardman, William Petherbridge, Alan Gibson, on crutches in his pyjamas, dressing gown and overcoat, Louis Edwards and Les Olive assembled for a board meeting at which Harold Hardman told his fellow directors that following his discussions with the Football Association and with Sheffield Wednesday, he had written to the FA to formally request that their Cup tie on Saturday be postponed until a suitable date could be found, with one suggestion being Wednesday, February 19, though that in turn would require the agreement of the Football League that their away fixture on that date against Aston Villa could be played later in the season. Harold Hardman told his fellow directors that he had also discussed the suggestion that two of the qualification rules for the FA Cup might be waived, given the tragic circumstances and the dire predicament in which the club now found itself, those two rules being that, one, any newly signed player would be immediately eligible to play in the Cup and would not have to wait fourteen days as stipulated by the rules, and, two, that any newly signed player who had already played in the competition this season for a previous club would be eligible to play again for United. The FA have been very good, said Harold Hardman, and I am sure they will try to co-operate and help us in every way possible. Every club in Lancashire, and many more beyond, has also offered us the loan of players, and we are deeply grateful. But quite honestly, I just don't know what will happen about next Saturday. I have no doubt at all that should the Cup tie be played, we could field a fairly strong side. But all our young players are still terribly shocked, and there will be very little training done this week as they will want to attend the funerals of the staff and their teammates.

*

Bill had wanted to leave Munich, to get the hell out of Munich more than anything he'd ever wanted before, but now, on the *Rheingold Express*, now bound for Holland, now Bill wasn't so sure, wasn't so sure he shouldn't have stayed back there in Munich with Bobby, in a bed next to Bobby, as the train lurched again, the brakes screamed again, and Bill and Harry both jumped then stiffened again, the sights and sounds of that bloody aircraft slewing all over that fucking slush-covered runway coming back to them both, punching them hard in the head, square in the face, with every lurch, every corner and every bend, speeding up and slowing down, braking suddenly, braking hard, in this compartment, this tiny compartment, the travel courier, that poor lass, not wanting to look at them, embarrass them both, see the sweat, the fear on their faces, both of them sweating, both of them shaking, unable to stop, Jimmy with his jokes to lighten the mood as best as he could, but the compartment just kept getting smaller, smaller and smaller with every bloody mile of this journey, this fucking journey from hell, as Bill tried to think of home, and Harry of his home, to put the thoughts of the crash out of their minds, but with every lurch, with every scream, back again, again it came, rocking Harry and Bill from side to side as on and on, hour after hour, the wheels rolled on, on and on, for days and days, it seemed to Bill, it seemed to Harry, they'd been travelling for days, lurching and screaming, from hell to hell and back again.

*

In the pouring, endless, biting, vicious rain, the thirty-minutes-each-way practice match had been a dirty, crunching, hard-fought game, and more than a handful of the lads were limping as they made their way back down the Chester Road towards the showers then the bath and home. But after the showers, the bath, Bill Inglis and old Arthur Powell asked some of the lads to hang back, to wait, the taller, bigger, stronger lads it was, Because Mister Olive, he wants to come and have a word, and so they sat around, the taller, bigger, stronger lads, waiting for the word from Mister Olive, who when he came he said, straight off he said, They're bringing back the Dead tonight, so we need you boys to help us set up all the tables in the gym, then when they're here, to help to bring, to carry them in, so you'll need to go back home to get your best suits on, then be back as quick as you can, so we best get a move on with the tables now, and Bill Inglis and Arthur Powell, they clapped their hands and said, Come on, lads, come on, boys, look sharp, look lively now!

But as the taller, bigger, stronger lads followed Bill Inglis and Arthur Powell out of the dressing rooms to the gym, Mister Olive stopped young David Gaskell, the seventeen-year-old reserve-team keeper, and said, David, you can get straight off back home. Mister Armstrong will run you back. He's in his car in the car park, waiting.

Why, asked David. Don't you need us tonight?

Mister Olive shook his head. No, we need you to come back again tonight. But it's not an easy thing to ask, I know, but we need you to also help sort out all Mister Whelan's belongings and then go round to Mister Taylor's digs, for their things, for their parents. Mister Armstrong's got some boxes in the car, and Missus Dorman will help you. So can you do that for us, David? For Mister Whelan and Mister Taylor, for their parents?

Yes, said David. Of course I will. I just put it in the boxes, right? Their stuff, all their gear?

Mister Olive nodded. Yes, if you would, David, then Mister Armstrong will come back to pick you up.

David nodded, picked up his stuff and followed Mister Olive out of the dressing room, down the corridors, out of the ground, into the car park and over to Mister Armstrong's car, Mister Armstrong inside his car, out of the rain. Mister Olive opened the passenger door, said he'd see David later, back at the ground tonight, as David got into the car and Mister Olive closed the door.

Hello, son, said Mister Armstrong as he started the car. Have you got everything, have you?

David nodded. Yes, thanks.

That's good, said Mister Armstrong as he pulled out of the car park. They drove straight up Warwick Road, across the Chester Road, turned right onto Talbot Road, passed the cricket ground, left down Byron Road, then left again onto Gorse Avenue –

Number nineteen, isn't it, said Mister Armstrong.

David nodded again. Yes, just here.

Mister Armstrong pulled up and parked in front of the large, semi-detached house, got out of the car and went to the boot. David got out, shut the door and followed him to the back of the car and the cardboard boxes in the boot.

Can I help you, Mister Armstrong, called Missus Dorman from the steps of the house. Do you need a hand?

No, you're all right, love, thanks, called back Mister Armstrong, handing David some boxes, David juggling the boxes and his own gear. We can manage.

David followed Mister Armstrong up the drive to the front door, the rain even heavier, even colder now, so dark Missus Dorman already had the light on in the hall. She said, Will you have a cup of tea, Mister Armstrong?

No, thank you, love, he said. I best get back, but there's some more boxes yet. I'll just go get them.

David put down the boxes and his own gear in the hallway. He glanced at Missus Dorman, her eyes still red. He didn't think she'd stopped crying since the minute she heard. She was looking down at the boxes on the carpet in her hall, chewing at her cheek, the inside of her cheek.

There we are, said Mister Armstrong, coming back with another couple of boxes. That's them all.

Missus Dorman shook her head. She said, We won't need all these boxes. I've already taken out and folded up and laid out all of Billy's things, and Missus Swinchatt, she said she already has all Tommy's things in boxes, so you can probably go pick them up now?

That's good, said Mister Armstrong, but, erm, I spoke with Duncan's mum and dad, and we think it's best if we gather up his stuff, too, you know, his things –

But I thought he was getting better, said David. I thought Mister Edwards was going to be okay, they said it in the paper, I just read it this morning –

Now, now, son, said Mister Armstrong, his own eyes red, so very red and black, sunken with grief and lack of sleep and hope. He will be fine, he will, but it's going to take some time, it will, so it'll be a while before he gets back here again, and so his mam and dad, they just think it's best to have his stuff, you know, for when he gets back home to them, or even to take it out to him, okay?

*

The Dead stopped off in London on their way back home that day. In the evening dark, the evening rain, the British European Airways Viscount 800 touched down at London Airport. Then four of the Dead were taken off the plane: Tom Cable, the BEA steward who was Manchester United mad, was going home to Swansea, Wales; Bela Miklos, the travel agent, was going home to Woking, Surrey; David Pegg, the England international, was going home to Doncaster, Yorkshire; and Liam 'Billy' Whelan, the inside-forward, was transferred to an Aer Lingus Dakota bound for Dublin, Ireland, and home. Then, after some delay, an hour late or more, the British European Airways Viscount 800 took off again, carrying the Dead, bringing the Dead, the remaining Dead in their seventeen, flag-draped coffins, home, back home, closer to home.

*

Harry, Bill and Jimmy had finally reached the Hook of Holland, disembarked from the *Rheingold Express* and boarded their night boat for Harwich, helped by the travel courier, who must have wondered what on earth she had done to deserve this thankless, most stressful of jobs, that poor woman who had dealt with their passports and customs, had found their cabin and their berths and had kept them in cigarettes and coffee, cigarettes and whisky, cigarettes and more cigarettes, all with time still to spare before they sailed at eleven that night.

But Harry didn't fancy sticking, sat in this cabin. No, bloody thank you, said Harry. I'm going to go have a walk about, stretch

122

my legs, find the bar, have a drink, a brandy or a rum or two to find my sea legs.

Find your sea legs, laughed Jimmy. That ferry from Belfast must be like a second home to you, son. But come on then, come on, Billy, let's go –

But Bill shook his head, sucking in air, glancing out of the porthole, then to the door of the cabin, blowing out his cheeks, and said, I'm not sure about this, Jimmy.

Not sure about what, son, said Jimmy.

Bill gritted his teeth. He said, The boat, Jimmy. This fucking boat. I just don't think it's a good idea.

So you fancy a swim, do you, son, laughed Jimmy. It's a bloody long way if you do. But then, more gently, kindly, softly, Jimmy said, It'll be fine, son, I promise you, believe me. We'll have a couple of drinks, just to steady our nerves, like Harry says – and remember, he's the expert – then we'll all have a kip, and before you know it we'll be docked at Harwich and almost back home.

Jimmy's right, said Harry. Few drinks and you'll be right, Foulkesy. So come on, let's go –

But Bill shook his head again, turned to the travel courier, that poor, long-suffering woman, and said, Do you know where they keep the life jackets?

They're all in here, she said patiently, calmly, opening one of the cupboards. Look, here you are –

Bill walked over to the cupboard, took out a yellow life jacket, unfolded and turned it over and around in his hands, examining its back and its front.

You going to wear that to the bar, are you, laughed Harry, but he was on his feet, too, taking out a life jacket from the cupboard, unfolding and examining its straps.

Bill didn't put the life jacket on, but he didn't put it back inside the cupboard. He clutched it in his hands and said, So where are all the lifeboats then?

123

There are five on each side of the ship, said the travel courier. Five lifeboats on the port side, five on the starboard side, and there are life rafts, too.

Can you show us, said Bill.

The travel courier nodded. Yes, of course I can. Shall we all go up on deck now?

Harry and Bill followed the travel courier out of the cabin, the life jackets still in their hands, along the narrow corridor, with Jimmy following on behind, then up some steps, through doors and lounges and out onto the decks at the stern, Jimmy lagging behind now –

He stopped by the taffrail to cup his hand, to try to light another cigarette, to let them go on ahead, to catch them up in a bit. He took a long drag of his cigarette, stared back at the shore, the lights here and there, then up at the sky, the night and its weather. He took another drag, his other hand in his pocket, always in his left pocket.

Jimmy had served in the Eighth Army. He had spent four years in North Africa as a Desert Rat, at Tobruk, Tunis and Sousse. He had been in Italy, too, in Rome after its fall, then seen out the rest of the war in Bari. He had seen a lot of things, those years in the war. Bad things and good, more good, kind things than you'd think. Known good luck and bad, but mostly, mercifully, good. If luck was what it was, such a thing as luck there was, then it had been good to him, he knew. Until now. He took a last drag of the cigarette, threw the stub overboard, into the water far below, then put his hand back into his pocket for his packet, another cigarette, but stopped. He took his left hand out of the other pocket, the beads of the rosary entwined in his fingers. He brought the beads up closer to his face, the crucifix, the figure on the Cross. He had rubbed it flat as he prayed, the figure, the face of Christ on the Cross, rubbed flat by the prayers he'd said.

Jimmy heard a bell sound now, then a whistle in the night. He felt the engines turn, the ship begin to move. The rosary, its crucifix in his hand, Jimmy looked at his watch, saw the time and closed his eyes, the figure, the face of Christ between his finger and thumb as he rubbed as he prayed. They'd soon be home, the Dead.

*

Oh, you're lucky to catch us, Bobby pet, said Cissie, at Jimmy's desk, on Jimmy's phone. I've hardly stopped to catch my breath all day, well, since I got here Friday, come to that. It's been non-stop, it really has. You wouldn't believe the number of telephone calls we get, you just wouldn't, and I can't tell you the letters, the cards and the flowers that come, oh, you should see the piles of post, Bobby, it's incredible, unbelievable, Bobby, and then there's all the tickets to sort out, you know, all that side of things like, and that's before all the other stuff, you know, with the poor families, all the things that need sorting, it's just heartbreaking, Bobby, it really is, to see them like this, everybody in bits, in pieces, you know, so it's good that I'm here like. But Wilf's been good, he really has, you know. He's taking poor Eddie's girl, Marjorie, is it? The poor lass, the poor thing. He's taking her out to the airport tonight, in fact they'll be out there by now, I should think. But they've had to ask some of the young lads, you know, to help with the coffins like, when they get them back here, to carry them into the gym like, and that took some setting up, I tell you, it took some arranging like, did the gym, you know? But you could just tell by their faces, them young lads, that's the last thing any of them wants to be doing, you know? But that's how it is, Bobby, you know, just how it is here, but how are you, pet, how is your head, is it any better like, do they know when you can be coming home? I mean, at this rate you're not going to be

125

back for any of the funerals, are you, love? Have they not told you anything more, the doctors like?

In the Rechts der Isar Hospital, in the office down the corridor, Bobby closed his eyes, gripped the telephone and said, No, Mam, no, not yet. But I'd better go.

Aye, me, too, pet, I'd best be off, said Cissie. They'll soon be back, they'll soon be here.

*

The Dead came home at half past ten that night. Finally, almost home, in Manchester at least, in the cold, the dark and rain, the British European Airways Viscount 800 touched down at Ringway Airport. The League Championship flag, soaked and sodden by the rain, was at half-mast in the cold, dark night above the terminal building, wherein below waited the relatives of the Dead, with the Lord Mayor of Manchester and the directors of United, all there to welcome back the Dead, heads bowed at the foot of the gangway as one by one the fifty-eight wreaths of red carnations and white tulips were carried from the plane, down the steps of the gangway to the waiting hearses. Then slowly, solemnly, one by one, covered in flowers, all covered in flowers, in red and white roses, red and yellow carnations, lilac and blue irises and lilies, white lilies, the Dead in their coffins, their seventeen coffins, were carried out of the hold of the plane and slowly, solemnly placed inside the backs of the seventeen waiting hearses. The hearses with seven of the Dead, with the journalists Don Davies, George Follows, Archie Ledbrooke, Henry Rose and Eric Thompson, with the former City keeper-turned-newsman Frank Swift and with the Manchester businessman Willie Satinoff, they would be leaving for private addresses, turning off at Trafford Bar, heading for their homes. But first the other ten hearses with the other ten Dead, with the journalists

Alf Clarke and Tom Jackson, with the trainers Tom Curry and Bert Whalley and the club secretary Walter Crickmer, and with the players Geoff Bent, Roger Byrne, Eddie Colman, Mark Jones and Tommy Taylor, led by an escort of police motorcycles, they set off in a cortège for Old Trafford, to the United ground, where these ten Dead would lie, would sleep tonight, in the gymnasium under the main grandstand, and although the hour was late, so very late, and the night so cold, so wet, so very cold and wet, hundreds of thousands of folk had gathered for hours, so many long hours, standing in silence, waiting in silence, to line the route of the cortège, the twelve-mile route from the airport to the ground, three, four, five folk deep on Ringway Road, Shadow Moss Road, Cornishway, Portway, Rudd Park Road, Brownlow Road, Brownley Road, Altrincham Road, Princess Parkway, Almouth Road and Princess Road, Mauldeth Road West and Barlow Moor Road, Manchester Road and Seymour Grove, where men now stood to attention or bowed their heads, hats and caps in hand, with tears upon their cheeks, as women fell to their knees in the mud, rosaries in hand, and tried to silence screams, to muffle cries, while children on their tiptoes strained to see, to catch a glimpse, a last and fleeting, final glimpse of the passing Dead, wondering who was who, in which hearse, which coffin was who, where was Eddie, where was Tommy, their favourite, the one they'd loved the most, as the cortège slowly passed, solemnly disappeared into the dark of the night, crawling on towards Old Trafford and home, closer to home, all traffic stopped en route. But not the clocks, the clocks no longer stopped, for now a clock close by chimed and struck the hour, the midnight hour, as the Dead in their hearses, their coffins, dressed in wood, decked in flowers, passed the thousands upon thousands more who had gathered as near to the ground as they could, held back by cordons of police, in cordons of silence, until sudden cries, desperate howls now slashed and pierced the night, in screams and wails of recognition that all they'd heard and read, the very worst they'd heard and read, was true, all real, as the Dead pulled onto the forecourt of Old Trafford and stopped beneath the stands. Then, one by one, one after the other, the coffins of Alf Clarke, Tom Jackson, Tom Curry, Bert Whalley, Walter Crickmer, Geoff Bent, Roger Byrne, Eddie Colman, Mark Jones and Tommy Taylor were solemnly, slowly taken out of the backs of the hearses, slowly, solemnly carried into the gymnasium, where hundreds and hundreds of wreaths and flowers hung from the bars on the wall, where two policemen were waiting to stand guard overnight, and where now, out of sight of the crowds, slowly and solemnly, gently and softly, borne on the shoulders, in the hands of the boys, the young lads left behind, the ten coffins of the Dead were placed upon ten tables draped in the black, black cloth of home.

II

BEFORE YOU FORGET

5

The light, the dawn came up, the wind, the waves went down, and Harry, Bill and Jimmy got up from their berths, left their cabin and went up on deck again, to stretch their legs again, to have another cigarette or ten, and to look, to search for sight of land, for Harwich ahoy.

Harry paced about, quick and fast he walked, into a jog, a little run he broke, turning and stretching, left and then right, up and down, his hands apart, a ball, an imaginary, invisible ball apart, bringing his knees up in a hop and a jump, then rotating his head one way then the other, eyes right, eyes left.

But as Harry went through his paces, Bill stood rooted to the railings at the bow of the ship, watching Harwich come closer through the fading night, rising up to greet him in the morning light –

That's a sight for sore eyes, is it not, son, said Jimmy, at the railing now, an arm around Bill's shoulder.

Bill nodded. He said, It isn't half, Jimmy. I tell you, you'll never get me to leave England again.

I felt exactly the same as you, son, said Jimmy. After the war, when I got home, when I saw the family, had a pint again, then went to Mass, I thought, that's it, this'll do me, I don't need anything more. But within a few weeks, Matt had called me, invited me up to Manchester, offered me a job, and there I was, son, on the move again, and it was hard on Winnie and the kids, I know it was, it must have been; I'd been gone for years, North Africa and then Italy, and then here I was again, on the move and gone again, up and away and off to Manchester. It'd be two years before they moved up to join me, Winnie and the kids, and they hardly knew me, the kids, probably wished they could have stayed down South.

Bill nodded again. I can't bloody wait to get home, Jim. I tell you, I'll never leave home again.

Well, you'll have to, son, said Jimmy, on Saturday, son, when we play Wednesday in the Cup –

Bill turned away from the horizon, home getting closer, coming nearer, turned to look at Jimmy, to shake his head, to start to say, No, Jimmy, I –

But Jimmy stopped him there; he gripped Bill's arm and said, I need you to be captain, son.

*

In the shadow of the main stand of the stadium, within sight at least of the double doors to the gymnasium, through the night, into the dawn, in the early-morning light, the drizzle, still they came, by bike or on foot, in their hundreds, their thousands, on their way to work or school to pause, to stop by the entrance to the ground, as close as they could to the gym, that place of exercise now a chapel of rest, a place of pilgrimage, of tribute.

Then, a little later and on throughout the morning, as the constant drizzle turned to fleeting sleet then back again to rain, one by one the hearses returned to the forecourt of Old Trafford, to pull up outside the double wooden doors to the gym, here to collect the Dead again, one by one in turn, to lift, to carry and then take away the coffins of Alf Clarke, Tom Jackson, Tom Curry, Bert Whalley, Walter Crickmer, Geoff Bent, Roger Byrne, Mark Jones, and then of little Eddie Colman –

Hello, Missus Colman, Mister Colman, said Cissie at the doors, the double wooden doors to the gym. I'm Cissie Charlton, I'm Bobby's mam.

Oh, hello, love, said Eddie's mam, taking, grasping Cissie's hand, holding it tight, not letting it go. I'm Elizabeth, but call me Liz, please. I'm Eddie's mam. It's lovely to meet you, it really is. Our Eddie's told us all about you, so much about you, hasn't he, Dick?

But Eddie's dad wasn't listening, he was looking at the doors, staring at the double wooden doors, thinking on what was within, the scene to come, all the scenes still yet to come, just wanting to get in then off back home again, get Eddie home again, if Eddie it really was –

Cissie said, Shall we go in, shall we?

Eddie's dad said nothing, but his mam blinked then nodded yes, so Cissie opened the double doors and showed them into the gym, guided them up to the casket, the coffin of their boy, their only son, one of the last two caskets in the room, then Cissie stepped back a step or two, tried not to watch but could not really not, as Liz reached out to touch the wood, the polished, varnished wood, to try to feel not wood, but flesh, her flesh and blood beneath, within this wood, if she could, she only could just touch and feel his flesh, once more to feel and hold him close, to hold and know –

Who's that, said Eddie's dad, gesturing at the other casket, the only other coffin left inside the gym.

It's Tommy Taylor, said Cissie.

Well, I hope they're sure, mumbled Eddie's dad. He'd heard, but wished he'd not, that there'd been complications in Munich with the identification of the Dead, which left him haunted by the thought, the fear that within this casket, beneath this wood was not their boy, their lad, but someone else's boy, their lad, and when he thought back on that night, the people who'd come to their door, most of whom he'd turned away, he wished now that he'd said yes when that airline official came to their door to tell them he was sorry, how sorry he was, but their

Eddie was dead, and though it was no consolation, he knew, said the bloke from the airline whose plane it was had crashed and killed their boy, their lad, Eddie had died instantly in the crash, so had not suffered, so he said, though how he knew, who knew, but the fella had then said that a plane was leaving in the morning to take the next of kin, and free of charge, of course, out to Munich to see the Dead, but Dick had shut the door on him and all, and their priest, who was at their house that night, and who said he was himself going out to Munich on that plane to give the last rites, he said, to them that had survived so far but might not yet the night, another day, this priest, he said, Dick, why don't you come with me? But Dick had shook his head and said, Why? What point is there in that? My son is dead. Nothing can be done. But now Dick wished he had gone out to Eddie on that plane, to see and be with him out there, then to bring him home without confusion, no mistakes of who was who and what was what, never letting their boy, their lad, out of his sight again.

Liz turned to look for Cissie, for the undertakers, to nod again to let them know that it was time, time to lift, to carry Eddie from this place, to take him home, and while they began, Cissie introduced Eddie's mam and dad to Missus Ramsden and her sister, Missus Taylor, who worked in the laundry, had done for years, but today had had to polish the caskets first thing, to help keep the dust from the coffins of the Dead –

Eddie says they call you Omo and Daz, do all the boys, said Eddie's mam. He's often mentioned you, hasn't he, Dick? But I do hope he's not been a bother to you, because we know what he can be like, don't we, Dick?

But Eddie's dad was not listening, he was watching the undertakers carefully, solemnly lift the coffin from the black-clothed table, solemnly, carefully carry the coffin out of the gymnasium, then carefully, gently place the coffin into the back

134

of the hearse, and softly, solemnly close the doors of the hearse, all the time thinking, I just don't know how they know.

He's not slept or eaten, whispered Eddie's mam to Cissie. Not a bite or wink since the moment we heard.

Cissie held and squeezed Eddie's mother's hand, then said goodbye to her and to his dad, his dad in bits, he really was, and that she'd see them later, on Friday, if not before, but to call her any time, day or night, with a reason or without, she was always here was Cissie, and Eddie's mam, she thanked Cissie, held and hugged her tight and said she'd call or see her soon, but that Cissie was always welcome to drop by, pop in, stop by, any time of day or night, it would help them if she could, and Cissie said yes, of course she would, she'd bring more of the cards, the flowers, as many as she could, that is –

Please don't bring no more flowers, said Eddie's dad. Please don't, love. The sight, the smell of them . . .

Eddie's mam smiled, she nodded at Cissie, and Cissie nodded, smiled back at Eddie's mam, watched his dad then his mam get into the back of the big black car behind the hearse, watched the hearse then the car pull away from the doors of the gymnasium, off the forecourt at Old Trafford, turn onto the Chester Road, Cissie not moving, waiting for that other hearse, that other car, coming down the Chester Road, bringing Tommy Taylor's mam and dad onto the forecourt, up to the double wooden doors, while the hearse and the car carrying Eddie's coffin and his mam and dad headed up the Trafford Road, that last, short drive over the Irwell to Ordsall and Archie Street, where Eddie's dog was sat waiting on the step for his master to come back home again, and Liz would tell Cissie later that when the coffin was brought in, when they set the casket down upon the table in the back room, Eddie's dog ran in, straight in under the table it went, and sat down beneath the coffin, which made Dick Colman think that this then must be their boy, their lad, within that wood, that casket on the table, it really must, back home in their back room at last. It must be him, he must be dead.

*

Bobby had his eyes closed, but he could still hear them. The wives and the girlfriends, the loved ones; Barbara sat with Dennis, Josephine with Albert, Ray's wife Betty and Kenny's fiancée Stephanie, by their bedsides, holding their hands, doing their best to cheer and perk them up, telling them how much they loved them, how much everybody loved them, or so it seemed. The news from home they were sharing, the stories in the press they were telling. How Manchester was stricken, the whole country in shock. How people kept on turning up at Old Trafford, just to be as near, as close as they could. His eyes closed, in his hospital bed, Bobby pictured the scenes in his head. The people wandering to the ground, aimless in their grief, with their red eyes, their white faces, staring up at the stands then to the turnstiles, thoughts of that pitch, its grass, those boots, those players who had grown up before their eyes, who had lifted their lives. His eyes still closed, Bobby smiled, nodded to himself and said, There has to be a match, as soon as possible a match; something for folk to try to latch on to, hold on to, after the storm, after the shipwreck, a piece of wood in a wild sea, to hold and cling on to; a match to help the players, the fans, the whole of the city, the country, a little bit of hope, a moment of escape to take away the horror, and Bobby opened his eyes and smiled, sat up in bed and was about to say, There should be a match, you know, as soon as possible, don't you think, lads? But when he saw Dennis, Albert, Ray and Kenny in their beds, in their bandages and casts, the anxious eyes behind the smiles of the women at their sides, when he thought of Johnny and Jackie upstairs with Duncan and the Boss, fighting battles just to stay alive, then Bobby shut his mouth, his eyes again, knowing there was no little bit of hope, no moment of escape, here or there, in Manchester or Munich, in hospital or home. But they must be home by now, thought Bobby, Bill and Harry and Jimmy, or almost home, and Bobby wondered if he should have gone back with them, left when they did, and Bobby began to wish he had, to think he better should.

*

Back on dry land at last, docked and through customs, on board the *Hook Continental* for London, Bill and Harry had thought this journey home could get no bloody worse, but the train from Harwich into London was no fucking better, going so fast Harry and Jimmy had to hold Bill down to stop him from pulling the emergency cord, but the scene that met them at Liverpool Street Station was the bloody worst of fucking all, a bucketful of gall –

Under bright, white-hot arc lights, the platform at the station was a heaving, surging push of reporters and cameramen, pushed and crushed right up to the doors of the *Hook Continental*, porters and policemen linking arms to try to hold back the hordes, to form a cordon, clear a path for Harry, Bill and Jimmy through the lights, the flashes and the pops, Harry and Jimmy leading the way, hands and arms up to shield their eyes, to parry the shouts, the questions and demands –

Harry? Harry? Give us a quote, will you?

Where's Bill? Where's Billy Foulkes?

But Bill, with his collar up, his eyes down, had stepped off to one side, ducked and weaved away, slid off to hide behind a van as the press pressed Harry and Jimmy up against a wall to fire questions in their faces –

Are you pleased Saturday's Cup tie's been postponed? That must be good news, is it not, Jimmy?

But what about Duncan, Jimmy? Is it true he's had a relapse? Have you had any news? Come on, Jimmy, come on. Have you not got a quote for us, Jimmy?

Aye, son, I have: if you don't get out of our bloody way, I'm going to piss on your fucking shoes!

*

The rain turned to sleet, then back again to rain, all day, the rain to sleet then back again, that day in Manchester, that first black day of that black week, that week of the funerals of the Dead, all traffic halted, the city stopped for a funeral procession of more than sixty cars which followed the hearse as it carried the coffin of Willie Satinoff from the Victoria Memorial Jewish Hospital up on Elizabeth Street, down the Cheetham Hill Road, into the centre of the city, where people stood, standing still under hats and brollies, watching in silence as the procession passed through the centre, the heart of the city, then out again along Princess Road, the long, long way out along Princess Road, until the hearse turned right onto Barlow Moor Road, then right again through the cemetery gates into Southern Cemetery, bearing the coffin of Willie Satinoff, who would forever be known as 'racehorse owner, Manchester businessman and friend of Matt Busby', but who was a human dynamo, they said, in business and in pleasure, who rarely touched a drop and was liked by one and all, always so well turned out, with a smile for everyone, and who, despite his horses and his wealth, his much more famous friend, was first and last a family man and fan, who loved his mum, his dad, his wife and kids, and Matt Busby and his boys, and who was just forty-seven years old that cold, wet day his body was lowered into that cold, wet ground.

*

The skies outside were still grey, still heavy, sleet and snow still falling on the city, but the world had changed in the night-time, just as Peggy had said it would change, and in the morning, when Frank had opened his eyes again, he had found himself in a different room at the Rechts der Isar Hospital, a bigger, lighter, private double room, with two beds, a high ceiling and a view out over the rooftops of Munich. The walls were painted in sky blue or warm yellow, to calm and to cheer, soft and mellow. There was a hand basin in a small alcove, two closets in the walls, chairs beside the beds and, at its head, attached to the wall, each bed had its own reading light and an oxygen cylinder.

On the sky-blue wall at the foot of the beds, someone had hung a framed photograph of Her Majesty the Queen and Prince Philip with Monsieur Coty, the President of France. They were standing on what Frank thought must be the balcony of the Élysée Palace, Her Majesty holding a bouquet of flowers, on what Frank guessed must have been the occasion of the state visit to France last April. Frank didn't know who had hung that picture there, but he was very glad they had, would like to shake their hand, for it cheered him up no end to see the face of Her Majesty the Queen, those flowers in her hand.

Frank turned to the other bed, saw Matt Busby in that bed, a plastic tent around his head. Matt was silent and still, unmoving, and Frank could not help but stare at Matt, to watch for his chest to rise, ever so slightly rise, then to fall again, but breathing, still breathing, with Missus Busby, his wife Jean, there beside his bed.

It's a lovely picture is that, said Frank.

Jean Busby turned around, she smiled at Frank and very quietly said, What picture, Frank?

That one there, said Frank, nodding towards the framed picture on the sky-blue wall at the foot of the bed. It's a wonderful picture of Her Majesty, it really is.

Jean Busby nodded, she smiled again, then turned back to Matt, to keep watch over Matt.

I don't know whose idea it was to hang it there, said Frank, but very thoughtful of them, don't you think? You don't know whose idea it was, do you, Jean?

Jean Busby turned around again, she smiled again at Frank, but shook her head and said, very, very quietly said, I'm sorry, Frank, I don't, no.

Here, Matt, laughed Frank, looking at the wall. You can't stay here, those are City's colours!

Matt grunted, then began to cough, and Jean sprang quickly to her feet, leant over Matt, then turned and left the room, returned again in seconds with white coats and tiny nuns who clustered around Matt's bed, over his chest, trying to soothe and ease the pain which racked his chest, racked and tortured the poor man, and Frank, he turned and looked away, and wished he had not spoken.

*

In the end, Bill had to ask a policeman for a hand, to help get him out from behind that van and over to the taxi, into the back, where Jimmy and Harry were cursing all the press and cameramen, Harry also cursing Bill, Where the fuck were you, Foulkesy? You're always running off.

Bill said nothing, just gripped the back seat of the taxi as it swung out of Liverpool Street Station and away, and tried not to scream, to kick at the seats, at the doors of this cab, tried just to think instead of Teresa, to pull, to keep and hold himself together as he gripped the seat tighter, and through gritted teeth asked, Is it the Lancaster Gate Hotel, Jimmy? Is that where we're off?

No, son, it's the Russell Hotel, said Jimmy. It's very close, we'll soon be there.

Well, that's good, said Harry. Don't think I could stand going back to the Lancaster Gate. Not now.

Jimmy nodded, then turned to the window, tried not to think of the last time they were down here, in London, only a week ago, just over a week ago, already a century, an age ago, as the taxi turned up Southampton Row and then pulled up in Russell Square.

Mavis and Teresa were sat in the window of the lounge of the Russell Hotel, looking out for Harry and Bill, coming, rushing straight out to meet, to hug, to hold Harry and Bill as they got out of the back of the cab into the arms of their wives, their wives who had thought they were dead, for hours had thought they were dead but now could feel they were alive, they really were alive, not just a voice on the other end of a telephone line, printed letters in a telegram, a glimpse, a fleeting black-and-white glimpse in a newsreel in the cinema –

Oh, we've been worried sick, they said, said Teresa to Bill, said Mavis to Harry. We've been out of our minds, going out of our minds . . .

Didn't I tell you I'd be bringing them back to you, said Jimmy with a smile, a hand at their backs, ushering them in off the pavement, away from the gawkers and the well-wishers, into the hotel. Back safe and sound to you both.

*

Later that day, that first black day of that black week, the rain and sleet still taking it in turns to fall on rich and poor alike, cats and dogs, the living and the dead, that day came the biggest funeral of them all, a funeral for a king, that self-styled 'Sports King of the North', Mister Charisma himself, Mister Henry Rose of Manchester, of England, the Wisecracker-in-Chief of the *Daily Express*.

That black afternoon, at half past two, the funeral cortège halted for two minutes outside the *Daily Express* offices in Great Ancoats Street, where thousands stood in silence on the pavements for a man who liked a flutter on any game going, a glutton for speed, a stranger to both brake and clutch. Henry was a man of flair and of flamboyance, a provocateur and a showman who revelled in the boos and hisses, both the cheer and the jeer, rising from his seat in the press box to raise his trilby to the crowd, who would have smiled at the copper who said, We knew he was popular, but by heck this is a tremendous farewell, would have smiled and nodded to himself, and everybody else, because Henry would have expected nothing less, no less than the thousands who lined the streets, that moment that silenced the heart of his kingdom –

Egotistical, Henry once asked himself. Well, why ever not? Why should one not be conscious of one's attributes as well as one's defects?

But Henry was not from Manchester or from the North at all. He'd been born in Norwich, in the last year of the last century, to parents who had fled to England from Ukraine to escape the Tsarist persecution of the Jewish population. His parents had then moved again, this time to Cardiff, where Henry was then raised, and forever after Henry, when speaking of his favourite subject, would describe himself as being both a Welshman and a Jew, devout and proud of both race and home.

The old South Manchester Synagogue, on Wilbraham Road, in Fallowfield, where Henry had worshipped, devout and regular, was where the day, that black day had begun, with a service and tribute from Rabbi Felix Carlebach, who said, Henry was a Rose that had no thorns. He was able to turn his potential enemies into fast friends. He was the King in his own world, and they crowned him with the crown of a good name.

It really was a funeral fit for a king, they said, was the biggest funeral procession ever seen in Manchester, they said, a cavalcade of mourning of two hundred cars or more, two mile long or more. Three hundred local taxis had also been laid on, or even four hundred, said some, but free of charge, they all agreed, to ferry the mourners out along Princess Road again, onto Barlow Moor Road to Southern Cemetery again, stars of screen and stage, of pitch and ring, journalist and broadcaster, officials from all sorts of sports, politicians of all shades and stripes, with Henry's family, his friends, his poor girl Elsie, some with trousers rolled or turned up to keep them out of the puddles and the mud, but all with heads covered out of tradition, in trilbies and homburgs, fedoras and bowlers, caps and berets, headscarves and veils, such an assembly of hats had never been seen, so they said, all there for the committal service, a hero's funeral –

I lived and died a hundred times during those agonising times, said Henry of the time he served in the First World War. The wind howled, shells whistled over my head, my brain was just numb. I could not feel helplessness, slowly becoming reconciled to the worst.

But whether it was a funeral fit for a king, for a hero, or not, whether thousands lined the streets to see and send Henry on his way or not, whether hundreds of taxis really waived their fares that day, for those going out Southern Cemetery way, whether it was all really so or not, the one thing on which everyone did agree, rich and poor alike, cats and dogs, the living and the dead, they all agreed that the skies, they wept for Henry Rose that day.

*

Despite the weather last Thursday afternoon, Neil Berry had been playing marbles out in the street, his street, Rochester Road, in Davyhulme, when his mother had called then shouted him in. He thought it must be the weather, the horrible weather, or maybe he'd done something wrong, but he couldn't think what that thing might be, it wasn't late, not late at all, and not yet time for tea. But when he got inside the house, his mother just sat him down and said, Your father's plane's been in some kind of crash. It's just been on the radio.

In his mind, Neil saw his father and his teammates, one by one, in their kits, their football kits, their boots, jumping from the plane, falling from and through the sky, then pulling at the cords, their parachute cords, coming floating down to land, hitting that ground, running, ready for the match. But before Neil could share his visions, say a single thing, his mother shushed him and his brothers, sat him, his brothers down again, demanding silence as they waited by the radio, the television for more news to come, as family friends, other players' wives, his Aunty Betty, who was the wife of Ray Wood and who lived on Royston Road, just by the school, they all began to gather at their home, though Neil still couldn't see why there was such bother, what was all this fuss, still thought his dad, his mates would surely just be on another plane, in their kits, their boots, back in time to play on Saturday again.

But the radio, the television news, it came through slow, so very slow, in bits and bobs, the room, the house full of people now, sat or stood where they could but always in silence, waiting and listening, and there'd be no watching *The Lone Ranger* tonight, Neil knew, it would just be the *Rupert* annual for Neil tonight, the one from Christmas with Rupert Bear flying through the skies, strapped in his seat beneath a big, bright-green balloon, with a propeller and a rudder at his rear, springs like legs and feet under his seat to bounce along the ground.

The boys should best go up to bed, said someone at some point that night, and so they kissed wet, worried cheeks goodnight and off they went to bed. But at some later point that night, Neil was told, he heard the news from someone, maybe it was his mum, that his dad, he was not dead, he was alive, he had

144

survived, which seemed a great relief, even quite a big surprise, but was no surprise at all to Neil, who'd seen his dad in his kit and boots, his red shirt, white shorts and parachute falling from the sky, smiling as he did, with a wink of an eye, raising his thumb to Neil as if to say, Can Rupert Bear do this?

That night, the next morning, and then only briefly, amid all the packing, the rushing around, would be the last times Neil and his brothers saw their mother for the best part of three months or more. She was going out to see their dad in Munich, which was where he was, they said, though Neil still did not quite understand why he would be there, though maybe it was to do with the Germans, the Nazis and the war. But wherever he was, his dad, whatever the reason his mum was off, Neil still had to go to school that Friday morning, down the silent street, across Canterbury Road and through the gates into the silent playground, where no one was playing football, marbles, anything at all today, everyone just standing there, in groups they were, in silence –

What are you doing here, said one of his pals eventually, shaking his head, the others just stood there staring at Neil or looking away, down at their shoes. His mates then took Neil gently by his arm, led him to their classroom and up to Miss –

My dad's been in a plane crash, said Neil.

I know, said Miss Thornley, then she started to cry, tried very hard not to cry, but could not stop herself as she took Neil gently by his arm and took him out of the classroom, down the corridor to see the Headmaster, Mister Shaw, who said, How do you feel, Neil?

I feel fine, said Neil.

That's good, said Mister Shaw. Now why don't you just take a seat outside my office, please.

Why, asked Neil, is something wrong? Have I done something wrong?

No, of course not, Neil, said Mister Shaw.

Okay then, said Neil, and Neil went and sat in the corridor outside the office, where all the children who passed by tried not to stare or smiled at Neil and all the grown-ups smiled and said, Hello, love, how are you, love, all morning he was there, until his Aunty Rene came for him, while Mister and Missus Thompson came for the twins, his brothers.

Neil stayed the weekend with his Aunty Rene and Uncle Harry, who lived just at the top of their road, on Lostock Road, who were not really his aunty or his uncle but friends of his mum and dad, Uncle Harry having played for United with his dad. But Aunty Rene, Uncle Harry and their son Ian, who went to Stretford Grammar, they were very kind to Neil that Friday, Saturday, Sunday, gave him fish and chips for tea on the Friday just like his mum, but with dandelion and burdock and some chocolate, too, though they never put the telly on, not even for the news, but Ian gave Neil all his marbles and said, Why don't you keep them, Neil, you can have them, if you like?

Can I really, said Neil. Are you sure?

Course he is, said his Aunty Rene, so don't forget to take them with you when you go, love.

Thank you, said Neil, but where am I going? Am I going to Germany to see my dad?

No, son, said Uncle Harry, leastways not yet. No, your granny and your Aunty Gwen, they're coming up to take you and your brothers down to stay in Folkestone.

Will we be going on the train, asked Neil.

I believe so, yes, said Uncle Harry.

It's like an adventure, said Neil –

It was an adventure, a real adventure at last, a ten-hour journey from Manchester down to Folkestone via Euston and Charing Cross stations, the three Berry boys with their grandmother and Aunty Gwen, the three Berry boys unable to sit still, up and down in their seats, in and out of the compartment, dashing here and there, up and down the carriage, turning black with soot and smoke and dust and dirt, then wide-eyed through the streets of London, then on to Folkestone, arriving in the dark, too late to see the sea, but Neil could smell it in the air, hear the gulls up in the night. But from the station, then they had to walk up a long, long and endless road, it seemed, up and down and round about it went, a viaduct looming up through the late-evening gloom at them, but then away again it went, until at last they came to a flight of steep stone steps leading up into a big and tall, old and ramshackle house, the biggest, tallest, oldest and most ramshackle house Neil had ever seen, even in the dark, the night, with four or five more flights of steep stairs within that smelt of damp and of the past, filled with pictures of old kings and queens, and things from long ago, but felt not like adventure's end but just the start of many more still yet to come.

The next morning, Neil and his brothers woke three hundred miles from home, in big, old beds of dusty, musty blankets, exhausted still, excited still, the sound again of gulls and of their aunt's dog, a Pekinese called Ching, who yelped, Hello, hello, and wagged his tail and then sneezed, Let's go –

On Folkestone beach, the Kent seacoast, there was snow on the cliffs, snow on the beach that first week they were down there, but every day Neil and his twin brothers, their Aunty Gwen and her dog Ching, they walked and played along the shore, in the bitter, biting-cold east wind, they did not care, even in a gale, rain or hail, sleet or snow coming in from the sea, without a care, the three Berry boys just loved to be beside the seaside, and Aunty Gwen, she tried her best, she really did, to make things normal and sometimes even fun, so said to Neil, Is there anything special you boys would like to do, seeing as it is half-term, you are on holiday?

Well, our mum takes us to the pictures every week, said Neil, which wasn't strictly true as it was only ever for the children's programme, and even then not every week, but yes, she often did, so it wasn't quite an outright lie, and his mum, she had been an usherette, and before he was a footballer, his dad was a projectionist in a cinema back in Aldershot, which was how they'd met, his mum and dad, and which was probably why Aunty Gwen smiled and said, Well, I know your mother likes the pictures.

Oh, yes, said Neil, and we were supposed to go this half-term holiday, she'd promised us, in fact, had Mum, which was not a fact at all.

But Aunty Gwen, she smiled again and said, Well then, I'd better have a look to see what's on then, hadn't I? Find us something suitable.

War films, said Neil. Mum usually takes us to see all the war films.

Although it's said, they say, that liars never prosper, that Tuesday afternoon, Neil found himself sat beside his Aunty Gwen in the dark and warm of the Odeon Cinema on Sandgate Road, waiting for the main feature to start, but first there was the news, the Pathé News –

'MANCHESTER UNITED TRAGEDY'.

There up on the screen, in black and white, before his eyes, Neil saw a mangled aircraft in a night of swirling snow, a German policeman stood beside the wreck, on which was written 'Lord Burghley' –

On the fringe of a Munich airport lies the wreckage of an airliner, intoned the Voice of Pathé, still smouldering from a crash in which twenty-one people were killed. Tragedy enough at any time, but in that plane were a group of young men who were almost the personal friends of millions: Manchester United, the finest soccer team Britain has produced since the

148

war. And seven of them died in the crash. Ten others, as well as their famous manager Matt Busby, were injured. Some so seriously that their lives hung in the balance. Busby's Babes, as they were affectionately called, were on their way home from Belgrade when the disaster struck. They were on top of the world. Their three-goal draw with Yugoslavia's Red Star team had put them through to the European Cup semi-finals. They had high hopes of the English FA Cup. Now those hopes are snuffed out, like the lives of seven of their finest players. Three days before, the press had carried pictures of a confident team leaving for Belgrade. Pictures which remind us that with them were eight of the North's finest sporting journalists, who would never see home again. Remember Matt Busby leading his Babes onto the Wembley turf for the Cup Final . . .

There, up on the screen, in black and white, before his eyes, Neil watched for his dad, to see his dad again –

. . . that brilliant day last spring? Roger Byrne, in the plain shirt, skippered them against Aston Villa. United were already League Champions and, that day, they came within an ace of bringing off the Double. Here's Manchester winger John Berry . . .

And there he was, up on the screen, in black and white, but alive again, before Neil's eyes –

. . . beating his man and passing to Tommy Taylor, a fine player then. Luck was against United when an accidental collision with Villa's McParland robbed them of goalie Ray Wood in the seventh minute. McParland soon recovered, but Ray Wood had to be carried off for a time. His place in goal was taken by Jackie Blanchflower, and splendidly, for Matt Busby trained his players to be versatile. Being a man short didn't prevent United from attacking again and again. Tommy Taylor was in there fighting, and Eddie Colman, too. Ray Wood soon came back to play on the right wing, and his colleagues concentrated on the left to give him a chance to recover. They kept up the pressure on the Villa goal, where a lesser man than goalie Simms would have been overwhelmed. Bill Whelan and Roger Byrne show Manchester United tactics at their best. Manchester's only goal came from a corner, which Duncan Edwards fed to Tommy Taylor for a magnificent header into the top of the net. Aston Villa won by a one-goal margin. But Busby's Babes had nothing to be ashamed of; they had lost to the only side in history to win the FA Cup seven times. No one could guess the tragedy that awaited the runners-up less than a year later: Duncan Edwards, injured; Bill Foulkes, injured; Mark Jones, killed; Ray Wood, injured; Eddie Colman, killed; David Pegg, killed; Dennis Viollet, injured; Tommy Taylor, killed; Roger Byrne, killed; Bill Whelan, killed; John Berry, in a coma, injured. At the time of going to press, Matt Busby was fighting for his life. The team secretary, Walter Crickmer, was killed.

Manchester, from the moment the news came through, was a city in mourning. Newspapers sold out as fast as they could be printed. It was as though every family in a city of three-quarters of a million people had suffered a personal loss, and so indeed they had. At Old Trafford, the saddest football ground in the world, the flag flew at half-mast, and on hundreds of other football grounds other flags were being dipped in sympathy. For this disaster is perhaps the most tragic single blow British sport has ever suffered.

'THE END'.

In the dark and warm, Neil turned to Aunty Gwen, and Aunty Gwen turned to look at Neil, and Aunty Gwen smiled and said, Would you like an ice cream, dear?

Yes, please, I would, said Neil, turning back to look at the screen, his eyes fixed upon the screen again.

Chocolate, is it?

Yes, please, said Neil. Thank you very much.

I'll be back in two ticks then.

Thank you, Aunty Gwen, said Neil again, his eyes still fixed upon the screen, the place where he had just seen his father in his shirt, his United shirt, beating the Villa man, passing to Tommy Taylor at Wembley last year, but Neil could not forget the sight of that plane at the start of the news, smouldering in the snow. It wasn't like Neil had thought at all, with their parachutes, in their kits and boots, fit and back and ready to play again, it was more like the scenes of war he'd seen, in comics or in films, of shot-down planes or bombed-out houses. It just wasn't like he'd thought at all. But before Neil could think any more, his Aunty Gwen was back with a chocolate ice cream, just as the screen turned blue, a bright Technicolor-blue sky through which soared a bird of prey, over hills and mountains of jungle and trees, and deep down within that jungle, with its exotic, squawking birds, Neil found himself before a graveyard, bamboo crosses in the ground, but hang on, what's this, there were train tracks through this jungle, too, the sound and the whistle of a train coming through the jungle, coming down the line, bringing in big, bright, bold, yellow letters the words 'The Bridge on the River Kwai' . . .

Neil took the ice cream from his Aunty Gwen, whispered thanks, then whispered, My dad was in the war, you know? He was going all round India in a truck, showing everyone films to cheer everyone up.

I know, whispered Aunty Gwen.

He didn't die, he came back.

Yes, love, said Aunty Gwen. He came home.

Aunty Gwen, asked Neil, what's a coma?

It just means your dad is still asleep, dear, whispered Aunty Gwen. That's all, dear, don't worry.

Neil nodded, turned back to the screen, the jungle and the war, but he couldn't help thinking, still kept thinking his dad had been asleep for a very long time, but maybe it was still night in Germany.

*

Frank knew he must not speak to Matt, to bother or disturb him, that Matt needed quiet, he needed rest, the doctors, the nurses and Peggy, too, they had all made that very clear, and Frank was not stupid, he knew that it was true. But Peggy and all the wives, they were not allowed to visit more than twice a day, and then not for long, not too long, depending on who it was and how they were, but usually not for very long, never long enough, and so whenever Peggy left again, had gone back to the Stachus Hotel again, Frank always felt so lonely, in that brighter, lighter, private room, with its walls of blue, sky blue and yellow warm, and despite the picture of Her Majesty the Queen, Frank felt so lonely, so terribly, terribly lonely, Matt silent and still in the other bed, the plastic tent around his head, more lonely than he had ever felt before, and Frank could not think why, had never felt this way before, on his way to war, or even as a child. But Frank could not stand it, he had to speak to someone. He reached behind him, above him with his one good hand, his unplastered arm, felt for the switch and pressed the button. Immediately, a doctor appeared and asked in broken English, jumbled German, what was wrong with Frank, what could she do? And in strange, slow gobbledygook, but with some useful gestures, Frank said, Telephoner my mutter, pleaser?

Minutes later, with a screen around his bed, a telephone plugged in, with a stern request to speak as quietly as he could, but with a kindly nurse holding the receiver to his ear, Frank was talking down the line to his mother back in England, listening as she said, When the doctors say I can, then I'm flying out to see you, son.

152

That would be wonderful, Mother, said Frank, wanting to say more, much more than this, but short of breath, and painful when it came, still struggling to breathe, so struggling to speak, to say anything more than, Thank you, Mother. I'll call again soon.

But before the nurse could take away the receiver, unplug the telephone again, Frank had one more call to make, one more call he knew he had to make, asked if he could please, please make that call, and the kind, young German nurse, she helped him connect the call, then held the receiver to Frank's ear again as, in his mind, Frank saw a telephone jangle on a desk in Manchester, the desk of his colleague, his pal Tom Simms, the northern sports editor of the *News Chronicle*, and Frank smiled as, in his mind, he saw Tom curse another ringing phone amid the clickety-clack of the typewriters, the rush to get the first edition through on time, and Frank smiled again as, in his mind, he imagined the shock Tom was about to get when he picked up that phone and barked, Sports desk?

Tom, said Frank, weakly, is that you?

But a voice Frank did not recognise, a young, uncertain voice, said, Hello? Can I help you?

Is Tom, Tom Simms there?

I'm sorry, said the young, uncertain, suddenly melancholy voice, but Mister Simms isn't here. He's gone to the funeral of Mister Rose of the *Express* . . .

How Frank came to know, he did not know, always later said he didn't really know, perhaps some chance remark, maybe a word overheard –

Hello? Hello . . .

But one moment Frank just knew, or could not pretend, no more pretend he did not know, could play that game no more, and maybe this was that moment then, as the kind, young German nurse took the receiver from Frank's ear, unplugged the phone from beside his bed and asked, Is everything okay?

I've lost my pals, said Frank, my colleagues, all great chaps, every one of them, and now they're gone.

*

Their son in acute danger, the parents of Duncan Edwards made a dramatic dash to Munich, where doctors were fighting to save the life of the young star, said the papers. They were driven at top speed from Dudley down to London, and though they arrived late, the Lufthansa plane was still waiting for them. They were taken straight out and on board, and within minutes the plane was in the air.

Meanwhile, in Munich, the doctors had called for an artificial-kidney machine. This machine, which looked like a giant washing machine, would clean Duncan's bloodstream. But the machine was being overhauled two hundred miles away in Freiburg, so a police car was sent out to the factory. The machine was loaded onto a trailer, the trailer attached to the police car, then the police car set off, travelling at speeds of over seventy miles an hour along the autobahn, racing to Munich and Duncan.

Racing through the European skies that night, Duncan's mum and dad, Annie and Gladstone Edwards, had never been on a plane before. Gladstone worked as a metal polisher at the Sankey & Sons ironworks in Bilston, and so his job had been classed as a reserved occupation during the war. He had been one of the lucky ones. But maybe each person only has a certain amount of luck in life, and when you've had your luck, that's it, thought Annie. Or maybe things are already mapped out for you, from the minute you're born, already decided from your first day to your last? Maybe that's why Duncan was kicking a ball 'fore he could walk, why if he had no ball, he was kicking the bricks in the street. People are watching you, she'd say, but he didn't care. He'd keep on kicking all the while he went on down the road. Maybe that's why he couldn't stop it, he couldn't help himself. It was already decided, already written for him. Why, then, when the clubs, all the clubs were watching him, he said, Well, Mum, he said, I think the best club I'd like to go in the country is Manchester United. So when she'd said, Well, if that's what you want to do and where you want to go, then said, You do it, you go, then maybe it didn't matter, wouldn't have made no odds if she'd said, or his dad had said, But why go there? Up there? Why not choose Wolves? Stay near and close to home?

But when their plane touched down in Munich, the wreck of that other plane, that plane that had almost killed their son, that plane still sat there, slumped in the snow, when Annie and Gladstone were hurried from their plane into the terminal building, then driven at speed from the airport through the German night into the city, straight to the Rechts der Isar Hospital, when they saw a man they had never seen before, waiting on the steps outside, who first introduced himself as Doctor Graham Taylor, a British European Airways medical officer, then Annie and Gladstone thought the worst, they were too late, their boy, their son was dead, but Doctor Graham Taylor whisked them from the car and with a smile he said, The machine has done its job, Duncan is slightly better now.

And as Doctor Graham Taylor took Annie and Gladstone inside the hospital, then down a corridor and into an elevator, up to the fourth floor, he said, While your son is still very seriously ill, a dramatic improvement has been seen since the artificial kidney was linked to his bloodstream, and so it would seem that the machine is working, filtering the nitrogen out of his bloodstream, and while it will take two or three days before we can know whether the present improvement can be maintained, Duncan has been conscious and even been talking.

What's he been saying, asked Annie.

Let's find out, shall we, said Doctor Graham Taylor as the elevator stopped, as the doors opened. But as he led them down a short corridor to the ward, he said, already in a low voice, Please remember when you're talking, your son knows of no deaths in the crash.

Then Doctor Graham Taylor smiled again and took them onto Duncan's ward, up to Duncan's bed, where there was Molly smiling, too, smiling as she said, Oh, Missus Edwards, oh, Mister Edwards, it's a miracle, it really is! Duncan asked for a drink and an apple, and he's had a glass of lemonade, haven't you, Duncan? And look, Duncan, look, love, your mam and dad are here –

Just get me out of here, Mum, said Duncan, whispered Duncan. I've got better things to do than lying around in here all day. I need to get back.

*

Manchester, Manchester, back again in Manchester, broken-hearted Jimmy Murphy came stumbling out of London Road, dragging with him his weather-beaten suitcase from the Broken Promised Land as sleet and rain took turns to stab, to scratch his face, his hands, before he tumbled down into the back of a waiting cab –

Hello, Mister Murphy, sir, said the driver, before he paused, then said, Is it, er, where . . .

Jimmy sniffed, wiped his nose, then said, Old Trafford, son, if you will, please, son.

Can I just say, Mister Murphy, sir, said the driver as the taxi spluttered back to life, pulled away from the station again, just say how very sorry I am, sir.

Jimmy smiled. Thank you, son, thank you, but then Jimmy slumped back in his seat, not keen to chat, not today, tonight, though he could feel the driver trying hard to think of what to say, the right words to say, but Jimmy knew he'd not, he never would, because there were no words, right words to say, and Jimmy turned to the window, glimpsed folk walking in the streets, stark white or sickly yellow underneath the lamps, the lamps all on, heads down under hats or umbrellas, heading home or to the pub, a cup of tea or pint of ale to wash away the day.

Thanks for them oranges, said the driver, suddenly. Them oranges the other day. They were lovely.

Jimmy smiled again. You're very welcome, son, but then Jimmy turned back to the window again, the streets of Stretford running down the glass again, and on the forecourt at Old Trafford, Jimmy thanked the driver, got out of the taxi, but he did not go inside the ground, up the stairs to the office, not today, tonight, Jimmy just stood there, looking up at the main stand, the bricks in the dark. Then Jimmy wiped and blew his nose again, picked up his suitcase and walked round to the gym, the double wooden doors to the gym. He opened the doors and stepped inside. The place was empty, the place was silent, the coffins and the tables gone, just the scent of flowers, the smell of varnish lingering still in the shadows, waiting there for Jimmy –

Hello, Jimmy, pet, said Cissie Charlton, stepping into the gym, coming up behind him. But then she saw his shoulders tremble, heard him sniff then say, not turn around, just say, Make us a cup of tea, will you, Cis, love. One of your special cups of tea, please, Cissie, love.

6

Jimmy's kids did not hear him get back from Munich, but in the morning, when they got up and came downstairs, they saw their dad through the kitchen window, in the back garden, out in the cold, damp morning, pacing up and down, wearing a path across their small patch of lawn and back, holding his rosary, its beads and its crucifix in his hand, rubbing at the figure and face of Christ on the Cross as he paced, as he prayed, first asking for forgiveness, then asking for comfort, comfort for others, asking for strength, strength for others, then strength for himself, the strength to help others, the strength to go on, to somehow go on.

But when Jimmy came back in, in out of the cold, out of the garden, wiped his shoes on the mat, he'd found that face of his again, put on that bravest face, a big and cheerful smile for their mum and them, especially for young Nick, who was still only ten. But Patricia, John, Phil and Jimmy Junior, they just wanted to help, to do what they could do, and Jimmy smiled and said, Well, I know poor Alma and young Les, they need all the help they can get, what with all the letters and donations, and Cissie Charlton, Bobby's mum, she's down here helping. But she'll have to get back, after the funerals, when Bobby gets back, and so it would be grand if you could come in, after school, after work, to help out, whenever you can.

Then Jimmy glanced at his watch, took a bite of his toast, a swig of his tea, then said, Crikey, I best look sharp and get changed, but I'll see you all later, either up at the ground or back here, though I can't say when.

But after his dad had got up from the table, gone upstairs to get ready, after Jimmy Junior had finished his own breakfast, gone up to get ready for school, Jimmy Junior passed his dad's bedroom, the door slightly ajar, and Jimmy Junior could hear his dad talking, speaking with someone, and through the crack in the door Jimmy Junior saw his dad on his knees by the edge of his bed, talking to God, speaking with God, praying and crying, in floods of tears, on his knees by the edge of his bed, in his Sunday-best suit, his dark funeral suit.

*

Each day the wives came from the hotel to the hospital, twice they came each day, to sit beside the beds, to hold the hands of the men they loved, if they were allowed and could, to hold their hands in flesh, or in spirit, and say, Come on, love, keep going, love, be strong, love, get well, love, it's going to be all right, love, please, love, please.

Even those that could not wake, they held their hands and said, over and over, like Missus Rayment said, Come on, Ken, come on, love. Time to wake up, love, time to get up, love. Come on, Ken, come on, love . . .

Or Johnny Berry's wife Hilda, his mother out here, too, to sit with Hilda beside poor Johnny's bed, Johnny wrapped in bandages, tubes in and out of every part of him, Hilda and his mother there to hope and pray he would wake up, to tell him of his sons, their boys back home, who were sending their love, their prayers, just waiting for Daddy to wake up, to come home, So come on, love, keep going, love, don't give up, love . . .

Beside Mattie's bed, in the silence of the room, Jean listened to Mattie breathe, and every now and then to grunt and try to speak, perhaps to try to ask the questions that she dreaded he would ask, and Jean would touch, would hold his hand, to softly, gently squeeze his hand and gently, softly say, Don't worry, love, don't worry, please. But don't talk, don't try to talk, love, please, just rest, love, please, just rest.

*

Joe came to pick up Jimmy, to drive them first to Old Trafford, both in their dark funeral suits, their black ties around their necks. Joe with more bad news for Jimmy –

Looks like Wilf McGuinness is going to be out for a while, the rest of the season, from what Ted says. But the lad's going to have to go in for the op. Ted says there's just no getting round it, despite . . .

Despite the mess we're in, aye, sighed Jimmy. He sighed again, then said again, Aye, Joe, it never rains but it pours, but maybe it's better to know now, have all the bad news at once, yeah.

Joe nodded. Maybe. But what's all this about Puskás and Czibor and Kocsis coming? Is it right?

I know about as much as you do, Joe, if not less, said Jimmy. But we'll find out soon enough –

Ferenc Puskás, Zoltán Czibor and Sándor Kocsis had all been key members of the Hungarian team that had humiliated England six–three in November 1953, in what the British press had called the 'Match of the Century'. Many of the morning papers were reporting that Puskás, Czibor and Kocsis had offered their services to Manchester United for the rest of the season.

Is there any truth in this at all, Mister Chairman, asked Jimmy at the ground, up the stairs, in the boardroom, across the table from Harold Hardman, in his dark funeral suit, a black tie around his neck, too.

Harold Hardman nodded. They have made contact with us, yes, through a third party, but it would seem to be a serious suggestion on their part, and of course we thanked them for their offer. But the board and I have been waiting to speak with you, and with Mister Busby, too, if you think there's any chance at all he might be well enough to speak about such matters.

I'm afraid to say that I fear it'll be a while before Matt is well enough to even think about such things. I spoke with Jean, with Missus Busby last night, and Matt is definitely a bit better, but the doctors are saying he needs complete rest, and will for a while, and of course he still does not yet know . . .

Harold Hardman nodded. Yes, of course, he still doesn't know. But what do you think, Jimmy?

Well, they are fantastic players, and you'll remember yourself, sir, that Matt did try to sign Puskás a few seasons back, but the problems back then would be the problems still now, would they not? The size of their wages, the issue of citizenship . . .

Harold Hardman nodded again. Yes, the board and I did discuss the issue of the FA ban on foreign players, whether we should ask them to reconsider their stance. But as you know, they've already agreed to a lot.

They have, said Jimmy, and so they should, some might say, but there'll be others who will start to grumble soon and then complain, you just watch.

Harold Hardman nodded. But you know they have agreed to postpone Saturday's tie until next Wednesday? And to play it under floodlights?

Yes, I know, said Jimmy, and that's good news, some good news at last, sir, but have they made a decision yet about the fourteen days and cup-tied players?

Yes, the fourteen-day qualification rule has been waived, said Harold Hardman, which is very good of them and an enormous help to us. But with any cup-tied player we might consider signing, we will have to discuss each player with the FA first, who will then decide each individual case on its merits.

Jimmy sighed. Oh, bloody hell, then that –

Now, hold on, Jimmy, said Harold Hardman, they have assured me they are unlikely to refuse our requests. But, of course, they have the other clubs to consider.

Jimmy nodded. I know, sir, but I was more thinking of the time, the time it will take. As you yourself know, sir, effecting transfers is a difficult business at the best of times, the length of negotiations, the snags that crop up, and that's after we've decided who we might need. I mean, we need to build as quickly as possible, I know, yet we still have to give every chance to our youngsters, for our up-and-coming lads to make good. We can't just turn our backs on them now, and we won't, I know. But at the same time, if we get any more injuries, then we simply don't have the numbers, we won't be able to fulfil all our fixture commitments, so I know we shall have to buy, I know. But then who shall we buy?

I know it's difficult, said Harold Hardman, getting up from the table, I know, but we –

Jimmy shook his head. We mustn't end up signing players just for the sake of signing them. It's vital that we get the right type of player to fit into our plans. They must be experienced, but young . . .

I know, said Harold Hardman again, on his feet, by the door, but, Jimmy –

Jimmy shook his head again. We can't force clubs to part with the players we might want, and most often the ones you want are the ones you can't get, and so even finding out who is available and who's not, who wants to come, will they then fit in if they do, then negotiating with their club, and now the FA, it's all just going to take so long, too long. I can't see how we'll have time –

Jimmy, said Harold Hardman, holding the door open, gesturing at his watch, we need to go . . .

Frank blinked, then blinked again, but try as he might he could not get his eyes to focus on the page, that bloody page. He'd read a sentence, maybe even two –

In 1909 the doctor warned Jessie Bader during her second pregnancy that the baby might not be born alive and that it would be risky . . .

– but first the letters, then the words, the whole bloody page would blur, would fade then fall away as his eyes stung, filled with tears, and Frank slammed shut the book and snapped, I know I talk too much, that's why they moved me out of there and into here, but how else am I supposed to pass the time. If you can tell me or these bloody German doctors, then please do, I'm all ears!

Now, now, dear, said Peggy. No one is saying you shouldn't talk or that you talk too much. As the doctors explained, it's simply that Mister Busby still needs constant care, but also quiet and solitude. It was their mistake to put the two of you together in that room in the first place, as they said. That's why they moved you.

Frank nodded, but still he worried Missus Busby had complained he talked too much, that that was really why they'd moved him five doors down and into Room 406, into here to share with Jackie Blanchflower. Frank knew Jackie, knew and liked him. His wife Jean was very friendly, too, always cheerful with a smile, but Jack himself was still quite ill, and the carefree, always smiling, ever wisecracking Blanchy of before the crash was gone, at least for now, it seemed to Frank, pain and shock still etched upon his face, there with fear and with despair, for the doctors said his kidneys had been badly damaged, along with the fractures to his right arm and pelvis. Frank could see it in Jack's eyes, the fear he would not play again, the despair at then what could or would he do?

163

I think they're worried, too, said Peggy, about Matt finding out, from what Jean and Sheena said, that one small slip of the tongue might tell him everything. They just don't think he's any state to know just yet.

Frank nodded. I was worried what I'd do, to be honest, what I'd say if he asked me. Because he has asked Jean, he's asked her twice what happened, I heard him.

And so what did she say when he did?

Don't worry, don't talk, just rest.

But he must know, said Jackie, from the next bed, suddenly and violently. The Old Man's not bloody stupid, he must fucking know, and if he doesn't fucking know, then he should know, we should bloody tell him, tell him what happened, because he needs to know –

No, Jackie, no, said Peggy, getting up from beside Frank's bed, joining Jean Blanchflower by Jackie's bed, trying to calm him. Missus Busby, the doctors, they think if he finds out too soon, if he knows before he's strong enough, then Matt won't want to go on, he won't try to get well, he'll just give up the ghost.

*

They went from funeral to funeral that day, that week, so many funerals those days, that week, on those black days in that black week; two yesterday, seven today, seven tomorrow, four on Friday. Shops had run out of black ties, florists could not keep up with the demand for wreaths and for sprays, the wholesalers had had to send to Holland for more flowers. But with flowers or without, in black ties or not, still the mourners came, on foot or by bicycle, chained and left their bicycles down the road and took off their clips, walked up the road, towards the church, or they caught a bus, or took a cab or shared a car, sometimes three or four wedged in across the back, and tried to think of what to say, what not to say, on their way out Flixton way, to that first funeral of that day, each man or woman thinking, or trying not to think, of Roger Byrne –

In their hundreds, their thousands they came out to Flixton, to line Church Road, to gather and wait on the cobbles before the mock-Tudor Church Inn, on the verges outside Saint Michael's Parish Church, hundreds and thousands who had never met or known Roger Byrne, but had watched him week in, week out for seven seasons now, had watched him come of age back in that Championship side of Fifty-two, then grow up to lead the so-called Babes, lead them as their captain to the title in Fifty-six, and then again last year, and he would have done again this year, they knew, these hundreds, these thousands, waiting outside Saint Michael's Parish Church, because they knew Roger Byrne, knew he'd have never settled for second, not Rog, their Rog, that was not his way, and who they could not believe, still not believe they would never see again, Roger running out of the tunnel, leading out the boys, tapping the ball up once, twice into his hands, then with one mighty kick high up into the air, up towards the Scoreboard End.

They carried Roger out of his quiet, suburban, semi-detached house, the club house that United had given them last year, just one year before, when he and Joy had married, and one last time they took him down the path and through the gate. They placed his coffin inside the back of the waiting hearse, its roof bedecked with flowers, the whole of Edale Avenue filled with neighbours and supporters, umpteen deep in places, some standing on other people's garden walls to get a better view as the hearse set off slowly, slowly made its way onto Sunningdale Road, then slowly left up Chassen Road, between the big, bare trees, slowly turning at the pub onto Church Road, all traffic stopped, and slowly on towards the parish church it went, followed by another car, then slowly by another with his wife Joy, his mother Jessie and his father Bill, then the Chairman and directors of United, the roofs of their black cars bedecked with flowers, too, and slowly, slowly followed by three other cars in black.

From under the bare, black branches on Church Road, the cortège turned onto the cobbles outside the Church Inn and stopped before Saint Michael's Parish Church, where policemen stood before the crowd of silent and respectful, decent folk who'd gathered, waiting there, hats in hand, with collars up, or at attention in their uniforms. But though the National Union of Journalists had called for reporters, sub-editors and photographers to refrain from covering the funerals of the Dead, 'beyond the mere fact that they have taken place', as 'anything more would constitute a serious intrusion into the private griefs of the bereaved', still between the melancholy sounds of muffled public grief there came the sound of cameras, clicking or rolling, held by men in raincoats stood on the low church wall or leaning back against a tree, snapping or filming as the coffin of Roger Byrne was lifted from the hearse and carried into the church, where his relatives and friends, old schoolmates and a few of his teammates got to their feet.

Because both him and Gordon Clayton were injured, and had not gone, and were still here, Wilf and Gordon had both been doing what they could, what little that they could. Gordon had gone straight round to see Mark Jones's wife June, had then helped Jackie Blanchflower's wife Jean as best he could, answering the phone, the door, before she went out herself to Munich. The next day, they'd both gone together to see Eddie's mam and dad, not that they'd known what to say, what on earth could you say, and had just sat in silence there, awkward and shocked, still stunned. But then Eddie's girl, Marjorie, she'd come round, had wanted to go out to the airport, to see the coffins when they came back, so Wilf had took her out there, Monday, when they came back, at least it was something, something to do, to try to help. But because they were injured, they couldn't train or do anything bloody much, Jimmy had asked Wilf and Gordon to make sure they went to every one of the funerals of the players, to go as representatives of the first team, standing in for the ones that could not make it, the ones who were not there. So here they stood, Wilf and Gordon, in Saint Michael's Parish Church, Flixton, as they carried in their captain, their leader, a player they both looked up to and revered, on and off the pitch, the man who set the standard, though he could be a right old so-and-so, could Roger, wouldn't half give the young lads some right old bollockings if he saw any sign of a growing, bigger head, a hint that someone thought they'd made the Big Time, that this was Easy Street, and not just with his tongue and all, he'd use his hands, his fists, would Roger, if he felt the need, he'd clipped and clobbered Wilf a couple of times or more, and though Wilf had cursed Roger bloody Byrne, Wilf knew himself he was a cocky little twat, noisier than most, and that each slap and punch from Rog had been one he had deserved, and that was why Wilf was standing in this pew, in this church in Flixton, trying not to see the coffin as it came past him down the aisle, just staring at the back of Jimmy's coat and Joe's, the backs of their heads in the pew in front of his, Wilf just trying not to cry.

But in the pew in front of Wilf and Gordon, with Sandy Busby there beside them, too, Jimmy and Joe were struggling, too, racked by the ifs, the onlys and the buts, the might-have-could-have-should-have-beens, as the vicar and the service tried to make some sense of what was and is and will be, and though both Joe and Jimmy knew there was no sense in the ifs, the onlys and the buts, the might-have-could-have-should-have-beens, still they racked, they plagued them both. Joe had seen Brian Statham on the way into the church, one of Roger's best friends from Gorton, Joe now dwelling on that day, almost fourteen years ago today, when he'd seen Roger and Brian playing for Ryder Brow Juniors in a Lancashire Amateur League fixture. Both were grammar-school boys, smart and good at any sport they played, and Joe had offered them both amateur forms. Roger had accepted, while Brian had turned Joe down, wanting to stick to the sport he loved best, cricket. Brian had gone on to play for Lancashire, had been selected for England and been chosen as one of the *Wisden* Cricketers of the Year, and though Roger had played two hundred and seventy-seven times for United and had been capped by England in thirty-three consecutive games, Brian was still here.

The thought that bothered Jimmy as he tried to sing the hymns, to still the mind, to heal the heart, their words he knew by heart, but still the thought that troubled Jimmy was that Rog should still be here, should not have gone, might not have gone. He'd had a knock to his ankle on Saturday, in the Arsenal game, a knock that had needed a lot of treatment, and a knock bad enough to make them change their plans, to pull Ronnie Cope off the list and put poor Geoff Bent on the flight instead, only there as cover, cover for Roger in case he was not fit enough to play. But if there was a doubt, and there was a doubt, then why did they risk him? If only he or Matt or Ted had thought things through, then they'd have surely seen it made no sense at all; if they were taking Geoff Bent along, why then bring Roger, too? Why not let Roger stay back home, here with Joy in Flixton, to get himself recovered, to rest up for Saturday, ready for the Wolves?

But then Jimmy smiled, so very briefly, slightly smiled as he thought of who or how they'd have told Roger he was not on the flight to Belgrade, that his services were not required, that he should stay back home in Flixton, rest himself up, ready for the Saturday. No, thought Jimmy, knew Jimmy, that was never very likely; he'd had cuts, he'd had bruises, all manner of aches and strains, teeth knocked out and stitches in his eyes, but he'd only ever missed one match, and even if they'd set his ankle, his whole bloody leg in plaster, Roger Byrne would have still been on that flight. He would have gone along just to see, to watch the game, to be there for the team; he was their captain, they were his team, they were his life.

In the pew at the front of the church, the pew closest to the coffin, Joy was trying hard not to think of what they'd lost, the times they would not have, trying harder to think of the times they'd had. But Joy and Roger had only been married six months. She'd only really known him for two and a half years, all told, and they'd never really seen each other very much, even after they got married. Roger was always either training, playing or studying. If he had a Monday off, he'd go to Salford Royal to study, go in there of an afternoon, if he could, if he had the time, and that was how they'd met, both studying to be physiotherapists. He'd always wanted to be prepared for the day his career, his playing days would end, and for Joy that day could not have come quick enough, the sooner he was out of football the better, she had always thought, that Roger had so much more to offer, and felt still, here in this pew, before his coffin, he had so much more to give, give to the world than this, outside of this.

The sitting down, the standing up, the sitting back down then the standing back up again was over now. Joy helped Roger's mother Jessie, his father Bill from the pew, back down the aisle again, stooped behind the coffin as they bore poor Roger from the church back out into the air, where still the crowds were gathered, waiting on the cobbles. The pallbearers placed the coffin back inside the hearse, as Joy and Jessie and then Bill got back into their car, the big black hired car, the sound of the hearse doors closing, its wheels on the cobbles, then the road the only sound, followed in procession by the other big black cars.

In the back of the car, the big black hired car, his mother Jessie was trying to be strong, as strong as she could, but there was a bitterness and an anger in her eyes, she knew, not at anyone, the pilot or the club, no, no, but if at anything, then it was at fate itself, the fate that had robbed her of her only son, their only son, that had done this thing to her, this thing to them; her husband, his father Bill, it was as if she'd lost him, too, had lost them both that night, for try as he might, she knew Bill just could not find the strength, could not be strong, this thing, he said, it made no sense, no sense at all. But Jessie didn't want to, couldn't think like that, fall into thoughts like that; she tried instead just to think of the times they'd had, the memories she had of when he was just six or maybe seven, and he was playing for the Abbey Hey Junior School team against another little school, and she'd gone along to watch him, thinking many of the mums, even some of the dads, they'd be there to cheer their boys along, it being a Saturday morning and the weather not that bad. But when she got there, Jessie was the only other mum, and apart from her and the teachers, there was just one other spectator, a dad who'd come with the other team of boys, and after a while this dad, he walked up to Jessie and he pointed and he said, See that little lad over there? He'll be a good footballer one day, you mark my words. And Jessie smiled and said, That's my son, that lad.

But his father Bill had no such thoughts, good or bad, he could not think a thing, his eyes just fixed upon the coffin of his son in the hearse up ahead, on the road up ahead, Manchester Crematorium coming up ahead.

But on the back seat of the car, the big black hired car, passing through Chorlton, along the Barlow Moor Road, as Joy desperately tried to find the words, to think of something, anything to help poor Bill and Jessie, but knowing there was nothing, nothing that would help, it was then the sudden, unwelcome, most unwanted thought struck Joy that she'd known Roger for just three Februarys, for only three, and that first February she'd known Roger, his car had skidded on some ice and he'd gone and hit a lamp post, then the second February he'd had to swerve to avoid a van coming down the Wilbraham Road, and he'd only gone and swerved into Matt Busby's neighbour's gatepost, of all the gateposts to swerve into, then this third and final February he'd only gone and died in a crash, and always around his birthday –

Roger Byrne died just two days short of his twenty-ninth birthday, just a few days short of knowing Joy was expecting their first child.

*

Bill and Teresa, Harry and Mavis, they slipped out of the Russell Hotel and into the enormous Rolls-Royce that Jimmy had booked to take them back to Manchester –

Don't be putting your foot down, Bill told the chauffeur. It's not a race, you know, we're in no rush.

The chauffeur touched his cap and said, Thank you, sir. Don't you worry, I will go slow.

But in the back of the Rolls, all the way back to Manchester, Bill kept gripping the seat, the inside of the door, straining to sit forward to tell the driver, sometimes even yelling at the man, Slow down, for Chrissakes, will you bloody slow down, man! You're going too fast.

And the chauffeur would touch his cap again, then again, and say again, I am sorry, sir, I really am, but I promise you, I'm going as slow as I possibly can.

And Mavis glanced at Harry, but Harry could only smile back at Mavis with a smile that said, What can I say, what can I do, I know we're going slow, I know; we'll be lucky to get back to Manchester by Christmas, the rate we're bloody going, but what can I do, what can I say, and Harry then turned, looked across at Teresa, smiled at Teresa with a different smile, a smile that said, Don't worry, love, don't worry, just give him time, he'll be okay,

Bill will be all right, you'll see, and Teresa touched Bill's hand, his hand that gripped the seat so tight, and rubbed and held his hand with a touch that said, Don't worry, love, I'm here, you're safe, we'll soon, or soon enough, be home, but Bill just shook his head again and said, It's all his bloody braking, I just can't abide the braking, thinking but not saying, never saying, It just brings it back again.

*

The first thing to say about it is that no one in Dublin called him Billy. They called him by the name his daddy gave him, the name his mammy called him, Liam. He was always Liam, always, and they were amazed when they read the paper that he was Billy, Billy Whelan, you know, he was Liam, Liam, and never anything else. But when they brought poor Liam back to Dublin, early on the Monday evening, on a freight plane from London, in with the dusk, the light leaving him with them, well, you should have seen the streets, you really should, the city just shut down. It was as if the President of Ireland himself had died, you know? And this in a town of funerals, mind. They had members of Aer Lingus AFC form a guard of honour as they took the poor boy from the plane, with officials from his former club, Home Farm FC, as they put his coffin, his remains inside the hearse, then in their heavy coats, with the black armbands on their sleeves, they walked in solemn step beside the funeral car, and when they got to Whitehall, there was a much larger guard, you know, a guard of honour waiting, made up of two, three hundred players, maybe more, former players and supporters, volunteers, all from Home Farm. But all the way along it was the same, crowds packed the streets, lined the five-mile route, in numbers you've not seen before, knelt on the pavement to say the Rosary as he passed by, all the traffic stopped, time and again, all along the weary way, the cortège accorded tributes from workers returning home, all the way the same, from the airport in, down to Whitehall, through Drumcondra, Phibsborough, and out to Cabra and the Church of Christ the King, close to the family home on Saint Attracta Road, number twenty-eight it was, the whole of the northside out on those streets, those roads he knew that were his home, the poor boy's home, for as his mammy said that night, Least now our Liam's home.

But his mammy, Elizabeth, she would never forget the nights he was taken from her, twice it was, she said, each time as sudden as the other. The first time was when Liam was playing one night for Home Farm, and so the story goes that Billy Behan, the famous Manchester United scout round here, he had Bert Whalley over from United to run the rule over Vinny Ryan, and Vinny was a great young player, he was all the talk, you know, always in the papers, Vinny going here, Vinny going there, Glasgow Celtic one day, United the next. Anyway, Liam was playing with Vinny that night for Home Farm, against Merrion Rovers it was, but at half-time, so the story goes, Bert Whalley, he turns to Billy Behan and he tells Billy, Forget about that boy Ryan, don't bother with him, get that lad Whelan, and as quickly as you can.

Now Liam's oldest brother Christy, who was like a father to Liam, because they'd lost their daddy early on, you know, and Christy, he went to watch Liam where he was playing, wherever it was, with the brother-in-law Michael, on their bikes they'd go, no matter where, no matter when, off they'd go, so he'd been at the match that night, had Christy, but he was already back home in his bed asleep that night, when suddenly the bedroom door flies open, and there's Liam shaking his brother Christy awake, telling him, Christy, Christy, can you come downstairs for a moment, please? There's somebody downstairs from Manchester United, and Christy, he opened his eyes and smiled and said, Well, it's about bloody time, and Christy gets up, puts on his overcoat over his pyjamas like and goes back down the stairs with Liam, and the first thing their mammy said was, Oh, Christy, they want to take him away, they want to take him from us, because there was Billy Behan standing there, you know, the famous scout and all, with Tom Smith, who was one of the main men at Home Farm, who looked after Liam's team, but cool as you like, Christy looks at Tom and says, Well, hello, Tom, what's wrong? What's going on? And Tom said, Well, this man here is Billy Behan, from Manchester United, and Billy, he puts out his hand, and Christy shakes his hand, and as he does, Tom says, They want Liam to go over to Manchester United, that's why he's here, Christy. And Billy Behan nodded. That's right, we want Liam to go over to Manchester United. But Christy looked at Billy, and Christy said, But what way do you want him? What's he going over for? If this is a trial, I'm not interested. He's too good for trials is Liam.

No, no, said Billy Behan. No trials. We want to sign him full-time, here and now, this night. He'll be straight into the youth team, playing Monday.

Well, I have no objections then, that's okay with me, said Christy, but he turned then to their mammy and said, If you want to let him go, I won't stand in the way.

Now Christy knew she did not want it, what mother ever does, so the thought of Liam leaving home and her did not sit well with her, not well at all with her, but she wanted it for Liam, if that was what he wanted, and so their mammy turned to Liam and smiled and said, Well, I suppose we'll have to let you go then.

That was all on the Friday evening, on a Friday night, and on the Sunday evening he was off and gone away, and they cried that night, did Christy and their mammy, and so did Liam, too, already missing home.

Well, they say he cried, and for sure he did, but that first Thursday he was there, over the water at Old Trafford, he was straight into the United youth team, you know, in for John

Doherty he was, playing in the first leg of the first-ever FA Youth Cup Final, helping United to beat the Wolves seven–one, the second leg then a two-all draw, but when you think back on that United side that won that first Youth Cup, then what a side it was: Gordon Clayton, Bryce Fulton, Paddy Kennedy, who'd come from Johnville, had he not, Eddie Colman, Ronnie Cope, Duncan Edwards, Noel McFarlane, Eddie Lewis, David Pegg, Albert Scanlon and then Liam, of course.

But, oh, he suffered with the homesickness, did Liam, oh, he really did, you know. He was always wanting to be home. One time he said to Christy, he said, I wish with all my life that this was over and I was coming home again. That stayed with him for many years, you know, the homesickness, it did. The problem he had was how to spend the days, you know, he'd train all morning, but they were done by one, and so then he'd go to the pictures in town, but he soon got fed up with that, you know, so the afternoons were a terrible drag they were. But there were things over there that happened, you know, and one of those things that helped him was when Christy and his good pal Sean Dolan came over on a visit.

Now Sean's brother Brendan, he was the manager of a canning factory that was owned by Louis Edwards, you know, the fellow who later went on the board, that became the Chairman at United, and Sean's brother Brendan and his wife Bid and their kids, they lived in a lovely big house out Stockport way, and Brendan and Bid, they invited Sean and Christy and Liam out there to Brendan's place one night, and they had a lovely big stew which Bid made for them, and Liam, he tucked into it, he really did, and so when they'd finished, when they were going, Brendan's wife Bid, she called Christy over, and she said, Now, Christy, did you see Liam eating the stew?

Yes, laughed Christy, he really lashed into it.

Do you think he'd like to eat more of them?

What do you mean, Bid, asked Christy.

Would he like to come and stay with us?

I'm sure he would, said Christy.

Now will you ask him then?

So when they were going into town, Christy, Sean and Liam, Christy said to Liam, What did you think of that dinner today? It was like Mammy's stew, was it not? Wouldn't you like to live with Bid and Brendan and their two lovely children? Now how would that be for you?

Ah, that would be grand if I could live with them, said Liam, it really would, you know.

Well, you can if you want, said Christy.

What do you mean, said Liam.

Bid told me to tell you that you can go and live with them, if that's what you want?

Is that right, said Liam, shocked and unsure. But if they're sure they're sure, then that's just great.

But great though that was, and help though it did, because he settled in quick, enjoyed being with their two children, taking them to the pictures, you know, that sort of thing, being more back into the family life, Liam didn't really have much time, was not long there before Munich. But at least at the Dolans' he was really happy, and he would also go to Mass, of course, and he was very friendly with Father Mulholland, he was a great friend to Liam, and Liam wrote home every week, sent Mammy three pounds a week, every week without fail, he would never forget, and he would telephone, too, the family two doors up from them on Saint Attracta Road, but still it weighed on them, you know, his words: I wish with all my life that this was over and I was coming home again.

That's why he was back as often as he could, you know, any old excuse, you know, like the time there was the five-a-side thing, quite big it was, with a good few international teams, at

Dalymount Park it was, you know. So Liam asked the Boss, could he take a team over from United, so Matt said yes, and so Liam gets Ray Wood, Eddie Colman, Duncan Edwards, he came over, too, and Albert Scanlon and Dennis Viollet, and some others, too, they all come over, and they're all staying at the Gresham Hotel, of course, but Liam, he's at home.

But the moment any rumour he was home, you know, the local children, they would find out and come knocking on the door, you know. Is Liam coming out? Are you coming out to play a match, Liam?

Have you got a ball, Liam would say, and they'd say, No, Liam, we've no ball –

And Liam would put his hand in his pocket, take out the money and say, Here, go up the bridge and get a ball, and I'll be out shortly.

Now that day he was back for the five-a-side thing was the same, he was outside playing ball with the kids, and out there so long, his mammy, she looked at her watch and she says to Christy, It's getting late, and he has still to get down to the ground to play. And she sends Christy out to bring Liam in, you know, to hurry him along.

Next goal is the winner, says Liam to the young ones, smiling, then when it's over, he comes running in for a quick wash and a change of his shoes, and then off he runs, you know, had to run to get down to Dalymount.

But then when he comes back home again that night, he says, Ma, what do you think of that then?

What do I think of what, says his mammy.

Two hat-tricks in the one day.

His mammy, she shakes her head, she says, What are you talking about, two hat-tricks in one day?

Well, laughs Liam, I scored a hat-trick out in the road with the youngsters, and I went down to Dalymount and scored a hat-trick against Shamrock Rovers, and with Eamonn Darcy in goal, so he was.

That was Liam, you know, always time for the young fellas, the little ones, you know, and he was the same in Manchester, they say. He was always the one who stopped to speak and sign their books, you know, whatever the weather, even if it was pissing it down, Liam would stand there in his belted grey gabardine mac and his trilby hat, dripping with rain, until he'd signed every last one of their books, until there was no one left waiting.

But the second time he was taken from them was, of course, the worst, and it was Charlie, Charlie Jackson, you know, who'd been the great mentor to Liam back in his Home Farm days, along with Tom, Tom Smith, you know, and he was a good friend of the family, was Charlie, but it was Charlie then who first came to them with it that day, that afternoon, that Thursday afternoon. Charlie worked in Guinness's and had heard the news down there, and the very moment he did, Charlie left his work to come straight up to the Whelan house in Saint Attracta Road.

Christy was sitting there in front of the fire, when he heard the gate opening. He looked up, saw who it was and called out to his mammy and sister Rita, who were in the back with the ironing, Well, here's Charlie!

But the moment she came through from the back into the front and saw Charlie standing there, Mammy knew something was wrong, because the first thing she did, she said to him, she pointed straight at the clock and said, It's three o'clock, Charlie, I know they're home –

No, Missus Whelan, said Charlie, looking at Mammy, shaking his head. I'm afraid they're not.

What's wrong, Charlie, I know they're home, said Mammy. They must be home, what's wrong?

They're saying there's been a plane crash, said their younger brother John, tearing into the house. It's in the *Evening Herald*, the Manchester United plane has crashed, a lad in the street in town was stood there telling everyone the news. But it can't be right, it must be wrong?

But the house was filling up, their sister Alice, she came straight round, came in, just stood there and looked at her mammy but did not say a thing as Mammy looked at Charlie, then the clock again, pointed and said again, But it's three o'clock, Charlie, I know they're home.

Poor Charlie Jackson, who'd come up to offer his condolences, to help in any way he could, but finds them all in there, while the whole of Dublin knows, and so poor Charlie ends up being the one to break the news to them, and so poor Charlie just shook his head again and had to say, you know, to say again, No, I'm afraid they're not.

Put the radio on, will you, Christy, said Mammy. If something's happened, it'll be on the radio –

Christy did as he was told, put the thing on, then fiddled with its dials, trying to get that crackly feed of the BBC, you know, with the house full, everyone silent, in complete silence, just listening to the crackly feed, the news filter through, straining to hear –

Here is the news. So far we know there are twenty-three survivors after Manchester United's air crash at Munich this afternoon. We're beginning with names of survivors. Of the crew of six and thirty-eight passengers on board, including a baby, these are the people so far known to have survived: of the Manchester United party, Matt Busby, manager, and the following players: Gregg, Wood, Foulkes, J. Blanchflower, Edwards, Morgans, Berry, Charlton, Viollet and Scanlon . . .

– to listen for Liam, knowing after the survivors would come the names of the dead, the house filled with such dread, not wanting to hear –

. . . the people believed to have been on the plane who are so far unaccounted for: of the Manchester United party,

Walter Crickmer, secretary, and Bert Whalley, coach, T. Curry,
trainer, and the following players: Byrne, Bent, Colman, Jones,
Whellan . . .

Whellan, pronounced the English voice of the English man
reading the English news, like in bell, not like you would if it
was Liam –

Taylor and Pegg . . .

'Unaccounted for' doesn't mean dead, said Mammy, they
didn't say dead, they never said dead. He could have wandered
off, concussed and confused, be in some hospital, not knowing
who or where he is.

But everyone knew, inside the house, they all knew, except
for Mammy, poor Mammy, who looked at them, at Christy and
John, at Alice and Rita, saw their thoughts, their fears in their
eyes, heard their thoughts, their fears in their heads, but she
shook her head and said, You're all wrong. 'Unaccounted for'
doesn't mean dead.

But then Joe Farrell from two doors up came with the
knock on the door, Joe's house being the only house on the
street with a telephone, you know, Joe being a taxi driver, and
Joe said, Christy, will you come with me, there's a call for you
from Manchester, from Old Trafford.

Father Mulholland, in Manchester, he knew the agony,
the anguish the family must be going through back home in
Cabra, and so he'd gone up to Old Trafford that night to find
out what he could, and when he found out the worst, he gave
the number of the Farrell house to Jimmy Murphy so Jimmy
could call and say –

Christy, we've had bad news, said Jimmy Murphy. Liam
didn't make it. From all that's left at Old Trafford, we send our
sympathies, wish you all our condolences, and please tell your
mother we'll be in touch again soon, and we'll do our best to
help you through all this.

Thank you, Mister Murphy, said Christy, thank you for calling, for letting us know, and Christy put down the telephone, went back to their house and tried to tell their mammy what Mister Murphy had just told him, but their mammy, she just shook her head –

I don't believe it, she said. He's made a mistake. He's been told a lie. If Liam was gone, then why's his name not been on the radio then?

But they tried to get their mammy to rest, you know, to lie on her bed, not just to stand or sit or fret beside the radio, you know, but Mammy, she insisted on the radio being on, that Christy sat and listened through the night, and Christy said he would if it meant she'd go upstairs to bed, to rest, if not to sleep. But later in the night, when his mammy had gone up at last, in that awful silence of that long night of waiting, there was another knock upon the door, and when Christy got back from the door, he switched off the radio set and went upstairs himself to bed, to sit upon his bed awhile, and as he did, his mammy came in to him and said, Christy, if he was dead, Liam was dead, wouldn't the police have come to us by now?

Christy sat on the edge of his bed, looked up at his mammy, his eyes wet, and said, Mammy, that was them just then, come with official notice Liam's dead.

But, Christy, are you sure they did, said his mammy. I never heard the knock.

Mammy, the policeman came, that was him just then, he's been. I wish he hadn't, but he did.

And he said?

He did.

Well, now we know Liam is with God then.

From the Friday morning till the Monday afternoon, when Liam came back home again, no one in the city, in Cabra, let alone the house on Saint Attracta Road, could tell you how they passed those hours that felt like days that felt like weeks that felt like months that felt like years that felt like they would never end, you know.

And their mammy was very strong, you know, she wasn't one to sit around and weep, you know? They'd had their share of grief or more, the family, lost their daddy back in Forty-two or Forty-three, their mammy left with the seven kids she was, then their sister Bridie, the eldest girl, she passed in Fifty-three, the year United first took Liam off away. But they were not a family that sat around and wept, you know. They grieved, of course they did, but then they just got on with things, you know, and that was down to their religion and their mammy, her strength and faith in God, her belief. God wanted Liam, that was all she'd really ever say, God wanted Liam.

But no matter how much they might have wished it was not so, was not this way, it was not possible for the Chairman, the directors, Jimmy, Joe, Bill Inglis, Arthur Powell or young Les to attend every funeral of the Dead. Thus it was agreed that when it came to poor Billy Whelan's funeral, then they'd send some of the young Irish boys back home, over the water, now that would be Joe Carolan, Jackie Mooney, Jimmy Sheils and little Johnny Giles, so they sent them back to represent the club at poor Billy Whelan's funeral. But if those four young boys had been hoping for a break from the grief back home, from streets that wept and rooms that shook, they found it stood there waiting for them here, from the airport into town, on every street, in every home, as desperate and as heavy as anything they'd left behind in Manchester.

But the other thing to say is, the city was not just in mourning for their own, that clouded hush not just for Liam, one of their own, but for all the boys, the English boys who'd died, you know, and that was quite a thing, when you stop to think: it was a very anti-English town, was Dublin then, you know, still less than forty years since the War of Independence, and not much more than ten since the Cunt Churchill talked of invasion, Cromwell and Craigavon in his ear, you know, and but one year before, almost exactly one year ago, the whole of Limerick and half of Ireland, so it seemed, turned out for the funeral of your man, killed on a raid up in the North, martyred for the cause, that was Séan South it was. But that was down to United, you know, the grief that the city, the country felt, because United would always give an Irish boy a chance, you know, that was known, not like some, you know, and that goes all the way back to Patrick O'Connell, and then if you think of Johnny Carey, and all the fuss was made of him, he was never out the papers here when he was there.

But you even had *The Irish Press*, the great anti-British paper, mourning the passing of 'so many great players', you know, not just an Irish one, and players of 'the garrison game', remember, which was itself a thing, that was their editorial, and then there was your man from Fianna Fáil, Oscar Traynor, who was then the Minister for Justice, and who was no friend of England, having fought against the Treaty as Brigadier of the Dublin Brigade of the IRA, though he was the President of the Football Association of Ireland, to be fair, you know, but there he was saying, Many of the players who have survived will carry on the traditions of the famous club.

The big part of this, you see, was that it was only a few months back they'd been over, had United, you know, in the September it was, when they were drawn against Shamrock Rovers in the European Cup; now that was some night, it really was, you could not hardly get up the lane to Dalymount, forty thousand were there that night, they said, but it was more, much more, you know, you had to fight your way into the ground, and just the Saturday before, United had beaten Arsenal at Old Trafford, with Liam scoring two, and people just could not wait to see them, see Liam, here in Dublin, at Dalymount Park, it was an incredible thing, everyone just praying it didn't rain and fall dark too soon, you know, with there being no floodlights and the six o'clock kick-off, and though it was your dreary, dull Dublin evening, with quite a wind as well, the air was just on fire that night, and it was Liam that set it afire, you know, he was brilliant, absolutely world-class, you know, one of the games of his life it was, scoring the second and the third, both in the second half they were, one a volley from a cross from Johnny Berry, the other with his head from David Pegg, and both Johnny Berry and David Pegg, they scored themselves, with Tommy Taylor getting two, United winning by six, you know, six–nil, and everyone had thought Shamrock Rovers were the best, but then you saw these fellows, and you just thought, My God! And Liam was one of the best of that team, you know. He was revered. Sixty, seventy years on, folk will still be talking about that team and about Liam Whelan, anyone will tell you that, and all around Dalymount Park, in the various parts of the ground, were the Whelan family watching their boy play that game of his life that night, but the one sad thing the night was when their Uncle Stephen, he turns to Christy and he says, You know something, Christy? If only your daddy was alive, that's the saddest part about it all, is that Johnny didn't live to get to see Liam.

But Liam, he was always bones, you know, from when he was a little boy, when he played in the playgrounds, out in the streets, with that team Red Rockets that went all over Dublin playing and were unbeaten here for years, but even then, back then, Liam had the pointed elbows and the knees, that frown above the nose, you know, the look that always seemed to say he was that wee bit cold and best be off, but then when you saw him play, with the control, the dribble and the vision, he'd leave teams, whole teams standing, just ghost straight through them, and then play the pass or shoot himself with that right foot of his, and what a foot was that, you know, a wand is what it was, that right foot of his, a wand, and to think there's people that will tell you with a straight face that Liam was a yard or two too slow, he lacked a bit of pace, but that's just nonsense and from ignorance, you know, it's a matter of record that he was the fastest sprinter that United had, but the boy played like a ghost, a shadow, you see. You'd be seeing him coming, thinking, Here he comes, ready to tackle him, just about to go into the tackle, and he's gone! And you're saying, Where is he? And he was around behind you and away, and you hadn't the faintest idea how he got there. He had that amazing ability, no one seemed to be able to get the ball from him, and you're left there thinking, Now how the hell does he do that? But it wasn't just the dribbles, you know? People are quick to forget Liam scored thirty-three goals in fifty-four games for United the season before, and from inside right that was, and not one of them a penalty, eight of them in eight consecutive games, more than even Tommy Taylor in the League, but if you still want to know how good the boy was, then ask anyone who saw his goal against Bilbao the year before, when he gets the ball in his own half, deep in his own half and all, then off he sets up the pitch, the pitch all mud and slush, coaxing the ball along through the heavy waves of mud, beating first one man, and then another, gradually gathering pace all the time, but then, with a shrug of the shoulders, a jink and a turn, he changes direction, wiggling his way diagonally across the field from left to right, until he starts to come, almost wander back in towards the middle, past five of their men, leaves them on their arses, but on he ploughs, on through the mud, but then with a touch to the right, then left, then right again, then, so precise and sure, an arrow from a magic bow he shoots, hard and true, into the top left-hand corner of the net and scores, and the people will all tell you, everyone who was there, about the time they showed that goal at the Savoy, up on O'Connell Street, on the Pathé News it was, and how the whole place just erupted, people out of their seats up on their feet, clapping and cheering, you know, forget the main show that night, what could beat that?

Then there was the games against the English, the night Liam nutmegged Duncan Edwards and he walked home from Dalymount, he did, with Joe Haverty and had a cup of tea with Mammy, and then they both went and got the number 12 bus into O'Connell Street and the Gresham, where the team were staying. That was the thing with Liam, you know? He'd just arrive home. No warning. No telephone call. He'd get the boat, or catch a flight, and just walk in through the door and say, Mammy, I'm home.

And Mammy, always as cool as you like, always said the same thing back: How long are you back for?

It hadn't even been that long since Liam had last been back, but a thing that caused not pain, because the pain was always there, but was still a thing for them, you know, was that Liam had gone to the Boss and asked to be excused from the trip to Belgrade. Liam was out of the side at that time, you see, with Bobby Charlton in his place, and so Liam knew he was never going to play, but it wasn't a sulk or anything of that sort, not out of anger, you know, it was just not that long since he'd got over a bout of the flu himself, knew his mammy had not been well herself, and so he thought it'd be better if he took himself off home to Dublin for a couple of days, you know, and then he's getting married that coming June to Ruby McCullough, who was a friend of the family and his sister Rita, they worked together at the biscuit factory, and there were always things to plan and do, not least of all to see the girl. But Matt, of course, he said no, you know, how would it look, and they might need him, you never know, and so that was that, off Liam went, on the trip, he had to go. God knows his own ways.

186

That night before the funeral, the house on Saint Attracta Road was open to everyone and crowded, and the fathers of the Irish boys from Manchester, the two that were from Cabra, they took them to the house, pushed their way in and through the folk to have a word with Liam's mammy and his brothers and his sisters, and though their poor mammy didn't really know where she was that night, still she held the hands of these two boys, she held them close, you know, and said, Liam often spoke of you both, always told us how you were getting on, and Jackie and young Jimmy, too, how you were all doing just grand, so don't you two give up now, you keep on with it, and for Liam, too, for he'll be watching out for you. But before you go away again, off back over there again, now you boys be sure to tell your mammy that you love her. Liam did, he always does. Remember that for me, will you, boys, and then remember this and all, that whatever else in your lives might be uncertain, be unsure, your mother's love is not, remember that. And with those words, she swore she felt her Liam kiss her then, felt his kiss, she really did, as if, as if her boy was never gone, not gone but here and with her still.

The day of the funeral, the Wednesday it was, they had to close the doors of the Church of Christ the King, on Offaly Road, because of the numbers, the fears of overcrowding, and Oscar Traynor, he was there, and all the representatives of the English and the Irish leagues, and your men from the GAA clubs, they were all there, too, you know, and that's a thing to think on when you think of it, you know. The coffin came in covered with a floral arrangement sent by the club, showing its Old Trafford ground and the pitch on which Liam had played, had dazzled and shone so bright, so very bright, complete with a ball, two goals and four bright-red corner flags, they said, and it was Father Mulholland, the great friend of Liam, who celebrated the Mass, Father Mulholland who Liam had asked to preside at his wedding to Ruby McCullough that coming June that never

187

came, and Father Mulholland, he was from up in Carrickfergus, they said, but a Catholic chaplain in the Royal Air Force, of all things, at a base over in Somerset somewhere, they said, but Liam thought the world of the fellow, and if he was a pal of Liam, then it didn't really matter what the hell else the fellow did.

O God, our refuge and our strength . . .

But outside the church, you could not move, the pavements packed so dense, so tight, you know, the whole of Cabra and the northside, there was not a vacant inch, you could barely move. But when the cortège then left Christ the King for Glasnevin, they had to get the Garda to move the mourners out from the road, you know, they'd all tumbled off the tiny pavements, so crammed they were, you see, and as the funeral procession passed Saint Peter's school, on Saint Peter's Road, the pupils all stood and bowed their heads, before the playground there, you know, where Liam played, the school where he would sit and stare at Dalymount, and dreamed of one day playing there, and all the other grounds and better lands, like his hero Johnny Carey, who had himself come up through Home Farm and always looked out for Liam, when he first went over there. But don't be thinking Liam was all days dreaming or thinking on the Lord, you know, in the sackcloth or hair shirt, forever with his beads; he liked a hand of cards, to sing a song, and drove a car was fit for scrap and nothing more, and was just a lovely, lovely man, apart from his talent, he was a nice guy, he was pure decent, he was, and it's lovely to be able to say that about a fellow, you know, not saying it because it's something he would want to hear, but saying it because it's true, Liam was a lovely, lovely man.

When they finally did get up to Glasnevin, well, there were rows and rows of people, men and women, young and old, for rows and rows, and you hear of all them big old funerals this old town has known, of O'Connell and Parnell, of Jeremiah O'Donovan Rossa or Thomas Ashe, Terence MacSwiney and

Arthur Griffith would be two more, and, of course, Michael Collins, the biggest of them all, the celebrations of loss this mopey old town has seen, but the gravediggers up at Glasnevin, those fellows will tell you they'd never seen so many mourners, not since that day they'd put Michael Collins in the ground.

But even at Glasnevin, at the graveside, still so strong, their mammy did not weep. It was only in the car, said Christy, then back at home, when all was done, only then she cried, but still her thoughts were for the living, cleaning out the fire at home, you know, turning to her daughter Rita, telling her Rita, Won't you look after Ruby? Please, look after poor Ruby, please.

Because Mammy, she knew that not only did God want Liam, but that Liam wanted God, that in his heart he was prepared, he was at peace, I know he was, said Mammy, Liam was ready for the end.

*

In his hospital bed, the hospital silence, Frank just could not stop thinking about the Dead, and most of all the Dead who were his friends, men he had known so long, their lives, their children and their wives, on different, rival papers, yes, but always friends, a gang of mates, the Brotherhood of the Press, some of the greatest journalists any man could ever hope to meet –

Take Donny Davies of the *Guardian*: well, he was a great broadcaster, and he didn't just write a report; he'd been an amateur international, and a county cricket player, so he wrote with knowledge, technical knowledge. But he was also an essayist. Then you've got Henry Rose, of the *Daily Express*, who was a great populist. Henry always used to say, People who follow sport want an argument, they want a discussion, so therefore I'm there! Let's find out what the person in the four-ale bar is arguing about, and I'll provide it. But then you've got George Follows, of the *Daily Herald*. Now George was a magnificent writer. He could have gone to Oxford, and he was just on the verge of going to Fleet Street, and Frank was in no doubt at all that George would have ended up the best sports writer he had ever known. On the *Daily Mail*, you've got Eric Thompson, who could also have been a professional footballer. But he was not only a good technician that way, he had a marvellous sense of humour, and he would illustrate his points with beautiful thumbnail sketches. They were special people. And then there was Swifty, who was a great personal friend of Frank, who was employed by the *News of the World* to give his opinions on games and who had a tremendous sense of humour, and not only that, but whatever he wrote, or got the ghost to write, always had the mark of authority. And Archie Ledbrooke was also a fantastic technician, both on cricket and on soccer, and he was doing marvellous work for the *Daily Mirror*, and when he expressed an opinion about players, players read him, because his opinion meant something. And then, of course, the two local paper men, Tom Jackson of the *Evening News* and Alf Clarke of the *Evening Chronicle*. Now Alf Clarke had been a very good footballer himself, but this was his club, Manchester United was his club, absolutely his club. He'd nearly missed the plane had Alf, thought Frank, remembered Frank. Tom Curry was counting the players, and they were a man short, and then suddenly a jeep came up, and it was dear Alf in the jeep. He'd been phoning the paper in Manchester to tell them that they were held up, and everybody was pulling his leg, and there was Alf, red-faced as he dived into his seat, started to fasten himself in, and within a minute Alf was dead. They all were dead.

How could it be, thought Frank, that Henry, Don and Alf had lived through two world wars, and George, Tom, Eric, Leddy and Swifty had all served in and survived the last one, too, only then to die like this, covering a football match in a foreign land.

There were so many funerals that day, too many funerals for one day. In Manchester, over in Dublin and down in Wales, too, where three people who had escaped the crash were at the funeral of Chief Steward Thomas William Cable. Curtains were drawn along the route to Saint Mary's Church, Brynmawr. Women in the streets sobbed, and men stood with bared heads. And among the mourners was Captain James Thain, and with him were Margaret Bellis and Rosemary Cheverton. Thirty more stewards walked in front of the wreath-covered hearse. They were among the sixty British European Airways employees who had chartered a plane to attend the funeral of young Tommy Cable that day, that lad who was, as everybody said, Manchester United mad.

There was 'no one so mad about sport' as Eric Thompson of the *Daily Mail*; he'd even written a best-selling book called *Mad About Sport*. He was known for his natty attire, always sporting a dicky bow, known, too, for his wit, his quips and his jokes, nicknamed 'the blue-eyed comedian' by colleagues and friends. A man with no enemies who illustrated his articles with his own cartoons and sketches, who contributed to match-day programmes and collected them, too. But that wet Wednesday, Eric Thompson was buried at Southern Cemetery, after a service attended by family, friends and fellow newspapermen, who all agreed the blue-eyed comedian was the J. B. Priestley of Manchester journalists, an avuncular and knowledgeable man, but with a humour broader than Priestley, and not nearly as acrid.

Archie 'Leddy' Ledbrooke of the *Daily Mirror*, the 'Man in the *Mirror*', author of *Soccer from the Press Box* and *The Fight for the Ashes 1948* and other books, had earned the byline 'The sports writer you must NOT MISS', but everybody missed Archie.

Archie Ledbrooke's funeral was held at the Church of Saint Michael and All Angels, Bramhall, Cheshire, 'just down the road from his home, where his widow and two daughters mourn'. The house was filled with flowers from neighbours, friends and strangers, and the streets outside were thronged with Manchester United supporters and fellow journalists and *Mirror* staff who had come to the village to mourn. Following a simple service, the packed congregation, silent and sad, drove to Stockport Crematorium for the final farewell. But when his wife Eileen and their daughters Helen and Jane returned to their home on Bramhall Lane, when they tried as best they could to go through the hundreds of cards, tried to read all the messages of sympathy, they came across a postcard of a river, and on its back it simply said: *This is the famous Blue Danube River. Not much snow here, but saw plenty on the way. Love Daddy.*

There was going to be a special *In Memoriam* service at Saint Bride's Church, Fleet Street, next Tuesday lunchtime, for all the journalists who'd died, but Geoffrey had still felt compelled, the urge to travel north to Manchester for Frank Swift's funeral at Saint Margaret's Church in Whalley Range, the man everyone will miss, but no one will forget, especially not Geoff.

Geoff couldn't really think of Frank as a journalist, not really, rather as a footballer and as a friend, the great distinction of his goalkeeping, the rich vitality of his nature: a big man was Frank, in every sense. But his bulk, the size of his fists could never mask his agility, his positioning, the accuracy of his throws, the shrewdness of his kicks, for Frank was to Geoff the greatest of all modern goalkeepers, save perhaps for Frank's own mentor, his great teacher Harry Hibbs. Frank had sought out Harry, asked him question after question, taking down his answers, studying then those notes. But all that homework, that hard work had paid off, and in spades: Frank made his League debut for Manchester City the day before he turned nineteen; just four months later, in April

1934, Frank won the FA Cup with City, and with Matt, beating Portsmouth two–one. But as he left his goal to walk towards the Royal Box, the ordeal of the match, the pressure of the occasion, it came up from the ground and hit young Frank square, and Frank fainted, laid out prone upon the Wembley turf. But Frank later added to his Cup medal with a League Championship medal and the Charity Shield, and fourteen wartime caps for England, and a further nineteen after, winning the Home Championship in Forty-seven and again in Forty-eight.

Perhaps, thought Geoff, Frank's greatest honour was when he played for Great Britain against the Rest of Europe, in what was then called 'the Match of the Century', at Hampden Park in Glasgow, before one hundred and thirty thousand, in the May of Forty-seven, with Great Britain in their navy shirts, white shorts and blue socks winning easily, six–one, that day.

But though Swifty was a showman, of that there was no doubt, beloved upon the terraces for his music-hall humour and theatrics, on and off the pitch, that North Country voice, its booming jokes, there was another side to Frank, a very different side, Geoff knew, born of the boy who had studied under Harry Hibbs, who never lost the urge to learn, sat at home each night with pencil and with paper, working out better angles to save the shots he'd missed, but there was still another, even greater side to Frank, glimpsed on one of his many hospital visits, the gentlest of giants stooped, bending over the bed of some sick and dying child –

Geoff would never forget the Sunday morning Frank took some of his fellow Manchester City players a hundred miles to visit a children's sanatorium. These children were all football crazy, but one poor child, ill for eight years or more, he had never seen a game, yet his scrapbook bulged with cuttings and pictures of his idols, and long after the players had left, that boy, he clasped, he clutched Frank Swift's autograph in his hand, and as the matron said to Geoff, I never dreamed a signature could be treasured, a visit mean so very much.

That was why Geoffrey was standing in Saint Margaret's Church in Whalley Range, watching poor Frank's coffin being carried out again, that man of contradictions, from this county of contrasts, of shawls and red roses, wooden clogs and droll wisdom, hard common sense and reckless generosity. A bright light had gone out of the world, knew Geoff, but only Lancashire could produce a man like Frank Swift.

*

From funeral to funeral they went that day, that week, too many to attend: they would have gone to them all, had they had the time. But they did what they could, the best that they could.

From Flixton, Wilf and Gordon drove back to Old Trafford to join two other cars on the drive over to Yorkshire. Three cars taking Wilf and Gordon, Colin Webster and Shay Brennan, Bobby English and Alex Dawson and a few others from the second team, all heading over the moors, Doncaster way.

Not far behind them came Joe and Jimmy, who had also stopped off at Old Trafford to pick up Cissie, after Flixton and the funeral of poor Roger Byrne, Cissie heading with them over the moors, Doncaster way, Cissie there to represent her Bobby.

But as they went from funeral to funeral that day, that week, on the way, between one funeral and the next, the mourning of the Dead, they had no choice but to speak of the living, and of the resurrection, of who Jimmy and Joe thought they might need, who was available, who they might buy or try to buy, and when that might be, Jimmy turning things over, names in his head, thinking back, thinking forward about who would fit and who would not, wondering about Mel Charles and Ivor Allchurch, both Swansea players who Jimmy knew from managing Wales, that part-time job that, yes, had saved his life, might well have saved his life, but left him with this, just this.

There's always Ernie Taylor, someone had said to Jimmy, though Jimmy couldn't think for the life of him who that might have been: was it Billy Foulkes on the train back home from Munich, or was it Joe, when he'd picked him up this morning, or the Chairman, Mister Hardman, when they'd had their meeting earlier that day, or even Paddy McGrath at poor Roger's funeral, but whoever had first put the thought in Jimmy's head, the more he thought, the more it seemed to make some sense.

Ernie Taylor was an inside-forward, one of the many positions where they needed extra help, and he'd been in two Cup Finals – in fact, for those with proper football eyes, he'd been the actual architect of Blackpool's triumph in the so-called Matthews Final, though that was a thought for another day – but Ernie was on the transfer list now, and Blackpool wanted shot, and, more to the point, as far as Jimmy thought, Little Ern had not played a game this season, least not a Cup game for Blackpool, and Blackpool were already out now, thanks to West Ham, so Ernie was not cup-tied, that was something, he didn't need no special dispensation, one less call to make or day to wait, provided, of course, Ernie Taylor did want to play for Manchester United, that is.

*

Jackie, said Frank, the other Frank, Frank Taylor, in his hospital bed in Munich. Are you awake, Jackie?

But Jackie was either fast asleep or playing dead, so Frank went back to the ceiling, staring at its shadows, those long, dark shadows and their fingers –

Maybe it had been thinking about his gang of mates, the pals he'd lost, the laughs they'd had on all the trips they'd had, but they had come upon Frank now, by dint of his own brooding, Frank knew, those thoughts of omens and signs, of things that might or might not have been, of roads taken and not taken –

Of United, in Europe –

Frank knew that a lot of chairmen and particularly the management committees, they lived in their own little worlds. They didn't want to be bothered with a lot of foreigners coming over, trying to be all clever. But they just did not have the vision to see that it was opening a door, both of showing our lads the technical skills that they needed to know, and also the fact that it could be a marvellous money-spinner, for the best clubs at least.

But Frank and his pals on the Manchester papers, they'd found it a tremendously exciting prospect, and he'd felt that for Northerners to do that, that showed London were a way behind the times, that Chelsea had turned down the chance of going into Europe! Frank knew it took a Northern team to have the bravery to do it!

And when Frank thought back now, even now, even here, bandaged up in a hospital bed, when he thought of those nights against Anderlecht, against Bilbao, both at Maine Road, of course, because Old Trafford hadn't its floodlights yet, then Frank knew, thought that United, that Matt had been right, until Frank remembered, remembered and thought of the Dead, the Dead and the omens, the portents –

People tended not to remember the first leg against Athletic Bilbao at the San Mamés stadium, La Catedral. People just remember the return leg at Maine Road, the deafening noise as Tommy Taylor inspired United to overcome the five–three loss in the first leg to win three–nil on the night, the sheer delirium and joy, everybody grabbing and hugging each other, utterly besotted, in love with that team of young lads playing such a wonderful, magical game that February night, the sixth of February it was, exactly a year to the day before the air crash.

But now Frank thought about it, the more Frank now dwelt and brooded upon it, back in Bilbao there had been an omen, a portent, a clear, clear warning of the disaster to come. The match itself had been played in a snowstorm, made of snow that seemed to thaw straight off, that turned the pitch to mud and slush. But after the game, the next day, when they came out to the flying strip, came to take off, they found the aircraft was coated, was covered with ice and with snow, and the pilot had refused to take off until Frank and all his pals and the young lads of the team and anyone else they could find had helped to sweep the snow from the wings; with brooms and with shovels on their shoulders, they had marched out from the airport building to the aircraft in what became known as Operation Snow Shift. It was treated as a big joke, everybody laughing and smiling, All right, Skipper, and that kind of thing. No one thought anything of it at the time, but now Frank did think about it, dwelt and brooded upon it. Frank knew it had been an omen, a portent.

*

It had come upon her that day, at some point last Thursday, before she knew, before they'd heard, the photograph, it came into her mind, the one of her brother David with the broom, the brush, when they were given sweeping brushes to sweep the wings and help sweep the ice and snow off the runway, maybe it had been the snow that day, but there it was, in her mind again, before Irene even knew. It had been Peter Whittell who'd first told them. He was only sixteen, a junior reporter, that's what they call it, on the *Doncaster Chronicle*, but they knew him from school and things, but his paper sent him up on the bus to their house on Coppice Road, Highfields. They didn't have a telephone, didn't have a television. Irene, her sister Doreen and their mum Jessie, they didn't even know their David was out of the country, and their dad Bill was at work at the pit. But Peter Whittell, he knocked on the door and had to tell them, I'm sorry, but your David's been in an accident. The Manchester United plane has crashed in a snowstorm at Munich, on their way home.

Irene and her sister and her mum, they turned on the radio to see if it was on the radio, and the radio just said the same as Peter had said, that there'd been a plane crash, and that was all they knew, for hours and hours. They didn't have any final names or numbers for hours, until, actually, it was six or seven o'clock on Friday morning until a policeman came to the house.

He was not an ordinary beat bobby, judging by all the gold braid on his uniform. They would never know who he was or where he came from, but he just said, Tha' David's dead, what dost tha' want doing with t'body?

Their mum, she was devastated, but their father, he said, There'll be no blubbering in this house, so Irene and Doreen, they had to hide their tears in their room or in the dark, at night, not let them be seen in the light.

But Irene still couldn't stop thinking of that photograph of David with the brush, of all the photographs it was that one that kept coming into her mind. There were so many other photos it could have been, he'd had that many taken. He was like a film star, was their David. They all were in their own way. The barbers in Manchester, they'd have all their photos on the walls so blokes could come in and choose which haircut they wanted. But more often than not, it was 'the David Pegg' they wanted. Because the press took photographs of them all the time, especially David. Photographs of them washing up and with tea towels in their hands, that sort of thing. They probably never had a tea towel in their hands in their life, most of them, definitely their David, thought his sister Irene, and he never would now.

But the funeral, the whole of the week before, it was like a film star had died. Highfields had never seen anything like it, never before, or since. Hundreds and hundreds of people came, from far and wide, they must have been in their thousands, in fact. They needed police to control the crowds and all the traffic, in the village, outside the church, Saint George's Church, all along the route to Red House Cemetery at Adwick, just outside Doncaster, where David was to be buried.

Twenty cars in slow procession left Coppice Road for Saint George's Church that sad and solemn day, and all along the way the shops were closed, the curtains drawn in every house. The wind whipped keen through Highfields, wrote Michael Parkinson in the *Yorkshire Evening Post* that night. Aproned women, miners in their pit muck, small boys didn't feel it. They stood bareheaded and sad. Above it all came the sad siren of Brodsworth pit buzzer . . . a requiem for David Pegg.

It was inevitable that David, a young man of such fine character, said the vicar of Woodland in his funeral address, should win for himself a place in the hearts of the people of this village, and indeed in the hearts of all who came to know him. Despite the honours that came to him through football, David remained unchanged. He remained humble; he remained the same, with loyalty and affection for his friends. Indeed, his loyalty to this village remained unchanged.

The floral tributes, they spilled out of the house and into the street, there were that many, and her mum felt bad, felt she should thank all the folk had sent all the flowers. She told Irene to get a notebook and a pen and write down where all the flowers had come from. But they were that many, Irene soon gave up, it was impossible.

Jimmy and Joe went back to the house, after the church, after the cemetery, just for a bit. Joe had been in this house, this room, a fair few times before, but not for a bit. Probably eight or nine years ago now since Joe had last sat here, in this house, this room, persuading David's mam and dad that their boy

199

should sign for them, the famous Manchester United. But his mam Jessie, she hadn't been that keen on David leaving school, worried if he did not make the grade, then what would become of the lad, her boy? The boy who might have been, who nearly was, that was no life, she said, not for the lad, her boy. But Joe had told her not to worry, United always made sure each and every lad of theirs, they had a trade to fall back on, if things went wrong, there was an injury or change of heart, on someone's part, and they'd already found an apprenticeship for David, as a draughtsman and joiner. But it was only when Joe brought Matt Busby over the Pennines with him to this house, this room, that David's mam's heart melted and she relented; with his charisma and charm, his politeness and honesty, Matt won the day. Bill and Jessie Pegg would never forget the moment when Matt put down his cup and said, Mister and Missus Pegg, I would stake my life that your David will make it as a professional footballer, of that I have no doubt.

His friends, his mates from United, they'd all come, too, and other mates from other teams, half of Sheffield Wednesday, so it seemed, but his friends, his mates from Manchester, they'd brought back his things from Missus Watson's house, the room he'd had in her house, packed up into four boxes in the boots of their cars. His records, his clothes and shoes, a clothes brush and a hairbrush, those things he'd left behind, now left behind again, with his mum, his dad, his sisters, left behind when his friends, his mates, set off back again to Manchester. They'd come in three cars, but left in two, leaving behind David's Vauxhall Victor, that car that used to cause such a stir when he drove it home, an even bigger stir when Tommy Taylor drove over with him, too, two posh new cars parked on a street where no one owned a car, a television, few even had a phone. David loved that Vauxhall Victor, and Irene loved it, too, loved those days when David drove it home, would park outside, when she'd rush out into the street, when she'd wash and shine that car for him, that car now left behind.

Cissie Charlton was there that day, too, Irene remembered, in the church and at the cemetery, then briefly back at the house on Coppice Road, there on behalf of her Bobby, who was still in Munich, in the hospital out there, and some people stopped Cissie to say, Hello, How do, and How's tha' Bobby doing then? At least tha' Bobby is still alive, they said, with their eyes, if not their mouths, and not in a mean or spiteful way, nor in a joyful or a thankful way, just as a matter of fact –

David Pegg was just twenty-two years old the day he died. He'd played one hundred and twenty-seven times for Manchester United and scored twenty-four goals. He had just the one full England cap, versus the Republic of Ireland, at Dalymount Park in Dublin, in May last year, playing alongside Roger Byrne, Duncan Edwards and Tommy Taylor, up against his old pal Billy Whelan, Ireland managed by Johnny Carey, too. And though the match was drawn and this cap was his only England cap, most people agreed David Pegg would soon succeed the great Tom Finney as England's finest outside-left.

*

The doctors had said Bobby was fit enough to leave hospital, well enough to go back home, that Bobby had in fact been fit and well enough a while, that it would in fact be better if he did, and Bobby agreed it would, it would, but before he left, he had one thing he had to do, one thing he did not want to do, so with heavy legs of dread and pounding heart of fear, Bobby climbed the stairs to go see Duncan and the Boss, to say, Goodbye, I'm off.

Inside his plastic tent, the Boss was fast asleep, and Missus Busby by his bed, she smiled at Bobby, gently, kindly smiled, but shook her head and softly, quietly said, I'm very sorry, dear, but he's just got off, and the doctors say he needs to sleep. But don't you worry, love, I'll tell him you were here, and that will cheer him up no end, it will, it really will, so thank you, love, but you just take care now, dear, have a safe journey home, love.

Thank you, said Bobby, quietly, softly, too, but I just hope he gets well soon, I really do.

Then Bobby turned, walked to where Duncan's mam and dad, his girl Molly were sitting by his bed, and now they moved aside so Duncan could see his mate, his pal, and though he was in pain, such pain, impossible to comprehend, Big Dunc threw back his head and laughed and said, Where the bloody hell have you been?

7

The bloody hell had he been, thought Bobby, where had he been? Under his blankets, in the bed downstairs, that's where he'd been, hiding, Bobby knew, hiding.

I've been waiting for you, whispered Duncan, waiting for you, Bobby, but all Bobby could do was try not to cry, try his bloody hardest not to cry, not to let Duncan see despair, the fear of death in his tears, his eyes, to try to keep Duncan calm, to keep him still, still here with him, with them, his mam, his dad and Molly here, but Duncan, he was restless, Bobby knew, lying there, wondering why he could not get up and at them, like he always did, why he couldn't get stuck in, like he always did, and Duncan said, he whispered once again, I've been waiting for you coming . . .

I've been waiting for you coming, the same, exact words Duncan had said to Bobby when Bobby first bumped into Duncan in the army, when Bobby had just arrived at Nesscliffe, the camp down near Shrewsbury, during their National Service, and it must have been killing Duncan to be doing his National Service, Bobby knew, when everybody else was playing football every day, and they'd all hated it, of course, didn't want to be doing it, but it must have been worse for Duncan, thought Bobby, because he absolutely loved the game. But he'd picked Bobby up outside the guard room, when Bobby first arrived, taken Bobby to his billet and said, Come on now, I've got your bags, I've got everything for you, it's all sorted out, I've been waiting for you coming.

But then when they'd got in, when Duncan had put Bobby's stuff down on the floor, they saw there was a spring sticking out of Bobby's bed, but Duncan just said, Don't worry about that, he said, I'll sort that out, and he picked the bed up and just walked straight out of the billet, and two minutes later, he came back with someone else's bed and said, There you go, Bobby . . .

Bobby turned his face, his head from the bed, towards the wall, away from Duncan, so Duncan couldn't see, didn't see Bobby trying not to cry, his hardest not to cry, but then Bobby heard Duncan whisper, heard him say, Get me out of here, Mum.

I'll get you out of here, son, said Annie, his mam. You've your car to look after, so you better hurry up and get better, get yourself home, hadn't you, son?

Just keep it on the road, Mum, whispered Duncan, said Duncan, for when I get home.

*

Daylight and darkness and sparks and things hitting him on the head, and he thought for the first time, I've done well, for the first time in my life, and I won't see my wife, my little girl again, but when he opened his eyes, there was his wife again, there in their bed beside him, his little girl again, there in the cot beside their bed, and there he was again, back home again, the home he'd fixed his mind upon, the thought of home, of getting home, back to this house, its rooms, these rooms where he lived, the smell, the taste of home cooking, the light in these rooms, the views from the windows, the garden and the trees, to be back here again, with his family again, his wife, his little girl again, that was all he had thought and longed for then, back then, last Thursday afternoon, one week ago today, in that seat, on that plane, in the daylight and the darkness and the sparks, things hitting him on the head, back then when he'd thought he was dead, he was one of the Dead, when all he'd wanted then was simply this, was simply home sweet home again, so why then did he feel, what was the word, the word he wanted, here at home, in bed, their bed, beside his wife, his little girl, the dawn out there, behind the curtains, in the rain, the rain upon the window pane, what was the word? Betrayed, thought Harry, was that the fucking word for this? Betrayed?

*

It was always snowing in Munich. Every morning when Jean awoke, got out of bed, pulled back the curtains in the hotel room, it was always snowing, it never seemed to stop. Downstairs at breakfast, with the other wives, the mothers and the girlfriends of the younger boys, they'd all remark and say, Not more snow again today! Then they'd all bundle up again, all trudge out to the taxis again, off back to the hospital and the men, the boys again.

But Jean did not complain, no one complained, they just got on with things, what things they could, as best they could, just hoping for the best.

Nor did Mattie complain, he never did. Even when they had to set his broken foot, and had to set it without an anaesthetic because of the condition, the state of his chest, his lungs. He just lay there silently as they set his foot, then lay there silently again when they'd brought him back into the room, had put him back into his bed.

Jean and Sister Gilda, they watched over Mattie, together or in turns, beside the bed in which he lay, silent, stretched out, the plaster on his right leg beneath the sheets, his head upon the pillow, waxy and pale and aged, his hair now grey, with streaks of white, a change that happened in one night, and Jean touched his face, his hair, stroked his face, his hair, and whispered, You are doing well, dear, you are getting much better, love . . .

But when Mattie coughed, when Jean saw the pain that shook and racked his lungs, his chest, it hurt Jean, too, to see him shake, to suffer in such pain, and Jean and Sister Gilda, other nuns and nurses, too, they'd do their best to end the spasm, to ease the pain, to help him back to silence, subside back into sleep.

Never once did Jean hear Mattie complain, but in her heart Jean worried, feared this silence was not born of bravery or of fortitude, but because he did not care, she worried, feared he cared no more for life, but wished for sleep, and only sleep, the endless sleep of death.

*

Thursday morning, and not quite yet a week, with some of the boys and Matt still fighting for their lives, on machines, in comas, most of the Dead still not buried yet, but the headlines had moved on, even in Manchester, in both the *Chronicle* and *Evening News*: the Rochdale by-election, the health of Winston Churchill, these were the front-page stories now, the health or not of the government, the former Prime Minister, life and death, living and dying all carrying on, but elsewhere now, and Jimmy was glad, relieved the circus had moved on for now, for Jimmy knew if they were ever going to get through this, somehow survive and carry on, then they would need space and time, quiet space and quiet time, to even make a start, let alone to try and see it through. But first there were the funerals to get through, seven more today, then the final four tomorrow, so many to attend, too many to attend, but Jimmy knew this black day in this black week would be one of the blackest, hardest days of all, but another black day he had to face, and Jimmy dried his eyes, he wiped his face, got up from his knees beside his bed, put his rosary back in his pocket, the beads, the figure and face of Christ on the Cross, and went to shine his shoes, and then to have a shave, a wash and find a shirt, then put on his suit, his tie again, his dark funeral suit and tie again, for the second time that week, black week.

*

If anything happens, then I'm ready for it . . .

Bill was sitting at the table, not eating his breakfast, staring out at the garden and the rain, then at the window frame, the tiny pools of rain leaking in.

His first job had been with Pilkington Glass, as a carpenter, but the pay had not been great, not great at all, so his dad had found him a job in a brass foundry, not far from their house in Rainhill. But the fumes were no good, they got to his chest, so he went to work as a painter and decorator, but the fumes were almost as bad. But around that time, he had his trial with United. He was introduced to the Boss, Jimmy Murphy and Bert Whalley, then he played the whole game out of position and thought he'd have no chance, that that would be that. But after the game, there was Jimmy and Bert again, and they asked him there and then to sign amateur forms with them, but after that, for a good few months, he never heard a thing, not a peep, so Bill went and did what his dad said he must never go and do and got himself a job down the local pit.

His dad had worked for years at the coalface, then had moved to surface tasks, was now the secretary for the miners' union for the North-West, and that was why his dad had never wanted that for Bill. Not that life, the danger and the hardship, the risk of death, every day that risk of death. But Bill had tired of going from job to job, an odd job here, an odd job there, tired of having no brass, never two farthings to rub together. But when his dad found out Bill had gone to work at Lea Colliery, as Bill had known he would, he'd not got mad, though he'd not been pleased, thought his lad had had more sense than that, but there might have been a part of him that was a little pleased, a little proud his Bill could take care of himself.

But then Bolton Wanderers wanted Bill, but Bill had to say he'd signed some form with United, so the Bolton man, he said he'd call and see what was what, that he'd get them to let Bill go, if they were not going to get back in touch, but within a few days, United did get back in touch; they'd obviously forgotten about Bill, but now they'd been reminded and remembered him, they wanted him again, and so from there things had moved on.

But around that time was when Bill had first met Teresa, it was at a dance in Liverpool. He was already with United, but she had no interest much in football or any sport, and that suited Bill just fine. But then, soon after they had met, she'd caught tuberculosis, fallen gravely ill, her life in danger, and she would have died, had it not been for a new drug that came along. But she still had to spend a year and a half in a hospital on the Wirral, in body plaster to prevent curvature of the spine, and Bill could only see her on a Sunday, but he never missed a trip –

Are you not going to eat that, love, said Teresa. It's going to go cold if you don't.

Bill turned from the window frame, glanced down at the plate, at the bacon, the toast and the egg, then looked up again at Teresa and said, That third time, you know, when everyone was scurrying about, swapping seats, going from the front to the back, the back to the front, Billy Whelan, you know, he was just sat there, across from me he was, and he just had this look upon his face, a look I can't describe, sort of tranquil and resigned, but calm, so very calm, and I could swear I heard him say, say something like, If this is the end, then I'm ready for it.

*

Ronnie Cope had packed his bag, was waiting for the taxi to come, when Jimmy pulled him to one side and said, Ronnie, the Boss has just rung through. Roger Byrne's been hurt, and he wants Geoff to go in your place. Ronnie was irate, or words to that effect, but Jimmy tried to calm him down and said, Calm down, son, calm down, it's only a trip out. But Ronnie shook his head, No, I'll see the Boss when he comes back, see about me future, I swear to God I will.

Geoff Bent had been to see the Boss about his future, just once it was, or maybe twice, before. He was a Salford lad was Geoff, from Irlams o' th' Height he was, had been the captain of Salford Boys and an outstanding prospect; quick to the ball and strong in the tackle, few got round Geoff Bent, hard as nails was Geoff, so lots of clubs came in for Geoff. But Geoff, he was an only son, and so his mam, she thought it best he stay near and close to home, and so Geoff went to United, which suited Geoff just fine, was in fact his dream come true, because young Geoff Bent, he was Manchester United mad. He'd been at United ten years all told, seven years as a professional, had made his first appearance in the first team back in December 1954, when United had beaten Burnley four–two and Colin Webster had scored a hat-trick. But in seven years, Geoff had only played for the first team eleven times, no more, and not once this season, least not yet, but then again, you never knew. Geoff was a full-back, see, could play left and right on both flanks. He would walk into almost any other team in the land would Geoff, but at United Geoff was cover for Roger Byrne on the left and Bill Foulkes on the right, and if one got injured, which wasn't often, or if Roger was off on international duty, then Geoff knew he always had a chance – that is, as long as he stayed fit himself; Geoff had already broken his leg twice, the last time just the year before. But that once or twice Geoff had been to see the Boss about his lack of first-team chances, about his future, what it had in store for Geoff, the Boss had said what he always said, said to everyone who knocked upon his door to ask about their future and what it had in store: There are no first-team players at Manchester United, son, there are only first-team probables.

And though Geoff was hardly ever even in the first team, just twelve times in seven years, he'd married Marion back in 1953, and in September last year, they'd had a daughter, Karen, and United had still allocated Geoff and Marion a club house, number one hundred and seventy-one Kings Road, not far from where Mark Jones lived with his wife June and their young boy Gary, just a mile or so from the ground.

But when Geoff had come back home on the Sunday night and said, I'm going to Belgrade tomorrow, Marion couldn't get over it, she was so shocked. But he said, I don't have to go, he said, the Boss said that if you can't manage, you know, I don't have to go. He said, You won't be able to manage on your own with Karen, will you? But Marion, she'd said, I will be able to manage! You go and enjoy yourself! But it was the first time he'd ever been like that, when she thought about it now, knew now, now it was too late, he just didn't want to go, not there, behind the Iron Curtain. Now it was too late, too late for Marion to say, You're right, you're right, I won't be able to manage on my own with Karen, not on my own, without you here, so please don't go, not there, behind the Iron Curtain, please just stay here, stay home with me and Karen then, forever here at home.

There weren't the reporters and their cameramen outside the house, but people in their hundreds still lined the street for the half-mile or so from Irlams o' th' Height up to the church in Pendlebury, and flags flew at half-mast on Salford buildings for Geoff Bent, and for Eddie Colman, too, another local lad, and local factories, pubs and clubs held collections for wreaths for Geoff, and for Eddie, too, those who remembered Geoff and knew his worth as a local Salford boy who had once jumped into Salford Canal, that was Geoff, the kind of lad he was, rescued another boy from drowning, awarded a medal for his bravery was Geoff, but most of all the people came to mourn Geoff Bent and say farewell to Geoff because they knew he was United through and through, loyal and true, packed on the narrow pavement outside the church, in its graveyard and inside the Saint John the Evangelist Church, on Bolton Road, Pendlebury; the church where Geoff had been christened, the church where he and Marion had married, where in its churchyard now his dad Clifford, his mother Clara, Marion and Karen buried their beloved son, husband and dear daddy Geoff.

Beside that newly dug grave, as they began to close the ground on her dear Geoff, Marion was angry more than sad, she was very, very angry. She could not understand why they were allowed to get on that plane after trying twice to take off. Marion looked up from the ground, the hole, the dirt in the ground, looked up at the sky, the clouds and the rain, and she shook her head, tried not to scream, They were all grown men, they could all speak up, and nobody said anything!

*

I'm saying to you now, Harry was saying to his bedroom wall, if anyone had had the courage to stand up and say, Here, this is crazy, then it wouldn't have happened.

Why didn't you then, brave man, said the wall.

Because like all people, said Harry, we're afraid to lose face in front of our friends.

Well, now you've got no friends, said the wall. Your friends are all dead, but least no one lost face.

Aye, said Harry, takes a brave man to be a coward, and he punched the wall once, twice in its face.

Harry Gregg in his house, Bill Foulkes in his, Harry and Bill both giving their four walls a talking-to –

Bill looked up at the wall again, shook his head and said again, If this is the end, then I'm ready for it.

Did you say something, love, said Teresa, coming into the bedroom, a pile of clothes in her hands.

Bill shook his head and said, No, I don't think so, no, I was just, you know, thinking aloud maybe.

Well, I'm going to put the kettle on, make a cup of tea, said Teresa, putting away the clothes. So are you going to come down and have a cuppa with me, love?

Bill nodded and said, Yes, I'll be down in a minute then, thank you, love. Thank you.

Teresa smiled at Bill as she left the room and closed the door, but then she stopped outside the door, to listen, to hear through the door, she thought, she swore, Bill talking to himself again, saying once again, What did you mean, Billy? What did you mean, If anything happens, if this is the end, then I'm ready for it?

And Teresa quietly went back down the stairs, picked up the telephone in the hall and quietly called Mavis, and Mavis agreed with Teresa, and Teresa agreed with Mavis, that it'd be better if Harry and Bill got out of the house, as soon as they could, the sooner the better, and went back to the ground, and back to work.

*

Tomorrow would bring the funeral of Walter Crickmer, while today brought the funerals of both Bert and of Tom, and it felt to Jimmy, and to Joe, to Bill Inglis and Arthur Powell, and to Les and Alma and all the staff at the club, no matter where they worked, that they were saying farewell to a part of themselves, huge, great parts of themselves and the club, parts you could never replace, for they were men you could never replace.

Bert and his good pal Tom, they were always the kindly ones, this pair of well-built, stocky chaps, in their white coats or very, very long grey shorts, in the changing rooms or on the training pitch, at the ground or at the Cliff, among the mass of players, knocking the ball about, they'd be the ones who'd spot the new boy, would wave to them, welcome them and say, Hello there, you must be Ray, or you must be Graham, must be Bill or Jeff, or Duncan, Colin, Wilf or Bobby, and whoever they were, these new boys would nod and say, That's right, sir, that's me, sir, and Bert would always laugh and say, Hang on now, he'd say, I'm not sir, he'd say, I'm Bert Whalley, is what he'd say, pleased to meet you, son, he'd say, we've heard a lot about you, we're looking forward to you joining the club, and then that new boy, that young lad, whoever they were, wherever they were from, he'd feel ten feet tall he would, and from that minute, he'd feel a member of the club, though he'd only been there five minutes, but already they'd made him feel he was part of the scene, and no matter how well they progressed or not, whether they made the grade or not, their doors were always open to these young lads, at the ground or at their homes, especially Tom's front door, just round the corner from the ground it was, where many lads lived in digs nearby, where they could always stop in for a cup of tea with Tom and his wife, a slice of cake, a piece of pie, a natter and a chat, a proper heart to heart if things were not going well, as well as they'd liked, as they'd hoped, there would always be an open door and a kindly, kinder word, a shot in the arm and boost from Tom. Aye, they were the very best of them were Tom and Bert, thought Jimmy, their heart and soul they were, were Tom and Bert.

Fifty big black old cars left Portugal Street, Guide Bridge, that Thursday morning, turned up Stockport Road and paused first there in Trafalgar Square, before the Methodist church, the home of the youth club where Bert Whalley had volunteered for many of his years. Then all along the way, up Stockport Road, past West End Park, through Chester Square, along Park Parade, all through Ashton-under-Lyne, then all down King Street, over the Ashton Canal and the River Tame, all the way to Dukinfield, the cemetery, the crematorium there, all the way along, thousands came out to line those streets of Ashton and of Dukinfield, where workers rose from their benches to stand at factory gates, with permission from their bosses, where shopkeepers came out onto the pavements, the local schoolchildren all lined up there, too, as busy as the Whit Walks it was, they said, but all stood without a sound, these silent thousands there, all there to stand, to mourn the passing of Bert Whalley, this lovely man of whom you'd never hear a wrong word said, who if you'd walked these streets with him, these streets of Ashton-under-Lyne, you'd not get so very far because everyone would want to stop to have a word, a chat with Bert, and although Bert would always stop to have a word, a chat, and though he was a Methodist lay preacher at Trafalgar Square and before he coached had played at centre-half, first for Stalybridge Celtic, then for United, Bert was himself a quiet man, a quiet man of faith.

In Dukinfield Crematorium, where his closest chums, his best and oldest friends, Jimmy Murphy and Joe Armstrong, stood with Sandy Busby, there to represent his dad, his father Matt, along with many of his old United teammates, Jack Crompton, Johnny Carey, Henry Cockburn and John Aston, as well as many other, younger lads, those boys Joe would first spot and Bert would then coach, along with Tom, poor old Tom Curry, and then with Jimmy and then with Matt, poor old Matt, and from Stalybridge Celtic, Bert's first and local club, there was old James Scullion, who had first signed Bert, back in Thirty-three it was, before the war, with former Stalybridge teammates, their former manager Ernest Ollershaw, there they stood, among the flowers, the flowers from Manchester City and so many other clubs, behind the family, poor old Bert's family, his wife, his daughter Linda, just eleven years old she was, her dad a father figure to so many boys at United or the local youth club in Trafalgar Square, but to Linda he was just the perfect dad, her dad, a lovely man, a quiet man, a smashing bloke and a Christian gentleman was Bert, they said, all said to her and to her mum, but to her, to Linda, he was her dad, just her dad, the perfect dad.

Oh, Bert, I'm sorry, Bert, thought Jimmy there, in the crematorium there, but not just there, not just then, he'd thought it everywhere, every hour of every day, last night as he'd tried and failed to sleep, this morning as the dawn came with the rain, that same thought there, night or day, day and night, just always there, the thought, You only went because I didn't, Bert, you're only dead because I'm not. That seat was mine, not yours. I'm sorry, Bert, I never should have not have gone . . .

But hard, too hard upon that funeral came the funeral of the other half of that white-coated double act, the funeral of poor old Tom Curry, and so with the service done for Bert, many of the big black old cars set off then from Dukinfield Crematorium back towards the ground, for Stretford and for Tom. For they had tried as best they could, had Jimmy with the help of Les, and of Alma and of Cissie, too, with the families of the Dead, to arrange these days as best they could, so people could attend as many funerals as they wished.

Tom 'Tosher' Curry had been at United for twenty-four years in all, but he was not a local man nor a young man. He'd been born in South Shields in 1894, had played two hundred and twenty-one games in ten years as a half-back for Newcastle United, then he'd moved this way to play one year more for Stockport County. When Tom finished playing there, at thirty-six or so, he went up to Carlisle United as a trainer there, then after four years there, Tom came at last Old Trafford's way, thanks to the ever-keen and canny eye of old Louis Rocca, who'd brought in Bill Inglis with Tom, too, both men working first under Scott Duncan, then for poor old Walter Crickmer, when Walter was the secretary–manager, and then with Matt, when Matt took charge, but Bill Inglis and Tom, they ran the dressing rooms, where they bandaged wounded limbs and egos, soothed aches and hearts, and so like poor old Walter, like poor old Bert, Tom was an institution, part of the fixtures and the fittings of the club, but made of flesh and made of bone was Tom, with a heart that burned with a passion for the club, the lads he trained, he coached, just like Bert's heart did, or Jimmy or Joe or Bill or Arthur's hearts all did, whether that lad was new that day or now a star, it mattered not to Tom, he cared for all the lads the same, for he loved them all the same.

But from this house in which he'd lived since Thirty-four, the house in Bedford Road, Firswood, just opposite Saint Teresa's school, the procession of big black old cars now left with Tom, went up the Great Stone Road to Gorse Hill Methodist Church, on the other side of Gorse Hill Park, and after the service at the church, close to the cricket ground, the cars all travelled back through Stretford again, through Chorlton, down Seymour Grove to the crematorium, Manchester Crematorium again.

In the porch, under its arch, out of the rain, among the mourners, Jimmy stopped, shook hands with Jack Crompton and said, It's good to see you, Jack, thanks very much for coming up, for coming back. How's life in Luton, son, you enjoying training, are you, son?

Thanks, Jimmy, said Jack Crompton. Thank you, and I won't ask how you are, but just remember, if there's anything I can do, anything at all, you just let me know.

Funny you should say that, son, said Jimmy, without a smile, but with the hint, the hint of a twinkle in his eye. There is something you could do . . .

Maybe it was the snow, the fact it was always snowing each time Frank awoke, looked out the window, there was always snow, more bloody snow. Or maybe it was the silence, the silence of the snow outside, the room, the hospital inside? But Frank had a feeling it was the calendar, the clock upon the wall, the watch not on his wrist but on the table by his bed, that watch, that clock upon the wall, they ticked and turned through the minutes, through the hours and the days, and the calendar, its dates then turned until here it was again, a Thursday come back round again, and so a week ago today it was, maybe why he was living it again, felt himself living through it all again, those scenes, those voices –

C'mon, Dad, shouted Frank Swift, his seat belt already fastened, pointing at the empty place beside him. I've kept this seat especially for you, so you get yourself sat down, back in the tail with me, Dad.

Frank had never known why Frank Swift always called him Dad; Swifty must have been a good six or seven years older than Frank, had been a hero to Frank, as a matter of fact, when Frank was a lad. Maybe it was because Frank looked or acted older? Maybe Swifty had thought him a fuddy-duddy? Frank had never known, and now he never would. But Frank did know why Swifty thought the back of the plane was the safest place to sit: it was said that in the war, when bombers crashed, more often than not the tail gunners were thrown clear and lived to tell the tale. But Frank himself had once read in some report on some terrible crash that the only person who had survived that particular time, they'd been sitting in a seat that faced the rear, and so perhaps that was why Frank shook his head and said, No, thanks, Frank. There looks to be a lot more space up front, in those rearward-facing seats.

What's the matter, laughed Swifty, you too good for the rest of us, are you? Well, you be like that, Dad.

Frank had been like that, had stuck to his guns, made his way up to the front of the plane, had sat himself down and strapped himself into one of those rear-facing seats at the front of the plane, all on his own at the front of the plane. Frank had hoped at least one of his mates, his pals from the pack, might have made their way forward to join him up at the front. But from his seat facing the rear, Frank could see them all sat at the back, see them laughing, see them joking, all eight of them sat together, Henry, Eric and George and all the rest of them –

There are plenty of seats up here, you know, shouted Frank, waving down to George Follows.

No point moving now, shouted back George. We're all sitting very comfortably here, thank you, Frank, and I'd only have to shift all my luggage.

It had seemed such a normal, jokey kind of conversation at the time, thought Frank, they all had seemed that way, all the conversations on the way that day, one week ago today, but now it seemed so strange, they all seemed so very strange, the conversations and the actions, the decisions and the choices of that day. Frank never normally would have sat at the front on his own, despite what he'd read about rear-facing seats, because he hated to travel alone, on his own, and the thing, the very thing he liked best on these trips were the times, the laughs and the jokes he had with his mates, his pals from the pack, so why then did he sit where he sat, alone at the front of the plane, looking through the porthole to his right, down through clouds where mountains reared out of the snowfields, rugged and fearsome, their crevasses dark and evil, they seemed to Frank at the time, wondered Frank, had they been carved in a fit of anger by some giant, demonical stonemason, Frank wondering if those mountains were the Dolomites? Or the Carnic Alps or the

Karamanhe? He leaned, reached forward in his seat, took the neat folders and maps from the pocket on the back of the seat in front of him and began to study one of the maps, but then Frank felt his stomach turn again, that mix of red wine followed then by white, followed then with beer last night, which at the time he'd known had not been wise, and why his stomach felt so very, very queasy, and that was really why, Frank knew, he'd sat up there at the front of the plane that day, all on his own, because he'd had a hangover and felt unwell –

Looking a bit green around the gills up there, Frank, shouted George, or was it Swifty, Henry, or maybe it was Eric, or was it Tom Jackson? Why don't you try and have a snooze? Read one of Alf's stories if you find you can't get off, best cure for insomnia you'll ever find!

And as if on cue, right on cue, a great, loud snore rose up from Alf Clarke, mouth wide open and fast asleep.

Been reading his own stories again, laughed George, all of them laughing, all of them joking,

all of them gone.

*

That black day, that black week, on and on, one after the other, hard after the other, the funerals came and went: workers and colleagues on the *Evening Chronicle* had left their presses, their benches and their desks, to stand in silence on the street outside Kemsley House, on the corner of Withy Grove and Corporation Street, many dressed in black, in sombre, funeral black, as the fourteen-car procession passed, bearing the body of Alf Clarke, the Man Who Bled Manchester United Red Blood –

He was United was Alf, a shareholder in the club, a close friend of Walter Crickmer, he was Vice-President of the Supporters' Club, and nightly, for six days a week, Monday

219

through Saturday, he published news of the club in the *Evening Chronicle* and the Saturday 'Football Pink'. Alf had his own page in the match-day programme, too, 'Casual Comments' in the *United Review*, because as Alf always said, There's only one team in this city, and you can't write enough about them . . .

Both Alf and Tom Jackson, his friend and rival at the *Evening News*, were trusted by Matt Busby, both being great advocates of the club, unashamed of their bias. Both men also liked to claim credit for coining the phrase 'Busby's Babes', a phrase, if truth be known, that neither Busby nor his Babes cared for much themselves.

But that black afternoon, that black week, it no longer mattered who coined what or when, or whether you bled red or blue, from Kemsley House in the centre, all the way out to the crematorium, people stood in silence, hatless, with heads all bowed again, and out at Manchester Crematorium, again mourners packed the chapel there, sportsmen and writers, from clubs and papers near and far, and men and women, young and old, who were his readers, were his friends, his many friends, and were his family, his wife and children, and though Alf was the man who was United, had bled Manchester United red, whose ashes would soon be scattered down towards the Stretford End, still that day, that afternoon, Manchester City, they came and they mourned, too.

Meanwhile, down Wolverhampton way, on Underhill Lane, at Bushbury Crematorium, the funeral of George Follows of the *Daily Herald* took place that black afternoon, on that black day, in that black week. He'd hailed from down that way, from Walsall way, had George, had started on the *Walsall Times*, moved then to the *Wolverhampton Express & Star*, then joined the Manchester offices of the *Daily Herald*, 'the working man's paper', moving up to cover the North-West soccer scene, becoming good pals with Jimmy Murphy and with Matt, always witty, always honest, and with a brilliant turn of phrase; it was George, some said, who'd first used the phrase 'the Red Devils', which both Matt and his boys all much preferred to 'Busby's Babes'.

He'd had two dreams had George Follows, for both the Red Devils and for himself: that he'd one day see them win the European Cup, and then that on another day he'd see his son Richard, who was then just ten years old, see him pull on that famous red United shirt and play for his blessed, hallowed Red Devils.

But the biggest funeral in Manchester that day, it was not for Geoff or Bert or Tom or even for Alf Clarke, it was the funeral at Saint Anne's Church in Saint Anne's Square for a certain Harry Donald Davies, better known to readers of the *Manchester Guardian* as 'an Old International', or to the readers of the *Boy's Own Paper* and the listeners of the BBC's Saturday tea-time *Sports Report* as Don Davies, or to his many friends as Donny, and to his wife and daughters as simply, only, Pop, and though the crowds who packed and lined the pavements and the streets, filled both the church and square outside, came as no surprise to most, they did come as quite a shock to Harry Donald Davies, the man himself –

Dead, he said. That can't be right, there's some mistake, I've much too much to do . . .

*

Bobby had left the hospital, or, well, they'd as good as kicked him out is what they'd done, but Bobby had not yet left Munich, still did not have the strength to face the journey back, and so they'd packed him off in a taxi to the hotel, the one where all the wives, the girlfriends and the loved ones stayed, but Bobby didn't like to go down to the restaurant, the lounge or the bar, didn't really want to show his face, his face that barely had a scratch, just a stitch or two, not when their husbands or boyfriends, their fathers or sons, were all laid up in bed, some still close to death, so close to death, while other lads, all the other lads were dead, all dead, so Bobby just sat upstairs, on his own, in his room, on his hotel bed, that hour and its minute coming round, wondering if he'd now forever dread that hour, that minute, every afternoon, or would it just be Thursday afternoons? And he'd used to love the afternoons, especially Thursday afternoons, those afternoons when they'd go to the pictures, when they'd walk into Manchester, to the pictures and back. Because it was boring on the bus. Let's walk, they'd say, and so they'd walk, and Bobby loved them walks, into town and back, the laughs, the fun they had. He didn't think he'd ever forget the first time they asked him if he wanted to go with them, never wanted to forget that first time Tommy and David had asked him to go to the pictures with them. Tommy Taylor was a big star, and David Pegg was in the first team, but Bobby had just arrived as a youngster, amazed even to be sharing digs with the likes of Tommy and David, sitting at the same table, eating breakfast and tea with them, it was like in a dream, he was living in a dream, he'd have to pinch himself just to make sure he was awake, that it was real, all real and true, but when they'd asked him then to go the pictures with them, when one of them had said, Are you coming then or what? And Bobby said, Yes, okay then, if you're sure, I'll just go get us jacket then, but all the way in, on the walk into town, Bobby had thought, Well, I'd better behave like a real professional footballer, and so when they got to the pictures, Bobby said, Oh, leave it to me, I'll get the tickets, and then he'd said, So where are we going to sit then like? And both of them said, Oh, well, let's sit in the best seats, and so Bobby said, Okay, he said, three best, please, and that was his whole wage packet gone in one go, and he'd thought, Blimey, it's a good job we're walking home.

When they were not carrying in the coffins of the Dead, when they were not serving as altar boys at the funerals of the Dead, or when they were not paying their respects to the Dead, Bill Inglis had all the lads come in, between the funerals, after one, before the next, to train and then to do their chores, around the ground, in the stands, beneath the stands, in the corridors, the changing rooms, to sweep, to clean, to do the things they always did, and that was why today Bill said, The skip is back from Munich now.

There it was, the skip, with the playing kits, the boots all caked in mud, week-hard mud and dirt and dust, from what must have been a very heavy, shitty pitch, and that was why Bill said, You need to unpack the kits, take them all down to the laundry room, then sort out and clean all the boots, the boots of them that survived, that is.

Nobby did as he was told, set about his task, unpacked the kits, the dirty shirts, the shorts and socks, took them down to the laundry room, but Missus Ramsden and her sister Missus Taylor, who the first-team lads all called Missus Omo and Missus Daz, though Nobby never dared, or never to their faces, they were not there, not in today. They were out at the funerals of Geoff Bent, Bert Whalley and Tom Curry, so Nobby left the dirty shirts, the shorts and socks in the baskets on the table there. Then Nobby went back down the corridor to the skip to start about the boots, to take and sort them out, the boots of the Living from the boots of the Dead, to start to brush and dust, to polish and then to shine.

But later, when Bill Inglis popped his head back in, in his funeral suit and tie, just to see how the lad was getting on, Nobby held up the boots of Tommy Taylor in his hands and said, What about the boots of them that didn't survive? What about their boots, Mister Inglis?

If you clean them, I suppose you can keep them, unless their mam and dad come asking for them.

Thank you, Mister Inglis, sir, said Nobby, and so he set about his task anew, cleaned and cleaned them till they shone like new, them boots, then stuck them inside his coat and took them home, went straight to his room and sat there then, on his bed, for hour after hour, turning those boots over and over in his hands, the leather and the laces, the studs, the odd bit of mud, the speck of dirt he'd missed, even them he loved, to think this bit of mud, that speck of dirt, they were from that pitch in Belgrade, that last pitch on which these boots had trod, these boots, the last boots Tommy Taylor ever wore, would ever wear.

*

Tommy used to play in borrowed boots at school, said his friends, recalled his mates. He didn't care, he didn't mind, he were from a football family was Tommy. His grandad Tommy, he'd played for Barnsley, his dad Charlie, his brothers, they all played football, too, and all big blokes, mind, and young Tommy, too, they called him Tucker, after Little Tommy Tucker, that lad who liked his tuck. But one day there were no boots to borrow, and teacher, he says, Here, Taylor, here, you wear these, and hands Tommy a pair of clogs, but Tommy shook his head, and thought, Fuck off, you play in clogs yoursen, and just walked off like, and teacher shouts, Taylor, you come back here right now or you'll never play for school again, but Tommy just kept on walking, didn't he, thinking, What makes tha' think I wants to lake for thee?

Like, Tommy liked football, had played for school, played for Barnsley Boys and all, but he didn't care, didn't mind if he didn't play, didn't lek for them again, he were more bothered about getting a job, a proper job was Tommy. He left school at fourteen to work at Wharncliffe Woodmoor Colliery, which everyone knows, even if they're not from round here, on account of disaster there that killed fifty-eight men; fifty-eight sons and brothers, husbands and fathers, who all left home for work, their shift that night, but didn't come back, home with the dawn, on August 6, 1936, when Tommy was just a lad of four years old.

But Tommy didn't go underground, with ghosts, in dark, he worked up on surface, which were hard enough, right bloody hard work it was, but least it were not in dark, not with ghosts. But he still liked odd kickabout did Tommy, with his mates from pub, up on Bog there, and so one day happened that local side round here, Smithies United, who played in Nelson League, they were a man short for a match and they asked Tommy if he fancied turning out for them like, and one telling of tale has it that first off, he says, Nah, I've got no gear, have I, says Tommy, but they says, Well, we'll borrow you some, won't we, daft lad, and then that first game he played for them, he was straight off spotted by some scouts.

But another telling of same tale has it that after playing in that first game, Tommy liked it like, and they liked him, so Smithies had him back again to play with them like, and it were third game he played for them, it were then that scouts were watching, from both Barnsley and from Hull, and both Barnsley and Hull, they liked look of Tom, offered him trials and amateur forms, but Tommy didn't fancy moving all way over to Hull, away from his family and his mates, so Tommy stuck with Barnsley, who paid Smithies a tenner for Tommy, who went straight onto ground staff down there at Oakwell, in winter of Forty-eight that were.

And Tommy loved it down at Oakwell, cleaning boots, working round the ground, any job you'd give him, he would do and do it well, and with a smile, and with a joke and all; he'd hide your shoes, turn a cold hose on you if he could, any chance he had, he just loved being round the place did Tommy, you'd have to kick him out to send him home. Full of life he was, always smiling, that cheeky, grinning face of his, but even then, back then, anyone could see he were an outstanding prospect like, never seen a lad could head a ball as hard and far as him, him and his brother Bill. In fact, there's them that'll tell you his brother Bill was the better boy with the ball, but pair of them were chubby lads and prone to fat, and with their Bill it didn't come off like it did with Tom, and so Bill didn't stay at Oakwell long, but Tom moved up fast, through B team to A team, and signed professional in summer Forty-nine it was, but hard on that he got himsen called up for his National Service, didn't he like?

Now Joe Richards, Barnsley Chairman, he had a plan to keep Tommy close to home by fixing him up at a local pit again; see, if you worked at pit, you were exempt from army like, weren't you? But truth be told, don't think Tommy much fancied either pit or army, but maybe because he'd been at pit and worked there once before, he didn't fancy going back down among the ghosts up there again, so Tom went into Royal Artillery, didn't he, and it were only really then, with his National Service like, that he got proper fit, and he could still play matches like for army and even sometimes for Barnsley. In fact, it were when he were in army that Tommy made his first-team debut, against Grimsby it were, and then he played again, few weeks later like, at home, at Oakwell, against Queens Park Rangers that was, when he scored that hat-trick that made everyone sit up, take note of him like, you know, and marked that name, Tommy Taylor.

But it was in army that he got himsen crocked and all, in his knee like, in a collision with a keeper from another army team it were, and proper crocked like, he needed two operations, was it? But he couldn't play for a year, best part of a year it were, and then when he comes out of army, comes back to Barnsley, he felt all right did Tommy like, but nowt seemed to go right for him, and he had his ups and downs with Angus Seed, the Barnsley manager back then. See, Tommy would sometimes say what others might only be thinking like, and he were not afraid to give a bloke a mouthful, if he thought they was wrong and he were right, and there were them that thought Tommy were getting that bit above himsen like, around this time; see, there's nowt folk round here hate worse than that, you know, big-headed and that, but this were when half the clubs in land were sniffing around after Tommy like, when Wednesday were saying they'd pay whatever, the world for him they would, they said, but one by one, they all went quiet on Tom, and then, after Barnsley got beat by Sheffield United, it were then Angus Seed goes and drops Tommy, sticks him in a reserve game, midweek match it were, but against Manchester United, their reserve team like, and, well, that were one of them moments, weren't it like? When world turns again, like that time when Smithies had asked him if he fancied a game, back when he was a lad and had just started at pit and forgotten about football like, and now he's dropped but playing midweek against Manchester United, and there's old Jimmy Murphy on the touchline, watching Tommy dominate game, out to prove old Angus Seed and all them doubters, them naysayers wrong like, Jimmy Murphy watching Tommy with a hat-trick make his point, and so there's them that'll tell you that were when Jimmy Murphy thought to himsen, This lad Taylor here, he could be just the lad for us.

Any road, either way, Tommy were back in Barnsley side that next Saturday, and scoring more and more, he just couldn't seem to stop, twenty-one goals in thirty games so far that season Tommy had, now this was Fifty-two to Fifty-three, that season like, but Barnsley, they were still struggling in the Second, even with Tommy and his goals they were going down, and then Angus Seed, poor bloke, he only goes and gets bronchitis, ends up dead he does, this bloke who'd won the Military Medal back in Great War, in Battle of Vimy Ridge, now dead after a bloody Cup tie down in Plymouth.

Now poor old Angus Seed, he dies in February, February seventh it was, Fifty-three, and Barnsley find themselves in no end of bother over money now, and so they end up putting both Tommy and Eddie McMorran up for sale, and Eddie goes to Doncaster, where Peter Doherty is manager, because Peter, he knows Eddie from managing Northern Ireland, and that's where Harry Gregg were, at that time, at Doncaster, but Doncaster only pay eight thousand, was it, for Eddie, while Barnsley are hoping for a lot, lot more for Tommy, and in end it came down to Cardiff or United, Manchester United, and Cardiff were offering more, prepared to break what were then record like, thirty-five thousand it would have been, whereas United, they were talking thirty thousand.

But Joe Richards, Barnsley Chairman, he'd give his word to Matt Busby that United had first dibs on Tom; see, United had had their eye on Tommy for a long while now like, and Jimmy Murphy and Joe Armstrong, they'd lost count of times they'd been to see Tom play. Fact was, last time Jimmy Murphy had been over to Oakwell, when he gets back to Manchester, he says to Busby like, so story goes like, he says, There were that many managers, chairmen and scouts in the crowd tonight, I thought I was at a meeting of the Football League, so if we still want that Taylor lad, we best get our skates on, Matt.

But thing was, see, Tommy didn't want to leave, anyone will tell you that; see, he was going steady with Norma then, Norma Curtis, as she was back then, a local Barnsley lass, and so Tommy didn't want to be moving far from her, from Norma like, nor from his mam, his dad, his family and his mates, so there were no way he were going down to Wales, all way down there, no way, not when he'd have stayed put if he could. But Barnsley Chairman Joe Richards, he had no choice, he always said he had to sell Tommy to save Barnsley, and so him and Tom, they went to talk terms, first at Royal Hotel, on Royal Street there, with Matt Busby, then over at Oakwell as things moved on, and Matt, he were that keen on Tommy, he agreed that Tommy could still live at home, even stick and train at Oakwell if he didn't like look of digs they'd lined up for him in Stretford, close to Old Trafford, and Matt would make sure as his family and Norma, they all had tickets for every game like, and just to take pressure off a bit, that little bit, instead of paying thirty thousand for Tommy, which was a big old price, they'd pay twenty-nine thousand, nine hundred and ninety-nine pound, and Matt, he give other pound note to Missus Wilby, who were Barnsley tea lady, and Matt says, Now how about that, son? Does that sound fair to you?

Aye, says Tommy, that does sound fair.

Well, you just sign here then, son –

Tommy signed for United on March 4, 1953, and next day, him and Norma had gone over to Manchester, to be given tour and have a look round, good look around, and it were funny, really, because after asking about living at home, training at Oakwell and all that, minute he saw ground, went round Old Trafford, met some of the boys, lads on team, he just felt right at home, seemed so at ease, like he were spellbound, like this were where he were always meant to be, and so he come back over with Norma, back to his mam's like, packs up his stuff, and next morning he's off back on train, his boots in a brown paper bag. Can you believe it? Tommy Taylor, the big new star, in all papers like, on TV, and there he is, carrying his football boots over to Manchester in a brown paper bag!

But three days later, at Old Trafford, in front of biggest gate of season, fifty-five thousand or thereabouts, three o'clock that Saturday afternoon, and Tommy's straight into first team, and it couldn't have gone no better for him like: Jack Rowley scores, and David Pegg, Tommy's new best mate, he gets two, and Tommy, he goes gets two himsen, and five–two United win –

'TAYLOR HAS THE LAWTON LOOK', said the headline in the *Daily Herald*, under which George Follows reported: *Enter the shy and smiling executioner, Tommy Taylor. The home-sweet-home boy from Barnsley, kisses all around from his family afterwards, is deadly in the penalty box. And Manchester United have bought a full £30,000 worth of goal-filled footballer, perhaps more. He looks a little like Trevor Ford – who were some player – a little like Jack Rowley, and in his ruthless execution near goal, he is a lot like Tommy Lawton.*

Rest of that season couldn't have gone no better for him either, really, like, living at Missus Watson's on Birch Avenue, sharing them digs at number five with David Pegg and Mark Jones, all Yorkshire lads together, house on fire they were, them and Jackie Blanchflower, and later Bobby Charlton, after Mark Jones and Jackie married like, playing in eleven more games, scoring seven goals, then getting himsen selected for England for summer tour of North and South America; all a far cry from Barnsley and from Smithies United, weren't it?

That summer, then, Tommy made his England debut against Argentina, in Buenos Aires, in front of hundred thousand, but after twenty minutes game was abandoned, it were raining that bad, and so his first proper England game were really one against Chile, in Santiago, few days later, when he scored and all. But he must have brought back weather, them black clouds and all that rain back with him when he came, must Tommy, because it weren't all plain sailing, blue skies and happy days like.

First off, things started to go wrong with Norma, didn't they like, you know, they were right young, weren't they, but Tommy, he had proposed to her, before he went off on England tour, but she'd said no, they were too young, thought they'd be better to wait a year or so. But then maybe he started to think, well, who knows what folk really think, but when he were away in America, he never got her letters and he thought she weren't writing, wasn't bothered about him like, and then when he come back home, there were rumours about him and other birds, you know, just lies like, but what with one thing and t'other, they broke up, didn't they, after a bit like, and then it weren't like Tommy ever had a bad season at United, far from it like, he were always top scorer, in League, if not overall, you know, and he were always making goals was Tommy, you know, for Dennis Viollet and then Billy Whelan when they come in, and it's funny like, when Dennis first come in team, he were so slight, Boss, Matt Busby, he pulls Tommy to one side and tells him, he says, Tommy, look after Dennis for us, will you, out there on pitch, but team itsen were in transition, wasn't it?

See, if you think back like, that first game Tommy played for United, when he scored two, well, were it something like seven of rest of team was over thirty or thereabouts? Any road, then there were that famous game, the one up at Huddersfield on Halloween, in Fifty-three? When Busby, he starts Dennis, Jackie Blanchflower and Big Dunc, who were what? Seventeen, was he? Now Jackie and Dennis had all played for first team before, and Duncan, too, but it were Busby bringing them all in, playing them with Ray Wood, Billy Foulkes, Roger Byrne, Jeff Whitefoot, along with Tommy and Johnny Berry, that's why this game is often said as being 'birth of Busby Babes', and also cos it were when Alf Clarke, in *Evening Chronicle*, had that headline, which Alf probably never wrote himsen like, but which said, 'BUSBY'S BOUNCING "BABES" KEEP ALL TOWN AWAKE', but Allenby Chilton and Jack Rowley, they were still in that side that day, and there were no place for Mark Jones or David Pegg, so it were still a time of transition, took them a while for things to come together like, but Tommy were still getting the goals like, but he were also having injuries, you know, lot of knocks, and that never really got sorted while Busby took him down London, that surgeon there, who finds there were a piece of bone like, floating about it were, and that were why he were always in such pain like. But once that got fixed, and he mended, well, he never looked back, did he, and team, too, they just kept on getting better and better like.

Mind you, Tommy always had his critics like, especially old Henry Rose, but Tommy always proved old Henry wrong, twice he made him eat his words did Tom. First there were time Henry said, If Tommy Taylor can score against Billy Wright's Wolves, then I'll walk back barefoot to Ancoats, so I will, which were where *Express* were back then. But sure enough, our Tommy goes and scores twice against Wolves, doesn't he, so old Henry, good as his word, he walks barefoot all way back into town, followed by half of kids of Stretford, so they said. Then other time were when Tommy had scored three for England, against Denmark that was, in December Fifty-six, it were, but Henry still were not convinced, or more likely he just liked to stir pot a bit, but Henry writes something like, If Tommy Taylor is the best centre-forward England have, then I am Santa Claus.

Now folk knew how Henry were, took him with a pinch of salt, he were just looking for a fight, sell a few more papers like, but Matt and Jimmy, they were not happy with that, because despite what most folk thought, our Tommy were never a bighead, there were no arrogance about him, in fact, opposite were true, he never really thought he were good enough for United, not when they'd first come calling for him like, and that were another reason he never really wanted to leave Barnsley. But fair play to Henry Rose, a few weeks later, after that second leg against Bilbao at Maine Road, under floodlights, on that night of nights, which were just an unbelievable experience, anyone who were there will tell you that, say same, cheering was unbelievable, it were deafening, and team were fantastic, and

Tommy, well, that were Tommy's finest night was that, anyone will tell you that, and they all admitted, did rest of team later, if they wanted a breather, they'd just boot it up to Tommy like, and he scored one, second one it were, from a quick free-kick from Eddie Colman, and Tommy took it, shakes off Garay and shoots left foot past Carmelo and in it goes, in off post, and then he made last one, too, third goal, and there were what, five minutes left? But Tommy, he picks up ball on right, again gets away from Garay, who were one of best there was at that time, but Tommy takes ball to by-line, glances up, spies Johnny Berry coming forward, and quick as you like, in a flash, Tommy cuts ball back for Johnny, who never breaks his stride, so perfect is that pass, he can just side-foot it home, the ball, and, well, everyone were jumping and crying and grabbing and hugging each other, it were night of nights, it really were, and Tommy's night, it really was, it were Tommy's night, *the greatest centre-forward exhibition I have ever seen*, wrote George Follows in *Daily Herald*, and fair play again to Henry Rose, he ends his match report in *Express* with, *Santa Claus salutes you, beard and all . . .*

And it were like Christmas, were 1957, the year they won Championship again, second year running, and did Tommy get something like seven goals for England, too, with that hat-trick at Wembley Stadium, against Ireland, and he were that good, you know, was Tommy, Internazionale of Milan, they offered sixty-five thousand quid for Tommy, which, if Matt Busby had said yes, which he never would like, but if he had like, that would've made Tommy most expensive player there ever was, at that time like. But it were also Christmas for Tommy, because it were also year he met Carol, who were a Manchester lass were Carol, and they went steady pretty quick like, and they'd got engaged and were going to get married in the June or July of Fifty-eight, that's what they were planning like, and he were just so happy, you know, just liked being with Carol, you know, in coffee bars and what have you, listening to music, because that were what he really liked, you know, listening to music, to his records like: Benny Goodman, the Platters, and his favourite was, what were it? That was it, it were 'Wheel of Fortune', remember that one? By Kay Starr?

That were why it brock his brother Bill's and his wife Audrey's hearts, that day they went over to collect their Tommy's stuff from his digs on Great Stone Road, number twenty-two it was, house he moved after Missus Watson and her husband had all that bother. But when Bill and Audrey went up to his room to get his stuff, his things, his records and his clothes, there was two little black and yellow *Teach Yourself* books on little table there, *Teach Yourself Public Speaking* and *Teach Yourself Maths*, and it brock their hearts, it really did, to think of their Tommy on his bed, reading them two books, thinking how he needed to improve, to better himsen like, when there really were no need, no need at all . . .

He really had it all did Tommy, their Tommy, all them skills he had, and he were so unselfish, with his talent like, all them goals he made, space he'd make for others, them balls he'd put, he'd place right at feet of Dennis Viollet or Johnny Berry like, and then there were all them goals he scored himsen, of course, one hundred and thirty-one in one hundred and ninety-one games for United, and then there were sixteen for England, and in just nineteen games, remember, with both feet and with his head; there never were a better header of the ball than Tommy, way he used to float, to hang in air, up there in air, and it used to amaze folk, folk would wonder how he did it like, but them that knew him, his brothers and his mates, we'd laugh because we knew all right how he did it like, because he'd never open a gate he couldn't jump would Tommy, and his mate Harry, he remembered this one time, and it weren't that long ago like, they come out of this house, and at bottom of this yard there were

234

this big old gate, and it were about five or six foot high, and all of a sudden, he set off running did Tommy and he jumped straight over top. Well, when Harry and others opened gate and went to other side, it were cobbled were street on other side, he could have brock his neck, and he were leant against wall laughing like, and Harry said, If Matt Busby had seen thee do that, he'd have gone potty like, you know, but that were just how Tommy was, always jumping stuff, you know, and Dickie Bird, who were a mate, were at school with Tom and kept up with him like, after Dickie got selected for Yorkshire County Cricket Club, you know, and Tommy were at Barnsley and then United, the pair of them, they stayed good mates, well, Dickie, he saw Tommy jump over many a garden gate or onto top of a snooker table like, and from a standing start that were, said Dickie, with no run-up or nowt, and so that were how Tommy could like float and hang there like, why they always used to laugh and say, By, tha' should've been born a horse should thee.

But no, ta, no, thanks, their Tommy would say, he'd always say, If I couldn't play football, then I'd rather I were dead, so maybe it were a blessing then, thought his little brother Bill, that black day, black afternoon, as funeral procession left their mam and dad's house, where folk stood four, five folk deep, in black, of course, many were, but some had come in red and white, colours of Barnsley, colours of United, and, you know, when them big black cars they pulled away, it was one week to the hour, the day since that plane did not make the sky, had failed to jump, to float, to hang like Tommy –

on a cushion, majestic in the air . . .

They buried Tommy Taylor over at Monk Bretton, in the cemetery there, after a short and simple service in the church up there, and there were thousands there that day, that black day, in that black week, from every local village, from Barnsley and beyond, from Manchester, of course, in cars again they came, they lined the streets again, from Smithies to Monk Bretton, all up Burton Road they were, filled the village, all around Saint Paul's, the parish church up there, where the Barnsley players formed a guard of honour and young lads stood in red shirts and white shorts, from his old school, Raley School, with a wreath they were, the Mayor and Mayoress of Barnsley, they came, too, Joe Richards, the Chairman of Barnsley, he were there, and Walter Winterbottom, the England manager, and Jimmy and Joe and Sandy, of course, and lots of others from United, too, and there were Dickie Bird, of course, and then his friends, his mates, who'd carried Tommy in, they carried Tommy out again, and in the graveyard, as they put poor Tommy in the ground, a bugler by the graveside there, the bugler sounded the last post.

*

That hour, its minute come around and gone again, Bobby pushed back the cover, the blanket and the sheet, the pillow from his face and looked up at the ceiling, the light and its shade hanging there, unlit and looking down on him. Bobby yawned, stretched out on the bed, the hotel bed, in the hotel room, looked at his watch, made double sure that hour, its minute had passed, had been and gone again, then reached for his cigarettes, his lighter, lit a cigarette, in the late, late afternoon light, smoked that cigarette, stubbed it out, in the twilight, the Munich twilight, then got up from the bed, his feet in his shoes, and walked over to the window, stood by the curtains, wondering should he draw the curtains, looking out of the window, staring out at the snow, the twilight and the snow, wondering if it always snowed in Munich, did it never stop, the snow, never stop falling? Bobby shivered, turned away from the snow, walked away from the window, the curtains still open, the twilight still here, and Bobby sat back down upon the bed again, kicked off his shoes again, then raised and swung his feet, his legs, and stretched out again upon the bed, that hotel bed, up in that hotel room, stretched out, waiting, but waiting for what, waiting and searching, but searching for who, searching the air, the light, the warmer air, the twilight, searching and asking, *Where are you? Where have you gone without me?* Tuning in and out, the radio, the songs in his head.

But then, as if by magic, there they were again, here they are again, not in his head, in his mind, but there in the room, here in the air, the light of the room, floating there, hanging here, before and around him, surrounding him now, Roger, Johnny Berry, Jackie Blanchflower, Ray Wood, Bill Foulkes, Tommy Taylor, Billy Whelan and Duncan, there's Duncan, here's Duncan and David, David Pegg, in their red shirts, but sometimes in blue, even in white, oh, what a good team, good players, a great team they are, young players, on the verge of things, all young players with the world, the world at their feet –

Tommy Taylor there, here with the ball, in the room, the hotel room, on its carpet, now the pitch, the ball at his feet, and Tommy gives it to Kenny Morgans, Kenny Morgans then to Duncan, Duncan squares it back and it comes out to him, to Bobby, and Bobby jumped, he springs up from the bed, so there he is to take the pass, the ball, and he's an easy side-footer then, into the back of the net, and Bobby falls, fell back onto his bed, in his room, his hotel bed in his hotel room, and Bobby smiles, and he laughed, he laughed out loud and said, I wish they were all as simple as that, but that was them, that's us, how they played, how we play, they were at them from the beginning, like we're always at teams, and they're so good, the players, his mates, so talented, they're certain to win the European Cup, certain to do it . . .

Then suddenly no more, the dream they started, gone again, from the room, the air, the light of the room, all gone again, the room cold and dark again, all that was good now

237

gone again, and Bobby cried, Where are you, he pleaded. Don't let it be true, let it be a mistake. You all think they're dead, but they're not really –

They're not really dead.

But then the plane is going down the runway again, just keeps going down the runway, and going down the runway, and doesn't take off, and is hitting a perimeter fence, and then that was it.

In that room, on that bed, in the cold and in the dark again, Bobby just could not put his mind to it, didn't think he ever would. He still could not believe it, really, what was happening, had happened, but it was a fact, he knew that, it was a fact. But the one thing he thought, he kept on thinking, still could not stop thinking then was, Well, why, why was I a survivor then, did I survive? When all the others didn't? Fate, just luck? Just luck maybe that I actually sat with my seat facing backwards instead of forwards? Is that it?

*

If they were to start again, Jimmy had said to Billy Foulkes, then before anything else, they'd have to find a trainer, now poor Tom Curry was gone, and Billy had come straight out and said, Well, why not ask Jack Crompton then? And it was not a bad idea, was a good idea, had thought Jimmy then, wondered why he'd not thought of it himself, now Jack was coaching down at Luton Town and by all accounts was doing well down there, and the Chairman there, he rated Jack, but Jack had been at United for over ten years, the keeper in the side that won the Cup in Forty-eight, then the League in Fifty-two, and he'd not even been gone that long had Jack, not yet two years, and so Jack seemed the man to ask, though Billy had his doubts if Jack would come back, but you never knew, said Jimmy, and if you didn't ask, then you never would, and when Jimmy had asked Jack, after the funeral of poor old Tom that day, Jack had said yes, without a second thought he'd said yes, and so that was a start, thought Jimmy, at least they'd made a start.

But Jack didn't put a body on the pitch, so they still needed players, and they needed them fast, but Jimmy hated that side, this side of football, the telephone calls, the negotiations, the chairmen and the boards, all the bartering and the haggling, the talk, talk, talk –

Give Jimmy the wind, give Jimmy the rain and a boy with a ball, and for hour after hour he'd work with that boy, in the wind, in the rain, do his best for that boy, for that lad, yes, he'd shout, he'd swear at that lad, but he'd never break his heart, never tell him he was no good, he'd not passed the test, not made the grade, no, that was Matt's job, what the Boss did –

So what are you going to do then, Jimmy, asked Paddy McGrath on the drive back from Barnsley, from the funeral of Tommy Taylor, up on the Moors, on the way back to Manchester. About signing someone then?

Jimmy shook his head, said, Well, between you and me, Pat, there's been a lot of kind words, lot of big speeches, you know, but it's all a lot of hot air, sweet bugger-all if you call them, you know? Swansea won't let Mel Charles go, or Mel doesn't want to leave, depends who you believe, but then they've said they want thirty-five grand for Cliff Jones, now where the fucking hell are we going to get thirty-five fucking grand from, eh?

But what about Ernie Taylor, said Paddy. Did you speak to Ernie yet, you call Blackpool yet?

Jimmy nodded, said, Oh, aye, I called Blackpool, asked if they still wanted shot of Ernie, and if they did, then to name their price, and they do still want shot and they did name their price . . .

Which is . . .?

Jimmy shook his head again, said, Well, they were being silly, asking fifteen grand, but we can get them down to ten or less, I'm sure. I mean, he's not playing, is he, the man's a burden, if he's anything at all to them.

But have you spoken with Ernie yet, asked Paddy. I mean, like I said, Jimmy, I know the man, I think we're friends, I can have a word, you know?

They'd come down from the Moors, passed through Hyde, Denton, going through Longsight now, back in Manchester now, heading to Old Trafford, when Jimmy looked at his watch, at Paddy, then said, You don't fancy a drive over to Blackpool now, do you, Pat?

Now, Jimmy, laughed Paddy McGrath, laughed Paddy for the first time in a long time. Am I ever going to pass up the chance of a drive out to Blackpool?

You're a saint, Pat, said Jimmy, you really are.

Paddy laughed again. Now, well, I don't know about that, but if I can help, Jim, I will, you know that.

And I thank you for that, Pat, said Jimmy, but would you mind if we first swung by Billy Foulkes's house, if you've the time? You don't mind, Pat?

I've all the time in the world, said Paddy. It's more about you, Jimmy, if you've got the time . . .

Jimmy might not have had the time – half the time he didn't know what bloody time it was; was it day or was it fucking night? – but Jimmy knew he had to call in and see how Billy Foulkes was doing, how he was getting on now Billy was back home again, his new captain, back home again in Manchester again –

I'm here with good news for a change, son, said Jimmy on the doorstep, in the hallway, the living room, inviting himself in with Paddy, the rain and the night. About that idea of yours, about asking Jack back, well, Jack said yes, and Jack said to tell you that he's looking forward to seeing you tomorrow morning,

Billy, back in training, at ten o'clock sharp, so I just thought I'd pop by to thank you, Billy, for that idea of yours, and to pass that on from Jack and see how you were doing, son.

Ten o'clock sharp, said Bill.

Aye, son, said Jimmy, if that's all right, and you've got no plans? Or are you busy, son?

No, he's not, said Teresa, bringing in a tray of tea, setting down the tray, pouring out the tea.

Jimmy nodded, smiled at Bill, and Jimmy said, That's good, that's great, now are you busy now, son, you've not got any plans for tonight, have you, son?

Bill looked at Teresa, shrugged, shook his head, then said, No, Jimmy, no, I don't . . .

Great, said Jimmy again, standing back up again, clapping his hands together. Then get your coat on, son, because me and Pat here, we're off over to Blackpool for a chat with Ernie Taylor, and it was you, was it not, who said I should give Ernie a call, was that not you, Billy?

Bill shook his head, uncertain and unsure, and said, Well, er, it might have been, I can't . . .

But you know Ernie, don't you, son, you know him well, I think you said?

Bill shook his head again. No, not really, Jimmy, I hardly know the man . . .

That doesn't matter, said Jimmy, Pat knows him very well, don't you now, Paddy? But you should still come with us, Billy, have a word as well, help him make up his mind, you being the captain now.

You mean, go with you now?

Yes, said Jimmy. Now.

What? In the car?

That is the plan, said Jimmy, yes.

But what about your tea?

241

Don't worry, we'll be wetting our whistles while you go get your coat on, son, said Jimmy, picking up a cup, then turning to Teresa, holding out his cup and, with a wink, he said, You've not a drop of whisky, have you, love, to put in this, just to warm us for the drive . . .

Either of you know why the Germans never bombed Blackpool, said Paddy. Go on, have a guess –

Paddy loved to talk about Blackpool, about how things were back in the war, things you wouldn't believe, the things he'd seen, no place like it back then, no place on earth. Every night in every pub was like New Year's Eve, that many airmen, both British and Yanks, and so many girls, some staying faithful, so many not –

They bombed Pendle, even tiny, little places like Oswaldtwistle and Edgeworth, but never Blackpool, said Paddy, putting his foot down again, making Bill jump, more nervous again. Made no sense, did it? They were making thousands of Wellington Bombers at Squires Gate, there were thousands of troops stationed or on leave there, but never a bomb dropped, not one single one . . .

Jimmy laughed, he said, Hitler liked the fish and chips, is that it? Go on, Pat, no idea . . .

He didn't eat meat or fish, said Bill from the back of the car, his hands, his nails gripping the seat.

How the hell do you know that, Foulkesy, laughed Paddy. But you're not that far off, Jimmy, because he did love Blackpool, did old Adolf, wanted to see a swastika flying atop the Tower and wanted the town to be a playground for his troops, come the glorious day that never came, that's why they never bombed the place.

They were coming into Blackpool now, in the evening, in the rain, both Jimmy and Bill looking out of the windows of the car now, into the evening, into the rain, thinking about

Germany, about Munich again, about the boys, the men, the friends they'd lost –

Ernie Taylor knows a thing or two about grief, said Paddy. He won't have to pretend and neither will you. He'll help you, and you'll help him.

Aye, you might be right there, Pat, said Jimmy, whispered, let's hope you are ...

*

Like I said on the telephone, said Ernie Taylor in his front room, with his wife at his side, and like I said to Paddy, I'm very sorry about everything that has happened to you like, you know, with the crash like, and I know you're desperate, and I still appreciate you asking us like, but I just don't think it would work, it wouldn't be right like ...

Ernie, I'm not asking you because we're desperate, said Jimmy, I'm asking you because I think you could do a job of work for us, a job we need doing, and one you would do well. I mean, you've two Cup medals on that sideboard over there, have you not, son? And if you'd stayed at Newcastle, you'd have had two more.

That was a long time ago, Jimmy.

Ernie, everything's a long time ago now, said Jimmy, that's just football, that's just how it is.

You know what I mean.

I know you'd help us steady the ship, said Jimmy, thinking, Steady the ship? Raise it from the fucking seabed is what you'd help us do, but then Jimmy saw again, out of the corner of his eye, that photograph in its frame, that smiling little lad, their son no longer here, and Jimmy, he sat forward in his chair, his seat, and softly, gently said, And maybe do yourself some good and all ...

Ernie Taylor, his stare into space, a far-off place, he groped, he reached for the hand of his wife as his wife, she groped, she reached for his, and as his wife, she squeezed his hand as he squeezed hers, she looked, she nodded, smiled at Jimmy, turned then to Ernie, said to Ernie, Why not, love, why not try?

*

Cissie had been looking for Jimmy, looking everywhere for Jimmy, had heard from Joe he'd gone over to Blackpool with Paddy McGrath, but then she'd heard from Les he was back, but when she'd gone up to his office, he wasn't in his office, so then she thought he might have gone home, but when she'd called his house, Winnie said he wasn't there either, she'd not seen him all day, not since the morning, so Cissie set off, walking around the ground, in the dark, in the night, and was it then she came across a shade, a shadow, at first, she thought, with the shape, the trace of Jimmy, but no, and if no, but who, then who? But then this nameless shadow man, he looked at her, at Cissie, this strange and sad but somehow happy man, and raised his hat and with a lonely, yet not unpleasant, smile he said, Forgive me, ma'am, forgive me, please, I should not be here, I must be gone.

8

Don, it seemed to Don, had fallen, stepped straight from the sky onto the ground, but where he walked now flowers sprung, it was strange, so very strange, the way the weather, the world was here, and made Don wonder, What was this Christian magic, this Lazarus spell, *and if it worked for Don, had worked on Don, then I wonder, Would it work for little thee and little me?* and with the flowers came the dawn, forever, always dawn, it seemed to Don, a soft pink, warm spring dawn, an eternal spring and always dawn which wrapped Don in a world of gentle storms of petal clouds, in a garden of wide-eyed, childhood wonder, even though the rain still fell, he knew, the cold outside it came, but Don could no longer feel the cold, the rain, in this garden, this world where all wounds were healed and all hearts loved, and only loved . . .

*

Even without the waiting hearse, the big black car for Mark Jones's wife June, their young son Gary, you'd not miss the place, that house on Kings Road, not today with all the people gathered there, under umbrellas in the rain, all the flowers in their hands, snowdrops gleaming gently through the gloom, with winter irises, their violet splashed with yellow, splashed with white, beside daffodils that glimmered, too, in hands or laid upon the ground, against the wall, a carpet of flowers leading up to their door.

Inside the house, the smell of the damp, the rain upon their clothes, the smoke from too many cigarettes, but most of all the flowers, all the flowers and the wreaths. Jimmy knew none who lived that week, those days, that black week, those black days in that hushed, damp city of the Dead, none would forget that smell of grief, of loss.

In that house once filled with so much life, in its back room there, where Mark Jones had sat and had his breakfast, lunch and tea, talked, laughed and loved over every meal with his wife June, where he'd played with their young son Gary, his dog Rick and all the budgies and canaries which he treasured and he bred out back, or where, when the day was done, he'd sit and smoke that pipe of his, listening to the radio, a bit of music or the news, where the Dean of Manchester now said some kind and thoughtful words, ones of comfort, if not for now, perhaps then for later, then the Dean conducted a short service in that back room there, with the family, the friends, the neighbours of Mark Jones all gathered there with Jimmy, Joe, Bill and Arthur, too, Les, his wife Betty, Ken Ramsden and the members of the United board, some stood out in the hall, the kitchen, even on the stairs. Then, when this first, short service here was done, lifted in his mother's arms their young son Gary, together with his mummy, they placed a wreath of red and white carnations shaped into a football on his daddy's, her husband's, coffin, then, still carried in his mother's arms, Gary followed his daddy out of the house, their family home, for the last time, down the path, through the gate, and watched as the coffin was placed inside the back of the waiting hearse. Then little Gary and his mother June got into the car behind, and the cortège began its slow journey over the Moors to Wombwell, Barnsley, taking Mark Jones from Manchester back to Yorkshire, his other home.

*

Matt, in his bed, his hospital bed, wasn't sure if he'd heard a knock upon the door or the envelope fall upon the floor, but when he turned his head, looked past the empty chair where Jean would sit, twice a day, there on the floor, over by the door, there an envelope it lay, and then, though it was a strange, unworldly thing and made no sense, he knew, Matt could not help but watch himself rise up from the bed, the hospital bed, then see, saw himself as he stood and walked towards the door, bent down, picked up that envelope from the floor, held and turned it in his hand, opened the envelope, took the letter from inside and read: *Dear Matt, No doubt you will be surprised to get this letter from your old pal Louis. Well, Matt, I have been trying for the past month to find you and not having your Reg. address, I could not trust a letter going to Liverpool, as what I have to say is so important. I don't know if you have considered about what you are going to do when war is over, but I have a great job for you if you are willing to take it on. Will you get in touch with me at 37 Craigwell Road, Prestwich, and when you do I can explain things to you better, when I know there will be no danger of interception. Now Matt, I hope this is plain to you. You see I have not forgotten my old friend either in my prayers or in your future welfare. I hope your good wife and family are all well and please God you will soon be home to join their happy circle. Wishing you a very Happy Xmas and a lucky New Year. With all God's Blessings in you and yours. Your Old Pal, Louis Rocca.*

Sit down here, Matt.

Matt looked up from the letter in his hand, saw Walter Crickmer standing over by the table, the one opposite his bed, and Matt smiled at Walter, walked towards him as he said, Thank you, Walter, and sat down there with Walter, beside him at the table there.

Now if you will just sign here, Matt, said Walter, taking papers from his briefcase, placing them on top of the table, then handing Matt a pen, a fountain pen.

Matt took the fountain pen from Walter's hand and smiled and said again, Thank you, Walter, and then Matt put the pen to the paper and began to sign his name, but as the pen moved across the paper, the paper turned to sand, to grains of sand, which one by one they blew and into dunes they grew, rising over the paper, the pen, covering Matt's fingers, his hand, then up his arm, over the top of the table, and Matt turned in shock to Walter, but Walter smiled, sadly smiled, it seemed to Matt, and said, *Requiem aeternam dona eis, Domine . . .*

*

Les Olive and his wife Betty, along with Alma, had been working sixteen-, seventeen-, eighteen-hour days since that day last week, dealing with all the telephone calls and the post, the issue of tickets and so forth, while helping the families of those who had survived, their flights and their hotel in Munich, the care of the injured, as best they could, at the distance they were. Les, Betty and Alma had also been helping the families of the Dead to organise the funerals, and Mister Stiles, who was young Nobby's dad and who was an undertaker up in Collyhurst, he had been a rock, he really had, and helped a lot. And as much as they were able, Les and Betty and Alma had been attending as many of the funerals as they could themselves. Les had wondered, half hoped that the more funerals they attended, the easier it might get, but that was wrong; if anything, it got harder. Because they were not the same, the funerals, how could they be? Each man was different, each funeral different from the last, some words the same, of course, parts of the service, yes, but each funeral was different, each man different, and there was always something that no matter how hard Les wished, he hoped it wouldn't, there was always something that tore into his heart, that kept it broken and in pieces –

248

Today, this black day, here in Saint Ann's Church, here for the funeral of Walter Crickmer, a man Les had known almost all his life, it seemed to Les, it was the sight of Jimmy Murphy's own son Philip, along with Nobby Lawton and young Nobby Stiles, assisting Father Edmondson as altar boys today, it was this sight, the thought of what this must be like for them, these three young lads, all these young lads, it was that sight, that thought that made Les sway, reach for the pew in front, the hand of his wife, to steady, try to keep his legs, his balance, or what was left of that, to not fall back or down, any further down.

Les had been just fourteen, younger then than Nobby Stiles, Nobby Lawton and Philip Murphy, when he'd first joined United, in Forty-two, and apart from his National Service, Les had been here ever since. He'd been a regular in the junior and reserve teams, playing in every position bar outside-left. He had only played twice for the first team, in April 1953, and both times in goal, when Jack Crompton, Ray Wood and Reg Allen were all either injured or ill. But United had won the first game, two–one away at Newcastle, and drawn the second game, two-all at home to West Brom, so United with Les in the side had never been beaten. But those were his two and only appearances, and all that time Les had been at United, he'd been working as an office boy, on the administration side of the club, and later that year, in Fifty-three, Les was offered and accepted a full-time position as assistant secretary to Walter Crickmer.

Walter Crickmer had joined United as the club secretary in 1926 and had been at Old Trafford ever since. Twice Walter had been the manager of Manchester United: first from 1931 to '32, then from 1937 through the war until 1945, when Matt Busby then took charge. But it was Walter, along with Louis Rocca, who had stopped United from going under in 1931, who had helped convince James Gibson to buy and save the club, and then, together, Walter Crickmer, Louis Rocca and James Gibson had founded the Manchester United Junior Athletic Club, beginning a policy which became the United creed, the tradition of finding then cultivating local young players, uniting the best of those junior players with the senior members of the playing staff through common, shared ideas and techniques, and it was Walter and Louis who then brought in Bill Inglis, Arthur Powell and poor Tom Curry to help implement their new and noble philosophy of youth.

In his second spell, those eight-odd years as manager-cum-secretary or secretary-cum-manager, whichever way it was, Walter Crickmer had been in charge for more than seventy games, winning more than he lost or drew, seeing United promoted straight back to the First Division in 1938 and nurturing the likes of Johnny Carey, Allenby Chilton, Stan Pearson, Charlie Mitten and Johnny Aston, but surely Walter's greatest task, his biggest achievement, had been seeing the club through the war, then rebuilding Old Trafford from the ashes –

Through the late summer, autumn, then winter of 1940, into the spring of 1941, the Luftwaffe had heavily, repeatedly bombed Manchester, Salford and Stretford, the worst nights of the Manchester Blitz being the week before Christmas, when two thousand incendiaries and high explosives fell from the air, killing over a thousand folk, injuring thousands more and damaging the cathedral, the assize courts, the Free Trade Hall, the Royal Exchange, Victoria Station and thousands and thousands of homes. But on the night of March 11, 1941, the Luftwaffe came back again, targeting Trafford Park, but bombing Old Trafford, too, reducing the main stand to a burnt-out shell, turning the terraces to rubble and leaving a deep crater in the middle of the pitch itself.

That March night of fire and ash, Walter was serving as a special constable, patrolling past the ground, first knocked off his feet, buried under rubble, but quickly on his feet again and dusted down, he rushed to try to reach the dressing rooms, at least to save the kits, the boots, anything he could, but the flames, the smoke were much too thick and, beaten back, Walter could only stand and watch the ground, Old Trafford, burning to the ground. But in that moment, stood there upon the ashes of the ground, the smoke still thick and biting in the air, Walter vowed to see the stadium, Old Trafford, rise, rebuilt again, and, from that moment on, he was consumed with and by the task, writing letter after letter to the War Damage Commission, and the Minister of Works, with help in the House of Commons from Ellis Short, and from City, who agreed United could share their ground, Maine Road, and the Cliff for the reserve sides of both clubs.

But Les Olive knew better than most that the restoration of Old Trafford, the return of football and the club to the ground, was achieved only after infinite amounts of discussion and negotiation, hours and days and weeks and months and years of hard, hard work, and that that glorious restoration, that winning return were both down to Walter Crickmer, thanks to Walter Crickmer, and only to Walter Crickmer, the man whose shoes Les knew now he had to fill, and Les again, he gripped the back of the pew in front of him, the hand of his wife, and tried to focus, fix his eyes upon the high altar, the stained glass, the Virgin, her Mother and her Son.

After the Requiem Mass, fourteen policemen led the funeral procession of more than two hundred and fifty folk, from the club, of course, but from all walks of life, Manchester life, parts of the city, the county and the country, bearing wreaths and flowers, all the way along, from Saint Ann's Church to Stretford Cemetery, where Walter Raymond Crickmer, aged fifty-eight, was there buried, a dearly beloved husband and father, *in God's keeping until we meet again.*

Harry's head was pounding, so bad it woke him up, it kept him up, so hard the pounding he could not go, get back to sleep. So up he got, out of bed, went to the wardrobe, quiet as a mouse he was, opened the wardrobe door, the drawer with his hankies and his ties, took out a tie and tied it tight around his head. He closed the drawer, the wardrobe door, and was about to turn, go back to bed, to try to sleep, the tie tied tight around his head, but then he spied the suitcase, there in the corner, on the floor. He'd meant to put that case away, out of sight and out of mind, but now he picked it up and, quiet as a mouse again, he took it down the stairs, into the dining room, put it on the table there, slid back and pressed the catches, lifted up its lid, and there they were again, looking up at him again –

Sometimes it felt a year ago, sometimes an hour, but it was what, a week ago today? No, maybe it was Saturday, the Saturday morning, when they'd taken him and Bill and Duncan's mate back out to the site of the crash, when they had them picking through the wreckage. He remembered the snow, the slush, the cold and the damp, the acrid, almost stinging smell of the smoke still in the air, some seats intact, as good as new, others mangled, smashed to bits, but Harry couldn't remember picking up a thing, taking anything from that wreck, packing it away, bringing it back with him, on the train and on the boat, but looking down into his suitcase, he knew he had, he must have done, because there in his case, staring back at him, there was a hat and toy –

The trilby hat Mark Jones loved to wear, he always wore, sometimes tilted at an angle, rakish like a star, other times he'd take it off, stick it on little Eddie Colman's head when they were having their sing-song, 'Frankie and Johnny' they used to like to sing, Big Jimmie Rodgers and Little Jimmie Rodgers they were, that pair, but Mark would always end his turn with that hat back upon his head, pushed back on that big old head of his as he'd belt out 'On Ilkla Moor Baht 'at' again –

But beside that hat Mark loved to wear, but would not, would never wear again, there was the toy, a little clockwork clown with a little clockwork drum, the present Mark had bought for his wee lad Gary, the young son he loved to bits, the toy, the present he'd never give to the son he'd never see again –

Harry picked up the hat, turned it in his hand, his hands awhile, then placed the hat back down over the toy, that clown and its drum covered with the hat, out of sight, of mind again, then Harry, he closed and shut and locked the case, picked it up off the table and turned to walk towards the door –

Where the fuck are you going with that, big man, said the wall. Hiding it away again, yeah, brave man?

The case gripped tight in one hand, his other clenched into a fist again, Harry turned on and to the wall and said, The fuck it's got to do with you, eh?

Should be giving them things back to the poor fellow's wife and kiddie, to June and Gary, yeah, big man. Don't want people going around saying, You know that Harry Gregg, he robs from the Dead –

Harry put down the case, tightened the tie around his head, then held his fist up to the wall and said, Listen, fellow, I'll be giving these back, don't you worry.

Well, isn't that good of you now, said the wall, and grand to know, so just make sure you do, 'stead of creeping round here like a thief in the night –

Don't you worry about me, said Harry, staring at the wall, fists still clenched, I know what's right and what's wrong, what needs to be done –

Harry unclenched his right fist, held a finger up to the wall, pointed then wagged that finger at the wall a little while, then nodded to himself, turned from the wall, picked up the case from the floor and walked out of the room, through the door and up the stairs, back towards the bedroom, where before the door Harry paused, took the tie off, off from around his head, then he opened the bedroom door, stepped inside into the room and saw his wife in bed, their little girl in with her now, beside her there, hugged tight, held close, both looking up at him with worried eyes of love –

And Mavis said, I thought I could hear you talking to someone, love . . .?

Harry nodded once, then twice and said, Aye, er, I called Jimmy, Jimmy Murphy, about training.

Mavis smiled, she said, And . . .?

And I'm going, going in now.

Mavis laughed, she pointed at the case. Are you planning on staying the night?

No, said Harry, holding up the tie. No, I was just sorting out some stuff, my gear, you know.

Mavis pushed back the covers of the bed, their wee baby in her hands, held their daughter up to Harry and said, Take our Linda for us will you, love, while I get my dressing gown on then go see about your breakfast.

*

Mark Jones, in his coffin, in the hearse, arrived back from Manchester in Wombwell, where there was not a house without drawn curtains and where it seemed the whole of Wombwell had come out onto the pavements to stand with heads bowed in tribute as Mark went first back to the home of his father Amos and rested there on Bird Avenue a short while with June and Gary, June back in Wombwell, where she, too, was from, a Wombwell lass, Tune Street was her street. Then, an hour later, around two o'clock, the cortège set off again, this time for Saint Mary's Parish Church, where it was four years ago he and June had wed, when Jackie Blanchflower had been his best man and half the team at least had been there, but not today, no Jackie, Duncan, Roger Byrne or David Pegg today, where now, in black, players and staff came from Barnsley Football Club, from Sheffield Wednesday and from Wolves, and from Huddersfield there was Bill Shankly, their manager, but from United there was only Wilf and Gordon and a few of the others, their eyes ringed and red, turned to the ground as they walked with heavy steps, stood in pews again, as Canon Adkins told the mourners packed and pressed inside Saint Mary's Parish Church that this had been the saddest week, he knew, but then he spoke, he tried to speak not only of the tears, the tragedy, but of the better, best of human qualities, of sympathy, of understanding, the kindness of our hearts, and he spoke, too, of the joy Mark had brought to so many people and the pride that the people of Wombwell, Barnsley and Manchester felt watching that young boy grow into the footballer, the man he was, a man untouched, unchanged by the honours and the fame he won, and then the words all said, the service done, Mark in his coffin was carried to the graveside for the committal there, and then was there interred, with his mother Lucy, who was but three months dead herself, but now was with her son again, together there in death.

In life Mark had been a Yorkshire schoolboy international, an England schoolboy international, and the captain of them both. He had played one hundred and twenty-one first-team games for Manchester United and won two League Championship medals. He had been selected as a reserve for England and was thought by many to be the natural successor to Billy Wright when he retired. He liked to wear a hat, an old man's hat, and smoked a pipe, kept birds, of the feathered kind, and liked to walk and shoot with his best pal, his black Labrador called Rick, and this all kept him that bit apart from the other lads, even before he'd married June, his sweetheart since he was sixteen, she was fifteen, and they'd had a little boy, their Gary, and all his mates at United, they called him Dan, after Dan Archer, the fellow on the radio, the old patriarch of Brookfield farm, but it was not to hurt or mock they called him Dan, it was from love, born of respect for a wise old head upon those broad young shoulders, but he was not a man you'd mock in any case. He'd boxed back when he was a boy, and carried with him still a scar, the air of the ring, its canvas and its ropes, the corner and the gloves, but he was not a violent man nor quick to raise his voice in anger, and only rarely ever did, but he was strong in the tackle, knew how to win and clear a ball, in the air or on the ground, could boot that ball clean over any stand in the land. He truly was a giant of a man, but not just in stature, nor only on the pitch, but off the pitch, and with his heart, that giant-sized heart of his. But all Mark had wanted was a family, to play football, yes, of course, but then later to retire from football, leave all that behind, and have a pet shop, run that with June, and have more time to walk and shoot with his best pal, his dog Rick, to then grow old with June, see their children grow up, raise families of their own, bring round the grandchildren to see the budgies and canaries their grandad kept in the aviary out back. But none of that would happen now, knew June; they would never run that pet shop now; he would never walk and shoot again with his dog Rick; his brother Tom would try his best to look after, care for Rick, but the poor dog would pine for Mark and die a few months on, and nor could June manage all Mark's budgies and his canaries, there being fifty-four in the aviary he'd built out back, not with Gary and her expecting very soon. So June would put an advert in the local paper, *Good Homes Wanted for Budgies & Canaries*, and then one by one, or in pairs, as she preferred, June would give away the birds to the many children who came to knock upon her door. And then, four months on from this day, this black day in this black week, June would give birth to a baby girl, their daughter Lynn, whom Mark would never see, would never hold and know, watch grow up with Gary, raise families of their own, bring round the grandchildren to see the budgies and canaries in the aviary out back. No, they would not grow old together now, knew June, not even for another hour, together one more day. She had lost him now had June, forever lost that lovely, kind and honest man, that great husband and dad, dead at only twenty-four, and June looked, she stared at those red and white carnations, shaped into a football, there on the damp, wet ground beside his open grave, and June, she could not help but clench her fists and think, What had football done for Mark?

*

Bill said goodbye to Teresa at the door, left the house, went down the path, through the gate and in the rain, that same black and heavy rain, Bill set off for the ground again, back to Old Trafford, and back to work again.

Morning, said Bill, when he got to the ground, and the staff, the players that were there that day, not at a funeral, beside a grave, they said, Morning, Bill.

Bill went over to the baskets, picked out some kit, got stripped and changed into the kit, then followed Harry and the rest of them, them that were there that day, back out into the rain, to jog up to White City in that rain, then to run a lap or two as they always did, they always had, then after some sprints, then onto the pitch they went to play, to kick again, a ball again, to trap, to pass the ball, to run, to head, to dive, to tackle and to scrap, to shout, arguing the toss about this, the toss about that, fighting about this, about that, something and nothing, a late challenge here, a foot left in there, you kicking a bit out of him, him taking a bit out of you, but he was soon up on his feet again,

257

you soon back on your feet again, yeah, you'd not keep Harry Gregg down for long, Harry on his feet again, nor Bill Foulkes, Bill back on his feet again, Bill and Harry back on their feet again.

See you tomorrow then, said Bill, after the bath, Bill changed and dressed again, and Harry, in his towel still, looked up at Bill from the bench, nodded once and said, Aye, see you then.

*

They had cremated Alf Clarke, the 'Man Who Bled Manchester United Red Blood', on the Thursday of that black week, then the very next day, they cremated Tom Jackson, his friend and rival on the *Evening News*, who had covered Manchester United for a quarter of a century, and was the 'Man Who Lived for United', who lived and died for United, lived and died together with Alf Clarke.

Alf and Tom, Tom and Alf, like Murray and Mooney, Stan and Ollie or Flanagan and Allen, Alf the slim one, Tom the rounder man, like peas in a pod, rivals, yes, but old friends first, for twenty-five years, together they had covered, followed, reported on and swooned over Manchester United. Alf had his 'Casual Comments' in the *United Review*, while Tom had his 'United Topics' in the match-day programme, too.

But while Alf, it's fair to say, he would not dispute, was consumed with a deep and serious, nigh on religious devotion to the United cause, Tom was the more cheerful, comfortable man to be about, always with a ready, happy smile, no less partisan in his passion for the club, but with the air of a man who felt just blessed, thankful to be doing a thing he loved to do, that thousands would give their right arm to do, paid to watch, to write about Manchester United every day . . .

Yes, Tom Jackson knew he was a lucky man, a very lucky man, and knew it because he'd known less lucky, much less lucky men and women, children, too, during and then in the aftermath of the war, in the work he'd done behind the lines, then seeing first-hand the concentration camps, the death factories, then tracking down the butcherers and torturers of those camps and factories, and had been part of the squad who had found and caught Irma Grese, who was never 'the Beautiful Beast' to Tom but always *die Hyäne von Auschwitz.*

The cortège of two hearses, one carrying Tom's coffin, the other bearing all the flowers, the tributes and the wreaths, left Tom's home in Kingsway, East Didsbury, towards the middle of that afternoon, that black afternoon, that last black day of that black week, went via Stockport Road, London Road, Piccadilly and Market Street onto Cross Street in the centre, where Tom in his coffin in the hearse halted, paused and stopped outside the offices of the *Manchester Evening News*, where the workers and Tom's colleagues on the *Evening News* stood in silence on the street outside, then, with a police motorcycle escort, the cortège, joined by scores of cars carrying his colleagues and other mourners, made its way back out of the centre of the city, through Albert Square, past Central Station, along Russell Street it went, on Chorlton Road, Brook's Bar, Upper Chorlton Road, Manchester Road, onto Barlow Moor Road and the crematorium, Manchester Crematorium again, where only the day, the afternoon before his pal, his friendly rival Alf, had come, brought with him sportsmen and writers from clubs and papers near and far, and now again today, this afternoon, many of those same men, same writers, from the same papers and same clubs, came this way again, with other, different men and women, but young and old again, those friends he'd never met but who'd read Tom every day, in the *Evening News*, every teatime, after work or after school, they read and felt they knew the man, Tom Jackson of the *Evening News*, here together with the friends Tom knew, Tom's many friends, his family, his wife and children, all there

259

that day, that afternoon, to say goodbye, farewell to the man, the colleague and the friend, the husband and the father who had lived for United.

*

Who was this Kraut, thought Frank, this jolly, stocky Kraut in his doctor's coat who strode in every morning, then twice or more at least each day, carried on like he owned the bloody place he did, was he the Camp Commandant this chap, thought Frank, with his Now zen, Jackie, *wie geht es Ihnen*, full of the old Boche blarney, *Guten Morgen, Herr Taylor*, sir, *wie geht es dem* leg today, and then he'd start to poke around in Frank's leg again, with his scalpel and his forceps and that ever-beaming smile of his, fishing out odd bits of metal, cleaning out the dirt, and though it never hurt, it only ached at worst, Frank always tried to see what was going on, what it was the man was doing to his leg, straining to listen, to catch the whispered words with his assistants and the nurses, and that was how, today, Frank heard him mutter, *Die Wunde hier am Bein hat eine Infektion . . .*

Infektion, infection, INFECTION, Frank swore, was sure he heard Kommandant Herr Otto Fritz just say, just now, in among his usual double *Deutsch*, and Frank, he felt his blood run cold, what little blood they'd left him with, had let him keep, as thoughts, as fears of gangrene and of amputation ran in horror, in terror through his veins, up his spine, to his mind, and Frank tried, tried not to scream, hard not to shout, I'd bet you'd like nothing more than to take an English leg, this fine old leg of mine, you filthy, sneaky little Hun! Well, by Jove, you'll not take this English leg, not without a fight you won't, I'll tell you that, you jumped-up Jerry Kraut!

But then Frank saw his wife, sat there beside the bed, saw her rise to her feet, the look upon her face, and in different

260

horror, different terror, Frank realised, knew all the things he'd thought, he'd said, he'd said aloud, and Frank felt his face, his cheeks turn crimson as his wife Peggy, she stood over, looked down on Frank, on his back, in his bed, and sternly said, Frank Taylor, you should be ashamed of yourself. Professor Maurer, his staff, every doctor, every nurse in this hospital have worked day and night, day in, day out, for hours without sleep, to save the lives of your colleagues and your friends, and moreover your own life, too, and never with a moment's grumble or complaint, with never a bad-tempered or sharp word. They really, truly are the kindest, most conscientious and professional group of men and women one could ever hope to meet, and though I know you're very ill, and so not quite yourself, still you really should be ashamed of all those things you've said, Frank, you really should . . .

And he was, Frank was ashamed, but still, yet still he was afraid, Frank was afraid he had gangrene in his leg, that they would come to knock him out, to put him under, then once he was under, while he slept, they'd wheel him out of this room, take him down the corridor, in the elevator to the theatre, and there they'd amputate, take off his leg, so when he woke, all groggy and confused and tried, then tried to wiggle the five toes on his right foot, there'd be no toes, there'd be no foot, no five toes and no right foot, and he'd whip back the bedclothes to find his whole leg gone, he had no leg!

Frank Taylor, said Peggy sternly once again, and Peggy had never once spoken sternly to Frank before, had never dared, in fact, but now still sternly said, You are being quite ridiculous. There is not the slightest chance that these doctors and nurses would ever do such a thing. They have gone out of their way to keep me informed, and they have done the same for all the other wives and families who are out here. And neither myself nor anyone else has had the slightest cause to doubt them.

Frank nodded, but said, That may be so, but my leg is infected, I know it is, I heard them say . . .

Yes, Frank, said Peggy, your leg is infected, but the doctors have assured me the infection is not gangrene, and so you should be thankful of that, and that you are not maimed or blinded, and that you are alive, and realise how thankful we all are that you are alive. What about poor George or Eric, or Henry Rose or Donny Davies? They're not here to complain, are they?

*

The Requiem Mass had ended, the hearse and cortège had left for Stretford Cemetery, but Philip Murphy, Norbert Lawton and Norbert Stiles had stayed behind in Saint Ann's Church to put away the vessels, to tidy up a bit, take off their vestments, fold and put away the cassocks and the surplices, then, stood outside the church, at its gates, in the rain, the rain again that never seemed to go away, Norbert Lawton and Norbert Stiles said goodbye to Philip Murphy, who was going to go back home then head up to the ground, and so maybe he'd see them then, see them later, but then as they were walking up the Chester Road, Nobby Lawton stopped at a bus stop, lit a cig and said, I'm going to get the bus from here, Nobby.

Are you not off back to the ground?

Nobby Lawton shook his head and said, I've got to go into bloody work, me, haven't I?

But what about Coly's funeral, said Nobby Stiles. It's this afternoon. Are you not going to go?

Nobby Lawton took a pull off his cigarette, then shook his head again. Boss said if I was serving, I could have the time off, but Eddie wasn't a Catholic, was he?

Wasn't he, said Nobby Stiles. Are you sure?

262

Nobby Lawton laughed. Course I'm sure I'm sure, and you'll find out I'm right and all, if you're off.

Course I'm off, said Nobby Stiles. It's Coly.

Nobby Lawton saw the bus coming down the Chester Road, took one last pull, then threw his cig into the road, and said, Well, say goodbye to him from me, will you, Nobby, please, and I'll see you tomorrow.

All right, I will, said Nobby Stiles, and yeah, then I'll see you tomorrow morning then . . .

But Nobby Lawton and his bus were already gone, soaking the younger Nobby's trousers, his best trousers, his socks and shoes as they went, and Nobby cursed, asked for forgiveness, sighed and shook his head, then off he set again, up the Chester Road, over the bridge, the canal, through Gorse Hill, thinking, Rain, rain, will you not effing go away and come again another day, until at last young Nobby came to Warwick Road again, turned right there and then was back again, at the ground again, but it seemed he was the only one –

No doubt, he thought, those folk who'd not gone on to Stretford Cemetery, they must still be over Yorkshire way, in Barnsley for Mark Jones, and so young Nobby wondered what to do because he didn't know now where Coly's funeral was going to be, which church it was, him thinking, assuming it was at Saint Joseph's, but if what Nobby Lawton said was right, then it couldn't be at Saint Joseph's then, could it, not if Eddie was a Prod, not that it mattered to Nobby, made no odds to him.

But as he walked around the ground, keeping close to the stands, the walls, their bricks, in their shadows, out of the rain, as best he could, young Nobby did not see a single soul, and every door he tried was locked, and Nobby thought, That's effing strange is that . . .

But on he walked, around and round the ground he went, how many times, he did not count, just thinking someone soon is bound to come, it's Old Trafford, not the bloody moon, and if not soon, he'd just have to go and buy a paper from the shop, because the papers printed stuff like that, about funerals, things like that, he knew they did, his dad being in the trade, but suddenly as he walked his feet just stopped, he didn't know why, they just stopped and would not budge, but then when he looked up, saw where he was, Nobby knew the reason why –

He'd come to that stretch of concrete beside the ground where every Friday afternoon, any other Friday afternoon, there would be twenty-two players here, the first team and the second string, in a game, a match in baseball boots, and they'd be shouting, they'd be swearing, laughing and joking, showing off with bits of skill or landing on their arses, magicking, summoning a world you could not wait to join, and Nobby would stand there, here on this very spot –

Transfixed –

Now what's with the long face, son, and on one so very young?

Nobby had such a fright, he jumped so much he was surprised to see his skin still on his bones, but was more puzzled than afraid when he turned to see a tiny little man, smaller even than young Norbert here himself, dressed in a cloth cap and plus fours, with a tartan travel rug over his left arm –

I am sorry, son, please pardon me, said the man, with a quick, apologetic touch up to his cap. I didn't mean to give you such a start, it's just you look so very sad.

Nobby squeezed and wiped his nose, then sniffed up and said, I've just been serving at a funeral and I'm off to another in a bit. I've been to that many this week, if you asked me how many, then I'd have to stop to count.

May I ask, asked this strange, oddly happy man, whose funeral it is you'll be attending next?

Nobby wiped his fingers on his trousers, sniffed up again and said, Coly, er, Eddie Colman's funeral.

Ah, 'Snake Hips' Colman, sighed the man. Oh, what a truly gifted young half-back is Colman! Each time I've had the good fortune to see young 'Snake Hips' play, he is the *premier danseur* in Manchester's ballet, and when he is in such a mood, we should have the Beswick Prize Band accompany him with snatches from *Swan Lake*, then we shall see the little fellow at his best, will we not?

But he's dead, isn't he, said Nobby.

Is he really, asked the man, this strange, oddly happy man in his cloth cap and plus fours, with his travelling rug, his finger raised. Then who, pray tell, is that . . .?

Dancing out of the rain, the shadows of the Stretford End, between the drops and puddles, across the concrete and the gravel there, a small and chubby cherub of a lad who, with a cheeky Salford grin, one swivel, a little wiggle of his hips, he sent the world a different, better way, made the world a different, better place, and what a glorious feeling it was, to be happy again, laughing at clouds, so dark up above . . .

*

Every time it rains, it rains Pennies from Heaven, Marjorie was singing to herself, but only in her head, thinking to herself, telling herself, trying to convince herself, Each cloud contains Pennies from Heaven . . .

He was always the sharp one was Eddie, with the drainpipe trousers and the winkle-picker shoes, and of course he had the sideburns down to here, the real Teddy Boy image, but he was never a Teddy Boy. But he always wanted to look smart, they all did, had to look smart, so say it was in the taxi, into town, they'd all be sitting on the edge of the seat so they wouldn't crease their jackets, keeping their legs out because they had to look flawless, absolutely flawless, when they got there, into town, the Cromford Club, the Continental or the Spare Wheel, and in they'd walk with a whistle and a swagger, but Eddie had his shuffle, always with that little shuffle . . .

That night Marjorie first met Eddie, he just asked her if she'd like to dance, and she said, Yes, and obviously she thought he was cute, and so she said, What do you do for a living, and now sometimes Eddie would say he was a painter and decorator, that was his favourite, and sometimes he'd say he was a docker, but that night he just smiled and said, I work in Trafford Park, and Marjorie, she thought, Oh, very nice, very nice . . .

Eddie was really chuffed, told his best pal Johnny, I've met this lovely girl, you know, and Johnny said, Oh, yeah, yeah? Yeah, yeah, said Eddie, yeah.

They just got sort of friendly, and then the week after they'd met, Eddie asked Marjorie to go out with him, and it just sort of went from there . . .

'Pennies from Heaven', that was his song, 'Pennies from Heaven', because he thought he had a great voice, Eddie, and after everything had finished on a Saturday, they'd all have a bit of a sing-song, and Bobby would get up, Bobby would sing, and Bobby did actually have a fabulous voice. He sounded a bit like Bing Crosby, or was it Frank Sinatra?

But try as she might, as hard as she could, singing that song to herself, thinking of the good times, and only the good times, the two years they'd had together, to keep herself strong, not just for herself, but for Eddie's mam and especially his dad, but try as she might, as hard as she could, singing that song, bloody song to herself, Marjorie could not stop thinking about the night she last saw Eddie, when he'd kept on saying, I wish I didn't have to go . . .

And she'd said, I can't believe it! You've got this fabulous job! You can go all over the place . . .

Marge, he said, I don't want to go.

*

He's done what, said Jimmy into the telephone, back up in his office, a cup of Cissie Charlton's special tea in his other hand, he said again, He's done fucking what?

He's disappeared, said Paddy down the line from a phone box in Blackpool, on the Golden Mile.

I know he's bloody little, said Jimmy, but he can't have fucking disappeared, Pat. He must be somewhere.

I know he must be somewhere, Jimmy, said Paddy, but I don't know where that somewhere is.

But you always know everything, Pat, you or your brother. You must be able to find him . . .

I'm looking, we're all looking, Jimmy, but his missus, she said he'd a call from Sunderland, first thing this morning, and then off he went, up and out the door, without a word, not seen hide nor hair of him since.

Jimmy shook his head. Jesus, Mary and Joseph, Paddy, as if I've not enough to deal with . . .

I'll find him, Jimmy, said Paddy, promised Paddy, bring him to you, you just sit tight –

It's Eddie Colman's funeral, said Jimmy, so I'll not be sitting tight, Pat, but dear God, please, have that little snake here waiting for me when I get back.

Jimmy put down the telephone, took a swig of Cissie's special tea, then picked up the phone again, dialled the North-East, got through to the Chairman of Sunderland Football Club and said, Ernie Taylor has agreed to sign for Manchester United, so hands off!

Now, Mister Murphy, said the Chairman of Sunderland Football Club, a military man he was, I must, in fairness, tell you that we discussed Taylor several weeks ago and have been in contact with Blackpool with reference to the price, and while we have no wish to cut across you in your grievous situation –

Good, said Jimmy, because it would be a terrible thing, would it not, if the press were to find out that Sunderland Football Club were stealing our players while we were still burying our dead . . .

*

That black day, that black week, the last of the funerals of the Dead was for the youngest of the Dead, and there were thousands and thousands out again that afternoon, black afternoon, in the rain, the pouring rain, on each side of the street, from Archie Street to Saint Clement's Church, off Hulton Street, on Groves Avenue, where last Thursday night his mam and dad had come to pray, just last Thursday night, to pray and pray, unanswered prayers, and after the service at Saint Clement's there, there were thousands, thousands more, stood all up Phoebe Street, along Regent Road, all along Eccles New Road, down Cemetery Road to the cemetery itself, through its gates and on its paths, thousands and thousands coming out of their factories, their offices, their schools and their homes, waiting for the cortège, watching it pass, in mourning black or United red, sheaves of flowers in their hands, they stood and wept as Eddie passed, some throwing flowers in his path, into the road, onto the hearse, a flower for a flower, all those flowers, fallen in the rain, then in the rain, the Salford rain, they buried Eddie Colman, the dear and only son of Richard and Elizabeth Colman, who was just twenty-one years old the day he died, had played just one hundred and eight times for United but who would forever be 'Snake Hips', 'the Boy with the Marilyn Monroe Wiggle', that little Salford lad who, as Jimmy

268

Murphy had once said, could make the rain, rain go away, the sun come down and dance with him and kiss his tiny Salford arse.

*

I once kissed the arse of Cliff Jones, fat lot of fucking good it did me, now the silly boyo's only gone and gone to bloody Spurs, but, Ernie, here and now, I swear, swore Jimmy, back up in his office, staring across the desk at Little Ernie Taylor, both men still dripping wet, half drowned from the rain and from the night, but Jimmy, with his finger pointed to his heart, he swore again, I swear I'll get down on my hands and bloody knees, in this office, here and now, and kiss those tiny little bloody feet of yours, or anywhere you please, if you'll just give me a season, till the end of this fucking season, please.

Ernie Taylor sighed, shook his head and said, I'm sorry, Jimmy, I am, but we've been thinking of moving back to the North-East for a while now, getting away from here, from all the memories like . . .

You think you're going to leave all your memories back here in Lancashire, do you, son?

You know what I mean, Jimmy. I can't even pass an ice-cream parlour, it doesn't come back, all comes back to us again, and everybody always knows, don't they? You know, I just pop out for a paper, a bit of distraction like, but the fellow in the shop, the other customers, they all mean well like, but they all know, don't they?

Ernie, I know they know, said Jimmy. But everybody will know back up in Sunderland, won't they? And then you'll have it all to go through again . . .

Ernie shook his head again. But it's not where it happened, is it, Jimmy? I just think we'd be better off away from here, up in the North-East like.

Ernie, listen to me, said Jimmy. Every bloody brick, every fucking stick of furniture in this place, every second of every minute of every hour of every day reminds me of all I've bloody lost, but you think if I fucked off to live in Timbuk-bloody-tu I'd forget? Forget my pals, forget Bert and Tom, and all them boys we've lost? The best men and boys you'd ever meet . . .?

Ernie said, Jimmy, please –

No, Ernie, you listen to me now, because bad enough as this all is for me, the same for everybody here, half of Manchester or more, but some of our young lads here, the ones we've left, they're hardly more than boys, Ernie, just young boys, and so I have to show them that we can go on, that we don't give in to grief, and so I need you, Ernie, need you to help me show them that we can go on, that life, this bloody life, it does go fucking on.

Ernie Taylor looked up at Jimmy Murphy, back across the desk at Jimmy, and Ernie wiped one eye, then the other, nodded and then said, Okay.

*

Poor Eddie's dad, said Cissie down the line from Manchester to Munich, you should have seen him, Bobby, the poor fellow is broken, love. His cousin Albert, too, his best pal Johnny. Steve Fleet and Wilf, poor Wilf, you should have seen them, Bobby, love . . .

Bobby on his hotel bed, his suitcase packed and at his feet, he swallowed then tried but failed again to speak.

And his poor mother, said Cissie, she told me, a few times she's told me now, how when Eddie left to go, he bent down to kiss her goodbye and he said to her, I'm going now, Lizzie, and he bent down, but she said, Oh, don't kiss me, Edward, she said, I've got a cold, and she can't forgive herself, you know, she wasn't to know, was she, but she just can't stop thinking, keeps thinking, I never even kissed my son goodbye . . .

Bobby put the phone to one side, his elbows resting on his legs, the tops of his legs, his face in his hands, buried in his hands, six foot under if he could, and Bobby shook, he shook and wept, shook and wept for Eddie, and for David and for Tommy, for Mark Jones, for Billy Whelan, for Geoff Bent and Roger Byrne, and for Bert and Tom, for Bert Whalley and Tom Curry, too, not knowing what else he would, could ever do.

*

I have never doubted that Manchester United's courage would help them rise again, declared Ernie Taylor, back out in the rain, the night, before the pressmen gathered there, with Jimmy Murphy, Harold Hardman and Louis Edwards at his side, Paddy McGrath and his brother back behind him in the shadows there. And I am more certain than ever after my experience tonight. I've met some grand people in Manchester tonight. It's nice to know there are so many fine people, like the United Chairman, Mister Harold Hardman here, and his fellow directors, left in the game. In fact, when I walked into the Manchester United office and saw Mister Murphy and other members of the staff, then the directors, I felt a surge of confidence. This is a challenge I gladly accept, a challenge I shall meet with everything I have, and if I can only help in some way to put this great club back where they belong, then I shall be satisfied. I knew many of the boys in the crash . . .

His eyes looking up into the rain, the night, above the stand, the ground, Ernie paused, swallowed then whispered, now said, And the first who springs to mind is Duncan Edwards, naturally enough perhaps, because he has been my opponent so often. And I have had my good days against him, and he has had his good days against me, but what a wonderful player. And thinking of Duncan, it only makes me wish I were a few years younger, that I could turn back the clock . . .

Ernie paused, swallowed again, whispered again, then said, For he exuded the spirit of youth, if ever a player did. And most players would feel honoured to play for his team, for United, and I feel a proud man, too, to play for them, too. I have always admired them, and naturally, if I were six or seven years younger, I would be even happier. But experience and youth do not always come together in the one player. But combined on the playing field they can work wonders. And so tomorrow morning, in training, I shall meet the boys, and I'm sure I shall like them, and I hope they will like me.

What about Sunderland, Ernie, asked one of the pressmen gathered there, in the rain, the night. Were you not tempted to head back there for a last hurrah?

Yes, said Ernie, nodded Ernie, and lots of people may be surprised that I have not held on until I had a chance to go back to the North-East and home. And it's true, it seemed at one time this week that this might happen. But then I sat down to think things over. And, yes, I was brought up in the North-East. I was born there. But surely if they wanted me so badly, they should have kept me there, never let me go? And then I thought about United's great traditions, and I thought, too, about the fine journalist friends from Manchester whom I knew so well, and my mind was quickly made up, and I said to myself, Ernie, it must be Manchester United. Let's see what can be done, and so to the fans I say, I will do my very best, and to the critics, We cannot be good all the time, so if I'm on the receiving end of it, fair enough, I can take it.

Jimmy, asked the pressmen, what was it that persuaded you Ernie was the man for you?

I saw Ernie play only once, said Jimmy, with a wink, a twinkle, in the rain, the night, when his side beat us, and he was magnificent. And that was quite enough to make up my mind, that memory alone.

Late that Friday night, after the funeral, the service at Saint Clement's Church, the burial at Weaste Cemetery, the cups of tea, the bottles of beer, the whisky and the brandy, back in the house here on Archie Street, the people, the well-wishers all now gone, his mam already up the stairs to her bed, just his dad, his cousin Albert and best pal Johnny, in their suits, their damp, wet funeral suits, their ties loose, collars unbuttoned now, in that room downstairs, oh, the times, the laughs they'd had in this room, the songs they'd sung, in the silence now, his dad, his cousin Albert and best pal Johnny, just sat round, staring at the table now, those objects gathered there, brought back from Munich, from the wreckage of that bloody plane and then given back to them by Wilf, in a paper bag, now on the table there, Eddie's wallet with its few pound notes, an apple and an orange, the quarter of tea and pound of sugar his mam had packed for him –

You know, he used to say, said his mam Lizzie from the doorway, in her dressing gown, suddenly standing there again, he used to say, You're the worst mum in the world, you are, you're a terrible mother, you are, because I'd never let him have a bike, because I was frightened of him getting hurt or killed on the road. But I wish now I'd let him have a bike . . .

*

Cissie was looking for Jimmy again, to say, Goodbye, I must be off, we're going to pick our Bobby up, our Jackie, his wife Pat and me, on Sunday like, but I'll be back and see you soon, and if there's anything you need, you just say, just let me know, you will do that, you must promise me that now, won't you, pet? But once again, Jimmy wasn't in his office, the empty cup upon his desk, that cup of Cissie Charlton special tea she'd made, nine parts whisky, one part tea, gone again, down in one again, no doubt, and so off she set again, around the ground again, in the dark, the night again, thinking of that shade, that shadow of a man she'd met last night, was it then, still wondering who that could have been, that strange and sad but somehow happy, nameless man, but then around the corner as she came, she saw Jimmy up ahead, there at last he was, was sure it was, in the darkness up ahead, pacing with his thoughts, alone there in the dark, the night, and Cissie was about to say, call out, There you are, Jimmy, I've been looking everywhere for you, pet, but then she stopped, watched him wander on, in a conversation with his shadow or maybe with that shadow man, deep in darkness and in conversation Jimmy was, and Cissie thought it better not to interrupt, and so she turned, she walked away again, left Jimmy with the shadows there.

*

In the shadows, in the dark, walking round and round the ground, in the dark of its shadows, Jimmy was thinking about the war again, those German bombers and the ruin of this ground, still a bombed-out shell it was when he'd joined up here with Matt in Forty-six. Some sort of pokey little dive of an office where Walter operated. But the business of the directors, all that sort of stuff, was carried on at Mister Gibson's office at his cold-storage firm in Cornbrook. Then Matt got hold of a Nissen hut, which the lads used for changing, but the practice pitch was a mile or so away. It was a right old topsy-turvy set-up, but they'd just got on with things, and the foundations had been laid, in many ways, by poor old Walter, Louis Rocca and Mister Gibson, all three of them now gone, helped by Bill and Arthur and poor old Tom, and perhaps the best thing Matt and Bert and Jimmy ever did was just to keep on doing what they were already doing here, just keep on keeping on, with Joe and all the other scouts they had, gathering the youngsters, whoever they were –

It made Jimmy laugh when he heard folk say United was a Roman club, and only Catholics need apply, that their best scouts, their greatest agents were all the priests of England, Scotland, Wales and Ireland, when most of their tip-offs came from teachers who were simply just United mad. But if that lad showed promise, then he was for them, whether he was a Muslim, a Hindu or, God forbid, an atheist. Because what they looked for was basic skill, an innate instinct which they could then help to develop. But most of all, for Jimmy and for Matt, for Bill and Arthur, for poor old Bert and Tom and Walter, for every one of them the most important thing of all was a genuine, heartfelt desire to want, to really, really bloody fucking want to play for Manchester United –

9

They called for blood, in the night, the German, Munich night, the doctors and the hospital, they needed blood for Duncan, to give him blood, to stop the bleeding, staunch the haemorrhaging, the haemorrhaging so severe that the nurses had dashed from Duncan's bed, from the ward, woken Professor Maurer, who rushed to the boy, and when he saw the boy, Professor Maurer feared the worst, called Gladstone, Annie and Molly back from the hotel to the hospital, and told them, Duncan is bleeding internally, suffering severe haemorrhages, and unfortunately, the use of the artificial kidney has reduced the ability of his blood to clot, which would stop the bleeding. We have already given Duncan one blood transfusion, but we will need to give him several more, I'm sure. So we are contacting registered blood donors, through police radio patrol cars, who, as we speak, are on their way –

Through the night, their lights and sirens, blue and red, howling, wailing through the German, Munich night, police cars rushed to the homes of donors, German, Munich donors, to knock upon their doors, rouse them from their sleep, their beds, bringing the donors and their blood, as many as they could, to the Rechts der Isar Hospital, to take their blood, as much as they could, to give to Duncan, give him their blood, to stop the bleeding, staunch the haemorrhaging –

Molly, Annie and Gladstone, in the chapel of the Rechts der Isar Hospital, on their knees, they prayed, oh, how they prayed and prayed that God would save their boy, Our Duncan, my Duncan, please, God, please . . .

Thank God, thought Jimmy, he could put away his funeral suit, leave it in the wardrobe, upstairs in Whalley Range, hoped it would be a long time now before he'd ever have to take it out and put it on again. And thank God, then, he was back in his training gear, his football boots again, back in the dressing room with what was left of him, what was left of all of them. But thank you, God, you left us even this –

Jimmy and Bill Inglis and Arthur Powell had gathered all they had, professional and amateur alike, at Old Trafford first thing that Saturday morning, then, all changed and ready, they jogged off up the Chester Road to White City for training and then a game again, a practice match, so Jimmy could see for himself, with his eyes, his own eyes, yes, but in among them on the pitch, in his gear, his boots, getting stuck in, playing alongside and among the likes of young David Gaskell, Alex Dawson and Mark Pearson, Ronnie Cope and Ian Greaves, Freddie Goodwin and Colin Webster, Bobby Harrop and Shay Brennan, to feel, to sense what they had and what they lacked, Jimmy keen to feel, to sense, too, how Little Ernie Taylor fitted in, how Billy Foulkes and Harry Gregg were doing, too, would they be ready or would they not for Sheffield Wednesday on Wednesday night, but thank God, thought Jimmy, for Harry Gregg, for there was Harry, diving here, leaping there, Harry was every-fucking-where, and thank God for that, at least, thought Jimmy, may God forgive me, please.

Meanwhile, up at the Cliff, in Broughton, by the Irwell, off Lower Broughton Road, on the ground where, once upon a time, under their brand-new floodlights there, Duncan Edwards had scored five, David Pegg had scored five, John Doherty had scored five, Eddie Lewis had scored four and four other lads had each scored one and Manchester United had beaten Nantwich

Town twenty-three–nil in the FA Youth Cup, but the Nantwich keeper, he'd played so well that Matt Busby had signed him on, but where at the Cliff today there was another game, early on that Saturday morning, some of the younger boys that United had in a match with nine boys who had been offered trials, from teams in the Manchester and District League and the Federation of Boys' Clubs, watched over by Joe Armstrong and Les Olive and a host of eager dads and most reluctant mams, and by Jimmy's young lad Phil, who knew a thing or two about who was good and who was not among the local lads, Phil helping Joe sort through all the letters that had come in, had flooded in, three tea chests full they had to sift and sort, from almost every man or boy, it seemed, had ever kicked a ball, all offering their services, their wonderous multitudes of skills to the A and B teams of Manchester United, so at least then United could fulfil their fixtures.

But after one half of watching these young boys today, Little Joe, he shook his head, walked over to young Phil Murphy and said, Hey up, Phil, lad, he said, said Joe, I think you best join in yourself –

So off Phil went, out onto the pitch to join Nobby Lawton and Nobby Stiles out there with Jimmy Elms and Frank Haydock, Johnny Giles and Reg Hunter, playing with or against these nine young boys who had been offered trials. But by the end of that second half, of those nine boys who had been offered trials, only one had caught Joe's eye, or two, if you counted Phil, and Joe knew there would be eight very disappointed boys tonight, eight even more disappointed dads, though some mams who'd think it probably for the best, but Joe knew that the most disappointed man of all would be Phil's own dad Jimmy, who'd been hoping against hope they'd find some wonder boy, from a letter in the tea chests, some boy who was so good, was just so good that the second you saw him, you knew, you just knew that here was a boy so good, he'd be playing in the first team well before he'd turned twenty, like Duncan had, like Bobby had.

Where are you going, Bobby?

I'm going home.

But how come you're going home and I'm not? How come you're walking away with your suitcase packed and I'm stuck here?

Bobby stared back at his face, his own face in the bathroom mirror, shaved and washed, hair brushed and parted, swept back and up into a bit of a quiff, the clean white shirt, the smart, straight tie, and Bobby shook his head, swallowed and then said, I'm sorry, Dunc, I just don't know.

*

Doctor Graham Taylor of British European Airways went to look for Gladstone, Annie and Molly, and found them on their knees in the chapel of the hospital. He led them back out into the corridor, sat them down upon some chairs and told them, The doctors have given Duncan several blood transfusions now, and it would appear that the bleeding has been halted, it's stopped, at least for now.

Oh, thank you, God, oh, thank you, cried Annie, in the corridor, beneath the harsh and brutal lights, her eyes up to those lights, the ceiling, the unseen and hidden sky above, where God, she knew in her heart, knew now He lived up there above, in heaven up above.

But Doctor Taylor did not want to raise hopes, hopes he feared would soon be dashed, and so he cautioned them that Duncan still remains dangerously ill, unfortunately, his condition still unchanged . . .

But what about the kidney machine, asked Gladstone. Will they have to use that again?

Doctor Taylor shook his head and said, I'm sorry, Mister Edwards, it's really too early to say. It was used for seven hours yesterday, as you know.

But is it helping him, Doctor, asked Gladstone.

Doctor Taylor nodded. Yes, absolutely. But the thing that is helping Duncan the most is his fighting spirit, his strong will to live. Neither Professor Maurer nor I, nor any of the doctors and the nurses, have ever seen such pluck. Being in such splendid physical condition, too, before the accident. All these things are helping Duncan.

Is he conscious, Doctor, asked Molly.

Doctor Taylor nodded again, said again, Yes, Duncan's been conscious all the time –

Can I see him then, asked Annie.

Doctor Taylor shook his head. I'm very sorry, but he's still very restless, so I've actually had to tell him to keep quiet, to try not to talk more than necessary . . .

I know, I see, said Annie, looking up to the lights, the ceiling again, that unseen, hidden sky above.

*

Back from White City, back at Old Trafford, out of his training gear, his boots again, back in his club blazer, his flannels and his smartest shoes, Jimmy met up with Joe and Les and Harold Hardman, too, to decide what it was that they next should do. Just tell me, Jimmy, please, said Les, where to go and who to watch, and I'll be there.

In his cramped, damp office, the rain so loud and heavy that he feared for the animals, Jimmy joked, We'll need another bloody ark if this keeps up. But if the games are on, they're not

280

called off, then me and Joe are going to head up to Turf Moor, see Jack Crompton, have a word with Jack, make sure he's all set for Monday.

Yes, said Harold Hardman, the Luton Chairman called me, Mister Mitchell, and –

He's not a happy man is he, said Jimmy.

No, he's not, said Harold Hardman, and had things with us been otherwise, he'd have never countenanced letting Jack come back.

Well, would that things were bloody otherwise, had been bloody otherwise, said Jimmy, yeah?

Now, now, Jimmy, said Harold Hardman, Percy Mitchell was one of the very first to offer assistance, and while letting Jack come back wasn't what he had in mind, he's been as good as his word, and he's kept his word.

Don't worry, sir, said Jimmy, I'll be the very picture of gratitude if I see him at Burnley.

But where do you want me to go, said Les again, diplomatically, saving Jimmy, sparing Mister Hardman.

Maine Road, son, said Jimmy, if the game is on.

Still thinking about Alec Govan then, said Les.

That's what everyone thinks, laughed Jimmy, and what I want everyone to think. But I want you to keep your good eye on their left-back, son, Dickie Neal Junior.

The lad they got from Lincoln, said Les.

The very fellow, said Jimmy.

Well then, I'd better go to Maine Road, too, said Harold Hardman. But I cannot see how Birmingham could afford to release anyone, not with the season they are having, the position they are in. Harry Morris will not be happy, I can tell you that.

Jimmy laughed, Jimmy said, Chairmen are never happy, Mister Hardman, sir, you should know that.

Later, Bobby would say, would write that Jimmy Murphy took him by train to the Hook of Holland for the ferry to Harwich, because no doubt that's what Bobby thought he remembered, how Bobby wished it had been; Bobby and Jimmy, Jimmy and Bobby, on the train, up through Germany, talking about football, only football, Bobby listening and learning from Jimmy, planning and scheming with Jimmy, on into Holland and onto the ferry, Jimmy with his silly jokes and tall tales of poop decks and shitty pitches, across the sea to Harwich, then up to London and on to home. But Jimmy was back in Manchester, at Old Trafford and then up at White City, that Saturday morning when Bobby and Nebojša Bato Tomašević got out of the taxi and followed the travel courier through Munich station, onto the platform and up the steps and onto the *Rheingold Express*; Bobby and Bato followed in turn by the press, shouting out questions, asking for photographs, and so after they had put their cases away, taken off their coats, Bobby and Bato stepped out into the corridor of the train, pushed down the window, leaning slightly out, Bobby with a cigarette –

You certainly look very fit indeed, Bobby, shouted the press from the platform. Have the doctors told you that you might be playing on Wednesday night?

Bobby shook his head, sort of smiled and said, No, I don't know. I don't know so much.

They probably won't let you, will they, shouted up the press. But bet you can't wait, can you, Bobby?

Bobby sort of smiled again, slightly shook his head again and said, It depends when I get home. Depends what I feel like when I get back home.

*

Bob Lord, the Chairman of Burnley Football Club, was not best pleased to see Jimmy Murphy and Joe Armstrong come through the gates of Turf Moor that pouring wet, torrential Saturday afternoon. But then again, Bob Lord was very rarely ever pleased. He was the butcher's boy who'd bought the shop, made his money and then, despite being spurned umpteen times or more, the devoted fan became the Chairman of the club he loved, perhaps the only thing he loved. Because Bob Lord did not like much, and he had a particular aversion to Manchester United; Hollywood United, that's what Bob Lord called them, and so Bob Lord was in no mood for sentimentalism when he heard Jimmy and Joe were darkening his doors that dark day, knowing as he did, because Bob Lord, he always knew it all, that the Catholic bloody Mafia were here to try to steal Brian bloody Pilkington from him, from Burnley Football Club. Well, he'd see about that would Bob Lord, because as he always said, never tired of telling anyone and everyone, Everything I've ever had in life I've had to fight for, but that's given me a maxim in life: if ever someone beats me in a battle, I don't blame them, I don't, I blame myself for letting them do it, and so over my dead bloody body will Jimmy fucking Murphy take Brian Pilkington from Burnley Football Club –

Because I feel sure that when all those League clubs announced they would help Manchester United in any way possible, they never for a moment assumed that Jimmy Murphy would plump for the star players of any club he fancied, and anyone who says I'm being callous is talking utter rubbish, bloody tripe!

Do United want to buy star players in order to win the League, the FA Cup, the European Cup, the Central League and the Youth Cup? Is that the plan? Because if they do, why don't they ask Preston for their manager Cliff Britton and let him take Tom Finney with him under his arm, and while they're at it, ask Manchester City for Trautmann, West Brom for Howe and

Barlow, Newcastle for McMichael? I mean, I ask you, would Blackpool have allowed Ernie Taylor to go if he had been five or six years younger? I bloody wonder.

Now I'm as sorry as anyone, lied Bob Lord, but United went into the European Cup with their eyes open, did they not? They weren't pushed into it, were they? And they made a lot of cash out of it, too, I can tell you that for nothing, and they won glamour and glory, which has attracted a lot of youngsters. Yet it is my belief that leading players are just what Jimmy Murphy wants now. But I can tell you that Pilkington will not leave Burnley, and give notice to any interested club, regardless of their circumstances, to keep their bloody hands off!

But that Saturday afternoon, under a bucketing-down, Bob Lord's beloved Burnley lost two–one at home in Jack Crompton's last game as trainer of Luton Town, and after the game, when Jimmy and Joe chanced upon Bob Lord, scowling and fuming and soaked to the skin, Jimmy smiled and said, Don't you worry, Mister Lord, sir, I don't fancy any of yours, sir, I really don't.

*

Bato Tomašević was a young attaché at the Yugoslav Embassy in London. Because it was not easy to travel from England to Yugoslavia, Bela Miklos, the Hungarian travel agent who was making the arrangements for the trip to Belgrade, had asked Bato to accompany him and the Manchester United team, to help with the police and customs, and Bato had jumped at the chance because Bato was in love. He had met an English girl called Madge, back when they were both students at Exeter University, and now they wanted to marry. So Bato needed to go back to Belgrade to ask for permission to wed. But the Yugoslav authorities refused his request, and so on the flight back from Belgrade to Manchester, Bato was left wondering what on earth he and Madge should do now.

But there had been laughter and jokes on the plane, the steward Tommy Cable had been serving whisky – hair of the dog for some, to calm the nerves of others – and Bato had been sitting in the front row, facing the steward, who had his back to the cockpit. But the third time they boarded, people started swapping seats, going from the front to the back, the back to the front, and Tommy Cable had said, Do you want to swap seats, Bato?

Yes, okay then, said Bato, and they did, they swapped, and Tommy had died and Bato survived –

Bato knew the crash had taken less than a minute, just seconds, but it seemed to last a lifetime,

before he blacked out.

Bato came round one hundred yards from the plane, still strapped into his seat, but when he got up, tried to get out of the seat, there was hardly a stitch left on him, his clothes, almost all of them, gone, blown off in the crash, even his shoes, his heavy and properly laced boots, were gone. He turned to look one way and saw white, snow, fields, everything fine, nothing wrong, then he turned and looked the other way and he saw the plane burning, people running, people moaning, drenched in petrol, faces and bodies bleeding, young, healthy men falling down. Dying. He saw hell, scenes Bato knew would stay in his mind, a hell he would never forget.

Bato turned away from the window of the compartment of the train, that view of a world of white, of snow, of fields, of everything fine, where nothing was wrong, and Bato looked at Bobby Charlton sitting there, across from him, next to the travel courier, who smiled at them both and asked, Is everything okay?

Bato nodded, smiled and said, Yes, thank you, it's a very nice train, very smooth.

Yes, it is, said Bobby Charlton, but then he leant forward in his seat, his arms on the tops of his legs, and he looked, he stared at Bato and said, I don't know about you, but I shall never, ever

285

get on another aeroplane again, even if it costs me my football career, I never will.

*

Restless in the night, the German, Munich night again, he tossed, he turned, cried and shouted out, in the German, Munich night, for in his sleep, his dreams he had the ball again, back at his feet again, at last, at last, let loose and free to play again, across those lunar fields of green, after the blossoms, before the rains, he roams, he romps, both bull and matador in one, with sleeves rolled up, his shorts hitched up, with graft, hard graft he takes, he wins the ball, then off he goes, pushes, surges forward through sunny glades of memory with the ball, a football or a tennis ball, a jam-jar lid or stone, until with grace, such grace he lifts or threads a pass, or with a cannonball, a rocket of a shot, right foot, left foot, even with his head, and boom, boom, he breaks the net again, and Duncan roars, in the German, Munich night, he cried and shouted out, Goal! Goal!

*

Matt swore he could hear voices, not in his head, but from outside the room, a voice he knew, it was Duncan, he was certain, he was sure, but Matt knew there was no point asking because no one ever told him anything –

My spectacles, love, he'd said to Jean. Do you know what happened to my spectacles?

And Jean had smiled, patted his hand and said, I'll ask, love, I'll ask, but don't be fretting about them now, please. When you're better, love, when you're stronger.

And then they'd come again, as they always came again, every day they came to set another of his bones, in his foot again,

286

bone by bone, day by day, the manipulation and repair, without anaesthetics, that was the drill, and it was cruel, though he knew they had no choice, but it was torture was the pain, and the old ward sister, she would lean over him and say, *Wunderbar, Herr Busby, wunderbar*, but Matt just shook his head and turned away and thought again, Why can't I die, just let me die.

*

From haunt to haunt Don went, criss-crossed the city, back and forth, weaving in and out, up and down the streets and places that he loved: the Park Works of Mather & Platt out at Newton Heath, the Free Trade Hall or the Kings Hall at Belle Vue, the Central Library or the university on Oxford Road, Maine Road or the cricket ground, until again Don found himself back again, outside Old Trafford once again, but suddenly swept up and then along, Don among the throng of people, queuing in their thousands there, six across in width, stretching for a mile or more back down the Warwick Road, corralled and shepherded by police mounted on horses black and brown –

I don't know about you, said the fellow pushed up against Don in the crush, but I'm busting for a slash. I've been here since gone midnight.

Gone midnight, said Don. That is impressive.

I just want to make sure I get a ticket, said the man. You must've been here a while yourself?

Well, yes, thought Don, said Don. Yes, I suppose I really must, though I could not tell you when –

You all right, are you, cock, asked the man. You're looking a bit pale, a Strangeways tan is that, he laughed, but then before his eyes, his own two eyes, he swore, though no one would believe him, ever believe a word he ever said again, the man watched as Don just dissolved into the crowd, the Sunday-morning air –

But Don was at the ticket window, bleached, he felt, but hanging on, a ticket somehow in his hand, he turned and walked away, over the bridge, the Bridgewater Canal, confused and lacking in direction, not sure why or if he should be here, when Don came across a little lad sat on the kerb, a scarf around his neck, United red and white, but with a bloody, snotty nose and a split and trembling lip, and Don asked, Whatever is the matter, son?

Some spiv, he thieved me ticket, said the little lad. I'd queued for hours, through the night, and me gran, she give me the money, she'll be so upset she will.

Now, now, said Don, there you go, and he gave the little lad his ticket. You take that.

The ticket in his little hand, the little lad, he blinked, stared at the ticket, blinked again then shook his head, looked up and said, But, mister, are you sure?

Yes, I'm sure, said Don, and passed the boy a handkerchief from his pocket, too, and said, But dry your eyes and wipe your face, your nose, your lip. We don't want to be upsetting your gran now, do we?

The little lad, he nodded, still staring up at Don, smiling up at Don, he said, Thank you, mister, thank you, but don't you want to go on Wednesday night?

No, said Don, no, I've seen United play, well, maybe a thousand times or more, so you go, son, you go, but you just keep that ticket safe now, in your pocket, and promise me you'll head straight home.

But the little lad stood up now, took Don's hand and said, But can I show you something first, mister, if you've got the time, will you come along with me?

Don nodded. Yes, I've got the time, I do have that, and so hand in hand they walked on up the road, led by the little lad, across the Ship Canal they went, up into Weaste, thousands with

288

them as they walked, tickets in their hands or hidden in their pockets, all the way up from the ground they came, from Old Trafford to Weaste Cemetery, to stand before the grave of Little Eddie Colman there, to stand in silence and in prayer, in prayer and thanks, and disbelief –

So 'Snake Hips' Colman is really dead, said Don, shaking his head, before the grave, beside the little lad.

Yeah, I know, said the little lad, I still can't believe it myself. Maybe I will on Wednesday . . .

Maybe, said Don, whispered Don, but Don suddenly felt cold, so very cold.

The little lad, he gripped, squeezed Don's hand and said, I just don't understand why some of the boys died and some of them didn't, do you, mister?

I'm sorry, said Don, shivered Don, but I don't.

It's just not fair is it, life, said the little lad.

I know, said Don, but that's why, when we can, while we can, we must be kind.

Well, I know you're kind, mister, said the little lad, turning from the grave of Little Eddie Colman to look up at Don. You're the kindest man I ever met –

But that man, that mister, the kindest man he'd ever met was gone, vanished into the air, the damp, grey, Salford Sunday air, and the little lad, he blinked then blinked again, stared at his hand, his empty hand, as if the man was never there, had never been, it was all a dream, a weird but happy dream, but then the little lad, he checked his pocket, and yes, yes, yes, the ticket was there, still there, in his pocket, safe and sound.

*

Bobby would later say, would write that when his mother and Jack collected him at the docks in Harwich, he felt a sense of relief. But Cissie and Jack were not at the docks that Sunday morning, they were waiting for him at Liverpool Street Station, the platform cordoned off but still swarming with pressmen and photographers, supporters and well-wishers, gawpers and ghouls, and when Bobby got off the train, stepped down onto the platform, he was a pathetic sight, thought Cissie, just standing there, beside his suitcase, looking so lost and all alone among the shouted questions from the press, the flashes of the cameras, the cheers and cries, the howls and screams from the crowd that surged towards the police, the station staff, and Jack, he'd had enough, he said to Cissie, Let's just get him away from here, or words to that effect, and Big Jack made skittles of the crowd, pressmen, cameramen, supporters or gawpers, Jackie did not give a fuck, he batted them away, bowled them over, picked up Bobby and his case, carrying their young 'un out of the station and straight to his car, then, to give the chasing pack the slip, like in a Hitchcock film, Jack drove Bobby with their mother and Jack's wife Pat to their Aunty Gladys's house in Huntingdon, where Gladys knew she shouldn't fuss, but she would have fussed anyway, over their Bobby and their Jackie, too, because she hardly ever saw them, not these days, not that much, now they were big stars, especially their Bobby, but it was hard not to fuss over their Bobby that bleak, winter Sunday afternoon, like he'd come back from the Dead it was, the Land of the Dead, and his Aunty Gladys, she touched his face, his cheek, her palm upon his cheek, and said, Oh, love, we were so worried, we really were, we all thought we'd lost you, didn't we, Cissie, love, we really did.

Bobby sort of smiled again, turned his face, his cheek away, looked to the window, the garden, and softly said, Yes, yes, Mother told me so . . .

But he was not listening, not really listening, staring out into the garden, the dirty English winter sky hanging low and heavy over the land, so low and heavy that it seemed to touch the ground, the grass, to dig down into the soil itself –

That's a nasty sky is that, said Jack, at his younger brother's side again. We best sup up and then get off.

Jack drove Bobby, Cissie and his wife Pat not back to Ashington, Beatrice Street and home, but up the A1, first to Leeds to stay the night with him and Pat, and on that long drive north, in some of the many tellings of the tale, Bobby turns to Jack, and Bobby says, I know you want to know what happened, and I will tell you, and so then as they drive, Bobby tells his brother the story of the crash, how he survived and others died, but when he's finished, Bobby says, Now I never want to speak of that again. I just want to forget about it all, okay?

But in other tellings, Bobby hardly speaks at all, he barely says a word, and Jack himself, he doesn't say much, and so on that long journey north to Leeds there were long, long silences, though Bobby said, would later say, I felt very close to him, close to Jack back then.

Early the next morning, the Monday morning, Bobby and Cissie got the train from Leeds back up to Newcastle, but in their carriage was a sailor who, Cissie later said, talked and talked about the crash, on and on he went, Oh, he did go on, but our Bobby just sat there, silent and withdrawn, he would not be drawn, not say a word. But then, at last, the sailor nodded off, thank God, and when Bobby saw him dozing, then fast asleep he was, Bobby turns to me, said Cissie, and says, Look, Mother, I am going to tell you about it now, but then I don't want it ever mentioned again, and then he tells me how the plane had attempted to take off three times, how he'd been thrown out of the plane, still strapped to his seat, but how he couldn't remember anything more until he woke up in the hospital, but how he'd been told afterwards that Harry Gregg, the goalkeeper, had found him wandering around, all covered in blood from the cut on his head, but Bobby couldn't remember that for himself, And so what I've just told you now, Mother, that is all I'm ever going to say, and it was all he ever did say, said Cissie. He never mentioned the subject of Munich to me ever again.

*

Jack Crompton had been pulling into his drive after training that Thursday afternoon, when a car had come screeching up, braking hard outside Jack's gate; it was Allan Brown, his neighbour down in Luton, who Jack was coaching in the Luton side, and Allan shouted, Jack! Jack! There's been a plane crash! United's plane has crashed!

But like so many folk that day, Jack had thought at first it would be something and nothing, just a burst tyre, the press making it out to be worse than it was to sell a few extra papers, like they always did. But Allan didn't think so, seemed to think it was more serious than that, said they best go inside, get the radio on and see what was what, and it soon became clear that Allan was right, that there had been a catastrophe on a major scale, that numerous people whom Jack knew personally as colleagues and friends, they had all lost their lives, and Jack broke down and Jack wept on Allan's shoulder.

For those first few hours, first days, as the news came through, worse by the hour, by the day, Jack hardly said a word, it was an age before he spoke again, but then the Chairman of Luton Town, Mister Mitchell, he called Jack on the telephone, asked Jack if he would come in to meet him in his office at Kenilworth Road –

Now then, Jack, said P. G. Mitchell, we contacted Manchester United, as you know, offering to help in any way we could. If we could be of any assistance, then they only had to ask. And now they have been in contact have Mister Hardman and United, but to ask if they could have your services, Jack, if you'd go back . . .

In truth, this did not come as a complete surprise to Jack; the day he'd left Old Trafford, after twelve years at the club, the Boss had told him then that he'd like Jack back one day as the club's trainer, but after he had first experienced the workings of another club, and Jack had believed the Boss, as he always did, thought Matt was being straight with him, as he always was, but Jack nodded and said, Oh, I see, sir.

Now then, Jack, we meant players, not you, Jack, but having made the offer to them, we must see what we can do. Now if you want to stay at Luton, we will be delighted, but if you feel that you want to go back to Manchester, we will understand, of course we will.

And so Jack was back, in the worst of circumstances, the very worst of times, but still Jack was glad to be back, for where else could he be than standing here, outside Old Trafford, in the pissing, pouring rain again, that Monday afternoon, back with Jimmy and with Bill again, Jimmy making jokes again, about Noah and his ark again, as two by two they watched the players file out of the ground and onto the bus, some players Jack knew, some he did not, as two by two onto the bus they went: Gordon Clayton, though he was still not fully fit, and David Gaskell, Ronnie Cope and Ian Greaves, Colin Webster and Freddie Goodwin, Alex Dawson and Mark Pearson, Bobby Harrop and Bobby English, Peter Jones and Barry Smith, Jack Mooney and Tommy Spratt, Reg Hunter and Harry Bratt, and Shay Brennan and Johnny Giles, And that's our lot, the best we got, said Jimmy, trying not to think, to dwell on all their yesterdays –

That team that won the Cup in Forty-eight with Jack in goal, Johnny Carey and John Aston, John Anderson and Allenby Chilton, Henry Cockburn and Jimmy Delaney, Johnny Morris and Jack Rowley, Stan Pearson and Charlie

Mitten, that same team, or thereabouts, that won the League in Fifty-two, with Jack again, but vying with Reg Allen, and with the likes of Tom McNulty and Billy Redman, Ernie Bond and Harry McShane, and of course there was John Downie, too, and Roger coming through, poor Roger Byrne and Mark Jones, too, poor Mark Jones, he'd played that season, too, along with Don Gibson and Jeff Whitefoot, and had not Jackie Blanchflower had a game . . .?

But Jimmy stopped, he shook his head, then shook his head again; he should slap his face, his own fucking face he should, he bloody would, lest he start to think again of Billy and Tommy, Little Eddie, David Pegg and Geoff Bent, and Johnny Berry and Duncan and Dennis and Ray Wood and Albert Scanlon and Kenny Morgans and poor Tom and poor Bert –

Where are you, he mustn't think, Jimmy knew he mustn't think, Where have you gone, that he should be thinking not of the past, the times that they'd had, but of the future, the times, the games to come. Sheffield Wednesday on Wednesday was just two days away, he knew, he fucking knew; he'd spent yesterday, Sunday, in a thousand forms of prayer, pacing in the garden or back up in his room, back at the house or here at the ground, listing all the players that they had, one by one, in his head or down on paper, over and over, again and again, in list after list, the players they had, had and had not, the positions they played, they could and could not, the holes, the gaps they had to fill, he had to fill, all down to him it was, he knew, in his head, then down on paper, in his pocket that other list of players, the ones he wished they had, and maybe could, you never knew, and there in the rain, the pissing, pouring rain again, Jimmy turned to Jack and winked at Jack and said, But don't forget Little Ernie Taylor will be meeting us there, and please, God, please, Billy Foulkes and Harry Gregg, they will do, too.

Any news on Charlton, asked Jack.

Jimmy glanced at his watch. The boy should be home by now, so I'll give his mother a ring later, find out the score. But he's still stitches in his head.

What about Wilf McGuinness?

Jimmy shook his head. He goes under the knife this week. Tuesday or Wednesday.

That is a pity, said Jack. A great shame.

Jimmy nodded, then Jimmy said, Like I told you, son, it's going to be a fucking long road back –

Then Jimmy, Jack and Bill climbed aboard the bus, which was the very bus that just two weeks ago, two weeks ago that very day had picked up Harry Gregg and Ray Wood, Billy Foulkes and Roger Byrne, Eddie Colman and Mark Jones, Duncan Edwards and Ken Morgans, Bobby Charlton and Tommy Taylor, Dennis Viollet and Albert Scanlon, Johnny Berry and Jackie Blanchflower, Billy Whelan and David Pegg, and, of course, Geoff Bent not Ronnie Cope, along with Matt and Tom and Bert and Walter and Matt's pal Willie Satinoff, picked them all up from this very spot on the forecourt here, then taken them out to Ringway Airport for the flight to Belgrade, with a stop in Munich to refuel.

But this afternoon, waved off by some supporters who wished them luck, the best of luck, they were not heading to the airport and the sky, they were driving to Blackpool and the sea, and not to visit but to stay, at the Norbreck Hydro Hotel, up on the North Shore cliffs, away from the supporters who meant well, Jimmy knew they did, but it was all too much, it really was, the fever, the hysteria, what with the press, the telly, too, it was just too much, they had to leave, to get away –

Jack, sat at the front with Jimmy and with Bill Inglis, he nodded and said, You're right, Jimmy, of course you are, but Jack was thinking, This is the quietest busload of footballers I've ever sat among is this, but yes, perhaps the hotel, the sea will do them good, the walks along the Promenade, the runs across the sands, the golf of an afternoon, if the sun it ever shines again, even take them to the Tower, watch the wrestling, let them let their hair down, even for a bit, for Jack could see they were all wound that tight by death and shock, by loss and grief that he had to get them somehow to unwind, or else, he knew, they'd snap, they'd break.

*

Duncan was improving, then Duncan was deteriorating, one minute on the mend, the next at death's door again, but then they'd come to them and say Duncan was 'satisfactory' again, after the artificial kidney had been used for five hours that day, they said, Duncan may not need the artificial-kidney treatment again today, and the doctor said, It's a good sign, that's a very good sign, and so Gladstone, Annie and Molly would put on their coats again, ready to go back to the hotel again, to go to bed with hope for once, for once with hope, not fear, nor panic or despair. But each time before he left, or at some point in the day, Gladstone would always without fail go along each day to see how Jackie Blanchflower and Frank Taylor were getting on, and Frank and Jackie would thank Gladstone, but then ask, How's your Duncan doing?

Not too bad, thanks, lads, Gladstone Edwards would always say, but don't you be worrying about him. We want to see you two up and about again.

*

Motionless, his back against the headboard, hands clasped about his knees, eyes full again of tears, for hours through the dark, while others slept; it was all right for them, his mother and the rest of them, they could all sleep, couldn't they, but he couldn't sleep, just couldn't bloody sleep, could he; it was the same here at home as it was back there in Munich, maybe even worse back here at home; it all seemed somehow nearer here, the sense of tragedy, the papers still full of the crash; they just couldn't seem to leave it alone, making a sensation of the tragedy, in spite of the loss and the grief, it was all just a sensation to them, hurting people who were already hurt beyond belief –

Bobby couldn't believe his mother sometimes; barely back he was, minutes, not an hour, not even seen his father, said hello, and the press, they were knocking at their door, and he'd said, in no uncertain terms he'd said, Send them packing, Mother, will you, please –

But she never listened to a word he said, no bloody wonder he hardly said a word, no bloody point round here, not when she always knew best, putting on her pinny, making sure she looked her best, telling him, Now, now, Bobby, they're only doing their jobs, a job you once wanted, don't forget, you're quick to forget, you wanted to be a reporter, didn't you, pet? That could be you out there in the street, knocking on the door –

You've no bloody idea, have you, he wanted to say, but didn't say; what was the point, the bloody point of saying anything to her –

She'd already invited them in, the bloody press, the cameramen, entertaining them, making them cups of tea, handing round the biscuits, but then they made him bloody pose with a cup of tea, and with her and all, of course, but never with a thought for those that had not, could not come back, how their mothers and their fathers, their brothers and their sisters, their wives and their kids, their loved ones and friends, how they might feel to see him staring out of their paper, with his mother and a cup of tea, a stupid smile across his bloody chops, not a mark, a single scratch on him, the mothers, the fathers, the brothers, the sisters, the wives, the kids, the loved ones, their friends, they'd all be thinking, How come he's safe and sound back home, with his mother and a cup of tea? Her with her smile, him with his grin, and a sheepish one at that, and well he might, because why him? Why the hell did he survive? What makes him so bloody special?

*

They had gone to bed with hope for once, but still they'd hardly slept a wink before they woke again to fear, to panic and despair, worried what the dawn would bring, the news of Duncan and the night he'd had. But again they'd do their best, as they always did their best, and so they rose and washed and dressed, then Gladstone, Annie and Molly went down the stairs to breakfast in the hotel dining room again, with Jean and Sheena Busby, Edith Rayment and Peggy Davies, Hilda Berry and Jean Blanchflower, Betty Wood and Barbara Viollet, Josephine Scanlon and Stephanie Lloyd, the fiancée of Kenny Morgans, and while they ate or picked at their German, Munich breakfasts, and missed a good old cup of English tea, a bit of bacon or fried egg, now that wouldn't go amiss, they chatted or they listened to the talk of Manchester and of England, of the weather and the news from home, then, as they always did, all of them always did, they went back up to their rooms for their coats and their hats, their scarves and their gloves, then they came back down the stairs again, out into the street, to board the special little bus that British European Airways had laid on, to take them back and forth each day, from the hotel to the hospital then back again, often twice a day, sometimes more, staring out of the windows of the bus at the people, at the shops, but with that nervous, nervous turning in their stomachs once again, wondering, worrying just what the day would bring, how Duncan would or would not be, then back off the bus again they got, back at the Rechts der Isar Hospital again, through those doors, down that corridor, to that elevator again, sick with the wonder and the worry now, as up they went, faint with premonitions, forebodings of ill tidings, fearing the faces, the looks on the faces of the doctors, the nurses when the doors of the elevator opened, their quick glance to the floor, their shoulders low as with a swallow or slight sigh they told them, We are sorry to have to tell you that, unfortunately, and despite all we had hoped, during the night we had to use the artificial-kidney machine again, and so this has in turn meant we have had to give Duncan another blood transfusion.

*

The back pages of the morning papers were full of 'scoops' about who would be coming to United, joining them in time to play tomorrow in the Cup, the talk again of Alex Govan and Dick Neal from Birmingham City, one paper certain that Paddy Fagan and John McTavish would be swapping Maine Road for Old Trafford and be on the United payroll 'before the week was out', while Reg Pearce of Luton Town was 'another almost certain to become a Manchester United player in time for the history-making Cup tie against Sheffield Wednesday at Old Trafford tomorrow night', along with the Bradford City outside-left Martin Bakes, the young Huddersfield half-back Ron Cockerill and Portsmouth's Scottish centre-forward Jackie Henderson, who was looking for a move, had been linked with Wolves, but said, Well, you cannot refuse to go to a club like United now, can you?

But Jimmy knew none of it was really true, because, quite simply, he didn't know himself. I just don't know, he said, know what to do. We have so little time, and the trouble is I cannot see any of these players, not for myself, with my own two eyes, so I have to rely on the opinions of others, the judgement of others –

And so that Tuesday morning, after breakfast in the hotel dining room, Jimmy and Jack, with Joe and Bill Inglis, took the players that they had out onto the golf course behind the Norbreck Hydro, in their dark maroon tracksuits, their black gym shoes, and then they put them through their paces there, the warm-ups and the exercises, then brisk games of six-a-side, Jimmy in among them, joining in again, the three hours of training, then back inside for lunch, Jimmy pleased to see Billy Foulkes and Harry Gregg, with their cases in the lobby, relieved to see them sitting down for lunch, quiet, yes, but chatting now and then with the rest of the lads again, and Jimmy smiled, because if Billy and Harry were here and fit to play, that would give him seven of the eleven –

Harry Gregg, the automatic choice in goal, then Billy Foulkes at right-back, with Ian Greaves in at left-back, then he'd have Freddie Goodwin and Ronnie Cope at four and five, with Little Ernie Taylor coming in at inside-right, then young Alex Dawson up front, thought Jimmy, up in his hotel room again, his makeshift office by the sea, pacing up and down again, wondering about Colin Webster, who had experience, and Mark Pearson, who had none, another inside-forward, but that would still only give him nine of the eleven.

*

There are at least three different tales of how things went with Bobby when Bobby got back home to Ashington, the house on Beatrice Street. In the first, the earliest of tales, one of Bobby's first questions on walking through the door was, Mother, is there a football in the house?

This is the story that accompanied photographs of Bobby out the back with a ball, in his best shirt and tie, his good trousers and shoes, behind the house on Beatrice Street, playing with four young local lads, two in Newcastle strips, two in Sunderland strips, the kits and the ball all helpfully provided by the gentlemen of the press. And it may well have been that story and those photographs which then prompted a telegram from Jimmy Murphy to Cissie, which, Cissie later said, urged her to tell her Bobby that if there's nothing wrong with him, then he should be back here in boots with me.

But that day after Cissie and Bobby had arrived home from Munich, after the photographs out back in the lane with the ball and the boys, after the reporters and cameramen had finally left, the moment Bobby came back indoors, so Cissie said, It was then Bobby announced, Mother, I'm giving up football for good. I've lost all of my mates and I never want to play football again.

This is the tale most commonly told, repeated and written in book after book, and in this tale, so the story goes, it is the local family doctor, Doctor McPherson, who talks Bobby round, brings him back to his senses, but thanks to Cissie, of course, because, Cissie said, Bobby was using his head injury as an excuse, an excuse not to play, not to go back to Manchester, a reason to lie up in his room all day, on his bed or on the floor, listening to those records, all those melancholy tunes, their depressing words, all day, over and over, enough to drive anybody mad they were, lying there on his bed or on the floor all day, refusing to go to the doctor's to have those stitches out, Well, thought Cissie, if the mountain won't go to Mohammed, so Cissie went to see Doctor McPherson herself, asked him to come call at the house on Beatrice Street, have a look at the wound, remove them stitches if he could, and have a word with Bobby if he would –

You know, Bobby, said Doctor McPherson, so said Cissie, I was in the Air Force in the war, and I saw many of my pals shot down, and the only thing to do about it then was to go straight back up again. Now your name is in football, and football is flying for you, and so my advice to you is that you've got to go out and kick a ball again, and go back to your team, and get up in a plane again, because there is nothing wrong with you that time won't heal. So I expect to see you at Wembley in May.

Then, soon after the doctor left, so the story goes, the tale that Cissie tells, Bobby's old pal Ronnie Routledge knocks upon the door of the house on Beatrice Street, a ball tucked under his arm, and he says, Fancy coming down the park for a kickaround?

And it's when he comes back later, said Cissie, from that kickaround down the park that Bobby says, Mother, I'm off back to Manchester.

But Bobby would always deny there was any truth in reports that said he'd said he'd never play football again. No, I never said that, said Bobby, that's just not what happened, not how it was . . .

*

In the afternoon, they left the players to themselves, some opting for a walk along the North Shore sands, others going back out onto the course for a round or two of golf, while the rain held off, before the light gave up, when in they'd have to come again, for another hand of cards, yet another hand of cards or a game of billiards, anything at all, not to pass the time, but to ward off time itself, dispel all thoughts of time, of past and future times; the horror of yesterday, the terror of tomorrow, the ghosts of yesterday, the game tomorrow, approaching, encroaching, coming closer and closer, hour by hour, closer and closer –

But Jack Crompton had no time for walks along the shore, rounds of golf or hands of cards; Jack left Blackpool without his lunch, picked up his car then headed straight down to Luton –

Be four hours there, four hours back, knew Jack, but if it meant they could get Reg Pearce, and Jack thought they could, so Jimmy thought they should, then it was time and petrol well spent, and he could pick up some more of his things while he was there, but as he drove, Jack kept thinking about the training that morning, the players they had, then about the players they missed, the lads they had lost, thinking about the last time Jack had played in United's first team, in October Fifty-five it would have been, at Old Trafford, against Huddersfield Town, when they'd won three–nil, a last clean sheet for Jack, but four of that team were now dead, Geoff Bent and Mark Jones, David Pegg and Tommy Taylor, who had both scored that day, four others in that side still in the hospital in Munich, Duncan Edwards and Johnny Berry, who had scored the other goal that day, both still so very ill, Jackie Blanchflower and Dennis Viollet, too, and Bill Foulkes had also played that day with Jack, Bill a lucky man to walk away, but Jack knew Bill Foulkes was not unscathed, still not sure if Bill should really play tomorrow, despite what Jimmy thought, he hoped, coming into Luton now, Jack just praying he could persuade Reg Pearce to come back up north with him tonight, to Blackpool then to Manchester, straight into the side for tomorrow night . . .

*

Physically, I have never felt better, said Harry Gregg, but I'll know how I really feel when I go out into the lights with the boys tomorrow. I think I will be all right because there is so much to play for. There will surely never be another game like this in the history of the game . . .

Harry didn't fancy a walk along the shore, maybe later on, but not right now. Nor did he want a round of golf, a game of cards with Bill. Not today, no, thanks. For now, at least, Harry was happy just to chat, to talk in the lounge with some of these new fellows from the press, the *Herald* and *Express*, or anyone who asked, it just helped to chat, to talk, at least for now –

How grand will it be to have the famous Old Trafford turf beneath our feet again. I cannot wait!

But can you win, Harry, asked the press.

We shall win if we can, but it is not even necessary to discuss the outcome of this game to look into the future. For the way ahead may be studded with disappointments, but we shall have our successes, too. But what a wonderful thing it would be if we can get a heartening start tomorrow night. And I am certain we will!

Then, with these words, a quick shake of hands, Harry was gone, up to his room –

At lightning speed, to lock the door, close the curtains, take off his necktie, wrap and twist it round his head, then pull it tight, tight –

You fraud, Harry Gregg, they said, the voices in the walls. The fuck you think you are? Who made you the spokesman for the Dead, the team? Ten minutes in the side, but there you are, with the big words, the big mouth, does that gob of yours ever shut? These ghosts are theirs, not yours, you hardly knew them, played, what, ten, eleven games with them, but that doesn't stop you, does it, Harry Gregg? The most expensive goalkeeper in history, but just a fucking fraud.

I'm sorry, I'm sorry, said Harry, twisting the tie tighter and tighter, round his head tighter.

Now, now, Big Man, said the walls, kindly, softly now. Stop with your blubbering, will you, please, for heaven's sake, and dry those beady Irish eyes of yours, we're only pulling your leg, winding you up, man.

*

Ronnie Routledge did knock on Bobby's door, that bit was true, but Bobby didn't remember any kickaround down the park, least not that day, not in his best shirt and tie, his good trousers and shoes. No, they went to the pub, did Ronnie and Bobby, and Bobby's dad and some of his mates, they were there, too, and the talk must have come round to the match, the Cup tie against Wednesday the next day, the talk about who Jimmy would pick, the team United would field, the news that Ernie Taylor had signed, big news in that part of the world, of course, but especially in Ashington, among the Charltons and the Milburns and their mates, all now reliving that glorious April day in Fifty-one, when Little Ernie Taylor, foot on the ball, surrounded on the Wembley turf by half the Blackpool team, plays a cute and cheeky back-heel for their cousin Jackie, Wor Jackie, to thunder the ball into the net for the second goal, which clinched the match, the Cup for Newcastle, and it was then it suddenly hit him, hit Bobby, as clear as day it was. He put down his pint and said, Father, I have to be at the match tomorrow night.

*

What is the fucking appeal of the bloody North-East, said Jimmy, Jimmy back in Manchester, Old Trafford, up in his office, Murphy's Bar, the bottles of beer on the desk, the telephone in his hand, asking Jack, still down in Luton, Do you fucking know, Jack, can you bloody tell me?

I tried my best, Jimmy, said Jack, I really did, but Reg just seems to be set on Sunderland. They've made a higher offer, too. Twenty thousand, I believe.

Twenty thousand quid, said Jimmy, laughed Jimmy, for Reg bloody Pearce?

He's very good –

The boy might well be very good, might well be the next bloody Bozsik for all I know, but we both know they're only doing it out of fucking spite are Sunderland, said Jimmy. You know that, Jack, I know that, just because they think we nicked Ernie off them. Well, give me those sixty-four inches of Little Ernie over a thousand foot of any other man, because you've seen him in training, haven't you, Jack, the little midget is a giant, is he not? The way he's cajoling the younger lads, but also coaching, encouraging, urging them on, and he's still got it on the ball himself, too, has he not, Jack, going deep for the ball, then slipping it forward, the quick, sure pass, straight to feet, oh, he's still the Demon Stoker, is he not?

Eight thousand quid well spent, said Jack.

Indeed, Jack, indeed, said Jimmy, I was telling the Chairman, Mister Hardman, the very same just now. I said, he's almost earned that back in training, has Ernie, the wise old head he brings, sure and steady as he goes.

Any news on Crowther, asked Jack.

Just that Villa want twenty-five grand for him, if you can believe that, said Jimmy, laughed Jimmy again. But we can get them down a bit, at least to under twenty. But it's the same old story, isn't it, Jack . . .?

He doesn't want to move?

He wants the night to think it over, sighed Jimmy. Apparently, he doesn't really want to leave the Midlands and home. Supposed to be a bit shy . . .

Have you had chance to speak to him yet?

I've not, said Jimmy, but whatever young Stanley says, come the morning, Eric Houghton has promised to have the lad call me first thing at the Norbreck.

Well, that's something, at least, said Jack, but then Jack paused before he said goodbye, reluctant to ask, but needing to know. Don't suppose there's been any change, any news from Munich, has there, Jimmy?

Not much, said Jimmy. You heard Duncan had to have another blood transfusion?

306

Yes, said Jack.

Well, we've heard nothing more since, though there's been a slight improvement in Johnny Berry's condition, apparently, but he's still on the 'danger list', they said, though Matt's still gaining strength.

Well, that's something, said Jack again, something at least, so I'll see you back in Blackpool then.

Aye, said Jimmy, I'll see you back there, son, and so you pop by when you're back, and we'll have a drink, another chat and another think about tomorrow –

I will, said Jack, I'll see you then –

But you drive carefully now, won't you, son, said Jimmy. Don't be rushing back, you promise me, Jack.

I promise, said Jack. Bye, Jimmy, bye.

Bye, Jack, bye, said Jimmy, the connection cut, the line now dead, the telephone still in his hand.

Jimmy put down the telephone, picked up his cigarettes, lit another cigarette, opened another bottle of beer, poured himself another glass, then there in Murphy's Bar, his office up the stairs, Jimmy asked himself again, What the fuck am I going to do?

Jimmy was the busiest boss in Britain, the papers all agreed, but what the papers didn't know, or wouldn't say, was how very little help he'd had. He got all these words, these gestures from all these other clubs, but where did words and gestures get him, what had they given him? Sweet Fanny Adams, that's what he'd got, despite all the big words, the gestures in the press.

He stubbed out his cig, downed his beer, got up from his chair and left his office, down the stairs to try and find a taxi or a lift back to Blackpool and the Norbreck Hydro, but outside in the dark, the damp, the press were still waiting for him there, asking, Jimmy, Jimmy, what can you tell us, what do you know, who've you got coming, who will be playing?

I'm sorry, boys, I'm sorry, said Jimmy, but I've nothing to announce. I wish I had, I wish I could, could tell you more.

But, Jimmy, Jimmy, asked the press, you must have some idea by now who will play and who will not?

Two words for you, boys, two words, laughed Jimmy: Keep fit! You all keep fit because I may yet need one or two of you boys tomorrow night.

*

Geoffrey didn't quite know why he'd travelled up to Manchester that day, the day before the game. He could have come up on the day itself, but no, he'd come up on the train first thing today, getting off at London Road. First he'd wandered down to Piccadilly, a pot of coffee in the Queen's Hotel, then round the Gardens under heavy skies that seemed to want to snow, but thought they'd better not, not today, nor tomorrow, but still showers of rain and sometimes sleet battled sunny spells before they scattered here and there across the city, its quiet, still muffled streets, and sent Geoff ducking into the Ping Hong on Mosley Street for a spot of early lunch that had turned out to be a long one in the end, sitting hidden in a corner there till almost three, yes, he was hiding there, he knew –

He knew it was going to be difficult to return to Old Trafford: difficult for every one of the sixty thousand crowd that would pack every square inch of the stands and terraces tomorrow night; difficult for the skeleton side that would have to carry the burden of the present; difficult, perhaps even more so, for the visiting players of Sheffield Wednesday; difficult, too, for those in the press box. Yes, the show must go on, he knew, and the stage would be the same, but nothing would be as before.

*

308

Jimmy, Jack and Joe and Bill had talked through half the Blackpool night, a bottle and a half of Norbreck whisky, too, picking one player, then another, thinking through the combination of him and him, but then what about him, why not try this lad here and that boy there, though that wasn't where he usually played, if they picked and played him there, but thinking, Yes, that might well work out might that, but then the doubts, the questions came again, his left was his weaker foot, did he even have a left foot, come to that, unpicking him again, that lad, that boy, thinking through yet another combination, searching for the balance, that balance that they still could not get right, not helped by the thought, the half-promise that they might yet have Stan Crowther in the side, if the lad said yes, and the FA then agreed, but time was marching on, the tide would soon be out, the dawn, the day be here, kick-off now but hours away, now down to Bobby English, they agreed, if they couldn't get Stan Crowther in the side, and then a gamble and a half in giving first-team debuts to Mark Pearson and to Shay Brennan, in at outside-left, Shay out of position, yes, and instead of Reg Hunter, but Reg was only just back in training, while Shay had been in training all along, and doing well, they all agreed, and more than that, said Jimmy, That boy, he shows no fear.

*

Duncan's life was hanging by a thread again, they knew, Gladstone, Annie and Molly knew, after a double crisis in the night. First, in the very early hours of the morning, the doctors told Gladstone, Annie and Molly, the artificial-kidney machine had broken down. However, technicians had managed to repair it on the spot, and there seemed to have been no adverse effect on Duncan's condition. But then came the second crisis, the doctors told Gladstone, Annie and Molly, because the level of poisonous nitrogen in Duncan's blood began to rise again, so the doctors had had to give Duncan direct person-to-person blood transfusions. But again, the doctors told Gladstone, Annie and Molly, Duncan had somehow found the strength to keep fighting on, the will to go on, and so again Duncan had somewhat rallied, his breathing even a little stronger now, and so they'd taken Duncan out of his oxygen tent –

Can I see him then, asked Annie again.

But the doctors shook their heads again and said, We're very sorry, but Duncan is still dangerously ill, still not quite back to where he was yesterday.

I see, said Annie again, on her knees again, in the chapel of the hospital again, but knowing Duncan would keep on fighting, keep on bouncing back, because he always did, her Duncan always did.

*

Shay Brennan fucking shit himself when Bill Foulkes banged on the door of the room first thing and shouted through the wood, Jimmy wants to see you, Brennan.

Fuck, fuck, fuck, thought Shay, jumping out of bed, washing his face, cleaning his teeth, pulling on his training gear, thinking, Fuck, fuck, fuck, how the fuck did he find out, then thinking, But then he always fucking does, him and the Boss, they always do, they'd been mad to think they wouldn't, they always fucking did –

Aye, you're fucked, Seamus, said his roommate, but don't be thinking of fucking grassing up the rest of us.

Fuck you, said Shay. If he knows about me, he knows about you. It was your idea and all –

But it's not me he's asking for –

Fuck you, said Shay again, going out the room, down the hotel corridor, the stairs to Jimmy's room, along another corridor, Jimmy's door already open, Jimmy on the telephone, Jimmy saying down the phone, Listen, son, if I didn't think you could play for Manchester United, if I didn't think you had what it takes to put on our red shirt, I would not be speaking to you now, but I know you're not sure, you don't want to leave home, but listen, will you at least do this for me, son? Will you come up with your boss today and have a chat with me, face to face, not on the phone, but face to face, then stick around and watch the match, the game tonight, will you do that for me, son?

Fuck, fuck, thought Shay again, standing there, shifting from one guilty foot to the other guilty foot, thinking, Whoever the fuck this is, please, dear God, say yes, or he'll be in an even fouler fucking temper –

Great, son, great, shouted Jimmy down the phone. Now you get your boss to call me back when he knows what time you're coming, and don't forget your boots . . . No, son, no, don't you worry, that was just a joke, my little joke, but I'll see you in Manchester, son, and soon . . .

Jimmy put down the telephone, clapped and rubbed his hands together, turned to Shay and said, Good morning, son, and how are you then this fine morning? Are you feeling well, son, are you? Fit and well?

I'm very sorry, Jimmy, said Shay, I –

Very sorry what, snapped Jimmy. What you very sorry about? Dear God, don't tell me you're crocked?

No, said Shay, no, but about last night . . .

Fuck last night, said Jimmy, are you fit, son?

Yes, said Shay. It was just a couple of pints.

Well, thank Christ for that, you're fit, said Jimmy, because you're in the team, you're playing tonight.

I'm what, said Shay. What?

But at outside-left, said Jimmy, not inside-forward, son, so you'll be wearing eleven.

Eleven, whispered Shay.

You'll be brilliant, son, said Jimmy, believe me you will, so you make sure your dad, he's there, your brothers and your sisters, too, you go call them now.

Yes, whispered Shay, I will, turning back to the door, the telephone by Jimmy's bed already ringing again.

*

It wasn't clear whose idea this was, but most likely it was the press again, but after lunch that afternoon, one of the doctors came onto the ward at the Rechts der Isar Hospital to tell Ray Wood, Dennis Viollet, Albert Scanlon and young Kenny Morgans that they would be able to listen to a special commentary on the match over the telephone.

That'll be good, won't it, said their wives, their loved ones by their beds, not sure, in fact, it would be good, but duty-bound, they felt, to be upbeat, to be polite, and Ray and Dennis, Albert and Kenny, in their pyjamas, their dressing gowns, in or by their beds, they smiled and nodded, polite and upbeat, too, but struggled to think what match was this, to pretend they even cared at all.

But on a different floor, Matt Busby, Johnny Berry and Duncan Edwards would never know the match was being played; Johnny and Duncan were too ill to be told, and Matt, of course, could not be told about the game because everything was still a secret to be kept from him, like the newspapers, his spectacles, the world itself, it seemed, a secret kept from him.

And as for Frank and Jackie down the corridor in Room 406, well, Jackie really didn't care, he simply couldn't give a fuck about a sodding football match or anything at all, he barely ate or drank a thing, but Frank, well, he would have liked nothing better than to have listened to that game later that night, the commentary over the telephone, the pictures it would have painted in his mind, the memories it would have stirred, but Frank still could not wash or feed himself, could barely read a paragraph, a sentence of his book, so whether it was on the orders of the doctors or someone simply just forgot, but like Matt and Johnny and Duncan, and Ken Rayment, too, lying in his bed, in plaster and in traction, Frank would know nothing of the game that night.

But back in England, Wales and Ireland, too, in Manchester and Salford, in Yorkshire and in Dublin, in Brynmawr and in Woking, in some of the houses, the homes of the Dead, their families, their loved ones, the ones they'd left behind, they drew their curtains, locked their doors, switched off their radios, their televisions, if they had one, put their hands to their ears, they closed their eyes and wished and wished, oh, how they wished they knew nothing of this game tonight.

*

Jimmy, said Tom Finney down the phone, the Preston Plumber on the line, I'm sorry to bother you –

Tommy, my old pal, said Jimmy, it's never a bother to hear from you, my old friend . . .

Well, I am a bother, Jimmy, said Tom, because I've a favour to ask of you, about tonight –

Don't tell me, said Jimmy. You want to leave Preston, come play for us tonight. Well, Tommy, my old pal, you're on! What time will you be here . . .?

Well, actually, said Tom, laughed Tom, I've a plumbing job on, but a pal of mine, he'd give anything for a couple of tickets for tonight, if you could, Jimmy?

I can and I will, said Jimmy.

Oh, Jimmy, thank you, said Tom Finney, that's very good of you is that, with all you've got on, and I just wish you the very

313

best for tonight, and my thoughts will be with you, and with Joe and with all the boys.

Thank you, Tommy, said Jimmy, but actually I do have a favour to ask of you, a huge one, if you could?

Of course, said Tom. How can I help?

Well, said Jimmy, first off, can you cancel that plumbing job, or find someone else, and then meet us in Manchester at the Queen's Hotel?

Yes, said Tom, but –

Well, you see, Tommy, I'm trying to sign Stan Crowther from Villa, said Jimmy, and so him and Eric Houghton, they're coming up for a chat, but the boy, he doesn't want to come, I know he doesn't, I mean, Eric's having to drag him up, but, Tommy, we need him, and I need him for tonight, in the side tonight, and so if you were there, the great Tom Finney, at the hotel, to help him make up his mind, you know, help sell United . . .

But, Jimmy, said Tom Finney, I play for Preston North End, I can't be seen to be helping one of our biggest rivals secure a transfer now, can I . . .?

Tommy, you're the most honourable fellow in football, said Jimmy. Everybody knows that, and they also know these are exceptional circumstances. I mean, if we both do our job and Crowther signs, the FA's making an exception, letting him play despite being cup-tied, so nobody's going to think any worse of you, Tom.

Well, okay then, Jimmy, if you think I can help.

Oh, thank you, Tommy, said Jimmy. You really are a pal. I'll see you at the Queen's at five.

Five, asked Tom. What time's kick-off?

Half seven, said Jimmy.

Bloody hell, said Tom Finney.

I know, said Jimmy.

They played table tennis for most of the morning, a bit of ping-pong when they weren't trying to sort out tickets for their mams and their dads, pals old and new, suddenly so many new pals, still trying to work out who would be playing and who would be not, Bob English and Reg Hunter still unsure if they were in the side or not, some lads telling them, Of course you are, of course you'll play, some laughing, Like, who else we got, Bob and Reg trying not to get up their hopes, trying not to read the faces of Jack Crompton and Bill Inglis, but wondering where the fuck Jimmy was, where the hell he'd gone now –

But Jimmy was here, Jimmy still there, wandering the corridors, the floors, up and down the stairs, down by the indoor pool or back up in the ballroom, the big ballroom and the smaller one, walking through the empty bars, the restaurant, into the ballroom again, the empty hotel ballroom. Jimmy sat down at the piano there, on the stool, he raised the lid and then began to play, key by key, note by note, picking out Chopin's Nocturne in E-flat major, but in the silences, those brief, short silences between the lonely notes, the chords, then time seemed to slow, to stretch out and wait, to pause awhile, waiting there for Jimmy, and only then, between those notes, those chords, he'd catch a glimpse, a sight of –

Mister Murphy, said a waiter. Excuse me, but the television people, they are ready for you in the lounge.

Jimmy nodded, put down the lid, got up from the stool and walked from the ballroom through to the lounge.

Faces he recognised, thought he knew, Fred being one of them, they shook his hand and sat him down, and then Fred said, Are you ready, Jimmy, shall we start?

Yes, Fred, whenever you are ready, I am ready.

Okay then, well, we know, Jimmy, that things have been

quite hectic for you these last few days. How do you think they're sorting themselves out now?

Well, these things take time, Fred, and as you know, we're in a terrible mess really, for players and so forth. And I'm trying to be with my lads here, and I'm also trying to contact players and clubs by phone. But it's a very, very difficult job indeed.

Right, obviously Harry Gregg and Bill Foulkes have recovered from the experience of the Munich crash, sufficiently to play tonight, in any event. But tell me, did you have any doubts about their selection?

Oh, no, not in the slightest. They're both full of beans and on top of the world, have been training hard and actually looking forward in a big way to tonight's game.

I see, said Fred. Now we all know your young reserve players have made quite an impact on the Central League this season and that several of them will be taking the reins tonight. How many of them exactly, Jimmy?

Well, it's five or six of them actually. Our big snag at the moment, Fred, is that these lads who are actually playing will have to play in the reserve side, and some in the first team, two or three years before their time.

Before their time, repeated Fred, whose name was not Fred, in fact, but Frank. Before their time.

Jimmy nodded, but then, suddenly, he got up from the chair, held out his hand and said, Thank you, Fred, but I'm sorry, Fred, I best get back to them.

Jimmy walked out of the lounge, walked into the lobby, saw Jack and Bill waiting there, the players in their groups standing there, and Jimmy looked at his watch and said, Right then, boys, we best get going –

*

Bobby's Uncle Tommy Skinner was happy to drive their Bobby down to Manchester. It was a long, long drive, three, four hours on these roads, and Bobby hardly said a word, but his Uncle Tommy was not the sort to be bothered by long silences, and Uncle Tommy knew their Bobby had a lot on his mind, Bobby trying to keep his mind fixed on the game that night, work out who Jimmy might play, thinking, Yes, there'd be Harry Gregg and Bill Foulkes, which was incredible to Bobby, it really was, and then, if they were fit, there would surely be Ian Greaves and Ronnie Cope, and Freddie Goodwin and Colin Webster, who'd all played for the first team before, and then, of course, Ernie Taylor would come in at eight, thought Bobby, thinking that Jimmy would probably bring in Alex Dawson and perhaps Mark Pearson, too, how Jimmy would have no other choice, not really, but wondering, too, about the likes of Bobby English and Bobby Harrop, and Reg Hunter and Reg Holland, how they must all be in with a shout at least; Bobby even wondered now and then why the hell he wasn't in the side himself tonight, he wasn't going to play himself tonight, even wishing now and then he was, a part of him, a quick glance at his watch, wondering what the team were doing now, would they be going to Davyhulme, to the golf club there, for the usual steak and chips before the game, would that still be the plan today? But those thoughts, those wonderings that way, they led to ghosts, he knew, the ghosts of smiles, of laughs, of games of cards, of billiards, of trips to the pictures and nights on the town, of songs round the piano and Paradise, aye, Paradise, the ghost of Paradise itself, and Bobby knew then why that other part of him, another part said, Playing? Tonight? What the hell are you talking about? Are you mad?

*

There were no jokers on the bus today, no pranks, no laughs, no saucy snaps, no racy books passed up and down the bus, no, not today, not even a hand of cards, just the sound of the wheels on the road, taking them back, the traffic and the weather, bringing them back, closer and closer, their eyes on the backs of the seats in front, the windows to their side, a sudden shift, a shadow out of the corner of their eyes that would give them such a start, the tap on the window that made them jump, would make them think, Was that a stone thrown up or what?

Through Poulton-le-Fylde, skirting Preston, then Bolton, down through Little Hulton and Eccles, closer and closer, until they were back again, in Manchester, at Davyhulme, the park and golf club there, new to some of the lads on the bus, the younger lads who'd dreamed of coming here one day, but not to Bill or Harry; this the place the first team would always come for their pre-match meal before each home game, and then again of a Monday afternoon, every Monday after training out here they'd come again for a round of golf or two, depending on the weather, or a game of billiards, snooker or of cards, enjoy a drink, a chat, and then the meal, late on Monday afternoon, with the Boss and Jimmy, Tom and Bert, often Bill and Arthur, too, all out here, the first team, the staff, all together, laughing and joking; there was even a Captain's chair where Johnny Carey, Stan Pearson and Allenby Chilton had all once sat, and where Roger, Roger Byrne, had last sat, just three weeks ago, before the last Cup game, against Ipswich Town, and then again the Monday after, the last time they'd all been gathered here: Harry and Bill, Roger and Eddie, Mark and Duncan, David, Tommy and Bobby, Dennis and Albert and young Kenny Morgans, Jackie and Johnny, Billy Whelan, Ray Wood and Geoff Bent, all gathered here that day –

But not today, nor on any other day again, as off the bus and in they came, these younger boys, reserve-team players, in the footsteps, the shoes of the Dead they tried to walk, across the carpets into the dining room, to sit at the tables, in the seats, the places of the Dead, the cutlery, the crockery once touched, once used by the Dead, but Bill Foulkes, he would not sit in the Captain's chair, not today, nor any day, and nor would he or Harry pick up a fork, a knife that day, they could not eat a thing, they just sat at that table with those younger boys, reserve-team players, instead, in place of the Dead, listening to the sound, the deafening sound of every clock in the land, of every watch on every arm, tick, round and round, nearer and nearer, round and round, closer and closer –

Jimmy was out of his seat, up and on his feet, his knife against his glass, tapping, ringing through the room, the players turning, looking at Jimmy, Jimmy on his feet, trying to remember all the things he'd planned to say about Sheffield Wednesday, how they played, calm and considered, not like he usually did, but more like Matt would do, then a few final words, reminders about things they'd said in training, how they themselves should play, but on his feet, his glass, his knife still in his hands, when he looked out across that golf-club dining room, all Jimmy could see were the faces of those who were not there, he knew were not, could not be there, but there they were, in their seats, their places once again, looking up at him, the faces of his pals, Bert and Tom, the faces of the boys, those boys he knew were gone, but here again today they were, looking, staring up at him, and Jimmy blinked, he blinked again, then shook his head and said, he tried to say, Play hard for the players who are dead, boys, play hard for the players still in hospital and play hard for the great name of Manchester United –

But Jimmy stopped, slumped back down, hard into his chair, before his legs, his heart gave way, the glass, the knife falling to the floor, his hands to his face, and Jimmy whispered, I'm sorry,

319

boys, I'm sorry, as Jack jumped up from his seat beside Jimmy and shouted, Come on, lads, let's go –

*

Stan didn't want to play for United. He didn't know how many times, how many ways he had to say it, but HE DID NOT WANT TO PLAY FOR MANCHESTER UNITED.

But it was as if they had some sort of magic spell, bewitched his boss, his chairman, or maybe they just wanted bloody shot of him, but here they were, driving him at breakneck speed up to Manchester, like he'd been fucking kidnapped was how it felt to Stan, bundled out of the car, into the posh hotel, surprise, surprise, the press, the cameras already there, they'd even roped in Tom Finney to give him the glad hand, the good word, how Stan was joining, The greatest club in England, in Europe, if not the world, Stan thinking, Oh, am I, Tom, is that right, and so you're signing, too, are you then, Tom? No, I didn't think you were. No, it's just old muggins here.

But then, at last, here came Jimmy Murphy, but not like the voice on the phone, the picture in Stan's head, but a softer, sad and crumpled man who looked like he'd just lost the world then wept himself raw, his eyes that red, this man who walked across the hotel lobby, his hand outstretched, he took and shook, gripped Stan's hand and said, just said, I need you, son. We need you –

Look, Mister Murphy, said Stan, it's a great compliment, I know it is, and so thank you, and I've nothing against United, I've always admired you, particularly after the way you played against us in the Cup Final last year, you know, with ten men, it was a courageous fight, it really was, but you see, Mister Murphy, sir, I've always been a Villa man at heart.

Jimmy Murphy, with tight hold of Stan's hand still, still he would not let him go, he said, Son, you don't understand, I need you now, tonight –

But, Mister Murphy, laughed Stan, even if I did say yes, it's already half six, and I haven't got my boots.

Eric Houghton, the manager of Aston Villa, he touched Stan's free arm and said, Don't worry, son, your boots are in the car, I brought them with me, just in case.

How very thoughtful of you, said Stan.

I just think you should help them, if you can, son, said Eric Houghton. Because they need you.

And you don't, thought Stan. Well then, I'm as good as gone here, the deal already done, and Stan sighed, Well, I just hope we can get to the ground in time.

Oh, don't you worry about that, son, said Jimmy, leading, dragging Stan Crowther out of the Queen's Hotel, I've arranged a police escort for us –

*

Now, as they drove down through Prestwich, Cheetham Hill, then into the centre of the city, Uncle Tommy Skinner began to wonder if this had been such a good idea after all. They stopped for a meal at a hotel in town, a place Bobby liked, said he liked and had been before, but the air, the atmosphere seemed to catch in his throat, even his Uncle Tommy, he found it hard to eat amid such a mighty swell of shock and sadness; after the meal, they'd planned to drive from the centre out to the ground, but back outside the roads were at a standstill, cars and buses bumper to bumper, blocking every route, so Uncle Tommy thought it best they leave the car and walk the rest of the way, if they could, and so through that bitter, biting twilight Bobby and his Uncle Tommy, hats on heads, the brims down low, their collars up, they walked among the crowds, the pavements all as packed, as blocked as the roads, bicycles abandoned, left on their sides, people tugging at sleeves, asking for spare tickets, touts selling some at daft, incredible prices, two-shilling or half-crown popular-side tickets going for a pound, even thirty shillings, but the search for tickets, the sound of the touts, all with London accents, so it seemed, they were the only voices, noises you could hear that night, walking there among the crowd, getting closer to the ground, many wearing black ties and armbands, red and white rosettes, red and white scarves, yes, but often with a piece of black cloth stuck or stitched on, Bobby thinking, Is this a seance or a football match, wondering again, Was this a mistake, a big mistake, a visit to a haunted house, Bobby and his Uncle Tommy edging slowly forward, gently parting, pushing their way through the crowd, Bobby wondering how on earth the team buses would ever get down these roads, through these crowds, even with the police, all the extra police, how then the team, the lads themselves would feel when they stepped off the bus and into this night, the emotions, the sensations coursing through its air, an almost constant, frightening, hysterical hum, so intense you could see, could taste it, so thick, it seemed, you wondered why Sheffield Wednesday would even bother coming here at all, what hope they had to even try to play on such a night as this, before a crowd like this; Bobby and his Uncle Tommy Skinner were at last inside the ground, through the players' entrance they'd come, they'd had no choice; the gates had been locked since half past five, they said, two hours before kick-off, but those locked outside, they did not go away, just stood and stayed, waited there, massed in muffled silence to listen to the cheers, the cries from those within; Bobby stood within, just inside the entrance there, he was about to turn to his Uncle Tommy, about to say, We best go up, get to our seats while we can, but then there was Jimmy, in his blazer and his flannels, with his shuffle and his smile, and his, Well, you are a sight for sore eyes,

Bobby Charlton, son, you really are! Now you're sitting with me tonight, you and your Uncle Tommy, but just come along with me now, son, into the dressing room, come say hello –

*

Ernie Taylor felt frightened, for the first time in fifteen years of League football, sitting in that dressing room, he was scared, but he also felt something unexpected, too, something he'd never thought he would feel when, just five days ago, still but five days ago, he'd agreed, reluctantly agreed to come here: he felt honoured. Ernie felt honoured, and humbled, too, by the devotion and the enthusiasm of these kids – because that was all they were, just kids – but their devotion, their enthusiasm, it shone through, had infected him, too, as he trained and played and talked and laughed with them, with Dawson, Pearson and Brennan, now changed into their kits, their boots, the same with the kids who were not playing tonight but who had still come into the dressing room, lads like Harrop, Hunter and Holland, urging, willing everyone on –

But perhaps it was easier for them, these younger kids, thought Ernie, easier than for the likes of Freddie Goodwin, Ronnie Cope, Colin Webster or Ian Greaves – Ian Greaves sat there in the place where Roger Byrne would have sat, in the shirt that Roger Byrne would have worn – all men who'd been around the team awhile, in and out the side, down the seasons, through the years, some even with a medal to their name, but who'd lost their places to lads now dead, pulling on shirts they knew they'd have probably never or rarely worn again, the shirts of men now dead or lying injured in a Munich bed, men they'd known, who'd been their mates –

Nor could Ernie imagine what was going through the minds of Harry Gregg and Bill Foulkes. Bill did not want to be the captain, that was clear, and Harry, well, he either said nothing or he never shut up; he'd looked right through poor Stan Crowther had Harry, ten minutes back, when they'd suddenly brought Stan in, introduced him round the room, then handed him a shirt, number 6, the shirt that Duncan Edwards wore, Harry staring at that poor lad as he pulled on that shirt, and for a moment Ernie feared that Harry would grab that shirt, rip it clean off Stan Crowther's back and say, That shirt's not yours, that's Duncan's shirt is that, but then, in the nick of time, thank Christ, back in came Jimmy Murphy, bringing with him Bobby Charlton, and Ernie wondered for a minute if Charlton was in the side, would play that night, but no, he'd just come in to see the lads he knew, shake their hands and say, Good luck, lads –

It'll be more than luck we'll need tonight, thought Ernie, sat there now with but minutes left to go, still frightened, still scared, because in fifteen years of League football, in all the years, the games he'd ever played, Ernie Taylor had never wanted to be on the winning side as much as he did tonight –

*

Down the corridor, out the tunnel, across the pitch, up the stands, onto the terraces, the names of the players echoed as over the tannoy the announcer read out the teams, each name greeted by a cheer, big, loud cheers for Harry Gregg and Billy Foulkes, but cheers for every name that night, for Greaves, Goodwin and Cope, an enormous cheer for Crowther then, for Webster, Taylor, Dawson, Pearson and Brennan, too, but still the team, the players stayed inside the dressing room as first Harold Hardman, Bill Petherbridge, Louis Edwards and Les Olive gathered on the pitch, their hats in their hands, they bowed their heads as the announcer now called for a minute's silence.

In the silence of that minute, the deepest, most profound silence that ground had ever known, some eyes were closed, some up beyond the lights, into the sky, some turned to the ground, to their feet or to their hands, the match-day programme clutched tight in some, where the names of the United team had been left blank, just a faint line of dots, the names of the players to be written above, filled in later, in pencil or pen, where were written there instead the words of the poet Laurence Binyon –

> *They shall not grow old*
> *As we that are left grow old.*
> *Age shall not weary them*
> *nor the years condemn.*
> *At the going down of the sun,*
> *and in the morning*
> *We will remember them.*

The moment, the second that minute was up, Bill Foulkes came running out of the mouth of the tunnel below the main stand, leading out the players into a blinding volley of flashbulbs and a wall of noise, wilder than anything that ground had ever known before, a roar so fierce the wonder was it did not split the sky apart, Bill turning right, heading down to the Warwick Road end of the pitch, where United always warmed up, they always had, then Bill came jogging back to the centre circle, more cameras, more flashes there as Bill shook hands with the referee and with Albert Quixall, the captain of Sheffield Wednesday; when he was a little lad, Bill used to dream that one day he would captain a great team like Manchester United, and now that dream had come true, but Bill just wished it hadn't, and he felt sorry, too, for poor Albert Quixall, he was shaking, almost crying as the referee tossed the coin into the air –

325

Heads, called Bill, and heads it was, and so Bill chose to attack the Warwick Road end, to let Wednesday kick off, and then Bill ran back to take his place, as the referee, Alf Bond, he checked his watch, then put his whistle to his lips and blew –

III

THE DEVIL'S WALTZ

10

From that first whistle, there started up a sort of shriek, a noise you'd never heard before, a shrill sort of involuntary, animal cry that had its peaks, sharp peaks, but which went on solidly throughout the match. Yet, at first, it felt as though you were not really watching a match, you were watching a film, actors playing the parts of people you knew, and the crowd as well, they seemed different, too, many more women than usual there that night, but then gradually the football began to take over. There was an early save by Harry Gregg, a well-won tackle by young Mark Pearson, but in their blue and white shirts, black shorts, Sheffield Wednesday began to try to play, to push forward amid the din, the howls, the shrieks, the sudden shouted names of the Dead on the air, as though summoning, calling them back, out of the night, a cross that Harry Gregg missed but which Ronnie Cope cleared, still the sense this was a fragile thing made of plasters and of prayers, this team of straw and hope, but then Ernie Taylor began to ask for the ball, running here, there and everywhere, making himself available more and more, demanding the ball, taking it, running with it, one minute sending Colin Webster away down the right flank, the next minute turning, swinging a ball out to Shay Brennan on the left, twenty-, thirty-yard passes, each as accurate as the last, then, having stretched the Wednesday midfield this way and that, Ernie would play a ball straight through the middle for Alex Dawson or Mark Pearson to scamper after and chase down, even having a shot himself, hitting the post early on, but constantly forcing, pushing Wednesday back and back. The ball into the box, to the head of Bill Foulkes, the ball pushed out by their keeper for a corner. The crowd shouting, cheering them on as Shay Brennan ran over to the left corner, and then Shay took the corner, right-footed, in it swung, somehow hanging over the goal, eluding two Wednesday defenders and their keeper, the ball either carried, wafted in on the cold night wind or sucked, willed in by the crowd behind the Wednesday goal, but somehow, somehow the ball was falling, had fallen into the net, as though an invisible Tommy Taylor had risen high above everybody else to turn it in, and Old Trafford exploded with another, different roar, shrill and shrieking still, but now in an exclamation of some kind of strange, reluctant joy, joy mixed with relief and with defiance, the tears of the happy sad, hats and scarves thrown up, up, up into the air. And though Wednesday kept on coming, and coming harder again after half-time, Albert Quixall stretching the United back line, one shot only just going over, still this scratch United side held on. Bill Foulkes tireless in defence, leading by example, Ronnie Cope winning tackle after tackle, landing on photographers gathered at the edge of the pitch, crunching into the barricades, but straight back up and on his feet again. The whole team chasing every ball, closing down every man, always running, they never stopped, always looking to push forward themselves. Bill Foulkes heading the ball clear, Stan Crowther, then Ernie Taylor quickly forward, the ball through to Mark Pearson, and Pearson shot, the ball spinning back off their keeper's legs across the goal, but only to Shay Brennan, who was there with a touch and then a shot, falling back as he scored his second. But still United came, still Harry Gregg turning every great save into another attack, Ernie Taylor taking the pass, releasing Mark Pearson down the right again, into the box, Pearson turning the ball back to Alex Dawson, who with a touch to get the ball from out beneath his feet then shot and scored. And six minutes later, when the referee blew his whistle for the final time that night, against all odds, all hope, Manchester United had won three–nil, and the crowd exploded again into one last, enormous, delirious cheer, hands upstretched towards the skies, the night, this wonderful, dreadful night when it did feel, it really felt the Dead were looking down on them, helping and supporting them, and out of the ground swept the crowd, on a tide of triumph and relief, into the arms, the embrace of the thousands still waiting in the shadows outside or in the streets leading away from the ground, out on their doorsteps, in their nightclothes, all asking, pleading, Who won, who won? Did we win, did we win? Who scored? What were we like?

*

Bobby had never known a game like it. He felt sorry for Wednesday, he really did. There was such emotion, it just dragged the best out of every player on the field, and they ran their socks off, they really did, and when the ball went in the net, the sound, the sound was just deafening, and Bobby thought, We're on our way, we're on our way, and he turned to his Uncle Tommy and he said, Well, this is ridiculous, me going back to the North-East from here.

He really thought he'd just stay on in Manchester now, he'd not go back tonight, he would not budge again. But soon again he'd changed his mind, thought it would be better if he did go back tonight, pick up his gear, his things, say goodbye to his mother, his father, thank them, the family for all they'd done, then come back down again in a day or two, yes, he thought, that would be best.

And at the final whistle, when they'd won the match, that was great, because it would release a lot of the tension, Bobby hoped, give people something to think about, other than what

331

had just happened, though Bobby dreaded to think what would have happened had they lost; he honestly thought Manchester would have died of a broken heart. But Bobby felt some of the pressure now lift from his own shoulders, too, felt perhaps the worst of the pain might be behind him now, at least be less than before, and Bobby turned to Jimmy and said, I'll be back in a couple of days, Jimmy, I promise.

Well, that's terrific is that, son, said Jimmy, like two wins for us tonight is that, son, hugging Bobby tight, telling Bobby, We'll be waiting for you, son.

I know, said Bobby, I know –

The moment he'd sat down in the stand, between his Uncle Tommy and Jimmy, Bobby knew he had to start playing again at the first chance he could. Not for himself, but for Eddie, David and Tommy, for Roger and Mark, for Billy and Geoff, for Tom Curry and Bert Whalley and Walter Crickmer, and for Duncan and the Boss and for all the lads still left in Munich. He would carry their memory every time he went on the field. He would play better than he had ever played before. He would try to help keep the team in the First Division. He would try to help drive the team towards Wembley. He would try to bring joy back to the fans who had seen this team grow and then die before their eyes. He would try to help to prove that there was life left in Manchester United –

Bobby would prove there was life after death.

*

A thousand miles away, deep in the Munich night, up on their ward at the Rechts der Isar Hospital, Kenny Morgans, Albert Scanlon, Dennis Viollet and Ray Wood took it in five-minute turns to listen on the handset to the commentary from Old Trafford, arranged by the *Manchester Evening News*, and when the final whistle went, it was said Ray Wood had the handset to his ear, and Ray yelled, We've won! We won! We won three–nil!

Back at Old Trafford, beneath the stands, Jimmy Murphy stepped out of the dressing room and told the waiting press, I have just been in tears inside there. Because I've just seen something wonderful, something which means more than even a victory deservedly won. We've all been privileged to see the beginning of a great build-up. Now we know the future will have its sunshine, too. So they were tears of joy tonight, my tears. I have always said that enthusiasm plus ability can beat anyone and anything, and I told the lads before the match, I said, Play hard for the lads who have gone, for those who are still in hospital and for the great name of Manchester United. That is what they've done, what they did, and Matt would have been proud to see these youngsters. For the first time in my life, I'm not ashamed to find my tears of joy cannot be forced back. This is the greatest day of my life, even after thirty years in football.

Behind Jimmy as he spoke, in the dressing room, there were more tears, drink, too, beer and champagne, for the photographers and camera crews there to record, to film the celebrations. But most of the drink went undrunk, just a sip with a smile for the cameras. But there was nothing to celebrate, nothing to cheer, all of them relieved to have won, yes, but still so sad, unable to escape the thoughts that they should not be there, that they had stepped into someone else's shoes, the shoes of the Dead; even Shay Brennan, the Man of the Match, everyone said, who loved a drink, any chance of a drink, he could not forget the lads, the friends, so many of the team were dead, that he was only there in that room because they were dead and he was not, and he just wanted to get out of that room, be gone and be home, and in the footage that was shot, the photographs that were taken in the dressing room that night, Well, it doesn't need

Harry Gregg or anybody else to describe it, all you've got to do is look at Foulkesy's eyes and look at mine –

Empty.

*

Bill had never cried, not since he was a little lad, but as soon as he came off the pitch, went back down the tunnel into the dressing room, he cried. He knew the lads had played their hearts out, they could not have given more, and it had been wonderful to skipper such a grand side. They had fought every inch of the way, and no one could say that Sheffield Wednesday had given them any quarter, shown them any pity at all. No one could say that they didn't deserve their win, and Bill liked to think that they did it for their colleagues who died at Munich. That was what Bill told the press after the match. But Bill was exhausted, utterly exhausted. It was as if he had some kind of flu or virus, the worst he'd felt since the crash, and it was only then, it seemed to Bill, after that game, later that night, that he knew that they were gone, the lads, his mates, that they were not coming back, an empty space where they once had been, but Bill had a terrible, nagging feeling that this was not at an end, perhaps might never end, that somehow worse was still to come, and Bill could not eat, still could not eat, and Bill could not sleep, still could not sleep, not that night nor the next.

*

That same night, Duncan had taken a turn for the worse, had shown signs of distress. But then again, the next day, there had been an improvement, however slight, but an improvement again, a sign of hope again. But Thursday night, Friday morning, the doctors noticed that Duncan's circulation was failing. A series of restorative injections produced some improvement. However, the improvement could not be maintained, his circulation failed completely, and at 02:16, Munich time, Duncan died –

Peacefully in his sleep, the doctors told Gladstone, Annie and Molly. With no pain –

But pain was all that Gladstone, Annie and Molly felt now. Pain, pain, pain –

Either stood in silent shock, unable to speak, unable to move, to understand how this could be, had come to pass, or curled up in a ball upon the floor, wailing, or shaking from head to foot, ceaselessly screaming, unable to stop . . .

But while the nurses, the doctors they did their best, they tried to help, again their best to help with embraces and with sedatives, there was no cure, no balm, no way to ease or stop the pain. Duncan was dead.

*

Late in the night, still at the ground, in his office up the stairs, Jimmy put down the phone and Jimmy cried, he howled, No, please, God, no, no, no –

He sagged forward in his seat, his head in his hands on his desk, and he wept –

He wept, he cursed, he raged, then wept again. He could not stop his tears, his tears of loss and grief, but tears of anger and of fury, too –

Fuck, fuck, fuck, he cursed and he raged. Why let the poor boy survive and live at all? Why do this to him, to his poor parents, to all of us? Why give us fucking hope where there was no hope, there never was . . .?

The greatest day of my life, Jimmy had told the press after the game on Wednesday night, what an idiot, what a fucking

335

fool he'd been to say such a bloody stupid, stupid thing. The greatest day of your life? Well, look at you now, Murphy. Where your mouth has got you now.

But he had seen something wonderful that night, he had, and he'd thought that it might, just might be the beginning of a great build-up, that the future might, just might have its sunshine, too, and he'd hoped, he'd prayed it could come true, it would be true. But at the centre of his prayers, the heart of his hopes was Duncan, always Duncan, that somehow, against all odds, against all reason, Duncan would not only survive, but rise and recover to play again. Not only to play again, but to captain and lead the team, a symbol of triumph out of disaster, of hope over despair, of answered –

The telephone on his desk was ringing again, ringing and ringing. Jimmy wiped his eyes, his face, he stared at the telephone awhile, then picked it up, listened to the voice on the line telling him that Manchester United and England had lost a great footballer, asking him if Duncan would have been the greatest footballer his club and country had ever known . . .?

Yes, said Jimmy, whispered Jimmy, the club and England have lost a great footballer. But I have lost a friend, a very dear friend. This is the final blow.

*

Professor Maurer knew they had to tell Ray Wood, Dennis Viollet, Albert Scanlon and Kenny Morgans. Their wives, their loved ones would be here to visit them soon, and they would know by now; the whole world knew by now, all except the survivors in the Rechts der Isar Hospital.

I have some bad news, said Professor Maurer. Duncan Edwards died early this morning.

What, said Kenny Morgans.

Unfortunately, his kidneys were so badly bruised that they just would not work, said Professor Maurer, and the artificial kidney and the blood transfusions just could not keep his bloodstream clean. But you should know that he was not in pain. He died peacefully in his sleep.

I just don't believe it, said Kenny Morgans. The nurse took me up to see him, just a few days ago. He was sleeping, but he looked okay, I thought the worst –

I know, said Professor Maurer, but it is incredible to all of us here that he survived for as long as he did. It was only his immense physical strength and superhuman will to live that enabled him to cling to life.

I can't believe it, said Kenny Morgans, turning to Ray and Dennis and Albert, can you?

Ray and Dennis and Albert had their eyes closed, raised to the ceiling or hidden behind their hands. They shook their heads and said, No.

*

Each morning, Cissie had greeted Bobby with the latest newspaper reports from the hospital in Munich. Some of the recent bulletins had been optimistic, and Bobby's hopes had grown again. But that Friday morning, as soon as she saw the headline, Cissie hid the paper before Bobby got up and came down, then she went to make him his favourite breakfast of ham, eggs and mushrooms.

But the moment he came down into the room, Bobby asked, Where's the paper, Mother?

It mustn't have come yet, love, said Cissie. You just get on with your breakfast, while it's still hot. Should make the most of them, before you –

Bobby pushed the plate away. I don't want any breakfast, he said. Duncan's dead, isn't he?

Frank Taylor knew something had happened, that something was wrong the minute that Doctor Taylor entered their room that morning. He usually came in with a spring in his step, a joke on his lips, doing his best to raise the spirits of Frank and especially of Jackie. But not that morning, that morning Doctor Taylor came in quietly, slowly, with the hint of a frown, not a smile, as he asked, Now then, chaps, how are we both today?

Can't fault the room service, laughed Frank, but Doctor Taylor only nodded, smiled at Frank, went over then to Jackie's bed, examined Jackie's arm again, said something like, Won't be long now, I shouldn't think, before Professor Maurer sets your arm, Jackie.

That's good, is it, asked Jackie.

Oh, yes, said Doctor Taylor, and then he looked across at Frank and said, Be your turn then, Frank.

I'd best keep my diary clear then, hadn't I, Doc, laughed Frank again, at his own joke again.

But Doctor Taylor only nodded, smiled at Frank again, went then towards the door, but at the door he stopped, he turned, coughed then said, There's no point keeping it from you both. You both are well enough. But I am afraid I have some bad news for you both. I know you'll understand, but Duncan couldn't quite make it. He died early this morning, very peacefully in his sleep –

Oh, God, said Frank. His poor parents.

I know you won't tell Matt Busby, said Doctor Taylor, but please be careful not to let anything slip. He's still too ill to be told anything yet.

Of course, said Frank. Loose lips, all that.

Doctor Taylor nodded, briefly smiled at Frank, glanced at Jackie, then said, I know you both understand. Everything that could be done, was done. I'll see you both later, and went then quickly from the room.

Frank turned to look at Jackie in the next bed, saw the tears rolling, streaming down his cheeks, the despair, the sheer, black despair being carved into his face, and Frank said, Stick it, son, stick it. We can't help Duncan now, he's gone. Think of your wife, she'll soon be here. Don't let her see you like this –

But Jackie Blanchflower turned his face away, reached out with his good arm, pulled the bedclothes up and over his head and buried himself in his bed.

*

Jimmy had no idea how they would, even could get back up again, keep on going now. But that Friday morning, Harry Gregg, Billy Foulkes, Ian Greaves, Freddie Goodwin, Ronnie Cope, Stan Crowther, Colin Webster, Ernie Taylor, Alex Dawson, Mark Pearson and Shay Brennan did get back up again, did keep on going, even Ronnie with a slight calf strain, Pearson and Brennan with their bruised feet and shins, all of them with their hearts broken all over again, they all got back up again, all ready to keep on going, and so Jimmy could pick the same team again for the League match against Nottingham Forest tomorrow; Murphy's Marvels, the press had called them in one paper, much to Jimmy's annoyance, Murphy's Chicks in another, Murphy's Mites –

No one seemed to understand that for Matt and Jimmy, for Bert and Tom, for Bill and Arthur and Joe, the performance of the fourth and fifth teams had always been as important as that of the senior teams, that the future of any club lies in its youngsters, and that was why, before the crash, they had a first-class Central League side which had included six full internationals. Yes, Brennan, Dawson and Pearson had all played well on Wednesday night, despite their youth, their inexperience, and deserved all the accolades, but Jimmy knew he was bringing them into League football too fast, far ahead of their time. It was one thing to blood a young lad into a team of experienced pros, but another thing altogether to promote a whole batch of them up in one go. But what choice did he have, what else could he do?

Because not only did he have to pick the first team, he had to pick a side to play Sheffield Wednesday in the Central League, over at Hillsborough tomorrow, and when he looked again down the list he'd written out, after he'd thought through the options once again, those endless discussions he'd had with Bill and Arthur, Joe and Jack, he could have bloody wept again, if he had any fucking tears left to shed. But that list was the best that they had, the only side they could name: Gaskell, Smith, Cummings, English, Holland, Bratt, Spratt, Harrop, Mooney, Giles and Hunter; of these eleven, only David Gaskell and Bobby Harrop were regulars in the Central League, three of them would be making their debuts, and the average age of the side would be seventeen. But what choice did he have, what else could he do?

*

Gladstone, Annie and Molly had asked if they could see Duncan one last time, to say goodbye, but when they saw Duncan lying in the hospital mortuary, Annie and Molly could not say goodbye, they could not let him go, they just could not, would not let Duncan go, and the doctors, the nurses, they came again with their sedatives, but with the orderlies, too, to help prise Annie and Molly away, away from Duncan, to get them back to the hotel, to pack in a daze, take them out to the airport and onto a plane and away, away from Munich, away from Duncan –

*Just get me out of here, Mum. I've got better things to do than
lying around in here all day . . .*

For a few brief, kind seconds, when she opened her eyes
Annie did not know where she was, why she was strapped into
a seat, on a plane, up in the sky, the air, but then those few brief,
kind seconds were gone and she remembered. She had never
said how good he was, nor Dad, they never said nothing to him
like that. They wouldn't, never did. She'd never even told him
that she loved him. But she did. She thought there was nobody
like him in the world. But she never told him –

I need to get back . . .

*

They had to open the gates early, at one o'clock that afternoon,
two hours before kick-off, there were that many people at Old
Trafford again, and then they had to close and lock the gates
early, thousands left outside the ground again, inside a post-war
record crowd of over sixty-six thousand for the League match
against Nottingham Forest. But it was a quiet, hushed and
sombre crowd that watched the Very Reverend Herbert Jones,
Dean of Manchester, and the Reverend Herbert Price, President
of the Free Church Federal Council, first lead out an official
party that included the Yugoslav Ambassador, representatives
of the Yugoslav Football Association and Red Star Belgrade,
the Lord Mayor and Lady Mayoress of Manchester, and the
Mayors of Salford and Stretford. They gathered on the muddy
pitch as the crowd removed their hats, their caps and bowed
their heads, and then the Dean of Manchester began the brief
interdenominational memorial service with prayers for the Dead,
the injured, their families, their friends and all who mourned,
and with a prayer for the club, too, and which concluded with
a reading from *Pilgrim's Progress* and then another minute's

silence, and in that silent, silent minute snow began to fall upon Old Trafford, the crowd, the pitch, and at the minute's end, when Bill Foulkes came running out of the tunnel, leading out the team, turning right, heading down towards the Warwick Road end again, at that very moment down in London, at the airport, a special BEA flight from Munich touched down, bringing the body of Duncan back home.

*

Jim Thain was the most hated man in England, a man most people seemed to wish was dead, wished his family dead, too, so he might then know how it felt, whom many would even murder if they could, judging from the letters he received, his wife, his parents, too, the things that people said to him, to them, when they stopped him or them in the street, on the rare occasions he or they now did go out. Some weren't best pleased with Busby either, believed Busby should have stopped Thain, the damn fool, but then again, Thain was the captain, the man in charge, the man who was responsible and thus the man to blame.

The British Airline Pilots' Association had stood by Jim Thain, at least, had been supportive, had complained that British European Airways should never have allowed Jim Thain and his surviving crew members to be subjected to such an 'exhausting and exhaustive grilling by the Press' in the immediate aftermath of the accident. The BALPA believed BEA should have prevented its staff from being subjected to 'such rough – one might even say inhuman – treatment'.

But Jim Thain just wished no one would speak to the bloody press, not even, or particularly, anyone from British European Airways. No doubt Anthony Milward, the Chief Executive of BEA, was a decent enough chap and had perhaps meant well, had probably tried to take the brunt of the press in order to spare

Jim Thain and his crew, but the things Milward had said to the press, they had only made things worse.

First, on arriving in Munich on the day of the crash, Milward had openly discussed the possibility of sabotage. Then, when Milward returned to London, he had suggested that the fact that a house was situated three hundred yards from the end of the runway meant that what very probably might have been a simple overshoot had become a major disaster.

Of course, these remarks had been reported not only in the British press, but in the West German press, too, and the West German authorities had been quick to issue an official retort, and for Jim Thain, a damning one, and one which was widely reported in the British press, too –

After a preliminary investigation, the West German Traffic and Transport Ministry said that the fact that the aircraft did not leave the ground was probably the result of ice on the wings and, they added, Captain Thain had yet to give a satisfactory explanation of why he did not discontinue the final attempt to take off.

It seemed to Jim Thain that Milward's bloody stupid intervention had given the Germans and their Chief Accident Investigator all the incentive they needed to contend for a particular result, hanging him out to dry in the process, blackening his name with the public, all in advance of any inquiry –

People have to blame somebody if they have something go wrong, said his wife, and I suppose you are the obvious person, dear.

I know, said Jim Thain. My biggest mistake was staying alive. But I'll be damned if I let them make a scapegoat of me –

Every waking minute of every hour of every day, Jim Thain went over and over, again and again, the events of that day, that hour, those final minutes, until Jim Thain was more sure than ever that the snow was thawing on the wings on the aircraft, more certain than ever that the aircraft's speed was retarded not by a failure in the engines but on the ground, that the large quantity of snow which had built up at the end of the runway had prevented the aircraft from accelerating, that the crash then occurred because of the amount of drag caused by excessive slush on the runway, and so Jim Thain would ensure that the German inquiry was in possession of every single piece of information with any bearing on the accident. He would submit his formal report. He would provide appendices that detailed take-off procedures. He would also provide reports dealing with slush and its observed effects on aircraft. His wife Ruby was a science graduate, and she would conduct experiments to prove there was no ice on the wings at the time of take-off, that the ice found on the wings of the wreckage formed after the accident. Jim and Ruby Thain would clear Jim's name, but not only for the sake of his reputation, his good name, but to help to determine the true cause of the crash, to help avoid another disaster, prevent more deaths, more grief.

For in the waking minutes, the hours of the night when Jim Thain could not sleep, he was haunted by the thoughts of Ken Rayment, his poor wife, poor family, the medical bulletins issued each day which reported a deterioration in Ken's condition and gave only cause for concern, not hope, praying in those minutes, those hours that Ken might live, his wife, his family be spared his loss, the grief. But in those same waking minutes, hours, Jim was haunted, too, by the words of Captain Hans Reichel, the Chief Inspector of Accidents, the exchange that he and Jim had had in Munich, two days after the disaster, when Jim suggested to Captain Reichel that the quantity of snow, the excessive slush on the runway had prevented the aircraft from accelerating and taking off –

Of course, Reichel replied, the captain should know his aircraft and under what conditions he can attempt to take off, wouldn't you agree, Captain Thain?

Throughout the last Sunday in February, there were memorial services across Manchester. First, at three o'clock in the afternoon, there was a Protestant service at the cathedral, attended by two thousand people, with many more outside. The Yugoslav Ambassador, Mister Vejvoda, and representatives of the Yugoslav Football Association and Red Star Belgrade attended this service, too, and heard the Dean of Manchester tell the congregation, Association Football is for millions what ballet is for others. It is a great art, and some of its greatest artists have been lost. Now it could be said, he said, that such things are just examples of mass hysteria or juvenile hero worship, as has been claimed, but between Manchester United and their support, and between sports writers and their readers, there is a family feeling unlike anything I have known. Then, at five o'clock, there was a Jewish service at the South Manchester Synagogue on Wilbraham Road, with special prayers for Henry Rose. Then there was an interdenominational service at a quarter to seven, at the Albert Hall on Peter Street, attended by one thousand, seven hundred and fifty people. Finally, there was a Roman Catholic service at a quarter past eight that evening, at Belle Vue speedway stadium, which drew a crowd of more than six thousand people for the Solemn High Mass at the King's Hall there. Ten double-decker buses were needed to bring the people from one Manchester parish.

But that Sunday, Jimmy, Jack and Joe, Bill and Arthur, Les and Alma did not, could not attend any of the memorial services in Manchester. Early in the morning, Jimmy went to Mass, as he always did, every Sunday morning, and then he went back to Old Trafford, as he always had, every Sunday morning, but not to sit and chat with Matt, as they always had, about the game the day before, all the games the day before, but to sit up in his office

345

with Jack and Joe, and Bill and Arthur, and Ted Dalton, the club physio, too, to talk over the games the day before, both the first-team and the Central League games.

We started well enough, said Arthur, really should have been three up, in fact, and that first half-hour Harrop, Giles, English and Bratt, they all played very well. But it was a heavy pitch, and they tired, of course, and once Cummings had to come off, then we didn't really stand much chance. It was two–nil when he came off, so four–nil flattered Sheffield somewhat.

Jimmy nodded, Jimmy said, I was thinking we'd take Bobby Harrop and Peter Jones back with us to Blackpool on Tuesday. That was a bad goal, the Forest goal, the way Wilson and Imlach combined. Not one of our boys was quick enough.

They were slow, yes, said Jack. Any news from Bradford about Blake?

Jimmy shook his head. No, nothing, but the good news is that Dennis and Kenny Morgans are out of hospital and should be home very soon. I reckon young Kenny might be fit enough to play again soon, too.

Meanwhile, downstairs, Les and Alma were hard at work still, still trying to sort through all the letters, still with help from Les's wife and Jimmy's kids and anyone else who cared to lend a hand, but still Les was working sixteen-, seventeen-hour days, and now he had the applications for tickets for the Cup game away at West Bromwich Albion to deal with, too . . .

You think Bobby Charlton will be back in time for West Brom, asked Bill, first looking at Jimmy, then at Ted Dalton.

Jimmy shook his head. I don't know, Bill. I just don't know. He told me he'd be back by now, but that was before, you know, before the news about Duncan.

*

Cissie couldn't stand it any more. She put on her coat, her hat and her gloves and went out into the snow. She trudged down the backs, round to see Bobby's friend Ronnie Routledge, and knocked on his door –

Hello, Missus Charlton, said Ronnie at the door. How are you, is everything all right?

Cissie shook her head, she said, No, it's not, Ronnie. He's up in his room with his records again. Morning, noon and night. He's barely said a word since Friday, since the news, like, and when I asked when he was going back, he said, I'm not. I said, You what? He said, I'm not going back, Mother, I'm not playing again.

Well, it's a shock to him, isn't it, said Ronnie, about Duncan. But I'm sure he'll come round.

Cissie said, Oh, you're sure, are you, Ronnie? Well, that's good, because you're going to make sure.

Me, said Ronnie. What can I do?

You can get your coat on, get a ball and get round to ours and get him out of that room and up the park for a kickaround is what you can do, Ronnie Routledge.

But it's snowing, Missus –

Snowing? This isn't 'snowing', said Cissie. What's wrong with you? A bit of icing sugar is what this is, and there's me thinking you were a goalkeeper, a bricklayer, too. Now get your coat on and come on.

Ronnie Routledge, who was on the books at Sunderland, and who was a bricklayer, too, sighed, got his coat down off the peg in the hall and then followed Cissie back round to Beatrice Street, stopping in on the way at Hirst North County School to borrow a ball –

I'll never smile again, until . . .

Bobby, called Cissie, going up the stairs, calling out again, Bobby, marching into his room. Will you turn this racket down! I've been calling you –

347

I'll never laugh again . . .

Bobby got up from the floor, went over to the record player, lowered the volume and said, What is it?

Ronnie's downstairs for you, said Cissie.

Bobby sighed. What does he want?

How should I know, said Cissie.

Bobby sighed again. Can you tell him I'm not feeling so good, I'll see him later . . .

No, I cannot, said Cissie. Tell him yourself.

Bobby sighed again, switched off the record player and followed his mother down the stairs.

You all right, Bob, said Ronnie.

All right, Ron, said Bobby.

You couldn't do us a favour, could you, asked Ronnie, holding up the ball. Boss has been on me back. Think I'm on me way out, to be honest. Could really do with a bit of extra practice like, if you didn't mind?

But it's snowing, isn't it, said Bobby.

Not really, said Ronnie. Not –

It's stopped, shouted Cissie from the back.

Bobby rolled his eyes, sighed again and said, Okay, then, Ron, and went to get his old boots on.

Sorry about this, said Ronnie, as they trudged up towards the park, the snow not stopped but not that bad.

Bobby shook his head, he said, Oh, don't worry, Ron. It's good to be out of the house, really.

You see the results yesterday, did you, said Ronnie. You see we lost at home to Burnley, did you?

Bobby nodded. Aye, my father told us.

Sounds like you should have beaten Forest, said Ronnie. Ernie Taylor was supposed to be brilliant again.

Bobby nodded again. Aye, my father said.

Up at the park, Ronnie took off his coat, put it down on the

348

ground, on the snow, and Bobby took off his coat, put it down on the ground as the other post, then Ronnie passed the ball to Bobby, and Bobby dribbled off up the park, in the snow, the ball at his feet, turning then, passing it back to Ronnie, Ronnie taking a touch, passing it back to Bobby, Bobby trapping the ball, hitting it back down the park to Ronnie, back and forth they passed the ball, until Ronnie took one ball on his chest, caught it in his gloves, kicked the ball back down to Bobby, shouting, All right then, Bobby, come on, let's go then –

And Bobby began to hit the ball, to strike the ball, to shoot at Ronnie, to try to score, again and again, ball after ball, Ronnie diving to his left, reaching to his right for ball after ball, again and again, Ronnie reaching to his left, diving to his right, Bobby sending Ronnie one way then sending him the other, after ball after ball, again and again, hitting, striking the ball, scoring goal after goal, for Eddie, for David, for Tommy, for Roger, for Mark, for Billy, for Geoff, for Duncan, for Duncan, for Duncan, until three hours later, when the snow was too thick, falling too thick, the light too faint, night falling now, Ronnie pleaded, Let's call it a day, Bob!

In the park, in the snow, in the twilight, with the ball at his feet, Bobby looked up, down through the gloom at Ronnie, head to toe in mud between the coats, and Bobby said, Okay then, Ronnie.

Bobby and Ronnie picked up their wet coats, said, Goodbye, see you later, then Bobby walked back down to Beatrice Street, stamped the mud and slush off his boots on the step outside, then took them off, went inside, saw his mother at the sink and said, Mother, I'm off back to Manchester tomorrow.

Are you, love, said Cissie, trying not to smile, to look too pleased. Well, your shirts and things are all ironed and ready for you. They're on your bed.

I bet they are, thought Bobby, going up the stairs to his room to pack, shaking his head as he went, saying under his breath, Thank you, Mother.

In London, on Tuesday lunchtime, at Saint Bride's Church in Fleet Street, there was a memorial service for Alf Clarke, Don Davies, George Follows, Tom Jackson, Archie Ledbrooke, Henry Rose, Frank Swift and Eric Thompson, conducted by the rector, the Reverend Cyril Armitage, and the Reverend Canon Mortlock and attended not only by the colleagues of the Dead, but by the many sportsmen whom Alf, Don, George, Tom, Archie, Henry, Frank and Eric had written about, had sometimes praised, sometimes criticised, and Walter Winterbottom, the England manager, gave the second address, and as he began to read from the Bible, Walter looked up at the tall church windows –

Snow had begun to fall again.

That awful afternoon, less than three weeks ago, Walter had been working in his office at Lancaster Gate when the telephone rang with the terrible news. He had played for United himself, of course, and knew Walter Crickmer, Tom Curry and Bert Whalley well. Big Frank Swift had been the goalkeeper when Walter had first become England manager, back in Forty-six. He had selected Roger Byrne thirty-three times and Tommy Taylor nineteen times for England. He might have capped David Pegg only once, but he was a boy with great promise. Now all three were dead. Dennis Viollet, Bobby Charlton and Albert Scanlon were players Walter was also considering for the upcoming World Cup that summer in Sweden, but all three were now injured.

But that afternoon, when Walter had heard that Duncan Edwards had not been killed, his heart had leapt. Duncan was the player whom Walter counted on more than anyone else in the England side. He was only twenty-one, but Walter had already selected him eighteen times for England. He was particularly impressed by the way that Edwards and Byrne played together. They were always in close touch with each other, one man constantly shielding the other. Byrne was the stronger individual personality, of course, more experienced and knowledgeable about tactics, the man with the greater football intellect. But Duncan, on the other hand, was indomitable, a boy who could respond to instruction and play any type of game to order. Just supremely in love with football, Duncan played with such tremendous joy that his spirit stimulated the whole of the England team. He was the boy whom Walter had always dreamed of one day finding, the dream made real. It was in the character and spirit of Duncan Edwards that Walter saw the revival of British football.

Last Friday morning, it was his wife who had heard the news first, who had had to break the news to him that Duncan had not made it, that he had passed away in the night. The feeling of dejection, the sense of loss, Walter had never known anything like it; it was overwhelming, almost unbearable.

He was a magnificent boy, always cheerful, always smiling, always ready for a laugh and a giggle; he was a lovely lad, and now he was gone.

*

It was snowing in Manchester, too, that morning, when Bobby arrived back at Old Trafford. But snow was just one of the many problems Bobby had, for although he wanted to come back to Old Trafford, to start playing again as soon as he could, Lance Corporal Charlton was still in the army, still with three months left of his National Service. But if the army medical officer passed him fit, Bobby was hoping to play in the Royal Army Ordnance Corps Cup Final at the Vauxhall Barracks, down in Didcot, on Wednesday afternoon. But Jimmy feared the Army Cup Final would be called off because of the weather, and Jimmy wanted to see for himself how fit Bobby was. So Jimmy had asked Bobby to stop off at Old Trafford to take part in a full-scale practice match, and in the cold, and in the snow, Bobby huffed and he puffed, his pace too slow, his touch not good, and at the end of the match, drenched in sweat and out of breath, bent double with his hands on his knees, Bobby gasped, he said, It's no good, Jimmy, I'm as slow as a carthorse.

Don't you worry, son, said Jimmy, you'll be fine. The minute the whistle goes on Saturday, all your old strength, your enthusiasm will be back, son.

Bobby sighed, he said, I hope so, Jimmy, I hope so. But what if the army won't release me to play?

Don't you worry about that either, son, said Jimmy. Alma has spoken with the War Office, and they've said that they'll deal with your case as quickly and as sympathetically as possible. So as soon as you get back to Shrewsbury, you go see your commanding officer.

Bobby nodded, he said, Thanks, Jimmy.

Don't thank me, son, said Jimmy, thank the good old British public. The army wouldn't dare not release you, if you were fit enough to play for us, so you just make sure you get back here in one piece, son!

I will, said Bobby, I will, and then Bobby said goodbye to Jimmy and to the lads, the team, that he'd see them again, be back as soon as he could, and the lads, the team, they said they'd see him then, just a shame he had to go, what a fag it was, they said.

But Bobby didn't mind, in fact a large part of him was glad, even if the Army Cup Final was called off tomorrow, because he'd rather be back at barracks than in Manchester, or even in Blackpool with the team, because if he was in Manchester or in Blackpool, Bobby knew there would be the pressure, unsaid but there, in the air, the pressure to go to Dudley, and Bobby knew he could not go, he just could not go, no matter how much he felt he ought to go, he knew he couldn't cope with his feelings in such a very public setting –

You're bloody hiding again, aren't you, Bobby, laughed Duncan. You're bloody ducking, aren't you?

On the train from Crewe down to Shrewsbury, his face to the window, the snow on the glass, Bobby closed his eyes and whispered, I'm sorry, Dunc, I really am.

You're like that bloody keeper, remember him, laughed Duncan, the Royal Air Force one?

Bobby nodded, he smiled. He did remember him. They were playing for Western Command were Bobby and Dunc, at Cosford it was, against the RAF, and Duncan was unbelievable that day. Maybe it had been a few days since he'd last played, but he just wanted the ball all the time, and there was one move, well, Bobby didn't think he'd ever forget that move –

First, Duncan demands the ball off his own keeper, then Duncan passes to the full-back, but Duncan asks for and gets it straight back, then it's Bobby's turn to get the ball and pass it straight back to Duncan, and all the time the RAF are in retreat, pelting back as fast as they can, and now Duncan passes it to the centre-forward, who holds the ball for a second or two, sees Duncan running into the box and rolls it into Duncan's path, and Duncan, well, he never breaks stride, he just shoots straight at the head of their keeper, who makes no attempt at all to save the shot, just ducking down, out of the way, as the ball rockets into the back of the goal –

I'm sorry, said Bobby again. I really am. I know I should be going. I'm a coward, Dunc, I know I am.

I'm only pulling your leg, laughed Duncan again. I wish I wasn't going myself, I can tell you!

*

A local Munich tailor had been into the hospital and had measured up young Kenny Morgans, Albert Scanlon, Dennis Viollet and Ray Wood for four brand-new suits. The tailor had then been back with the suits a week or so later, and they had tried them on, had had the necessary adjustments made, and now young Kenny, Albert, Dennis and Ray all had fine new suits ready for the day they could leave hospital, they could set off back for home.

That day came first for young Kenny and Dennis. They were allowed to leave hospital, but on condition that they would fly back to England, not travel by train. Professor Maurer and his staff felt that a journey home by train would be too strenuous for them.

Before he left the hospital, Dennis asked if he might go and say goodbye to the Boss, and Professor Maurer and his staff agreed, but only on condition that Dennis made no reference to what had happened, and Dennis nodded and said, Of course, whatever you say, Doc, then in his new suit Dennis went upstairs to the fourth floor and Room 401 –

Hello, Boss, said Dennis, sitting down beside Matt Busby's bed, trying not to show how shocked he was to see the Boss looking so old, so very old and grey. I've just popped in to say goodbye. I'm going home.

Matt Busby gave a little nod, a little smile, then said, That's great, son. You're feeling better then?

Oh yeah, said Dennis, I'm fine.

Matt Busby gave another little nod, another little smile, and said, So you're going home then, son?

Yeah, yeah, said Dennis. Me and Kenny Morgans, we're going back together, tomorrow.

Matt Busby nodded, smiled again and said, Kenny is going home, too, is he? Well, that's great.

Yeah, said Dennis. It's great.

354

But then Matt Busby said, And so how are you getting home then, son? You and Kenny?

Well, said Dennis, we're flying, I think.

Matt Busby reached out, grabbed then gripped Dennis by his arm and said, Don't do that, son.

Okay, said Dennis, okay, I won't –

Don't let Kenny fly either . . .

Okay, said Dennis again, I won't –

You tell him from me . . .

I will, said Dennis, I will.

You promise me . . .

I promise, said Dennis.

Matt Busby released his grip, let go of Dennis, and his head back on his pillow, Matt Busby closed his eyes and sighed then said, That's good, son, thank you, son.

I'll see you later then, Boss, said Dennis, getting to his feet, Matt Busby nodding once, his eyes still closed, exhausted by the effort, seeking sleep, an exit, as Dennis left the room, went back downstairs to where his wife Barbara was waiting with young Kenny and his fiancée Stephanie, and Kenny asked, How was the Boss then?

He didn't seem that good, said Dennis.

Why, said Kenny. What happened?

He said we're not to fly back.

Barbara nodded, she said, He's right, you know?

Yeah, said Dennis, I know, I know he's right.

So what are we going to do then, asked Kenny. I can't stay another day longer in here. I can't . . .

Stephanie shook her head, she said, You won't have to, dear. Professor Maurer said if you didn't want to fly back, then you could stay in the hotel for a few days, until you were a bit stronger . . .

Barbara nodded, then asked Dennis, Did the Boss say anything else, love, ask about anyone else?

No, said Dennis, he didn't.

Kenny shook his head, Kenny said, That's strange, don't you think? He was in a room with Duncan, wasn't he? And with Johnny, too, when we all first came in.

It's not strange, said Dennis. He knows.

*

The black days were back again, had never really gone away, though that Black Wednesday in the Black Country, the world was white at first that day, with sleet, with snow, but then was turned to grey and black and into slush and mud by the thousands upon thousands, five thousand, it was said, who from the dawn had braved the cold, the sleet, the snow, the slush and mud to line the streets of Dudley, from the Priory Estate and Duncan's home, three hundred wreaths laid out across its tiny lawn, in reds and whites, some shaped as footballs, some as a number 6, past Duncan's old school on Wolverhampton Street, where pupils stood in tribute on both sides of the road, all along the way to Saint Francis Parish Church on Laurel Road, they stood waiting, in the cold, the snow, for the moment when all traffic stopped, hats and caps came off, heads bowed as the cortège passed slowly, slowly by.

There were many fellow footballers, football folk and various dignitaries among the three hundred mourners packed inside the church. Jimmy was there, of course, with the United directors and some of the players. Gordon Clayton and Bobby English had been asked to be two of the pallbearers, but a snowstorm had delayed them, so it was Peter McParland and Pat Saward who helped the England captain Billy Wright, Ray Barlow, Don Howe and Ronnie Clayton bear Duncan's coffin on their shoulders into Saint Francis Parish Church.

In the front pew, Gladstone, Annie and Molly sat side by side, inconsolable. Behind them sat Mister and Missus Dorman,

Duncan's landlady and her husband, invited down by Annie, and who wept as though they themselves had lost their own son –

He was a boy of whom any mother would be proud, Missus Dorman had told the *Manchester Evening News*. He did not smoke, he barely drank. He was a clean and tidy lad who preferred watching television to publicity-seeking. He liked to spend hours cleaning his car. But he never liked flying. He always seemed to go quiet a couple of days before flying.

Talent and genius we shall see again, the Reverend Catterall told the congregation of Saint Francis Parish Church, but there will be only one Duncan Edwards. This superb and modest athlete lived and loved his life among us to the full and would have undone no part of it. And it is now fulfilled. Go forward, Duncan Edwards, from this place, rich in achievement, honoured and loved by us all, forward into the dawn.

The pallbearers bore Duncan's coffin on their shoulders back out of Saint Francis Parish Church, then the hearse carried Duncan's coffin the last two miles to Queen's Cross Cemetery, where the police had to hold back the crowds as the funeral cars passed through the gates, three thousand people straining for a better view. Beside the open grave, the wreaths stretched for thirty yards in each direction, north, south, east and west.

But in the bitter, biting wind that cold, bleak, snow-swept day, Gladstone, Annie and Molly did not, could not see the crowds, the wreaths, they saw only Duncan's coffin being lowered into the winter ground, laid there to rest with his little sister Carol Anne, who had died of meningitis at just fourteen weeks, when Duncan was but ten years old, and that day, when Annie and Gladstone had had to tell him his sister was gone, that Carol Anne would not be coming home, Duncan had gone and sat outside upon the step and sobbed and sobbed.

*

Matt had heard the terrible cries, the howls of grief, heard them echo down the corridors, through the wards. Days later, he could hear them still; Matt knew what had happened, must have happened, he was certain, he was sure; he had heard the whispers outside his room, the low, sad voices from his doorway, and so when the kindly German priest next popped in to say, Hello, and how are you today, Matt? Would you like to share a prayer again together today, Matt? Matt shook his head, and Matt said, Tell me, Father, how is Duncan Edwards today?

Later that same day, in the early evening, when Jean came back again to visit Mattie, for the second time that day, she sensed straight off that something was not quite right, the air heavy in the room. But she sat down beside his bed, touched his hand, smiled and said, You're not wearing your new spectacles, dear?

Jean, I know, said Matt. I know Duncan is dead. I want to know the rest, I want to know the worst. For my own peace of mind, Jean, please. You have to tell me.

This was the moment Jean dreaded would come, but knew had to come, Sheena and Sandy, Professor Maurer and all of his staff, too. How many times had they discussed what it was they would do, what Jean should say when this moment came? But now it was here, she just nodded, Jean nodded and whispered, Okay.

Roger Byrne, asked Matt.

Jean shook her head.

Mark Jones, asked Matt.

Jean shook her head.

David Pegg, asked Matt.

Jean shook her head.

Billy Whelan?

Jean shook her head.

Geoff Bent, asked Matt.

Jean shook her head.

358

Tommy Taylor, asked Matt.

Jean shook her head.

Eddie Colman?

Jean shook her head again.

Walter, asked Matt.

Jean shook her head.

Tom Curry, asked Matt.

Jean shook her head.

Bert, asked Matt.

Jean shook her head.

Willie Satinoff?

Jean shook her head.

Frank Swift, asked Matt, Henry, the press boys?

Jean shook her head again. Just Frank Taylor.

My God, whispered Matt, my God, what have I done, and turned his head, his face away from Jean.

Jean gently squeezed Mattie's hand, then let go, stood up and said, I'm just going to go find Professor Maurer, dear. I'll be back in a minute, love.

I don't need a doctor, thought Matt, those poor kids, those other lost friends, their faces here before him now, their wives now widows, their children now orphans, parents burying their sons; how could he ever face the loved ones of the Dead?

11

He came out of the mist, the fog and the snow, off the hills, the moor, cut and bleeding, his clothes torn and ripped, and when he fell through the doors, they thought he was a ghost, from the war, from before, but he gasped, he said, Can you help me, please, there's been a crash.

The six station engineers working up at the Independent Television Authority transmitter at the summit of Winter Hill, high on Rivington Moor that day, they had not heard a thing. The snow was that heavy, the fog that thick that morning, they were already wondering, worrying how they'd get back down, back home that night, so when the doors swung open, this figure comes in out of the fog, in off the moor, giving them the fright of their lives, he did, his face covered in blood, his clothes in tatters, telling them there had been a crash, their first thoughts were, How on earth could this chap have got a car up here in all this snow?

But then it dawned on them: he did not mean a car had crashed, he meant a plane had crashed, and Mister Jarvis, who was in charge, he told Alan Sucksmith to call the police station down at Horwich and let them know, then Mister Jarvis told the rest of the staff to gather up all the blankets and the cushions they could find, the two stretchers and the first-aid kit. Then they left Frank Grindley to prepare the beds they had, while the rest of them followed the man, who said his name was Howarth, he was the first officer, followed him back out onto the moor, into the fog, the snow, tracked the drops of blood he'd left, his footprints in the snow, four hundred yards, until they came upon the scene.

The day after Duncan had been buried in Dudley, and three weeks to the day since the BEA Elizabethan had crashed on take-off at Munich Airport, thirty-five men in a party of Manx motor traders who were flying to Lancashire to visit a factory died after their chartered aircraft, a Bristol Wayfarer owned by Silver City Airways, crashed into the side of Winter Hill, a one-thousand-five-hundred-foot ridge above Horwich, Lancashire. Only four members of the party and the crew of three survived.

Bill Foulkes switched off the news, the television and the radio, put the paper in the bin and said, I will never fly again, he swore. I will not fly again.

But Manchester United were still in the European Cup, they'd reached the semi-finals, that was the reason they were, well, in the mess, the state they were, and how or even if United would fulfil their commitments in the European Cup were questions that the Chairman, Mister Hardman, had now to address –

We are not keen on the prospect of long train journeys across the Continent, said Mister Hardman, but if we draw Borussia Dortmund and Milan, and Borussia get through, then our tie will quite definitely be on. However, if we have to travel to Milan, Budapest or Madrid, then I can say that our chance of continuing is only fifty–fifty at very best, because we do not plan to fly to any of the remaining European Cup games.

I am not afraid of flying, said Harry Gregg, when Harry was asked by the press. I never have been, I never will be. But what happened at Munich was terrible to see, so to put it bluntly, no, I don't want to fly right now. But how I shall feel later, well, I cannot say.

Harry, Bill and Bobby had not spoken about the crash, they never did, they never really would, but in the dressing room one day, after training, Bill said to Bobby, If we have to fly to Madrid, Milan or Budapest, are you all right with that, are you, Bobby?

I don't really fancy it, said Bobby, but knowing if they could somehow, somehow still win the European Cup, well then that would be the best thing they could do, the greatest gift they could give the Dead.

But over the water in Brussels at the draw for the semi-finals of the European Cup, when Sir George Graham, the Secretary of the Scottish FA, who was representing Manchester United, explained that the club did not want to travel any more by air, he was given a surprisingly sympathetic hearing by the organising committee, and it was decided to 'fix the draw' so Manchester United would play either Borussia Dortmund or Milan, travelling to the away leg by train.

'THIS IS CARRYING SENTIMENT TOO FAR', said the headline in the *Empire News & Sunday Chronicle*.

Listen, we had not looked for any favours, boys, said Jimmy to the press, we never look for favours, but we are grateful for this wonderful gesture, but Jimmy knew he would have to get down on his knees with his beads again and just pray that Dortmund beat Milan, Milan being almost five hundred miles further by train.

Bill had loved flying, he really had. Nothing had bothered him, he was never afraid. Never thought about the Superga air disaster that had wiped out the entire Torino football team in a crash in a thunderstorm in 1949, killing all thirty-one people aboard, the players, club officials, journalists and crew. Bill had never given it a second thought. He could have gone for a ride on a kite and loved it could Bill, he just loved flying that much, the thrill, the excitement of it all. Honestly, the plane could have flown upside down for all he cared. But not now, not any more; all Bill wanted to do now was to somehow wipe the memory of Munich from his mind, but it just would not, would never go away. He would rather forget the European Cup, too, if he was honest, if he could, but at least now the talk of flying was at an end, at least for now. That is a load, a great weight off my mind, Bill told the press, and an extremely helpful arrangement. So I think United should definitely go on with the European Cup, but at the moment I just don't want to fly.

*

The snow hung over the sixth round Cup tie against West Bromwich Albion at the Hawthorns that Saturday. But Jimmy knew another postponement wouldn't help them, it'd be just yet another fixture to rearrange, not least more work for poor Les, and there'd be folk who'd say it was only putting off the inevitable, anyway.

Back at the end of October, United had played West Brom at the Hawthorns in the League. It had been a tight, tough old game, but West Brom had won four–three, and that was against a United side of Ray Wood, Billy Foulkes, Roger Byrne, Freddie Goodwin, Jackie Blanchflower, Duncan Edwards, Johnny Berry, Billy Whelan, Tommy Taylor, Bobby Charlton and David Pegg. Jimmy had played for West Brom himself, more than two hundred times in all, been to Wembley with them, too, in the side that lost to Sheffield Wednesday in the final of Thirty-five, and so Jimmy always kept a keen eye on West Brom and Jimmy knew they were a good team, built on the core of the side that won the Cup in Fifty-four, that finished second in the League that season, too, just four points behind Wolves, five points off the Double. A lot of folk had West Brom down as favourites for the Cup this year, too, fancied them to go all the way, not least their own manager, Vic Buckingham –

With every respect for what Manchester United are, what they have been, and what undoubtedly one day they will be again,

363

Vic Buckingham had declared in that morning's papers, we are going to try and keep them in the waning stage. We have worked out no special plan and we are not watching any particular player. We shall be fighting all eleven United men, and there will be no singling out crash survivors or lads who had never played in a first-class match ten days ago. We will treat the new United at the highest level, but I don't think they will have the answer. The crowd, the background at Old Trafford, the desire to live up to the great men who are gone, this has carried them through against Sheffield Wednesday and against Nottingham Forest. But that cannot go on indefinitely. As I always say, talent does what it can, but genius does what it must . . .

Six–nil he says they're going to beat us, said Jimmy in the away dressing room at the Hawthorns. Because of the weather, it had taken them four hours to get down from Blackpool. The last mile had taken another half-hour because of the crowds on Halfords Lane, fifteen thousand United fans had come down, they said, banging on the side of the coach, urging the team on, filling the ground, the stands above the dressing room. Six-fucking-nil, can you believe it, said Jimmy, looking round the room at Harry Gregg, Billy Foulkes, Ian Greaves, Freddie Goodwin, Ronnie Cope, Stan Crowther, Colin Webster, Ernie Taylor, Alex Dawson, Mark Pearson and Bobby Charlton, Jimmy shaking his head in disgust. The gall of the man. Well, fuck Victor! You get out there and you fucking fight! You show them we don't need their fucking sympathy. You go out there and fucking win!

*

They had had to give Matt two shots of morphine to help him sleep, at least to rest, to try to numb, to stop his thoughts. But when he woke, it all came back. He had another small operation, to remove fluid from his right lung, but when he came round, there it was, waiting for him again. It would never go away, he knew, Matt knew, it would always be there, it could never be undone.

They could fix him up, get him well enough to leave this place, go back to Manchester. But he would not go back to football, of that he was convinced. He swore to himself, I will never go back to football.

*

The roar that greeted United when they came running out at the Hawthorns, as loud as a clap of thunder overhead, made Geoff wonder if this was not the Hawthorns but Old Trafford, and the tumult took the Albion by surprise, threw them off their stride, for within minutes Little Ernie Taylor pushed the ball out to Dawson, who crossed for Charlton, and Charlton shot, the shot blocked by Howe but fell then to Ernie Taylor, who fired the loose ball home, and the crowd, or at least, it seemed to Geoff, its largest part, went wild, their cheers carried for miles on the high winds. But then the Albion came back, Gregg twice parrying from Kevan, before Allen finished off a corner kick from Whitehouse to bring the home side level. Yet still Taylor and Charlton, backed by Crowther and Goodwin, continued to make United play, Taylor beating men as if they did not exist, they were not there, though Dawson failed to round off one great opening. But then, just before half-time, from twenty yards out, Taylor left Sanders's crossbar shuddering, and this time Dawson rose to head in the rebound amid an ear-shattering commotion.

With a touch more such steadiness from Dawson, and Pearson, too, in attack, at the critical moments, when two–one up, United could have sewn up the match. But with an hour gone, having produced the game of his life, Taylor had played himself into the ground, and Charlton, too, began to fade, and with no Edwards and no Colman to gather scattered forces, United were losing their shape and poise. Now the Albion roused themselves to a thundering rally over the last twenty minutes, when each receding minute seemed like an eternity and left Geoff wondering how Gregg and his battered companions could hold on to even part of the spoils as wave after wave of attacks pounded against Gregg and Cope and the others, until it seemed that all would be swept away and lost.

In the final barrage, driven by Howe, Allen volleyed another United clearance back goalwards, hitting Gregg's legs, only for Horobin to touch the rebound forward towards the goal-line as Harry Gregg dived again, scrambling to clear the ball off the line, helped by Ronnie Cope, who scooped it away off the line. But with his whistle straight to his lips, the referee blew and awarded a goal, and Harry Gregg tore towards him, other United players surrounding the referee, too, as hundreds of schoolboys and youths charged onto the pitch, the police struggling to stop them, clear them away, the United players continuing to protest, The ball never crossed the line, it never did, it never did, and Harry Gregg, he was that mad was Harry Gregg, he tore off his glove and threw it at the referee, who really should have cautioned Harry Gregg but turned a lenient, sympathetic eye on the 'Hero of Munich', and minutes later that was that; the game was drawn two–two, but only just, by the span of a hand, the width of a glove, it was as near as that, and with his heart still pounding, thumping in his chest, up in the press box Geoff thought, Well, if it is going to be like this again on Wednesday, in the replay under the steep floodlights at Old Trafford, then Lord, dear Lord, all our nerves will be in shreds.

*

Matt was shaking, his fingers, his hands, his arms. He took off his spectacles, tried to put them to one side, his fingers, hands and arms still quivering, he pushed the newspaper off the bed onto the floor. There were no more secrets any more. He knew from Jean that Captain Kenneth Rayment was still unconscious and dangerously ill. Jean had said that they were using blood transfusions, injections and packing his body in ice in the fight for his life. She had spoken of the man's poor wife, too, how sorry, how worried she felt for the woman, the hours and hours she spent by his bed, pleading, Come on, Ken, come on now, time to wake up, Ken, time to get up now.

But Matt had just read in the newspaper that the Munich district attorney was preparing charges against the pilot and co-pilot of the Elizabethan airliner. The newspaper said that the trial would most probably be held in Munich, and if the district attorney believed that the pilots acted carelessly, then the charges would be manslaughter. Manslaughter, manslaughter, Matt had read the word again and again, over and over, Manslaughter, manslaughter, and Matt could not help shaking, he just could not stop shaking.

Matt had flown many journeys, had got to know the sounds. There was nothing unusual when the drone of the Elizabethan's engines exploded into a roar and the big aircraft charged along the runway. Aye, there was a wee bit of tension, a twist in the stomach, there always was, that feeling that surely even the bravest had of, God help us, this could be it, so as he always did, Matt had begun to pray, until the aircraft was up in the safety of the air –

But that day, they had not taken off. The roar of the engines returned to a drone, the aircraft turned around and idled back along the runway to try again . . .

That bit of tension was now a lot of tension, that twist in the stomach now a knot, the prayers more urgent as they roared

367

along that runway once again. But again the roaring stopped, the drone returned, and they turned again, idled back again to try –

Again . . .

Why on earth had he not said anything, had he not spoken up? He was the manager of the team, for heaven's sake. Chelsea had heeded the Football League's advice and had not entered the European Cup. But he had not heeded the League's advice when they had the chance of going into Europe. It had been his decision to take Manchester United into the European Cup. If he had not taken them into Europe, the Dead would be with their families, their loved ones still. He should never have allowed the pilot to make that third attempt at take-off, he knew, and he had known at the time, on the day, as they sped on and on and on and on in the great din of the engines.

*

I'm not like Matt Busby, fumed Jimmy, raged Jimmy after the match, in the tunnel, the dressing room, on the coach, all the way home. He had had it up to here with some of the press, some so-called football people, too. People who should know bloody better, people talking fucking shit, claiming Manchester United were trading on the disaster, making innuendos about sympathy from the opposition, teams not playing hard but going soft for fear of injuring a United player, upsetting the manic United support, the talk that every team that takes on United will get no cheers for beating a so-called 'shadow side'.

Bollocks, fucking bollocks is that, Jimmy thundered, Jimmy stormed, all through Sunday, into Monday, on to Tuesday, I've been in football for over thirty years, and the way the lads fought beat anything I have ever seen in that time, better even than that fantastic game against Bilbao. The boys were magnificent, every one of them. This was one of the greatest performances in the history of Manchester United. One of the greatest games most of that crowd will have ever seen.

Now we don't like picking out individuals at Old Trafford because Manchester United has always been essentially a team, and I hope we will always continue to put the emphasis on teamwork. However, Ernie Taylor has been exceptional since the moment he arrived. He answered our call in our hour of need, and the marvellous way in which he has settled down with us shows you that the boys were glad to see him. He has been a natural at Old Trafford. He plays the type of football we like, and with so many youngsters coming into the first team, it is important that there is someone able to help them play the right brand of soccer. And anyone who has seen Ernie's careful working of the ball, watched him spraying defence-splitting passes in our last two games, they will know Ernie Taylor plays football, they will know Ernie is no kick-and-run player.

Stan Crowther has been playing himself into the side with great care, too, and I reckon he will become a firm favourite at Old Trafford. He was not particularly keen to leave the Midlands, yet in our plight and search for experienced players, he said yes, he would come to Manchester. But then, you see, the spirit at Old Trafford has always been something OUT OF THIS WORLD, and all the boys have been pulling together magnificently. When I asked Bobby Charlton to play on the left wing today, which meant a switch for him from inside-right, he said, I will play anywhere you want. That's Manchester's spirit, the United spirit for you.

But there were some in the press who were saying, Manchester United fans are suffering from mass hysteria. They are behaving like those groaning morons who idolise whichever skiffle hero happens to be the noise of the moment, but Jimmy was having none of that –

I'm not like Matt Busby, no, said Jimmy in the morning, then at noon, again that night. No, Matt can keep quiet when I know he's really upset, even when I know he's really wild inside. But I will not keep quiet when I hear the supporters made the victims of cheap criticisms and ridicule. The Manchester United fans have shared our successes. They have been the proudest supporters in the country. Of course they stuck out their chests and boasted that they belonged to Manchester United. We had the good fortune to give them something to boast about! And I hope we will be able to carry on making them proud, and noisily proud, because our fans are fantastic, shouting us to Wembley. All we ask is to be allowed to play our own way and try and get to Wembley.

*

I will never go back to football, Matt told Jean again.

Jean had lost count of the number of times Mattie had told her, I will never go back to football.

Even before I knew the rest, before you'd told me the worst, I'd had half a mind not to go back. But now I am certain, I will never go back to football again.

Professor Maurer had warned Jean and the family of the possibility that Mattie would suffer a form of delayed shock. But because Mattie had been noting which boys had been to see him and which had not, putting two and two together, and had probably then worked out for himself what had happened before he asked Jean, the shock was perhaps less than they'd feared.

But Professor Maurer had also warned of the inevitable depression that would then set in, that all they could do was to hope it would not be too acute or last too long, that they should just listen to Mattie, not try to challenge or argue with the things he might say, no matter how mixed up, how horrible those things he thought or said might be, they should just listen –

You don't believe me, I know you don't, said Mattie. You think I'll come round, I'll change my mind. But I'm telling you

370

now, Jean, I swear to you, Jean, my mind is made up. I will never go back to football.

I do believe you, said Jean.

But you don't agree then, do you, said Mattie. I can tell, it's written all over your face, Jean.

It's not a question of whether I agree or not, is it, said Jean. It's your decision, love.

But you don't support it then?

I just don't think you are being fair to the people who have lost their loved ones. And I am sure those who have gone, too, they would have wanted you to carry on. And then there's the boys who are trying to keep going – Billy Foulkes, Harry Gregg, Bobby Charlton . . .

*

Once again spivs had made a fortune, seven-and-six tickets going for seven quid. For most folk, though, the only hope was to pay on the gate, and so folk had started to queue from noon, all through the afternoon they came, they queued, in the rain, the heavy rain again, until the queues stretched not yards, but miles, the pavements crammed, the roads jammed. Once again the gates were opened early, hours before kick-off, but once again the ground-full bells soon began to ring, and once again the gates were locked an hour early. Once again there were thousands, some said thirty thousand, left outside, so many thousands left milling, swarming around that they stopped running trains from Central Station to Warwick Road, many older, long-time United and West Bromwich Albion supporters never even getting near the ground, queuing for hours to get on trains that never came, and now would never come, six thousand supporters left stranded in the city centre. But at Old Trafford, for those locked outside the ground, there was

371

no hushed and sombre silence, there was shouting, there was violence –

People continued to push frantically forward, hoping to find a turnstile still open, while younger lads tried to scale the walls. Police grabbed them, hauled them down, dragging them away, and while some lads struggled with the coppers, others steamed in to help their mates, their pals, threw objects at the coppers. Mounted police tried to regain control but were almost pulled from their saddles as other gangs of lads now set about the locked gates, pulling two clean off their hinges. But inside, they were met by a wall of police reinforcements –

In all my twenty-two years controlling crowds at Old Trafford, I have never seen anything like it, said Chief Superintendent Frank Waddington of the Manchester Division of the Lancashire County Police. My officers tell me the trouble was caused by youths and a few hotheads. There was no need for drastic action, and all of the men, I believe, handled themselves extremely well in what could have been very difficult circumstances.

*

It was as if people round here had lost their heads, their minds, thought Vic Buckingham, inside the ground, under the stands, in the away dressing room at Old Trafford –

Listen, lads, he said, looking round the away dressing room that night. Of course, we were all stunned by the crash, and I know you are all very sympathetic to them, I know you want Manchester United to rise again, and I am sure they will again be a great team one day. But not today, not tonight, no fucking way will I let it happen today, here tonight, because it is my job, your job, our job not to let them become great again at our expense, the expense of West Bromwich Albion Football Club. Because what can we do for those who were killed? Nothing. Of

372

course, for their dependants, we do as much as we possibly can. But then on with the game –

So I want you to go out there and knock the fucking stuffing out of them, because believe you me, right now, this minute, that's what Jimmy Murphy is telling them to do to you. So fuck this crowd, this team, just get out there and win this game!

*

Blink and you would have missed it. Half the press box probably did, smiled Geoffrey, their eyes down on their portable typewriters, thirty seconds from the end, believing extra time was around the corner, their copy delayed. But they certainly heard it and then looked up, and, Well, thought Geoff, how does one describe such scenes? The flurry of waving figures, the great crowd, agitated and at explosive point. The steep floodlights splintered on a scene perhaps best called 'tribal'. Geoff could not help feeling sympathy for poor Albion, and they themselves might have won at the last breath, for it was one of those matches, had it been a boxing match, in which no more than half a point separated the contestants at the end. But it is the end that matters, and it was the deathless, deathless spirit of these young men from Manchester that carried the day at the crisis. Yes, perhaps the tie lacked the full quality of football, certainly before half-time. But at the change of ends, when the United had the breeze at their backs, there were some flashing moves and counter-moves, thrust and parry, all at a searing speed.

But there was no denying that the setting itself was like some hothouse, and had been all evening long, the battle fought out to a ceaseless, thunderous roar. It was this, together with Manchester United's heart, a fine defence and the artistry of Taylor and Charlton in attack, that won a victory that will go into the history books, and to think that exactly a month ago today, the club had seemed to have been destroyed. Now a new miracle really did seem to be happening.

Geoff had already noticed that the people of Manchester now looked at one with warmth and pride in their eyes. Rightly, deservedly so, because Manchester United now had something more than just a faith to hang on to in the days ahead, and he believed, Geoff really did believe that if Manchester United, the new, now went all the way to Wembley, well, then it would unquestionably be the greatest and most dramatic achievement in the realm of any sport in history.

Oi, Geoff, shouted Desmond Hackett again, sitting on the press-box steps, his typewriter on his knees. For the umpteenth time, who was it bloody scored?

*

The moment Colin saw the ball go into the net, everything seemed to start spinning, everything in a dizzying whirl. There was champagne, beer in the dressing room, Jimmy with a bottle in his hand, telling everyone, That'll teach Vic Buckingham to talk about six or seven goals, teach Vic to keep his fucking predictions to himself, everyone patting Col on the back, hailing him the hero, the man of the hour, and the next morning, when he awoke, Colin thought at first it must have been a dream, he'd dreamt it all, but then he remembered, he remembered, and in his heart Colin wished he had just dreamt it all, he wished it was all just a dream. Not the goal last night, but this whole last month. A bad bloody dream. He'd watched the coffins come back, helped carry them into the gym, then been to the funerals, eight in what? Eleven days, was it? His mates in them boxes, in the ground. He just couldn't get his head around it, it was doing his head in, he knew, but he couldn't stop thinking about it, just couldn't stop himself. Not just him obviously, everyone. Everyone was on edge. Folk went on

374

about the great spirit, all that, but it was cobblers. People barely spoke, they dared not speak, didn't know what to say, what could you say? He'd been over to see Tommy Taylor's mam and dad, his brothers and his sisters, and sat with them awhile, they were distraught, heartbroken, of course they were, but they'd ended up consoling him, their arms round him, sat there in their house in bits again. But at his digs in Manchester, or at the ground, or at the hotel in Blackpool, he just always felt bad-tempered, easily annoyed, and over nothing much at all, just stupid little things, mainly, most of all with himself, the mistakes he made, the way he let his mind wander here and there, then irritable all the time, many days he could barely, hardly keep his anger in. He knew he'd always had a quick temper, it was one of the reasons he thought the Boss always seemed to have a doubt about him. He'd give him a run in the first team, but then Colin would go get in some scrap, some scuffle, like the one in Prague, and then sure enough, he'd find himself back in the reserve team come next Saturday. But if it was bad before, his temper, it was worse, much worse now, and Colin knew, in his heart he knew why; he knew it didn't matter that he'd scored, it was just a tap-in from three yards out anyway, the tea lady couldn't have missed, the easiest goal he'd ever scored, but Colin knew no matter how many goals he scored, how well he played, it didn't matter, nothing fucking mattered any more; he'd never raise, bring back the Dead.

*

The *Manchester Evening News* had made a special arrangement with the Rechts der Isar Hospital again and had organised another minute-by-minute commentary service for the sixth round Cup replay so that Albert Scanlon, Jackie Blanchflower, Ray Wood and Frank Taylor could all hear the news of the match as it happened.

375

Jean and the doctors had asked Matt if he would like to listen, too. But Matt had shook his head and said, No, no, I have no interest in that at all.

But late that evening, it must have been almost half past ten, Matt heard a sudden, raucous cheer from a room somewhere down the corridor, and Matt guessed they must have won, and Matt closed his eyes again, he tried to sleep again, but still he could not help but wonder what had happened, who had scored, and in the morning, when Jean came again to visit, as she always came to visit, every morning, afternoon and evening, Matt sighed, then said, I suppose they must have won then?

Who, dear, asked Jean.

United, said Matt.

Oh, yes, said Jean. We did, one–nil.

Do you know who scored?

Now then, who was it, said Jean, turning to pick up the newspaper, trying not to smile, let Matt see her smile, opening the newspaper. Well, this is what the man in *The Times* wrote, said Jean, and began to read aloud: As for the goal, I can only try to tell the story in a series of easily recognisable pictures, in the manner of a strip artist with his panels. There was one minute left. It was all the world on extra time, when suddenly West Bromwich Albion threw themselves into a final assault. Allen chipped a through pass down the left to Horobin. The winger was shepherded aside by the powerful Cope and some at this point, on quiet reflection, might have considered there was an obstruction. But no, the ball came loose to Goodwin, who found Taylor somewhere near the half-way line. Taylor dummied, darted to the right like a little goldfish, and lofted a beautiful through pass to the last precise inch down the right touchline. And there already gathering momentum was the match winner. It was Charlton who had moved across field and with fiery pace swept past Williams down the right up to the by-line, squeezing past the giant frames of Barlow and Kennedy down the by-line, in towards the near post, and there was his short diagonal pass leaving the Albion defence wide open and defenceless. Webster moving in from the left flashed the ball home and the explosive point of a night that will never be forgotten in Manchester was reached.

I see, said Matt, as Jean folded up the newspaper. So it was Colin Webster then, thank you, love.

Jean smiled, she said, Sounded very exciting.

But who's this Taylor, asked Matt.

Jean smiled again, she said, Ernie Taylor, you know, dear? Who was at Blackpool?

Aye, said Matt, and then again, I see.

I think I heard it was Paddy who first mentioned, who suggested Ernie to Jimmy.

Aye, they're pals, said Matt, yes.

Jean smiled, she said, But how are you feeling today, dear? Your cough, it seems a wee bit better?

Yes, said Matt, it's not too bad today.

Jean smiled again, she said, You know, dear, Professor Maurer and some of his staff, they've been invited to Manchester by the club, and the club thought it would be nice if you could record a short message for them to play before the game on Saturday, letting the crowd, all the supporters know how you are doing, how you're getting on, and thanking Professor Maurer and his team, you know? But only if you're up to it, love?

No, said Matt, I'd like to, if I can.

Jean smiled, she said, That's great, dear, that's great. I'll let the club know. I think the *Empire News* it is, they will come in and record the message.

Okay, said Matt, and then Matt said, We must be in the semi-finals of the Cup then now?

And Jean smiled, smiled again, leant over Matt, kissed the top of his head and said, *We* are, love, yes.

Just stay in the compartment a while longer, will you, boys, the police inspector told Dennis Viollet and Kenny Morgans, young Kenny Morgans, as he was now universally known, when their train pulled into Liverpool Street Station. Just while we clear a corridor for you through the crowds so we can get you to your transport.

Dennis and Kenny could not believe the crowd that had gathered at Liverpool Street Station to greet their return from Munich. It was hard for them to fathom why, after a month, a month to the day; were they hoping there had been a mistake, that the other lads, the Dead, would step off the train and say, Surprise, surprise!

But even with the police holding back the crowd, when Dennis and Kenny stepped down from the train, people still broke through the line to shake their hands or pass them flowers, to wish them well, it seemed, just to wish them well, and one older lady, she ducked down under a policeman's arm and rushed to hug young Kenny, held him, squeezed him tight and said, It's me, love, it's your mum, but then she was gone again, back into the crowd, lost and swamped by reporters and photographers, could they not just leave them alone for five bloody minutes, with their questions and their flashes, but the police and station porters now jostled the journalists, manhandled the cameramen out of the way, moving young Kenny and Dennis away, off into their separate cars, to go their separate ways –

Dennis and Barbara had decided to go back to Manchester by car, but young Kenny and his fiancée Stephanie travelled back by train, and when they got off the train at London Road, there were no crowds, no reception party, no one even seemed to recognise them, and as they walked out of the station into the thick, thick Mancunian fog, young Kenny pulled the collar of his coat up over his mouth to keep out the smog and felt relieved, he thought it for the best, it best there was no fuss.

*

Twenty-five doctors and nurses from the Rechts der Isar Hospital, led by Professor Maurer and his wife, walked out of the Old Trafford tunnel to a huge cheer from the sixty-three thousand supporters before the League game, against West Bromwich Albion yet again, snow falling on Old Trafford yet again, the cheers only getting louder as Professor Maurer and his party gathered on the pitch, embarrassed by the photographers, blinded by their flashes, and then the Chairman, Harold Hardman, introduced the members of the party to the crowd, each member waving shyly to the crowd, Mister Hardman expressing the admiration and gratitude of the club for all that Professor Maurer and his staff had done and were doing for the injured. Then Bill Foulkes, Harry Gregg and Bobby Charlton came out onto the pitch, each carrying a bouquet of red and white flowers, presenting the bouquets to the party to yet more cheers from the crowd. But then Harold Hardman asked for quiet, said they had a special message for the crowd from Munich, and the whole ground fell suddenly, utterly silent as over the loudspeakers came a familiar, yet strangely haunting, haunted voice, falling with the snow upon the crowd –

Ladies and gentlemen, I am speaking from my bed in the Isar Hospital, Munich, where I have been since the tragic accident of just over a month ago.

You will be glad, I am sure, to know that the remaining players here, and myself, are now considered out of danger, and this can be attributed to the wonderful treatment and attention given us by Professor Maurer and his wonderful staff, who are with you today as guests of the club, said the voice upon the still winter air.

I am obliged to the *Empire News* for giving me this opportunity to speak to you, for it is only in the last two or three days that I have been able to be told anything about football, and I am delighted to hear of the success and united effort made by all at Old Trafford. Again, it is wonderful to hear that the club have reached the semi-final of the FA Cup, and I enclose my best wishes to everyone. Finally, may I just say,

God bless you all.

And then the voice, that familiar yet strangely haunting, haunted voice, was gone again, leaving tears with snow upon the cheeks, the faces of so many in the crowd, the crowd still hushed, still sombre as into the snow, the biting, bitter wind, United now kicked off, but this time they did not, could not win, nor even draw, despite the best efforts of Bobby Charlton, running here, there and everywhere, every inch of ground, position on the pitch he seemed to try to cover, but Little Ernie Taylor could not help him, not today, limping from early on, a strain in the muscle of his thigh, and West Brom scored, and scored, and scored, then scored again and won four–nil, and for the first time since the tragic accident of just over a month ago, Manchester United lost, and as the still hushed, still sombre crowd made their way home from Old Trafford, in the snow and in the wind, in the evening papers they read that while Johnny Berry was now considered out of danger, the day before in Munich gangrene had been found below the knee in the left leg of Captain Kenneth Rayment, and the only possible way to save his life was to amputate, and so that night, while Professor Maurer and twenty-five doctors and nurses from the Rechts der Isar Hospital, along with players and officials from Manchester United Football Club, attended a civic reception and dinner at Manchester Town Hall given by the Lord Mayor of Manchester,

Captain Kenneth Rayment had his left leg amputated from above his knee.

*

Are you still planning on leaving United, Ray?

Ray Wood and his wife Betty got off the train from Munich at Liverpool Street Station, to a lot of shouted questions and bursts of flashbulbs from the reporters and photographers gathered there. But there were no other people waiting, no crowds of well-wishers for Ray and Betty, but some passers-by, when they realised who it was surrounded by the press, they shook Ray's hand, they wished him well as they were passing by, one even said, I hope you stay on at United, Ray, but if you don't, you come play for us, for the Arsenal, son!

Before Munich, before the crash, Ray Wood had wanted to leave Manchester United. Ray knew the Boss had never really trusted him since Wembley, the Cup Final last year, that the Boss thought he'd lost his nerve since that shoulder charge from Pete McParland had knocked him out, had broken his jaw and fractured his cheek, that was why the Boss had bought Harry Gregg from Doncaster in December, paid twenty-three grand for Harry had the Boss, made Harry the most expensive keeper in football history did that, and Ray had not played for the first team since, not once, so Ray had read the writing on the wall, he wasn't stupid, what with young David Gaskell coming through in the reserve team, too.

Ray plucked up the courage, went to see the Boss, told the Boss straight he wanted to leave, asked him for a transfer there and then, but the Boss had just smiled at Ray and said, well, what had the Boss just smiled at Ray and said? Back at home, when Betty asked what had happened, what the Boss had said, Ray couldn't really say, but thought it was something like, Don't

381

you worry, son, I'll see you right, you'll be all right, you don't worry, son. And that was that, left at that –

Well, I'm suffering from double vision, Ray Wood told the press at Liverpool Street Station, and it may take three months or more to clear up, the doctors reckon. So I shall be out of action, out of soccer until next season, anyway. But since the disaster, I have given up all hope of moving to another club. I am going to stick with the lads and do all I can to help them.

*

Jimmy had known it couldn't go on, it wouldn't last. You cannot pitchfork third-team players into the electric atmosphere of Cup football, play them out of position, then expect them to do that week in, week out in the League as well. No, at some point they will run out of steam, drop to their knees and not be able to get back up again. But though Jimmy had seen defeat coming, could even point to certain reasons – reasons, not excuses: the ceremonies before the kick-off, the injury to Ernie Taylor, in particular – no reasons ever made a defeat any easier to swallow or digest. United had slipped down to sixth in the League, too, though it was true they'd played three less games than City or Luton, who were both above them now. But those three games in hand, they were a problem in themselves, when to play, how to fit them in; they would have no choice now but to play at least one midweek game a week until the end of the season. And just to compound a bad day, the reserves were well beaten at Preston, and that was after Jimmy had strengthened the side, surprising many by bringing in Warren Bradley, Derek Lewin and Bob Hardisty, three amateur but experienced players from Bishop Auckland, and yes, Bob Hardisty might well be thirty-seven or however bloody old he was, but Jimmy didn't care how fucking old Bob was; Bob had been England amateur international captain, and more to the point, Jimmy knew Bob, knew Bob would be a great help to Jimmy with the youngsters in the reserves; even if Bob ended up just standing there, prompting them, Jimmy knew he'd be helping them, teaching them. But the defeat at Preston only confirmed to Jimmy what he already knew: there were going to be a lot of hard lessons coming their way now, now the well of sympathy was drying up.

*

The army insisted that Lance Corporal Charlton must play in the postponed RAOC Cup Final at Didcot, on the Friday afternoon, the day before United travelled to Turf Moor to play Burnley in the League. Bobby didn't mind, he didn't complain, he scored three goals, he made four, and the Seventeenth Company, Nescliffe, beat the Fourth Training Battalion, Blackdown, seven–nil and won the Army Cup. Major-General Richmonds presented Bobby with his medal, then Bobby said goodbye to his army teammates, got into a car and was driven back to Manchester, ready for the game at Turf Moor the next day.

United had brought a lot of supporters with them to Turf Moor that sunny Saturday afternoon, but in the shadow of the Pennines, the dark and silent mills, 'Murphy's Marvels' would need all the support they could get, because the sunshine wouldn't last for long, not round here, that was for sure. Jimmy had not dared risk Little Ernie Taylor, and so perhaps Bob Lord's Burnley 'Butcher Boys' sensed a chance for a much-needed win, or maybe they'd just had it up to here with all the bunkum still being said and written about Manchester bloody United, felt a meal had been made of Munich, the mourning overdone, gone on too long, well, today they'd give them something new to cry about –

Early on, Harry Gregg dived at the feet of Brian Pilkington and the 'Hero of Munich' got a boot in the mush for his bravery and needed treatment. But soon after, when a patched-up Harry went up for a ball with Alan Shackleton, Harry thought there had been an elbow in there, aiming at his face again, and Harry didn't like that; Harry went for Shackleton in a scuffle in the box. But once again the referee didn't put Harry in the book, he just had a word, turned a lenient, sympathetic eye again, and the Burnley crowd, some in that crowd that day, they didn't care for that, and for the first time that Saturday afternoon, as clear as day, there were shouts in the sunshine of IT'S A PITY THEY DIDN'T ALL DIE!

Minutes later, Doug Newlands went in hard on Ian Greaves, and this time the referee did get out his notebook and take down Newlands's name, and soon after he had his notebook out again, evening up the score, taking down Stan Crowther's name after Stan had squared up against Les Shannon, who seemed to be out looking for trouble that Saturday afternoon, and Shannon found it soon enough again when Mark Pearson tackled him. Now Mark Pearson was only seventeen, he really was a Babe, and Jimmy loved Mark Pearson, he really did. He never shirked a tackle, chased down every ball, won back balls he'd lost, he was a fighter, not a quitter, a Jimmy Murphy type of boy, but with his dark hair and long, Latin sideburns, his build and strength, the way he put himself about, there had already been talk in the press that young Mark Pearson needed to tone it down a bit, get his act together and start to show more respect, so when young Mark Pearson clipped old Les Shannon, put Les on the ground, Shannon wasn't having that, not from some seventeen-year-old bloody hooligan, Les straight back on his feet, his fists up and raised, jostling, pushing Mark Pearson, young Mark Pearson not backing down, no, he stood his ground. But the referee was having none of this, he said, and sent young Pearson packing, Straight off you go, but not Shannon, only Pearson, and head down, off young Pearson went, to boos and jeers, the police having to protect him as he went, the cries again, the abuse, You should have died at Munich, you!

In the first minute of the second half, things went from bad to worse as Jimmy McIlroy beat Harry to score, and then with only ten men and twenty tiring legs, despite Bobby doing all he could, all he possibly could, despite the taunts still upon the air, Pity you ever came back from Munich, Charlton, in the seventieth minute Alan Shackleton scored, and then two minutes later, local lad Albert Cheesebrough scored a third and Burnley won three–nil, with very few handshakes at the end –

You cheating fucking bastard, raged Jimmy, storming into the Burnley dressing room, squaring up to Les Shannon. You dirty, cheating fucking bastard, getting young Pearson sent off like that, he's only fucking seventeen, the boy, you're a fucking bully is what you are, Leslie Shannon, should have been you that was off, not him, and if not for that, then for that fucking tackle on Bobby Charlton, you could have broke his leg you could, you dirty bastard, you should have been off for that, half of your fucking mates and all, you're a fucking disgrace, the bloody fucking lot of you!

Jack Crompton dragged Jimmy out of Les Shannon's face, hauled him back down the corridor to the away dressing room. But soon after, when a Burnley official came knocking on the door, bearing a tray of sandwiches for their visitors, meat sandwiches from the shops of Chairman Bob himself, as was customary in these parts, Jimmy told the player closest to the door to tell that Burnley Butcher and his boy exactly where they could stick their bloody meat fucking sandwiches.

*

Teddy Boys, shouted Bob Lord from every paper in the land, Manchester United were running around playing like Teddy

Boys this afternoon. If we allow this lot to carry on like this, and ride roughshod over the rest of us, well, it will put the whole structure of organised League football at stake. It looks to me like they don't like losing, but they'll be losing the sympathy a lot of the public have given them if they carry on like this, in this unsporting way, and they'll do a great deal of harm to the game, too. Everybody was grieved by the terrible tragedy at Munich, but I am afraid that the public spotlight focused on the new United, all they have had to withstand in recent weeks, well, it seems to be a bit too much for some of these young men, and some of the players, well, they seem to be losing their heads. I know Manchester people are still swayed by what happened in Munich, but it isn't a good thing for the team or for the game. There is too much sentiment about Manchester United in Manchester, and to put it bluntly, they need to remember there are other clubs in football than Manchester United.

Now Jimmy was no saint himself, a man of many faults, he knew, and aware of every one of them, but Welsh and Irish as he was, the thing about the English that always got to Jimmy, not all of them, but many, particularly the richer they were, the richer they got, was that they just could not seem to be nice for more than five bloody minutes, it just didn't seem to come natural to them; you could guarantee any praise would be always quickly followed by abuse, sympathy by mockery or worse, a simple act of kindness by an act of utter selfishness, as though they regretted any good they did. They just seemed a very petty, jealous people, more naturally given to hate and spite than love and kindly acts. No wonder they needed all their fabled manners and codes of conduct, otherwise they'd slit each other's throats, and God help you if you weren't from round here, then they didn't even bother to pretend to be nice. Still, Jimmy wasn't going to let the Burnley fucking Butcher get away with talk like that, not when his bloody team had started all the trouble, all the bother anyway, going in on Harry Gregg like they did, Shackleton and Shannon coming at young Mark Pearson, both with fists up.

It's a shocking thing, boys, it really is, said Jimmy to the press when they called him up, as he knew they would, up in his office at Old Trafford, late on Saturday night. Disgraceful to be coming from the chairman of a football club, it really is, you must agree, it's not worthy of the game, and to be honest with you, boys, I wouldn't even bother to answer such an outburst. I've more on my mind. But I have to defend my players, reply on behalf of the boys, and I can tell you, we object most strongly to the remarks about Teddy Boys. They are totally unjustified. We have played five matches since Munich, and until the Burnley game I cannot recall one single incident to which anyone could take exception. They have all been played in a sportsmanlike manner. Our club has a record, on and off the field, as second to none in sportsmanship. But we don't like losing? Well, no one likes losing, not even Bob Lord, but when defeat comes, we are not upset. Why should we be? I've been on the losing side many times over thirty years, and always been taught to accept defeat, and that is what I tell my lads. When things happen on the field, you leave them on the field and forget them later.

You see, boys, after the Munich disaster, we did not expect to win a match. Not a single one. But it is not about winning or losing. All we want to do is to keep the flag flying until the end of the season, when we can then start to reconstruct. So the question of losing does not enter into it. You shake hands, as many did on Saturday. We have no excuses for our defeat. But Mister Lord's remarks were totally unjustified, a shameful thing to say, and I take the strongest exception to these comments.

Jimmy put down the telephone, opened another bottle of beer, poured himself another glass and smiled. That'll tell them, thought Jimmy, show them they can't be talking shit about Manchester United players in the press, not while I'm about, no,

387

not while I'm in charge, but then Jimmy started to think about Matt again, about what Matt would have done, Matt would have said, and Jimmy knew Matt wouldn't have done what Jimmy did, said what Jimmy said, no, he'd have played it cool would Matt, a quiet, hard word that would have put Bob Lord in his place, or maybe he'd have just turned and walked away, not deigned to get involved with the Burnley Butcher, not stoop that low and get dragged down, and Jimmy took another drink, filled the glass again, just wishing Matt would hurry back, would soon be back, spare him all of this, this world of boardrooms, directors and the English rich, their money old and new, it didn't seem to matter which, Jimmy just wished, he wished Matt would soon be back, please, God, please.

*

Jim Thain put down the telephone, paused a moment in the hall, then went back into the sitting room.

His wife Ruby looked up. Who was it, dear?

It was Doctor Taylor, calling from Munich, said Jim Thain. Ken didn't make it, dear. He's dead.

Oh, no, said Ruby. Oh, poor Mary.

Yes, said Jim, but Doctor Taylor said she took the news very bravely, she was being very brave.

She will be, said Ruby, for the children, I'm sure.

Jim Thain nodded, poured them both a drink, thinking of Ken's children Stephen and Judy, just nine and six years old they were, how often Ken had spoken of them both, how Stephen already had dreams of being a pilot, of being just like his daddy when he grew up, and Jim Thain put down his glass, he closed his eyes.

You mustn't blame yourself, dear, said Ruby at his side, his side again. Ruby knew that Jim was haunted by the fact that before the flight, he'd suggested to a BEA chap that Ken should be his first officer on the Belgrade trip. Ken had been off work awhile, he'd had a hernia operation, so he'd not been back flying long. But Jim and Ken were both keen on poultry farming. Jim had already gone into business, and Ken was keen to follow suit. Jim had thought the trip to Belgrade, being four days there and back, would give them ample chance to chat –

Ken wanted to go, said Ruby. He was delighted, dear. He'd flown the team to Spain last year, had he not? Mary said he liked flying Manchester United, and he'd got to know some of the officials, the players, the press on that trip last year. He was grateful to you, dear.

Jim nodded. Jim said, Yes, Ken said their son was now a supporter of Manchester United.

He was grateful to you, dear, said Ruby again. But now we have to fight for Ken, to clear his name as well, for Mary and their children, too. We have to prove neither of you were to blame. People have to know the truth.

*

Harry was having trouble telling what was real from what was not, what had happened and what had not. Before the game at the Hawthorns, against West Brom, when the team had got off the bus there were thousands waiting outside the ground to cheer them on or simply stand and gawp, but Harry had seen this fella step from the crowd and stop Stan Crowther in his tracks, and Harry marched straight up to the man and said, I think it's me you're looking for? The man looked Harry up and down, then said, I just wanted to say that I'm glad you're okay, son.

In the dressing room, Stan Crowther had asked Harry, Who was that then? That bloke in the crowd?

Why? What's it to you, said Harry.

Nothing. I was just asking.

You should have been a peeler then, said Harry, you like asking questions so much, PC Crowther.

Fuck off, said Stan Crowther, I was only trying to make conversation. I couldn't give a shit who it was.

Well, it was my father, PC Crowther, said Harry, standing over Stan, looking down at Stan. And I can't stand the man. He left my mother with six kids, and she still loves the man. But I despise the cunt and –

Harry, shouted Jimmy Murphy, leave the poor lad alone and get yourself changed, will you?

But now Harry didn't know if that had been his dad or not; he'd thought it was, could swear it was, but now he wasn't sure, wasn't sure he'd even said all that to Stan, the shit he thought he'd said.

Then, at Turf Moor on Saturday, he could swear he'd seen his father in the crowd behind his goal, could have sworn he heard him say, Pity that you didn't die with your pals, isn't it, Harry Gregg, but when Harry had blinked and looked again, the man was gone or his face had changed, but his father wasn't there, just some Burnley cunts laughing, shouting, Forgotten where you are, have you, Gregg? You need your head seeing to, you do, Gregg! This is Turf Moor, you stupid Irish twat!

But again, now Harry didn't know if this had happened or it hadn't, what was real and what was not. But the headaches were real enough, he knew that was a fact, they had not stopped, they'd just got worse. He could hardly sleep, they were that bad, even with his neckties tied tight around his head most nights Harry could not sleep, thankful only he was in Blackpool now, so Mavis wouldn't know and little Julie wouldn't see. But before the League game against West Brom, the one they lost four–nil, he'd had to grip the sides of the tunnel to keep himself upright, and Bill Foulkes had seen, and Foulkesy had later said that night, What's wrong with you, mate?

Nothing, said Harry. Just a headache, you know.

You get them a lot, do you?

Sometimes, you know, said Harry. Why?

You should probably have an X-ray or something, shouldn't you? Case it's more than just a headache.

I'm all right. Don't you worry about me.

Bill Foulkes shook his head, he said, You should go see someone, mate. Get it looked at properly.

Get what looked at properly?

Bill Foulkes laughed. Your head, mate.

Fuck you, said Harry, and half swung for Billy Foulkes but missed, almost broke a finger on the wall.

You daft bastard, said Bill Foulkes. What the hell did you do that for? I'm only trying to help.

Well, Harry Gregg doesn't need your help or anybody else's help, thank you very much.

But there was one other thing that was a fact, that was undeniably, indisputably true: Harry Gregg had picked the ball out of the back of his own goal ten times in the six matches since he'd got back from Munich, and not all of those times were down to Billy Foulkes or Ronnie Cope or Ian Greaves, the referee or anybody else, no matter what Harry might have shouted, cursed and sworn blind at the time. No, some of them goals were down to Harry Gregg, he knew, knew all too bloody well, and so at Blackpool, on the beach, Harry was out on the sands on his own, throwing the ball about, as high as he could into the wind, then jumping to catch it, throwing it backwards or forwards, flinging himself after it –

What the hell are you doing, son, shouted Jimmy, jogging across the sand towards Harry. You'll break your fucking neck carrying on like that, you will!

I want you to drop me, Jimmy, said Harry. I'm playing shit, I know I am. I'll lose us the Cup.

Now you listen to me, said Jimmy, reaching out, grabbing Harry by his training top. I'll tell you when you're playing shit, son, and I'll tell you when you need extra training, so you get yourself back inside that bloody hotel now, you raving, fucking mental Irish loon!

Harry nodded. Okay, Jimmy, I –

Go on, said Jimmy. Fuck off . . .

Back up in his room, sat up on his bed, the tie back round his head, Harry heard a knock upon his door, whipped the tie off from round his head and said, Yeah?

It's me, it's Bill, said Bill.

What do you want?

Just open up, will you?

Harry sighed, got up from the bed, opened the door and said again, What do you want?

Here, I brought you these, said Bill, and he handed Harry a small jar of pills and said, A mate of mine, Norman, he was in a bad car crash a while back. He had bad headaches after, couldn't sleep, so the doctor gave him these to help him sleep. They've helped me.

Harry looked at the tiny jar, read the label, *Phenobarbitone*, and said, Thanks, Foulkesy, thank you.

*

Johnny Berry had been on the danger list, unconscious ever since the crash. At first, the doctors had not thought he would survive, he would not live, even Professor Maurer had said, Johnny Berry is in the hands of God. Many were the days, early on, when the press reported that his wife, Hilda, fair-haired and pretty, had gone in to see Johnny, but had left with tragic, worried eyes. He had had operations, many operations, yet he remained unconscious and dangerously ill. But then slowly, day by day, slight improvements began to be seen in Johnny Berry, though he remained unconscious, on the danger list, still listed as critical. But still, day after day, Hilda went from the hotel to the hospital and sat beside his bed, held his hand and whispered, Hold on, John, please, for me and for the boys, for Neil and Paul and Craig, please, John, please. And slowly, day by day, Johnny began to respond to stimuli, more and more, and day by day, he started to maintain a very slow rate of improvement, and even though he was still unconscious, still dangerously ill, even though he had some very restless nights, still he maintained the improvements, day by day, and the good nights began to outweigh the bad nights, and Johnny began to show signs of regaining consciousness, but still Johnny could not keep down food and liquid taken by the mouth, and Johnny was given fluid intravenously to improve the functioning of his kidneys, help his kidneys filter out certain poisonous substances from his blood, and still the hospital said that Johnny Berry remained unconscious, on the danger list. But then, one day, it was a Monday, the second Monday in March, the hospital announced that Johnny Berry had maintained the improvement shown in the last two days, and now, at last, more than one month after the crash, Johnny was fully conscious and talking a fair amount, though the hospital was quick to add, John Berry is still on the danger list, and it may be a while yet before John can speak clearly or answer doctors when they ask him who he is and what he does. But Hilda Berry didn't care how long it took, she knew who he was and what he meant to her and to their boys, and Neil and Paul and Craig, they were just happy Daddy had finally, finally woken up, because he had been asleep so long, they'd begun to wonder if their daddy would ever wake up again.

*

The body of Captain Kenneth Rayment was flown back from Munich to London on Monday, March 17, and two days later, on a day of light snow showers, perhaps the last of the year, smoke and soot heavy in the air, the funeral of Captain Rayment was held at Saint Mary the Virgin, on Overton Drive, in Wanstead, east London, where Ken had been born in 1921. After the funeral, the body of Captain Rayment was driven to the City of London Crematorium, at Manor Park, for cremation there. During the war, Captain Rayment had shot down five German fighters, one Italian plane and a V-1 flying bomb. He had been mentioned in dispatches and was awarded the Distinguished Flying Cross in 1943. But since the crash, his family had received unkind, hateful letters and his children had been taunted, been bullied, and there were no crowds standing two, three deep outside Saint Mary the Virgin in Wanstead or along the route to the City of London Crematorium that day, no heads bowed, no flowers thrown upon the hearse as it passed, but his family, his friends, his colleagues, they were there, and they remembered what Rosemary Cheverton had said when the air stewardess had seen Ken last. He was so brave, she said, so very brave, still trapped in the cockpit, in tremendous pain, and they were trying to cut him out, but Ken just smiled and gave us all a wink.

*

Jimmy was not Matt, he knew, he knew, he fucking knew he was not Matt. He should have never risen to the bait, or stooped that low, whatever way you put it, he knew, he knew, he should have just kept his big fat fucking Welsh gob shut is what he should have done, he knew, he knew. But Butcher Bob had written to the fucking FA with a list of grievances about Jimmy Murphy and some of the other staff and players of Manchester United

394

Football Club, the referee would also be submitting a full report of all the incidents he had witnessed at the 'Battle of Turf Moor', and of course, Mister Harold Hardman, the Chairman of Manchester United Football Club, he didn't like any of this, not one little bit, no matter whether Jimmy was in the right or in the wrong, Mister Hardman never liked to see the good name of Manchester United brought into question, no matter who was doing the bringing, no matter who was doing the questioning, it mattered not –

You stupid fucking so-and-so, thought Jimmy again. Why could you not be more like Matt, you stupid fucking so-and-so, and Jimmy sighed again, just thankful that Mister Hardman had still agreed to let Jimmy sign Tommy Heron from Portadown, even though Tommy had a groin strain and would not be fit to play for a while.

But at least Little Ernie Taylor had been over to the Norbreck and had trained a little on the sands. But Ted Dalton had told Jimmy what Jimmy already knew, that Little Ernie was still touch and go, but then Jimmy told Ted what Ted already knew, If Ernie isn't bloody fit for Saturday, then we'll be out the fucking Cup.

I know, Jimmy, I know, said Ted, I'm doing all I can, and so is Ernie, rest assured, he's doing his best.

Jimmy had his rosary in his hand, he held it up to Ted, he said, The Big Man must be sick of me and all I ask of him, but I just pray Ernie's fit to play.

But whenever Jimmy started to feel sorry for himself, to curse his lot, the slings and arrows of another bloody shit fucking week, then Jimmy knew what it was he had to do, so Jimmy went back up the stairs to his room at the Norbreck Hydro, and Jimmy sat down on the edge of the bed, and Jimmy took out his old address book, and Jimmy picked up the phone, dialled numbers he would have dialled more often had he had the time, he really would, that was not a lie, that was the truth, and then he spoke, he listened, had a chat, then said goodbye, put down the phone then picked it up again, dialled another number, spoke and listened, had a chat, said goodbye for now, put down the phone, picked it up again, and did this time and time again, eight, nine, ten, eleven times, and then this week, it didn't seem so bad, his week, nothing bad about his week at all, not compared to the weeks and weeks and weeks and weeks of the families of the Dead.

Then Jimmy went back down the stairs, walked around the hotel, up and down its corridors, to stretch his legs, to clear his mind, then in the ballroom, the empty hotel ballroom once again, once again at the piano, on the stool, Jimmy raised the lid and began to play again, a little bit of Chopin, a touch of Grieg, a spot of Liszt, but no more show tunes, not tonight, those nights, those days were gone, but still a little Chopin, Grieg and Liszt, they helped him try to settle down his thoughts, his doubts, his worries, thinking of his own wife, his children now –

Jimmy hadn't seen Winnie, some of the kids, in he didn't know how long. The last time he had been back home, with the dawn, sat in the room, his wife Winnie, she'd come down in her dressing gown and said, I think you've got the wrong house, have you not?

No, he said, I've not, he said. This is where I want to be, where I always want to be.

I know that, love, smiled Winnie, but you're doing what you have to do, what must be done.

Well, I'm not making a very good job of it, said Jimmy. I wish I was more like Matt.

Well, I'm very glad you're not, laughed Winnie. And I might not know much about football, but I do know every other team in England, bar three, are wishing they were in the semi-finals of the FA Cup with you, and so, in the very worst of circumstances, I'd say someone was making a very good job of it, James Patrick Murphy.

*

In the dressing room at Villa Park, in the last minutes before Billy Foulkes would lead them out, Jimmy went from player to player, from Harry Gregg to Billy Foulkes to Ian Greaves to Freddie Goodwin to Ronnie Cope to Stan Crowther to Colin Webster to Alex Dawson and Mark Pearson, making individual points to each of them, but mainly just encouraging each of them, telling them, Remember, boys, remember, no game is ever won until it's lost, don't any of you forget it now!

But when Jimmy came to sit with Ernie Taylor and then with Bobby Charlton, Jimmy didn't have that much to say, knew he didn't have to say that much. Bobby was no more a boy, he was playing like a man, and a man possessed at that. He seemed ten times the player he was before the crash, which made no sense, but it was as though the talents of every lad who'd died had filled his boots, his legs, his brain, his heart and soul. He was just playing out of his skin, the boy, out of his skin, game after game, still playing for the army, too, a game every other day, sometimes two, three games in a row, but Bobby didn't seem to mind, it seemed to Jimmy that Bobby would not have it any other way –

Listen, kid, said Ernie Taylor, leaning into Bobby, my thigh, he said, it hurts to walk, let alone to bloody run, so when I look up, all I want to see is your fucking arse disappearing up that field, giving me something to aim at.

Okay, said Bobby –

And in the twelfth minute, with a forward touch from Ernie Taylor to put him clear, Bobby shot from the edge of the penalty area and hit the top corner of the Fulham net, and the

397

tight, pressed crowd, almost all on United's side, or so it seemed, they went wild. But just a minute later, a pass from Langley split the United defence for Stevens to smack Fulham level, and Johnny Haynes, the London architect, born in Kentish Town, he now took command, and with control and patterns, Fulham played, and with eight minutes to half-time, Haynes and Lawler combined to release Dwight, who found in turn that bearded pirate Jimmy Hill, streaking through the middle, there to put the Fulham two–one up. But the fates, the gods, call them what you will, they were not with Fulham Football Club that day, and with half-time but a stride away, Langley fell, injured in a tackle with Dawson, and was carried on a stretcher from the field. In injury time, Taylor shot, the shot was blocked by Cohen, but the rebound found Bobby, who shot again and scored again to bring the sides level once again.

In the second half, to a great roar from all sides of Villa Park, Langley reappeared, hobbling onto the field. He had to switch from left-back to outside-left, but still he played a part, a nuisance to United, an inspiration to Fulham who forced a leaping save from Harry Gregg, and then another save, another save and yet another save from Harry Gregg. But meanwhile, down the other end, in the other goal, Tony Macedo flew towards his top corner to flick over a header from Webster, then turned a swift, low stab from Bobby round his post, then again at full stretch he caught another rocket from Bobby, which astonished even Bobby, left him standing, applauding the Fulham keeper, honours even as the two sides left the field at Villa Park.

*

Hulme born and bred, a Hulmerist he was, his right leg still well plastered, his skull still surely fractured, Albert Scanlon tottered off the London train at London Road, helped by his wife Josephine, and Albert breathed in deep, sniffed up the air and said, Smell that, will you, love.

I'd rather not, said Josephine, who was expecting their second child quite soon now, putting her pretty new scarf up to her mouth, squinting to see even a couple of yards ahead, the fog, the smog it was that thick.

Well, that smells like home to me, said Albert. That smells like Manchester that does.

Welcome home, Albert, came a muffled voice from out the gloom, a shuffling figure who said, Now then, Albert, my cab's for you, this cab's all yours, yeah, it's on the house, I'm at your service, Albert, day or night, free of charge. You just call me, and I'll be there.

Well, thank you very much, said Albert. That's very kind indeed, he said, shambling after the driver, with his one good leg and pregnant wife, through the thick fog, into the back of the cab. We could really use the help.

Now then, Albert, lad, said the driver as they set off on their way back home, is it right that you met the Lord and Lady Mayor of Manchester in Munich, that you took them boozing in some beer cellar, is that right, is it?

Yeah, it is, said Albert. But it wasn't my idea, it was all arranged, all planned like, you know.

Josephine coughed, she said, The Lord Mayor and the Lady Mayoress were in Munich to thank the doctors and staff and people of Munich for all they have done.

It's funny, though, isn't it, said the driver.

Yeah, said Albert, it is, yeah.

What is, asked Josephine.

Well, you know, said the driver, it's not that long ago, is it, since we were all bombing and killing the hell out of each other. Just shows, doesn't it?

Yeah, said Albert, it does.

Shows what, asked Josephine.

You know, said the driver, how times change.

Yeah, said Albert, looking out of the taxi, out into the fog, the smog, its shadows and its shapes, the ghostly, haunting shadows there and shapes. They really do.

*

The replay was down at Highbury, which was almost home for Fulham but far for United, far and unfair, an outrage, some would say, but more than that, it was the memories that worried Jimmy. Highbury would be a haunted place, the whole trip to London, the same hotel, that dressing room, that pitch, it might all get to some of them, feared Jimmy, get the better of some of them.

Billy Foulkes already had the flu, looked like death warmed up he did, but he said, I'll play, Jimmy, you know I will, there's no way I'll duck out now.

Ted Dalton had worked miracles on Ernie Taylor's thigh again, and on Alex Dawson's ankle, but Jimmy had also brought Bobby Harrop and Shay Brennan down to London with them, because both Jimmy and Jack knew they'd been lucky to hold Fulham at Villa Park, that they'd need more than luck this time.

A lot of folk, folk in the press, folk at the bar, they also knew United were not playing well, that for seventy minutes at Villa Park they had been outplayed by a good Second Division side, so no wonder they were being beaten in the League, hit for three or four each time. Murphy, folk said, in the press and at the bar, he should drop Alex Dawson for a start, Pearson, too, bring back young Kenny Morgans; if he was fit enough for the reserves, scoring goals for them, why not pick and play him in the first team then?

But Jimmy thought Kenny had not yet got back his appetite, his hunger for the game, looked like he was happy in the reserves, and Jimmy worried young Kenny might never get that appetite, his hunger back, never lose that feeling that he just didn't care any more, that look in his eyes that said, What is the fucking point of this?

No, Jimmy had a better plan: he would give young Mark Pearson a rest, bring young Shay in at outside-left. But hang on, hang on, thought Jimmy, what if he switched Colin Webster and Alex Dawson, bringing Colin inside, pushing young Alex out right, still wearing number 9, but giving Alex more space –

Do you follow what I'm saying, you with me, are you, boys, said Jimmy in the Highbury dressing room, just minutes before kick-off.

Colin Webster and Alex Dawson both nodded, both said, Yeah, Jimmy, yeah, okay then, Jimmy.

You see, son, said Jimmy, gripping young Alex Dawson by his arm, I have this feeling that if you have that bit more space, you'll score three today you will.

Well, one would be nice, laughed Alex Dawson, but if you think so, if you say so, Jimmy.

I do, son, said Jimmy, I do.

*

The crowd was a lot less than expected, less than forty thousand there inside the Highbury ground that mild and misty, damp and dismal afternoon, the game controversially being shown live on the BBC –

From the first minute, the commentator gasps, the action and his accent clipped, United are hammering away at the Fulham goal, they are not going to give keeper Tony Macedo a moment's peace, attacking again down the left wing, Seamus

Brennan takes a corner for United, Colin Webster gets to it, gets it to Alex Dawson and it's in! Manchester one up, but now Fulham counter-attack. The ball comes to veteran Arthur Stevens, and that's the equaliser! Fulham try again, but United left-half Crowther gets it clear, and Dawson's there to put Manchester back into the lead. But this isn't going to be an easy job for either side. The Fulham boys have plenty of fight in them. Jimmy Langley crosses to Chamberlain, and it's two-all. Macedo busy again, in a tussle with Colin Webster. Now it's their dangerous winger Brennan on the move again, Macedo runs out but fumbles it, and Brennan scores!

The second half, Fulham are a goal behind and battling hard to catch up, but they've got Munich survivor Harry Gregg to reckon with. Out to Greaves, who clears. Bobby Charlton moving in on the left wing again, he centres, a tussle before the goal, and Dawson shoots and scores his third, United's fourth!

Two goals down, things certainly look black for Fulham now, but for the moment, their defence holds, and now they're hitting back. A tussle in the United goalmouth, right-winger Roy Dwight taps it in, and that's four–three! United are determined to increase their lead, but Macedo is fighting them off. Time and again they come back. Over to the other end, Fulham inside-left Haynes has a shot at goal, but Gregg gathers safely and gets it clear. Haynes again, Roy Dwight shoots, but it's offside! Hard luck! A certain amount of debate over the ref's decision. But now United are attacking again. Fulham try to clear, but the ball goes to Bobby Charlton and out to the right wing, back again to Charlton, who runs in for a shot and leaves Macedo helpless! So the astonishing Babes have done it again! And it is to be an all-Lancashire Cup Final.

And that mild and misty, damp and dismal afternoon, it did seem to Jimmy, seemed to Bill, seemed to Harry, and very much to Bobby, too, that Highbury was a haunted, spectred place that day, but the ghosts, the spirits that played, they'd helped them on their way.

*

Goodbye, said Frank. I'll see you at Old Trafford or at Wembley, not in the stand, but out on the pitch, son.

Jackie Blanchflower smiled, he nodded, said again, I'll see you later, Frank, but Jackie knew he'd not see him from the pitch again. Jackie didn't think he'd ever play again, wasn't sure he wanted to play again. He didn't even want to watch a match, especially not United, because it wouldn't be United, would it? How could it be? Tommy had been his best mate, the best pal he'd ever had.

And that same mild and misty, damp and dismal Wednesday afternoon, when Jackie and his wife Jean arrived back at London Road, his right arm still in a sling, United had sent a taxi to meet them, take them home. United had even offered them tickets to the game at Highbury that afternoon, which Jackie had declined. But the driver had the radio on, tuned to the commentary of the game. Because I knew you'd want to hear, he said, and you'll be pleased to know you're winning.

But in the back of the taxi, Jackie shook his head, he said, Can you turn it off, please just switch it off.

After the match, straight after the match, after he had picked up Alex Dawson in his arms, hugged that lad and held him tight, ruffled his hair and said, What did I tell you, son, what did I say? Then Jimmy was straight down the tunnel, the corridor, up the stairs, through the handshakes, the pats on his back, into an upstairs room, one with a telephone, the door shut now, silent here, Jimmy dialled the hospital, called Munich from Highbury, and Jimmy said, Jean, love, Jean! Hello, love, Jean. I'm just calling to say we won, love, we won, you probably know, but we won, love, we won. I just wanted to make sure Matt knew, he knew, he knows we won, we won! Is he there, love, can I have word with him, with Matt?

I'm afraid he's not so good today, Jimmy, dear, said Jean. But he knows you won, he does, his eyes lit up, they did, said Jean. A little bit they did, and he said how proud he was of Harry Gregg and Billy Foulkes and Bobby Charlton, in particular, those boys who were with us in the plane crash, he said, their performance was wonderful, and he said for me to tell you, Jimmy, he was delighted, and he said, tell him to keep it up.

*

As they left the Highbury pitch that afternoon, as the sporting men of Fulham shook their hands, slapped their backs and wished United luck, the very best of luck, Bobby had his head bowed, he did not speak, a few folk even said he looked distraught, though they could not think, not fathom why, why would he look distraught? United were in the final of the Cup, the FA bloody Cup, doesn't get much better than that now, does it, Bobby, lad? Come on, Bobby, smile, why don't you smile? You scored a goal, you're in the Final?

*

Nobby believed in miracles, he really did. He was an apprentice at Manchester United, for a start, clearing the snow from the pitch, cleaning up the washrooms and the gym, yes, but playing in the FA Youth Cup and in the practice matches, too, all those practice matches with the reserves and the first-team boys. But every night before he said his prayers, then went to sleep, Nobby would go under his bed and get out Tommy Taylor's boots from there, wrapped up in a cloth they were, and Nobby would look at them, he would stare at them, wipe off any speck of dust on them, then Nobby would say a prayer or two on them, very special prayers, before he wrapped them back up again, put them under his bed again, then he'd kneel down beside his bed and finish off his prayers. But that night before the semi-final replay of the FA Cup, when Nobby had gone under his bed for Tommy's boots, they were not there! They were not there! He looked and looked, he searched and searched, but they were not there, they'd gone. He couldn't find them anywhere! But that next day, that afternoon, United won, they beat Fulham five–three, were in the Final of the Cup, and when Nobby got back home that night, went up the stairs, looked under his bed again, there they were, back where they always were, and Nobby's heart, it raced and raced to think what this could mean, it was a miracle! These were holy, magic boots, they really were, Tommy Taylor's boots, and Nobby wanted to tell the whole world about the Miracle of Tommy Taylor's Boots, how they had disappeared, gone off down to London, helped Alex Dawson score a hat-trick, helped

405

Shay and Bobby Charlton score, too, but when Nobby went and first told his brother Charlie, he just laughed and said, You're as blind as a fucking bat you are, they'll have been there all the time, and so after that, Nobby never told a soul, a living soul, but Nobby knew what he had seen or not seen, and so Nobby knew what he believed.

*

Three days after Manchester United had beaten Fulham and reached the final of the FA Cup, they travelled to Hillsborough to play Sheffield Wednesday once again. Sheffield Wednesday were bottom of the table, but that last Saturday afternoon in March, Roy Shiner scored the only goal and Wednesday beat United. Two days later, Manchester United went back to Villa Park to play Aston Villa in the League. Aston Villa were fourth from bottom of the table, but on that last day in March, Aston Villa beat United by three goals to two, the winning Villa goal a most contentious one at that, Jackie Sewell scoring in the dying seconds of the game, but with Pete McParland, who else could it be but that man who'd robbed United of the Cup last year, clearly offside in the build-up to the goal. But though Harry and Bill and Ronnie Cope, they'd all protested strongly, the goal still stood, and again United had lost in the League. But it was just Jack Crompton on the bench, in charge that day, Jimmy not at Villa Park that day, not there to storm and rage.

*

It was not Matt Busby who stood out in the rain, the wind, the sleet and snow, morning, noon and night, teaching boys to trap, to pass, to shoot, ball after ball, hour after hour, day after day, season after season, turning young boys into pros, that was not

Matt, that was Jimmy, Bert and Tom, Bill and Arthur, that was us, not him, not Matt, by the sweat of our brows, the mud on our boots, we turned those boys into men, football men, so every team at every level at the club was stocked with the finest football boys and football men in the land, if not the world, and that was down to Jimmy, Bert and Tom, Bill and Arthur, not to Matt; nor did he spot those boys, that was Joe and all the other scouts, travelling up and down the land, every afternoon and evening of the week, that was Joe and all his scouts, not Matt; he rarely even watched them play, these boys, he just turned up at the end to sell the dream and seal the deal, that was Matt, what Matt Busby did, he sold the dream.

But as he journeyed over land and sea, by train, by boat, then train again, Jimmy knew whatever rancour, bitterness he sometimes felt, it was not really felt, not really meant, or else, why else would he be travelling thirty hours over land and sea, by train, by boat, then train again to see the man he knew, more than ever now he knew, the man who was the Boss and his very good, dear friend, and the moment Jimmy clapped eyes on Matt again, Matt with his own eyes closed, on his back, on his bed, in that private room, both his legs in plaster still, face etched and aged with pain and grief, hair now white, fifty going on eighty was how he looked to Jimmy now, a faint, pale grey shadow of the man he once had been, and Jimmy's heart it hurt, it bled, it really hurt, it really bled for him, for Matt, because Jimmy, too, could see that huge and heavy stone upon Matt's chest, that just as Jean had said, it weighed, pressed down upon his chest, his ribs, had crushed and broken his heart, that huge and heavy stone of guilt.

Hello there, Matt, old pal, said Jimmy, sitting down beside his bed, touching, patting his hand, watching Matt open his eyes, blinking then turning to Jimmy –

Hello, Jimmy, said Matt. Well, this is a surprise, a nice surprise, but what are you doing here, Jimmy?

Well, I've come to see you, haven't I, said Jimmy. Just, you know, to keep you in the picture like.

You didn't fly, did you, Jimmy?

No, Matt, no, said Jimmy, no.

That's good, said Matt, that's best. But it must have been a long journey for you then? You must be tired, Jimmy, you must be exhausted?

Ah, you know me, Matt, said Jimmy, couple of those beers, these German beers, and I'll be fine.

They're very good, said Matt.

So I hear, said Jimmy, yeah.

So who's looking after the team then, asked Matt, while you're here, Jimmy?

Jack, said Jimmy, Jack Crompton, you know, Jack's come back, he's been great has Jack.

Ah, that's great, that's good to know, said Matt. And that really is an incredible thing it is you've done, getting to the Final, Jimmy, you know? Just fantastic. It really is. Well done, Jimmy, well done.

Well, I can't take any credit, said Jimmy, I really can't, Matt, it's all down to the lads themselves, the way they played. If I'm honest with you, I didn't think they could pull it off. I knew they would respond, but I just didn't think it would be enough, that they could play like that, like they did at Highbury, they really did play good football, Matt, you would have been proud, you really would, and you should be, Matt, you should be proud. Because it's down to you, you know, the years of planning, the foundations you laid, giving me and Tom and Bert and Bill and Arthur and everybody else, giving us the time, the space, the chance to encourage all these youngsters, that was your policy, Matt, that was down to you, and at Highbury, last Wednesday, those young reserves, they did you proud, and so I just hope, I pray it will be possible for you to be there at Wembley, Matt.

But Matt had closed his eyes again, a tear from the corner of his left eye rolling slowly down his cheek, now from his right eye, down his right cheek, too, another tear, then another tear as Matt whispered, I'm sorry, Jimmy, I'm sorry, but I can't, I can't . . .

No, Matt, no, said Jimmy, reaching out again, touching, holding Matt's hand. Don't say sorry, Matt.

But it's all my fault, said Matt, his eyes open now, wet and open now, looking at Jimmy, telling Jimmy, I'm the one to blame, Jimmy, it's all my fault –

No, said Jimmy, no, Matt, no, no one says that, no one thinks that, it's just not true –

But some of them boys, they should never have been on that plane, Jimmy –

No, Matt, no –

No, Jimmy, no, there was no reason to take so many players. Half those boys, they were never going to play, you know they weren't, but it was me who made them come –

But that was me as well then, and Bert and Tom, we all sat and talked it through, Matt, we all did.

But it was my decision, Jimmy, you know it was, and so it's my fault they're dead, those boys –

Don't say that, said Jimmy. No –

David Pegg, said Matt abruptly, suddenly, you know his mother, she never wanted him to be a footballer, Jimmy, she never did. And she was right, Jimmy, she was right. But I sat there in their front room and I told her, I swore to her, I said, I would stake my life your David will make it as a professional footballer –

And he did, Matt, he –

But he wasn't going to play, Jimmy. He'd not played a game all year –

You ever see the way that boy drove his car, said Jimmy, how fast he went, the speeds he went. He gave me bloody kittens did that lad, death could have been round any corner –

409

But it wasn't, Jimmy, was it, said Matt. Death was on that plane, where he should not have been. Geoff Bent, the same, Geoff, too. We knew Roger would play, come hell or high water, we knew Roger would never shirk a game, a game like that. Bill Whelan, too, he never should have been on that flight, Jimmy, never. But I made him come, I –

It was his job, said Jimmy, Billy knew that.

No, Jimmy, no, I made him, forced him to come. He came to me two, three days before, he said his mammy had the flu, he'd not been well himself, could he go back to Dublin, see his mammy, his fiancée, too, but I said, no, Jimmy, I told him, no, how would it look. 'How would it look,' what was I thinking, Jimmy? Bill Whelan should have been in Dublin with his poor mammy, Jimmy, you know he should, his death is down to me, just me.

Jimmy sat back in his chair, his head back, put his fingers to his face, wiped his own eyes, his cheeks, then sighed, then said, I saw their Christy at Highbury, I invited him over for the replay, I saw him then.

You invited him over, whispered Matt, said Matt. That was good of you, Jimmy, very good of you. How was Christy then, how is their mammy, did he say?

Well, it was strange for him, of course, said Jimmy, watching the team without their Billy, said he was a bit overcome at first, but Christy said how glad he was he came. A few of the other families, you know, they've been to matches, we've invited them, me and Les, and they all say they're glad they came, that's what they say.

And his mammy, asked Matt again.

Well, she has her faith, you know, and Christy said it's helped her a lot, and she was asking after you, Christy said, and he was, too, you know, just wishing you the best, Matt, wanting to see you home.

That's very kind of them, said Matt, whispered Matt. Very good of them.

I tell you, Matt, people just wish you well, want to see you home again, back at Old Trafford, at work again.

Matt sighed, he said, I dare not tell you, Jimmy, what I've wished for, what I've wanted.

Well then, don't, said Jimmy.

Matt nodded, Matt said, But what I want now, Jimmy, what I have to do now is speak to the families, Jimmy, as soon as I am well enough, I must go round and see all those who are bereaved and then try to do whatever it is I can for them, that is all I want to do now.

*

In the houses, the homes of the Dead, they did their best, they really did, but the lights were off, the power gone. Every time they had come home, Roger and Geoff, Mark and Liam, Duncan and Eddie, David and Tommy, they had always brought such energy, such light with them, especially the boys who had moved to Manchester, away and far from home, Mark and Liam, Duncan, David and Tommy, it had always been an occasion whenever they came home, with their stories, their tales, their jokes and the laughs. Oh, they were such happy, brightly coloured days, it sometimes seemed the rest of them, their brothers and their sisters, their old friends, their mates from school, the lives they lived, they were in black and white compared to their brothers, their friends at the famous Manchester United, and so when they left, went back to Manchester, to their digs, their other mates, it sometimes seemed they took half of the light back with them when they went, left them in the black and white, the shadows and the dark until they'd come again, back home again. But now they'd never come again, back home again, and no matter how they tried, and try they really did, hour after hour for day after day, some of those hours that felt like days, those days that felt weeks, in the houses, the homes of the Dead, the light, it just kept leaving them, it would not stay, would not come back.

*

Each of the few days Jimmy spent in Munich, at the hospital with Matt, as Jimmy came and went, reporters asked him, How is Matt, how is he doing, when will he be out, when will he be back, will he be back for Wembley and the Final, is that when he'll be back, Jimmy?

Fuck off, will you, spat Jimmy, said Jimmy, with your questions, will you, your constant bloody questions, can you not leave us alone, give us a moment's peace, five fucking minutes would be nice, you know?

All right, Jimmy, calm down, will you, Jimmy, we're only asking, doing our jobs, and in the papers, their newspapers, the press, they wrote, Mister Murphy was not in the mood to be interviewed after his thirty-hour sea and land journey to the Rechts der Isar Hospital to put Matt Busby back in the football picture.

But on the last day he was in Munich, Jimmy popped in to see Frank Taylor once again, see how Frank was doing, how Frank was getting on, and to ask Frank to do his best, the best he could to keep up Matt's spirits, help cheer up Matt, if Frank could, and help with Johnny Berry, too, please, whatever Frank could do.

Of course I will, said Frank, you know I will, Jimmy, you can always count on me. But there is one thing you could do for me, if you wouldn't mind?

Of course, my old pal, you just name it.

Well, Jimmy, said Frank, some of the boys in the press, the fellows who've flown over, they'd really like to have a word, hear how Matt is doing, and so they've asked me if you wouldn't mind?

412

Well, go on then, okay, said Jimmy, with a sigh. Just for you then, Frank, my old pal, and so when the press filed into Frank Taylor's room, when they'd taken their pictures of Jimmy in a bedside chat with Frank, when they asked Jimmy about Matt again, Jimmy said, We are all tremendously thrilled to see the progress Matt is making. He's obviously getting his teeth into football again, and that was why I came over. I wanted to tell Matt all about how the young boys are playing, how we got to the Cup Final, and how we hope to win at Wembley. Now I'm just hoping and praying that Matt can get back home for the Final. It would be the greatest moment of my life, if Matt could be there with us at Wembley.

But what Jimmy wanted to say was, You haven't a clue, not one of you, not a fucking clue. That man is broken in body, but in spirit, too, crushed and drained by grief and guilt, thinking only of the Dead, their families, the ones they left behind.

*

Albert had had his plaster off at Old Trafford, and Ted Dalton thought it safe enough for Albert to start to walk, then to jog, then run again, laps of the pitch, and as he ran around the pitch, Albert could not help but think of the games he'd seen, he'd played upon that pitch, thinking of Roger, who Albert had admired more than any man he'd ever met, how hard Mark Jones was on the pitch, but how gentle he was off the pitch, as gentle as a mouse he was, and then there was Duncan, of course, and he was simply magic was that lad, he could do anything, but how Billy Whelan, he never knew how good he was, and then Albert remembered this one time, well, it must have been a few times, but this one time in particular that came back to Albert now, jogging gently around the pitch, when dear old Bill Inglis sidled up to him, when Albert was doing laps, and with

413

his ever-present Woodbine between his fingers, Bill whispered, all confidential like, Albert, you know that David Pegg, well, you could get his place, you know. He's not fit to lace your boots, so you just keep at it, son, then you'll get his place. But Albert knew old Bill's tricks, knew Bill would be straight off, sidling up to David, whispering, all confidential like, I tell you, Dave, you need to watch it, son. You know that Albert Scanlon, well, he's been going round saying you're not fit to lace his boots, that he'll have your place he will, and he's good, you know, he's the nephew of Charlie Mitten is Albert, football's in his blood, so you best keep at it, son. But him and David, they laughed about it later, impersonating Bill, that confidential whisper, that Woodbine in his hand.

But here was Albert now, in the drizzle, on his own, jogging gently around the pitch, keeping at it still, not sure why he was keeping at it still, but after he had done the laps then had a bath, a wash, changed out of his training gear into his usual clobber, Albert thought he'd go see a picture up in town, called up his new mate George the cabbie, asked him if he minded giving him a lift up town, and George said, No worries, Albert.

But when George and his cab arrived to pick up Albert from the ground then run him into town, this fella comes out of the office, says, Albert, can I have a word? And he says, this fella Albert didn't know from Adam, he says, Albert, now you've had your plaster off, you're back walking properly, the club won't be able to pay for your taxi any more, you'll have to stop using it.

What are you talking about, said Albert. The club aren't paying for it anyway, it's free, it's on the house, out of the goodness of George's heart. It's got sod all to do with the club, so sod all to do with you.

Well, that's okay then, said the fella, face now as red as his club tie. Just as long as there's no confusion, that everything is clear.

414

Albert dropped his cig on the ground, opened the door to the cab and said, No, there's no confusion, pal, everything is very clear, clear as a crystal fooking ball.

*

Now Johnny Berry was allowed up and about, just for a few hours each day, Johnny would come into Matt's room, sit down by Matt's bed and say, I tell you this, Boss, you really find out who your friends are, don't you, Boss. I thought Tommy Taylor, some of the other lads, I thought they were my mates, my pals, but all the time I've been in here, lying here, they've never come to see me once, not even called or written, not even once, can you believe it? Now you've always said to me, Boss, a man's gotta do what a man's gotta do, so I hope you won't mind, but when I get back, first thing I'm going to do is give Tommy and some of them other lads a piece of my mind. Call yourself friends, I'll say, you must be bloody joking. If that had been you lying in hospital, I'd have been straight round, and as often as I could. But I tell you this, not now. I wouldn't cross the road if you were on fire. I wouldn't, I tell you.

And every day Johnny came into the room, sat down by his bed and said all this to Matt, the pain Matt had felt when he'd had the surgery on his lung without anaesthetics, when he'd had his foot reset one bone at a time, each time without anaesthetics, all that pain was nothing, nothing to the pain Matt felt hearing Johnny saying what he said, not knowing what had happened, Johnny's mind not right, a fragile thing, the doctors said, they could not take the risk, could not tell Johnny why Tommy had not been to see him yet, why Tommy would never come to see him now, why they dared not stop Johnny Berry telling Matt, Tommy Taylor is some friend of mine, he's not been to see me once.

415

On Good Friday, Manchester United played Sunderland, who were second from the bottom of the League, and Bobby Charlton scored, Alex Dawson scored, but still United could only draw two-all at home. The next day, Easter Saturday, Manchester United played Preston North End at home, Preston who were now second in the League, and for this game Jimmy rested Alex Dawson and Shay Brennan once again, brought back young Kenny Morgans, his first game back since Munich, and Jimmy gave Tommy Heron his first start at outside-left, and United drew nil–nil. Two days after that, on Easter Monday, Manchester United played Sunderland again, this time up at Roker Park, and for this game Jimmy was forced to play Mark Pearson instead of Tommy Heron as Tommy did not have permission from the League to play that day; Tommy's transfer from Portadown had come only after deadline day, in extenuating circumstances, but Sunderland were in danger of being relegated, so it would be unfair to let him play that day. Jimmy also rested Stan Crowther, brought back Wilf McGuinness, his first game back since his cartilage operation, and Colin Webster scored twice, and Manchester United won a game in the League at last that day, beating Sunderland two–one away, their first win in the League since that dreadful day, two months ago, in Munich, in the snow.

But from the crowd at Roker Park that day it was not just curses, names that came United's way, coins and cans were thrown that day, at Ian Greaves and Harry Gregg, and Harry, he turned to the crowd at Roker Park and shouted, What am I? Some kind of dog you starve, you beat, you kick, you stone? Is that what you effing think of me? He wanted to rip the turf up off the pitch, with his fingers, his bare hands, hurl huge chunks of sod back at the crowd, throw it over them, the whole effing pitch if he could, and bury them he would, if he could, as Harry shouted, You don't know me, the things I've seen, you've never seen the things I've seen, and I hope you never will, you effing bunch of so-and-sos.

*

That Easter Monday, after United had beaten Sunderland, Bobby went to see his mam and dad, and his brother Jack, he drove up to Ashington for their belated family Easter, too. The next day, the Tuesday afternoon, Jack and Bobby went to the pictures in Ashington, saw *The Duke Wore Jeans*, with Tommy Steele and June Laverick, at the Wallow on Woodhorn Road. And when the film was finished, as they were walking back to Beatrice Street, Jack bought an evening paper, and as he always did, he read the Stop Press first, and suddenly, right there in the street, Jack let out a whoop of joy, began to do a jig, hooking Bobby by his arm, waltzing him around, telling him, You've only gone and been selected for England, kiddo. You're playing against Scotland at Hampden.

Let us go, will you, Jack, laughed Bobby. Everyone's looking, you're embarrassing us.

Jack laughed, he boomed, But you know who else will be pleased? Brace yourself, kiddo –

Bobby, shouted Cissie, coming down the back of Beatrice Street, you'll never guess –

He knows, said Jack.

Didn't I tell you, said Cissie, grabbing Bobby, hugging him, kissing him, didn't I always tell you, didn't I always say! I knew it –

But the thing was, the thing that Bobby would never say, never dare tell anyone because he knew how it sounded, but he'd known all along this day would come. It had been his mother who'd warned him of the perils and pitfalls, gone on and on at him about the need for an education and a trade, the ever-present risk of injury, the high chance of failure. But Bobby had known that was not going to happen to him, and somehow, don't ask him how, he had known it since he could first kick a ball.

Every morning, before he set off to the pit, not knowing if he would come back home again that night, his father always checked aloud his pockets and his satchel: Bait, bottle, lamp, tabs, he'd say, and then with a last tap upon his right trouser pocket, he'd turn to Bobby with a wink and say, And nae brass.

Bobby was proud to be his father's son, the job he did, under the ground, in the dark and in the heat, the dangerous, back-breaking work he did for Bobby, his brothers and their mother. But Bobby knew that would not be him, would not be Bobby; he knew he would be selected for England Schoolboys at fifteen, that he would score two goals against Wales at Wembley; he knew then every First Division club would come banging on their door on Beatrice Street, but ever since he listened to the FA Cup Final on the radio in 1948, when Manchester United beat Blackpool four–two, he knew he would only play for Manchester United; he knew then if he listened to everything Jimmy Murphy told him, did everything Jimmy said, he knew then Matt Busby, the Boss, would pick him for the first team, that he would score goals, win medals, then an England cap; these were ambitions, yes, his dreams and his wishes, he'd even repeat them to himself whenever he pulled a wishbone with his brothers, but he knew he didn't need superstition or some kind of special luck, he just knew they would come true, that it was written in the stars: Bobby Charlton would play for Manchester United and England; he was untouchable, he would play forever. But then came Munich, that aeroplane, that place, the things he'd seen, the friends he'd lost, and when he'd woken up that next day, in that hospital in Munich, his first thought had been, How wrong could you be, Bobby? No one, least of all Bobby bloody Charlton, aged but twenty-one, ever knew what tomorrow, let alone the future, would bring, or take away again.

I knew it, I just knew it, said Cissie again. Oh, well done, love, well done, pet, really. Congratulations, pet!

Bobby smiled, he said, Thank you, Mother.

Be you next, said Cissie, taking Jackie's arm, squeezing Jackie's arm. You just see. You watch.

Jack laughed, he laughed, Don't talk daft, Mother. Never in anyone's wildest dreams but yours, Mother.

*

Five days later, Manchester United went down to London again, to White Hart Lane this time, where Stan Crowther and Ronnie Cope returned to the side in place of Bobby Harrop and Wilf McGuinness, but United lost one–nil to Tottenham Hotspur, dropping down to ninth now in the League. But there was some good news that day from Munich, where the Rechts der Isar Hospital announced that: Matt Busby will be released from hospital next Thursday. He is to leave Munich by train, arriving in London on Friday morning. The other two survivors still in hospital, John Berry and Frank Taylor, are improving daily, but the hospital spokesman could give no indication as to when they might be discharged.

The British Embassy in Bonn also announced that: Professor George Maurer, Chief Surgeon at the Rechts der Isar Hospital, has been appointed an Honorary Commander of the Order of the British Empire in recognition of his services to the victims of the Air Disaster. The honour is intended to symbolise the appreciation and gratitude, not only of the injured, but of the many thousands of British people who have anxiously followed the progress of their recovery.

Back in Munich, there was one last announcement from West Germany that day: Judge Walter Stimpel, forty-one years old and a former German World War II Luftwaffe flying ace, would be heading the German inquiry into the Manchester United air crash. The inquiry will meet in Munich on April 29 and 30, probably at the airport where the United plane crashed. Judge Stimpel will be assisted by a professor and a civil airline pilot. The hearings will be attended by observers from the British Ministry of Civil Aviation and British European Airways. Captain James Thain has written to say he will be in Munich to appear as a witness. Judge Stimpel said he did not yet know how many witnesses would be called, but he wanted to keep their numbers as low as possible. The detailed findings of the inquiry would be sent to the West German Transport Ministry, which would pass them on to the British Ministry of Civil Aviation. But unlike maritime boards, said Judge Stimpel, we will not be concerned with fixing the blame on anyone, merely finding the causes of the crash.

*

In the end, Johnny Berry left the Rechts der Isar Hospital two days before Matt Busby. He was the only one of the players who'd survived the crash who flew back to England, arriving back in Manchester on a British European Airways Viscount. But two male nurses had to sit behind Johnny and Hilda Berry on that flight, one with all the medicines Johnny needed, the other with a bag of tranquillisers, just in case. Johnny still knew nothing of the crash, the death of his friends, his pals. He thought he'd been in a car crash, or seemed to think he had, that was the reason he had a broken pelvis, a badly broken elbow, injuries to his jaw that meant the removal of all his teeth, and a badly, very badly fractured skull. There was no way that Johnny could travel home by train and boat and train again, he was not strong enough. But the doctors, the nurses, they were concerned, worried that the flight itself might bring it back, that his amnesia would vanish, be gone, and Johnny would remember, it would all come back to him. But Johnny did not remember, it did not come back, at least not yet, and on landing at Ringway Airport, he was taken straight to Manchester Royal Infirmary so more work could be done on his jaw and his teeth, where the doctors said, He is quite comfortable, though it's impossible to say when he will be released.

For now, Hilda Berry felt it best their boys, they wait to see their dad, not come visit him just yet, maybe wait a week or two, but Bill Foulkes and Dennis Viollet, they came to see Johnny, how he was getting on, and Johnny said, Not so bad, he said, not too bad, he said, but you know I could not sleep a wink last night?

Oh, why was that then, asked Bill.

Well, you know that Tommy Steele, said Johnny. He was in this room, strumming away, all night he was, strumming his guitar, singing them blues . . .

*

The day after Manchester United drew three-all with Portsmouth, down on the coast at Fratton Park, ten weeks exactly since he'd first arrived, Matt left the Rechts der Isar Hospital in Munich. His right leg in plaster, walking with the help of two crutches and looking already very tired, Matt thanked and shook hands with the nurses and the doctors who lined the corridors of the hospital to say goodbye to Matt and Jean and wish them well, the best of health, but the warmest thanks and the longest handshake were for Professor Maurer at the end, when Matt said, Thank you, Professor. Thank you for everything you have done. Thank you for making me well again, and Professor Maurer smiled and patted Matt's hand, and Matt said, Don't forget, you must come to London to see the Cup Final, and Professor Maurer smiled again and said, If you'll be there, I will, and both men smiled and laughed for the cameras, the reporters, and then Jean shook hands, she thanked the professor, too, as the nurses helped Matt into his heavy winter coat. Then, in his coat, but with no hat, Matt limped on his sticks out to the car that took Matt and Jean to the waiting press conference at a nearby hotel, organised by British European Airways, and where Matt sat with his right leg up, resting on a chair –

Do you have any idea yet, the press asked Matt, when you will be able to take over your job again?

Matt shook his head a little bit, then said, quietly said, At the moment, I say next season. This season lasts for only three more weeks, so it's impossible for me to take over in this short period of time. Besides, Jimmy, Jimmy Murphy is doing a wonderful job. He'll keep it at least until the Cup Final. I will not attempt to take any part in management until after that. Jimmy had to take over when things looked extremely black, and the boys have responded wonderfully well to him, they really have. And I have to say, the development of Manchester United has had a great influence on my own recuperation, and it has helped me quite a bit, it really has.

What about the Cup Final, the press asked Matt. You think you will be there?

Matt shook his head a little bit again, then said, quietly said again, At the moment, it's too early to say whether I'll be able to go to Wembley, but I hope so. If I can, I'd like to lead United into the stadium.

But beyond the Cup Final, the press asked Matt, what of the future, Matt?

Matt sighed a little, then said, almost out of breath, it seemed, but still he said, Well, I think I will still go for nursing the Babes, but plan to buy other players, too, players to replace the lost ones, the ones we lost, you know, like Tommy, Tommy Taylor, you know. But I'll continue to rely on young players. But there is a big gap to be filled, you know, and it will take a little time.

That was supposed to be the end of things, the last question before they left for the station, but someone from the press, they asked, shouted out, Do you think you will ever fly again with Manchester United, do you, Matt?

Matt seemed to freeze, frozen in that seat, his right leg up on another chair, but then his hand came up, his head went down, his head held in one hand, he said, he whispered, I would not like to answer that now. Maybe in a little while things might seem different. But only time will tell, yes, only time will tell.

*

Harry was playing for Northern Ireland against Wales, down in Cardiff, in a British Home Championship game, and Harry thought Jackie might want to come with him, the change of scene might do him good, get him out of the house, from under Jean's feet, out of Manchester, too, away from here, See all the boys, you know, your Danny, and I know Peter Doherty, he'd love to see you there.

Yes, said Jackie. He already called.

Harry nodded, he said, So you coming then, are you, Blanchy? Your Danny, he'd be pleased, yeah?

Yes, said Jackie again. He already called.

Harry nodded again, he laughed. Did he tell you how I stopped this shot of his on Saturday, but then how Bobby Smith, the dirty sod, he charges into me, bundles me over the line, the dirty sod, but the referee, he'd got a pair of balls on him for once, gave a free-kick, and so he should. He tell you that, did he, your Danny?

423

No, said Jackie. He said you lost.

Harry tutted, he said, We'd not have lost if Stan bloody Crowther could control a fucking ball with his feet and not his hand. I told him, You after my job, are you, Stan? That reminds me, did you know Ronnie Reynolds, he's wearing contact lenses now, yeah? Your Danny tell you that, did he? No, I bet he didn't, they kept that quiet. But as we were coming off the pitch, I went to shake his hand, and the fella is weeping, and I said, Ronnie, what the hell you crying about, you bloody won! It's these new contact lenses, Harry, he said, and this bloody wind, he said, my eyes won't stop watering, I cannot see a bloody thing. I said, Well –

Harry, said Jackie, I'm not going, and I'm not going to Sweden either, or to Wembley. I've to go back into hospital in June, for an operation on my arm.

Harry shook his head, he said, You could still come down to Cardiff with us, still go to Wembley if you wanted. Maybe take your mind off things, you know?

No, said Jackie, I've to avoid all crowds.

And who the hell told you that?

The doctors, said Jackie. Who'd you think?

Harry shook his head again, tried not to shout, just say, Doctors? The hell do they know? They don't know you, Blanchy. You box, you fight. Avoid all crowds? You're a professional footballer for Chrissakes, man!

Am I, said Jackie. You sure about that, are you, Harry? Well, a lot of good it's done me then.

*

It had just gone three on a grey, overcast April afternoon when a big black Humber car provided by British European Airways brought Matt and Jean back home to Kings Road, Chorlton, Manchester. They had travelled on the *Rheingold Express* to the

Hook of Holland, then on the overnight ferry to Harwich, then by car all the way back here, in this big black Humber, Matt with his right foot in a big sock up on a pillow in the back.

Now Matt swung his leg, his foot off the pillow, tried to get himself with some help out of the back of the car, onto the pavement, where a crowd of thirty children, neighbours and well-wishers had gathered, outnumbered by the press, and on his crutches, his hands not free to wave, Matt nodded, he smiled, he said, Thank you, thank you, everybody, and then he hobbled, he limped through his gate, and in his garden, on its path, almost, almost home at last, Matt stopped again, out of breath, he leant on his two crutches, turned and thanked the well-wishers once again, still gathered on the pavement on Kings Road, and Matt joked with the press, the photographers, he said, Are you all right then, lads? How have you been while I've been away? Did you miss me, boys?

But Sheena, she had seen enough, she came out of the house, took her mum and dad inside, with one last wave, into the house they went, the hallway lined with flowers, bedecked with cards, the front and back room, too, their pet poodle jumping up, yapping with delight as Sheena led her dad to his usual favourite chair, sat him down, got him settled, his foot up on a cushion, the dog upon his lap, and when Sheena saw her father, saw her daddy sitting there, back home again at last, she could not help herself, she broke down, she wept and said, I'm sorry, Dad, I'm sorry, I thought you were never coming back.

*

Neck to toe in plaster still, Frank was all alone in Munich now, in the Rechts der Isar Hospital, now Matt and Jean had gone. Frank had seen more of Matt, much more of Matt these last few weeks, either sitting on his balcony on a sunny day or, day by day, learning to walk again, pale and shaking on two sticks, he would come in to see Frank, sit down and rest and have a chat, but then before Frank knew it, Matt had come with Jean to say goodbye –

Hello, my old pal, he'd said, as he always said. Just hope you won't be long now following Jean and me back to England. You must be longing to see your boys.

But be sure to come and see us, Frank, said Jean, when you get back to Manchester.

Later that day, Frank asked Professor Kessel, What are the chances of me following Matt and being back for the Cup Final, Doc?

I know it would be nice to see your friends again, Frank, said the doctor, a kind and always cheerful, very friendly man, but, young man, he said, one finger raised towards the ceiling, the sky, the heavens above, each and every day, you should thank Him above, who ordained where it was you sat in that aeroplane that day.

*

The day after Matt Busby came home, United played Birmingham City at Old Trafford. There had never really been any expectation that Matt would be at the match that afternoon, not after the arduous journey of the last few days, and it was a good job he did not try, he did not go, because within two minutes of kicking off, Birmingham were one–nil up and went on to win the game two–nil, and so it was now three months since Manchester United last won a League game at home, at Old Trafford.

But that afternoon, there was some good news to the north, when, at Gigg Lane, up in Bury, Dennis Viollet scored for the United reserves in his first competitive match since returning from Munich –

I feel tired, said Dennis after the game, but I also feel confident that with a couple more games, I can be fully match fit and ready for Wembley, if I am selected, of course. But I think if I play in one of the midweek games and again on the Saturday, then I'm sure I would be ready to play in the Final. It just depends on these next few games, how they go, but I make no bones about it, I'm desperately keen to play if I can, what with having had to drop out of last year's Final with a groin injury. But then again, if Jimmy, if Mister Murphy, he thinks I'm not ready or someone else can do a better job than me, I shall have no complaints and I'll sit out another Cup Final, knowing it is in the best interests of Manchester United. After all, the lads have done well enough up to now in the Cup without me, and I know the Cup Final team will be picked entirely on merit and current form, and that alone, that is as it should be, the Manchester United way.

Still further north, at Hampden Park in Glasgow, there was more good news that afternoon, unless you were one of the five million good people of Scotland or Matt Busby, back in Chorlton, who had been the manager of the Scotland national football team until that first Thursday in February. Now Scotland did not have a manager, they had Dawson Walker, who was the man with the sponge at Clyde. So perhaps it was no great surprise that England won four–nil that day, but what pleased so many folk, English- and Scotsman alike, was that Bobby Charlton scored on his England debut, in front of a crowd of one hundred and thirty thousand people, with one of finest goals surely ever seen at Hampden, volleying a perfect centre from Tom Finney from twelve yards, a thunderbolt that hit the back of the Scottish goal before their keeper Younger could even raise a hand; the keeper's only action was to run out to shake Bobby Charlton by the hand. Well done, son, said Tommy Younger, that was a fantastic goal.

Last season, in the November, Wolverhampton Wanderers had come to Old Trafford, and David Pegg had scored, Tommy Taylor had scored, and Liam Whelan had scored, and United had beaten Wolves three–nil that afternoon, three of the one hundred and three goals United scored on their way to winning the League that season.

Eighteen months later, on April 21, Wolverhampton Wanderers came back to Old Trafford. This was the match that United would have played the Saturday after they returned to Old Trafford from Belgrade, the match they were so desperate to get home for, the match they had been so desperate to win.

On Thursday, February 6, as the Elizabethan was attempting to take off for a third time that afternoon, Wolves had not lost a game in the League and were top with forty-two points, while United had already lost four times in the League, including a three–one defeat at Molineux, and were third with thirty-six points. Still, if United were to beat Wolves at Old Trafford on their return from Belgrade, then all at United were confident that they could catch Wolves and win the League again, a third season in succession. But as it was, since that afternoon in February, Wolverhampton Wanderers had only lost one match, and on Saturday, when United were losing again at home, and Bobby Charlton was away scoring for England, Wolves had beaten Preston North End, without Billy Wright or Bill Slater, and so when Wolverhampton Wanderers arrived at Old Trafford on that Monday evening in April, Wolves were the new Champions of England.

Once again, Matt Busby was not strong enough to attend the match that night, but Matt insisted that the United players form a lane from the tunnel and applaud the players of Wolverhampton Wanderers onto the pitch, and so Bill Foulkes, seventeen-year-old David Gaskell, who was playing instead of Harry Gregg, who was sick in bed with flu, Ian Greaves, Freddie Goodwin, Ronnie Cope, Wilf McGuinness, Alex Dawson, Shay Brennan, Colin Webster, Dennis Viollet, in his first senior game since Munich, and Kenny Morgans stood and clapped as the new Champions of England took to the pitch, and then Dwyer, Stuart, Jones, Clamp, Wright, Flowers, Deeley, Broadbent, Murray, Booth and Mullen promptly thrashed the old Champions four goals to nil.

*

Matt knew he could not hide away at home forever, in his favourite chair, with his foot propped up, or in the garden, if the sun came out. He knew he'd have to go back to the ground, face Old Trafford, the people there and not there. He'd have to face the families, too, he knew, and the sooner the better, too, he had to force himself, he knew. He talked with Jean and Sheena, thought it best he go in one afternoon, not when the players were about or the crowds there for a match, just to see the place, the staff again, but he had to do it and do it soon, he knew. So Matt called up Paddy McGrath, asked if he'd not mind giving him a lift, help him with the stairs and things, and Louis Edwards said he'd come in, he'd be there that day, too, to help and lend a hand.

So two days after United had lost to Wolves, the night they would be playing Newcastle at Old Trafford, but well before the game, just after lunch, Paddy McGrath called at Kings Road, Chorlton. It was the first time Paddy had seen Matt since Munich, and when Matt saw Paddy, standing at his door, he came towards him, hobbling on his sticks, and with his sticks still in his hands, he reached out, hugged Paddy, held him tight and said, Thank you, Paddy. Thanks for doing this.

Paddy helped Matt into the car, then Paddy drove them the short way to the ground, but Matt did not really speak, say much, and Paddy just talked about the weather, the shows that were on in town, trying to keep the conversation light, knowing there were tears in Matt's eyes, already tears, and as they came, got closer to the ground, crossed the bridge, Old Trafford straight up ahead, Matt did not look, he did not, could not look up, and Paddy wondered if he should ask if they should turn around, go back to Kings Road and try again another day, but then Paddy heard Matt sigh, felt Matt steel himself, wipe the tears away, off his cheeks, from his eyes, but not the ghosts, they were still there, those young, red ghosts.

Louis Edwards was waiting at the main entrance to the ground, the doors wide open, and with him stood Jimmy and Jack Crompton, little Joe Armstrong, young Les Olive and dear, dear Alma, and Paddy helped Matt from the car, and on his sticks, Matt came towards them all, shook their hands, hugged Alma and said, I cannot thank you all enough, he said, his voice breaking, his eyes watering again, for all you've done.

It's just so good to have you back, they said, all said. Welcome home, Boss, welcome back.

They all then went inside, helped Matt along to Ted Dalton's medical room, where the staff had been asked to gather so Matt could say hello and thank you all, to all the staff, the office and the ground staff, the ladies in the canteen and the laundry, all so pleased, so happy and relieved, with tears of joy, they were to see the Boss walk in, old as he looked, through hell it seemed he'd been, but back again, at Old Trafford once again.

Then Matt coughed, he cleared his throat to say a few more words, how United would go on, that the great days were not behind them, no matter how long and hard the road back, United would rise again –

But before he'd hardly said a word, Matt broke down, he could not go on, it was just too much, all too much, Matt sobbing, terrible, heaving, painful sobs as Jimmy and Jack helped him from the room, down the corridor, out into the stands to get some air, and they got Matt sat down in a seat in the stand, with Jimmy and Jack at either side of him, Matt with his hands to his face, his cheeks, his eyes, Matt wiped away the tears again, then shook his head and said, I'm sorry, Jimmy, I'm sorry, Jack, and straight ahead he stared, out onto the pitch, that empty, silent field.

But then, to their surprise and his own, especially his own, Matt turned to Jimmy and said, If you don't mind, I'd like to stay for the game tonight. Would that be all right with you, Jimmy?

You don't need to ask, said Jimmy, you know you don't, Matt. But if you're not too tired, is all I'd say. I wouldn't want you to be overdoing things, pushing yourself too hard, and nor would Jean.

Matt shook his head. No, but I need to see a game, Jimmy, here at Old Trafford, I know I do, and I want to, Jimmy, I do, I really do, and the sooner the better.

You want to come in the dressing room, too, asked Jimmy, have a few words with the boys?

No, no, Jimmy, no, I won't do that, not today, tonight, I won't. I'll just sit and watch the match.

All right, said Jimmy. But if you change your mind, you just say, and then he and Jack helped Matt back inside, helped him up to the boardroom, poured them all a drink, and a stiff one at that, and later on Mister Hardman joined them. He'd brought Matt and Jimmy the special badge the players would wear on their shirts at Wembley a week on Saturday, showed them a golden eagle atop a crown, part of Manchester City Council's new coat of arms, though Jimmy squinted, then said, Looks more like a phoenix than an eagle, does it not, sir?

Later, Jimmy introduced Matt to Keith Dewhurst and David Meek, who were writing about United now for the *Evening Chronicle* and *Evening News*, and now also for the *United Review*, just as Alf Clarke and Tom Jackson had done before, before, and Matt looked sad, they thought, so very sad, so very tired and frail, but still he gripped, he shook their hands and said, I know Keith, good to see you again, son. I hope you're well. And pleased to meet you, David. Let's hope we win.

The attendance was low that night, only twenty-eight thousand or so there that night, but when the Old Trafford crowd saw Matt Busby come out and slowly, slowly on his sticks make his way to a seat up in the stands, the reception that they gave the Boss, it was a great, tremendous cheer that echoed, echoed round the ground, across the pitch, that field. But it was a spartan, quiet and ghostly crowd that watched that match with Matt, that match that Matt, he tried, he tried to watch, not think upon the games, the boys now gone, that last time Newcastle had come this way, when David Pegg had scored twice, Bill Whelan had scored twice and Dennis Viollet had scored twice as well and they had won six–one, or the year, the season before that, when Dennis had scored twice again, David Pegg had got another goal and Tommy Taylor had got one, too, and John Doherty had scored that day and United had won five–two. No, no, thought Matt, I must not think on that, as Matt tried again, he tried again to watch the match before his eyes, see Ian Greaves, not Roger Byrne, see Crowther, Cope, McGuinness, Dawson, Ernie Taylor and Colin Webster, not Mark Jones, Geoff Bent, Eddie Colman, Duncan Edwards, David Pegg, Bill Whelan or Tommy Taylor, and be thankful there was Harry Gregg and Bill Foulkes, Bobby Charlton and Kenny Morgans playing once again, be thankful United were playing good football, too, they were the better side, that there was Ernie Taylor setting up Alex Dawson to hook the ball into the net from twelve yards out, and for almost all the match they really were the better side, that when Newcastle equalised with just two minutes left upon the clock, a goal and point that would keep them in Division One, United were unlucky, desperately unlucky, they had been robbed. But Matt, he did not want to dwell, to think on luck and theft, but to think instead of all the things he'd hoped, really wanted to have said: how United would go on, that the great days were not behind them, that United would rise again, so don't dwell upon the ashes, think only of the phoenix.

After the match, Matt told Keith and David and the other members of the press, It is great to be back at Old Trafford and to see so many familiar, friendly faces, and the welcome was tremendous, it really was. During my last fortnight in Munich, I got terribly homesick. I wanted to see a match at Old Trafford as quickly as I could, and so this has been a real tonic for me, it really has. It has helped me considerably, and I'm certainly hoping to be fit enough to get down to Wembley now.

But later that night, after Paddy had driven him back home, helped him into the house, after Matt had sworn blind to Jean and Sheena he was fine, a wee bit tired was all, that it had been a good thing, a good day at Old Trafford, it really had, when Matt got into bed, his foot propped up on a spare pillow at the end of his bed, Matt found it hard to sleep and not to cry, lying there in the dark, seeing those young, red ghosts again upon that empty, silent field.

*

Two days after Matt Busby returned to Old Trafford, Manchester United travelled down to London to play Chelsea. It was United's fourth League game in seven days. It was also the last League game of the season. In the first League game of the season, back in late August, against Leicester City, the newly promoted Champions of the Second Division, away at Filbert Street, the United team that late-summer day had been Wood, Foulkes, Byrne, Colman, Blanchflower, Edwards, Berry, Whelan, Taylor,

433

Viollet and Pegg. In the seventieth minute, Byrne passed to Edwards, Edwards passed to Pegg, Pegg set up Viollet for a shot which was deflected to Whelan, who scored. Minutes later, now from the right, Pegg hit a perfect cross for Whelan to score again. Five minutes after, again from the right, this time Berry hit another perfect cross for Whelan to complete his hat-trick, and United won three–nil. But in the last League game of the season, down at Stamford Bridge, the United team was Gregg, Foulkes, Greaves, Goodwin, Cope, Crowther, Dawson, Taylor, Charlton, Viollet and Webster, with Charlton switching to centre-forward, Webster at outside-left, Dawson out on the right and Viollet back at inside-right, and though United lost again, to a youthful Chelsea side, they played quite well, dominant for much of the game, with Webster shining on the left and Viollet looking fully fit again, and so there was much speculation that this would be the side that took to the Wembley field just one week from today, when United would be back down in London once again to play Bolton Wanderers in the Cup Final.

*

Tickets for the Cup Final were already changing hands at twenty, thirty times their face value, twenty-five-shilling tickets going for twenty-five pounds, so begging letter after begging letter filled the sacks of the Old Trafford postmen, but they were not the only kind of letters that the postmen brought. Back before the semi-final, Harry Gregg had had letters offering him two hundred, five hundred pounds if he would throw the match, let Fulham win, but Harry had just put them straight in the bin, Just from a crank, he'd said, and regularly there were letters addressed To Whom It May Concern, which, wrote Ernie Taylor in his column in the *Evening Chronicle*, Listed all our sins and those of our parents, in language that is earthy to say the very least, and which suggest that we are only playing on sentiment, that the other sides are just letting us win. Little Ernie revealed that such letters were pinned up on the Old Trafford noticeboard to give the players a laugh. But there was nothing funny, no funny side to the many, many letters that Dennis Viollet was now receiving.

When he had come round, properly round in Munich, in that hospital bed, Dennis had hated football, really hated football, wanted nothing more to do with it, and for day after day, week after week, lying in that bed, he did not change his mind, he really fucking hated football, the very thought of it, he was done with football, through with it. But then when he got back to Manchester, Fallowfield, the place where he was born and raised, went down to the ground, the club where he'd come up through the ranks, when he saw the lads, how hard they were all trying, how hard Jimmy, especially Jimmy, but Jack and Joe, Arthur and Bill, how hard they were all trying, well, then Dennis changed his mind. He would train as hard as he could, do the best that he could to be fit and ready for the Final, to play if he could, help United win the Cup, do it for the club, yes, but do it for the boys, the friends who could not play, the ones they'd lost, like Jimmy said, and win the thing for them, the Dead.

But now every day, with every post, these many, many letters came, all addressed to him, all telling him how unfair it would be if Dennis were to play in the Final, unfair on all the young lads who'd battled through against all odds, the letters said, You are only going to play a stinker, Dennis, you know you are, and let the side down, you know you will, and then you'll never forgive yourself, will you, Dennis, so don't play, Dennis, just don't play!

Last season, Dennis had played in every round of the Cup except the Final, missing out with a groin injury, so he could sympathise with anyone who played in the early rounds but missed out on the big day itself. But last season, it had never

435

entered his head that it was unfair that Bobby Charlton was playing in the Final, that it was only his second game in the Cup. It didn't cross his mind. And this season, in the third round of the Cup, Dennis had scored a hat-trick at Workington, and he'd been in the side that beat Ipswich Town in the fourth round. Dennis could not understand how anyone might think he did not deserve a place if Jimmy picked him to play in the Wembley side, could not believe that someone would then pick up a pen, take out some paper and write a letter, put it in an envelope, buy a stamp and post the thing, not just once, but twice, three times a day, a supporter, so they said.

*

I just want to know why, said Marion Bent.

Matt had come to say sorry, just as he had come or called to say sorry to all the other families of the Dead, their parents, wives and loved ones, but it was only Marion, the widow of Geoff Bent, with their baby daughter Karen in her arms, in their house on Kings Road, Stretford, it was only Marion who said what Matt knew all the other families of the Dead must think, must surely want to say: Why did you let them all get back on that plane again, after trying twice, failing twice to take off? Why did you or no one else speak up? I mean, you are, you were all grown men, you could all speak up, but nobody said anything, I just can't understand why.

He said, I'm so sorry, Marion, I'm so sorry. It is my fault, I blame myself. I should have said something. But how would I have felt if that captain would have been telling me, my lads, how to play football. That's how I would have felt, telling him how to fly his plane.

Well, I wish someone had, said Marion Bent, looking down at her daughter, Geoff's daughter, their baby in her arms, wiping

436

a tear from her eye, from her cheek, wish someone had told him not to fly his plane that day.

*

We are all on the same side here, said Judge Stimpel. This is an inquiry, not a trial, we are looking for cause, not blame. But whatever Judge Stimpel said, however honourable his intentions, Jim Thain knew the airport and the airline were looking for a scapegoat, for someone to blame, and Jim Thain knew they were looking at him.

The British party flew out to Munich the day before the inquiry was to open, all stayed together at the Four Seasons Hotel: the four officials representing British European Airways; Jim Thain and his own representative, Captain Gilman, and Captain Key, who would represent the late Ken Rayment, all of whom were employed by BEA, but Gilman and Key were there as representatives of the British Airline Pilots' Association. The Germans had also suggested, kindly suggested the British should bring along a man from the Meteorological Office, and that in itself told Jim Thain all he needed to know about the way things would go, the way fingers would point.

The inquiry opened at ten sharp on the morning of April 28, out at Munich airport, in a conference room on an upper floor of what looked to Jim Thain like a barrack block, with guards on the doors. But inside the room, sat facing one another across a very long table, the interpreter in a glass booth at one end, the atmosphere was friendly, very friendly, matey, in fact, very matey –

Everybody present here today, began Judge Stimpel, in some capacity or other, is concerned with aviation, and so all of us here today are only too aware of the ever-present dangers, which no amount of experience, no technical developments can ever wholly eliminate. So I hope I can assure all those who were personally involved in the events of February 6, especially Captain Thain and the gentlemen from BEA, that the members of this commission feel a close comradeship with them. We will try to carry out this investigation objectively and in accordance with our duty, of course, but also with a deep interest and understanding of your personal fate.

But then Judge Stimpel called on Captain Reichel, the Chief Inspector of Accidents, to read his report on the investigation he had carried out, in which he emphasised his discovery of a layer of ice on the starboard wing of G-ALZU, as the Elizabethan aircraft was referred to throughout, and added that: It was ascertained that no action had been taken to rid G-ALZU of ice while it was on the ground, prior to take-off. He spoke of the sixteen other aircraft that had landed at or taken off from Munich between fourteen hundred hours and eighteen hundred hours that day, how the reports on the condition of the runway from those pilots all stated that braking action had been good or fair, that snow and slush was cleared before take-off from the lifting surfaces of all aircraft which were standing in the open a long time during their stop in Munich, all apart from G-ALZU.

Captain Reichel did admit, There were varying opinions on the snow conditions on the runway. However, the snow had fallen on a non-frozen and very wet base, so that it had subsided to form a layer of slush. Yet, insisted Captain Reichel, citing the landing of his own aircraft seven hours after G-ALZU had failed in its third attempt to take off, our comparatively light aircraft rolled, unimpeded by the snow, right up to the end of the runway, and no snow had been cleared from the runway.

It was an inquiry, not a trial, they had said, they were looking for cause, not blame. But there could be no doubt about what and then who Captain Reichel felt had caused the accident, what

438

conclusions he wanted the commission to reach. So when Judge Stimpel then asked Jim Thain to read his own statement, to tell them everything he had observed that day, what conclusions he himself had reached, Jim Thain already felt he was on trial, a man accused and in the dock, but with none of the benefits an actual, proper trial would have brought him: prior access to statements, lists of witnesses, the right to call his own witnesses, to have a lawyer, a defence.

In the conference room, sat across the long table from him as he read, the commission listened to Jim Thain in silence, except for one moment after he'd said, Before the first attempt to take off, I observed the snow was thawing on the starboard wing of the aircraft.

You didn't see anything from the steps of the BEA office, did you, asked Judge Stimpel. This was when you came closer to the plane?

I can't remember making a point of looking for snow when I was standing on the steps, said Jim Thain. It wasn't until I got closer to the aircraft that I looked up.

So you saw it from the ground, from below, asked Judge Stimpel. You didn't climb onto the wing?

Oh, no, from below, said Jim Thain.

There were no more questions until Jim Thain reached the end of his statement, when Judge Stimpel then asked him to talk the commission through a normal take-off for an Elizabethan aircraft, in normal conditions, and which Jim Thain did, at some length, answering questions about V1 and V2, the nose wheel and the angle of wing to ground, whether or not he had felt the tail wheel touch the ground during that fatal third attempt –

Quite truthfully, replied Jim Thain, it would be difficult to feel the tail wheel if it was touching, but if you were to ask if I thought the nose wheel was very high, the answer would be no, no, I didn't.

439

But after Jim Thain had finished speaking, Captain Reichel then called witness after witness, in person or via statement, to contradict or cast doubt upon all the things Jim Thain had said –

I was able to see the upper surface of the aircraft plainly from the second floor of the main building from not more than fifty yards, one said, and the snow remained on the wing. After the mechanic had given the 'all-clear' signal to taxi, I told colleagues I was surprised that the aircraft was not de-iced before take-off.

It struck me that halfway along the runway, the pilot was trying, with all his might, to get the aircraft off the ground. The nose wheel was high in the air and the emergency tail wheel was on the ground.

The remarkable thing was that the tail bumper had been in contact with the ground over the last three hundred metres, wrote one witness who had been quickly on the scene, had seen the wheel tracks in the snow. Obviously the pilot was desperately trying to pull the machine up off the ground, or trying to stop it . . .

For the next two days, on and on the statements came, in person or in writing, on and on they went, and on and on Captain Reichel hammered and drove home his point, the conclusion he'd already reached: the cause of the accident was ice on the wings, ice on the wings, ice on the wings, the wings . . .

At one point, Judge Stimpel did intervene with 'a last question': Would Captain Thain like to make a statement on what he believes caused the accident?

Well, from the investigation that I have done, replied Jim Thain, I feel the cause of the accident was slush on the runway and not ice on the wing.

About slush and the whole state of the runway, we shall talk in detail later, Judge Stimpel assured Jim Thain. You will have a chance to say more about it yourself.

But the statements and the questioning became more and more confused, jumping from subject to subject, seemingly at random: the house at the end of the runway; boost surging and unsticking; the height of the nose wheel again; again the slush, the spray on the runway –

We shall keep this question in mind, so that we can come back to it if necessary, said Judge Stimpel, closing down that line of discussion again. But I'm afraid we are getting too far from the question of ice –

The Question of Ice; it always seemed to come back to the Question of Ice –

I said to my colleagues, said one young witness, why are they not removing the snow from the wings?

Yes, it need not be ice, said another expert witness. Even a cover of wet snow on the wing can be enough to stop a plane from leaving the ground.

During the attempted take-off, said another, in a familiar, rehearsed echo, it struck me that the pilot was trying for all he was worth to unstick the aircraft.

On and on the statements came, they went, crucial points, alternative avenues still being missed, not pursued, not followed up, while other statements just muddied the waters or, worse, cast further doubts –

In regard to V1, said one of the gentlemen from BEA, there is no instruction which says that the take-off must be continued or not continued.

I feel that I ought to put in front of you an instruction which does deal with the position of the pilots. It has nothing to do with the authority of one or the other for decisions, but just for the completeness of the record, said another of the gentlemen from BEA, handing over the document with the instruction that required the captain of the aircraft to always sit in the left-hand seat.

Jim Thain could hardly believe it; he had been the captain of the aircraft that day, but he had been sat in the right-hand seat, and BEA knew he had and why he had. He could barely contain his anger as he told Judge Stimpel and the commission, Regarding these instructions which have been brought to your attention and which you will find requires the person in command to occupy the left-hand seat: in this particular accident, I was operating within United Kingdom legislation, exercising my prerogative as commander, sitting in the right-hand seat, ordering Captain Rayment to occupy the left-hand seat.

I make no point of this at all, sir, said the gentleman from BEA. I am not suggesting it has any importance at all in the circumstances of the accident, but British European Airways do not want it to be thought that anything we have is not available to the commission.

Then why bloody bring it up, Jim Thain wanted to shout. Why bloody mention it at all? But he knew why, knew full well why –

British European Airways were hanging Jim Thain out to dry, stabbing Jim Thain in the back, casting any doubt they could upon his competence, his character, making sure the whole damn world knew what and then who, who was to blame.

The question of ice on the surface of the aircraft, whether it was the reason for the failure of the aircraft to become airborne, has been discussed thoroughly, Judge Stimpel told the press of the world. And a number of questions need further clarification. Apart from the problem of ice, the commission discussed a number of possible additional causes of the accident. Here, too, supplementary investigations will be necessary. As soon as these further investigations have been concluded, the commission will resume its inquiry.

The commission wishes to stress the fact that the present stage of the investigations admits of no definitive conclusions as to the cause or coincidence of causes responsible for the accident.

But Jim Thain knew no one was really fooled, no one deceived; three words in the judge's statement had said it all:

442

'possible additional causes'. That told him everything he needed to know, what he'd known all along: they had already decided on the cause, already come to a conclusion, a verdict; they knew then who was guilty, who was to blame; it was him, it was Jim; they had made up, already made up their minds.

*

Jimmy was sick of doubt, the constant thoughts, the permutations in his head, the beads in his hand, between his fingers, round and round they went. Width, width, width, that was the thing about Wembley, Jimmy knew, you couldn't win there without playing to its width, so you needed wingers, and that was what they did not have, now David Pegg was dead, Johnny Berry not knowing who or where he was, and Albert Scanlon still with that bandage wrapped around his head. That just left young Kenny Morgans, and up to the Newcastle game, Jimmy had been pushing and pushing young Kenny, bringing him back as fast as he could, always in his ear, urging young Kenny on, On for the Dead, son, the lads who are not here, promising young Kenny Wembley, a place in the team.

But then, after the Newcastle game, Matt had said, Young Kenny looks so thin, so frail. I hope the boy is not pushing himself too hard, Jimmy, and Jimmy knew that Matt, the Boss, was right, young Kenny was just skin and bone, no wonder the boy played in fits and starts, the odd spurt here, the odd spurt there, but most times young Kenny just was not there, he was a ghost.

So Jimmy had rested Kenny for the game at Stamford Bridge, brought back Dennis Viollet, put Alex Dawson out on the right again, tried Colin Webster out on the left, and Colin had had a good game, but still . . .

Round and round the thoughts went in his head, and not just about the FA Cup, what side to name, he had to discuss the

443

Welsh squad for the World Cup with the selectors, too, as if he didn't have enough to do, and those discussions would feature young Kenny, too, whether to take him to Sweden or not, and more and more he was thinking not, best not, best let the boy rest, still . . .

Round and round the thoughts went in his head, the beads in his hand, between his fingers, followed him to Blackpool, back to the Norbreck Hydro, where from Monday until Friday, the week before Wembley, Jimmy had brought the boys again, for peace and quiet, some kind of sanctuary, the light training on the golf course, the jogs across the sands, keeping them away from the constant demands for tickets, the endless speculation in the papers, but, of course, the press came, too –

If you caught him on a good night, late at night, Jimmy would talk and talk, often keep folk up all night. He'd drink whisky and hot water with you till the dawn, fill the ashtrays, stain the walls with nicotine, as he talked about the war, the things he'd seen, the things he wished he'd never seen, but then he'd turn to music, the composers that he loved, why you really ought to hear Sibelius's String Quartet in D minor, not just his Fifth Symphony, if you want to know the measure of his genius, and talk of genius would then lead back to football, the players he'd played with and against, the best ones he'd ever seen, how fucking great Hughie Gallacher, Alex James and Tom Finney really were, how no one really knew just how fucking good Tom was, how little people knew. But just imagine a world without Tom Finney or Beethoven? What a heartless, ugly place that would be.

But catch Jimmy on a bad day, early in the morning, well then –

Excuse me, Jimmy, said one of the new young press boys, the ones they had brought in to fill the shoes of the ones who'd gone, good pals of Jimmy, some of them, fast friends like George

Follows, whom Jimmy missed, he really did, those men who knew what was what, how football really worked, what football really took, not like some of these new young boys, some of whom, it seemed to Jimmy, had never seen a match before Munich, but this particular new young lad, he smiled, he said, I'm very sorry to bother you, but –

Then don't, piss off!

But then that better, bigger part of Jimmy sighed and shouted, Steve, Steve, I'm sorry, my old pal. Get back here with you. What is it, my old friend?

Well, I was just wondering if you'd be willing to share your thoughts on the team for Wembley, you know, whether you will be risking Dennis Viollet?

'Risking' Dennis Viollet, said Jimmy, scoffed Jimmy, shouted Jimmy. Go on, get out of here, go on, fuck off, will you, Steve or Kev or Dave, or whatever your fucking name is, 'risking' Dennis Viollet . . .

Jimmy had had enough of this, was sick and tired of this. He called a press conference then and there, that Tuesday morning, four whole days before the Final, and said, I was hoping to hold back until Friday, just to keep Bolton guessing, but I can't hold back any longer. Every night since the semi-final I have been going to bed and seeing a new team line up at Wembley. I reckon I would have gone on picking and repicking the team until I finished up having eighteen players trotting out there.

I tell you, boys, it's the toughest thing I've ever had to do, and I hope I never have to do this job again. So many of these lads, they have played their hearts out, but you just can't pick them all and, of course, you can't leave one out without a twinge of conscience.

But this is the best permutation I could produce, these same boys who looked so good against Chelsea last Saturday. I am just thankful this tough job is over now.

Then Jimmy led the press out onto the golf course, where Harry Gregg, Bill Foulkes, Ian Greaves, Freddie Goodwin, Ronnie Cope, Stan Crowther, Alex Dawson, Ernie Taylor, Bobby Charlton, Dennis Viollet and Colin Webster stood waiting to pose for the photographers in their Cup Final kit, with its special new badge.

What about the lads who didn't make the team, asked one of the press. Mark Pearson, Kenny Morgans, Bobby Harrop, Wilf McGuinness and Seamus Brennan? How did they take the news when you told them, Jimmy?

Well, I told them in a private conference, earlier this morning, said Jimmy, and they were disappointed, of course they were, they want to play, of course they do, but young Shay Brennan, he said, That's all right by us, Boss, you know best. Just give us a ticket for Wembley and we'll be shouting our heads off for the other lads!

Then Jimmy turned away, took out and lit a fag, yet another fag, and with his other hand inside his jacket pocket, his beads back in his hand, between his fingers, Jimmy muttered, May God forgive me, please.

*

Bolton Wanderers were used to being the Bad Guys, the team no one wants to win, the nation hopes will lose. In 1953, it was Blackpool the whole world wanted to win, watching on their brand-new televisions, bought ready for the Coronation, that so-called 'Matthews Final', when Bolton were actually three–one up at one point, still winning three–two with three minutes to go, before they obliged the country and duly lost four–three. But that was then, and this time Bolton, its club and its people, they seemed in no mood for any form of sentiment –

On Cup Final day, wrote in one reader to the *Bolton Evening News*, I hope Bolton will beat Manchester United to a frazzle! I shall be hoping for a blow that will shatter the prayers of the distinctly unhealthy and morbid sensation mongers whose sentimental partisanship is no more than wallowing in momentary misery.

I am really disgusted with the day-by-day sentiments expressed by the national press about Manchester United, wrote in another. If Bolton do win, the papers will say they beat a poor team, but if they lose, the Munich to Wembley team will be toasted everywhere. All I can say is, 'Carry on Bolton, get 'em beat and bring the Cup back to Bolton!'

In the weeks leading up to the Final, such letters filled the *Bolton Evening News*, railing at the national mood, the emotions on display. Even Alderman Vickers, the Labour leader on Bolton Council, felt compelled to say, While I am sure everyone in our town is very sorry about the disaster which overcame Manchester United, we would remind people that at Winter Hill, near Bolton, there was a similar disaster which left forty orphaned children in the Isle of Man, and little national coverage was focused on this tragic event. In other words, let us not have emotional sentiment at Wembley, but football!

In this, Alderman Vickers was supported by Alderman Taylor, the Conservative leader, who agreed, As things stand, there is a real danger that Bolton Wanderers will be playing the rest of the country!

Some of those fellows who died at Munich, said Nat Lofthouse, the captain of Bolton Wanderers, they were among my pals. Just a few weeks before the disaster, I was having a drink with them at Old Trafford, after they had thrashed us seven–two!

*

There had been singing on the team bus again, jokes returning to the dressing room, pranks at the Norbreck Hydro. It was Dennis and Albert who had brought back the songs, the jokes and pranks; it was Dennis who led the singing on the bus back from Highbury after beating Fulham in the replay, bursting into the 'Manchester United Calypso'. Once again it was no longer wise to leave your shoes out for a shine in the corridor overnight. Even Bobby had bounced up and down on Ronnie Cope's bed, used it as a trampoline, until Ronnie woke up and Bobby remembered, then Bobby didn't speak for a week.

But then the Boss came back, frail on his sticks, a haunted, sickly king, and the clock went back, the jokes, the pranks, the songs all stopped. You never knew when the Boss would turn up again, and you didn't want him to hear you laugh, to see you smile.

And here he was, he came again, hobbling up the Norbreck steps, the Boss driven over, watched over and supported by Louis Edwards and Paddy McGrath –

You here again, Paddy, my old pal, said Jimmy, fresh from training, still in his training gear.

Here to help, said Paddy. You know me, Jimmy, and Matt, he wanted to come over . . .

Aye, Jimmy, said Matt, sitting down in a chair in the hotel bar, closing his eyes for a minute, catching his breath, then, opening his eyes again, he said, I thought we could have a wee chat about Wembley, Jimmy?

Of course, Matt, said Jimmy.

I see you've named the side, said Matt.

Aye, said Jimmy. I thought it best, the speculation, you know, it was getting to everyone.

Aye, said Matt. You've no doubt seen all this speculation about me and Wembley, too, whether I will be leading the team out or not. There's some people saying it'll make the whole thing too emotional, if I do.

Well, that's bollocks is that, said Jimmy. Every Wembley occasion is an emotional one. The bands, the singing, the Cup

448

at stake, what else could it be? But it would be the grandest day of all for me, if you would lead the team out, side by side with me, Matt.

I'd love to lead my team out, with you alongside me, Jimmy. But it's a long walk, a long stretch from that dressing room to the centre circle. I'll only know on Saturday morning, when the doctor tells me yes or no.

Well, let's hope it's yes then, said Jimmy, and we can walk out together, side by side.

Aye, said Matt.

Jimmy nodded, Jimmy smiled at Matt, and Matt nodded, smiled back at Jimmy as there they sat, in the sudden silence, the afternoon shadows of that hotel bar, until Louis Edwards coughed, then said, Why don't me and Paddy go take a walk outside, Matt, while you and Jimmy have your chat about that other thing?

What other thing, said Jimmy, but Louis Edwards and Paddy McGrath were already walking away.

Matt leaned slowly, still painfully forward, patted Jimmy on his arm as he said, It's nothing so dramatic, Jimmy. You know Louis, know Paddy.

Yeah, said Jimmy, I do.

Well, they tell me there are rumours about you being offered other jobs, you know, a manager's job?

There are always rumours, said Jimmy. That's football. Football is a house of rumours. Gives the hangers-on something to do, to talk about.

So there's no truth, then, in these stories that there are two big clubs coming in for you, Jimmy, one in the North, one in the South? Maybe a few others, too?

They may want me, said Jimmy, for all I know, but I've had no calls from anyone, and if I did, I would tell you straight. But I'm not interested, Matt, I'm not.

This time in charge, it's not whetted your appetite then, asked Matt, his cheek resting on his hand.

No, nor the Welsh job either, said Jimmy, then he smiled, laughed a little, then said, You know, Matt, the other week, Wales were playing Northern Ireland at Ninian Park, and I should have been there, I know, but it was the same night that we were playing Portsmouth away, and I just couldn't leave the boys, and so I called up the Welsh FA, asked to be released for that match, and of course they said yes, of course . . .

Matt swallowed, he sighed, then said, It's a good job you didn't ask them to release you for the Israel game, or you'd have been on that plane with me.

I know, said Jimmy, I know, and poor Bert would be here today, not me, and I think about that every day, many times each day, but that's why I could never leave, Matt. My heart is at Old Trafford, and all I want to do is to help you pick up the pieces, Matt, and start all over again, just like we did in 1946.

*

This was the best place in the world, thought Bobby, the sauna at the Norbreck Hydro. He'd sit in here and sweat and sweat; sweat out all the dirt, the tiredness, all the impurities and weaknesses, all those things he did not like, but best of all, it was a place cut off, within these wooden walls, it was a world apart, a place where no one but the players came, a world where no one made demands on him, up close and in his face, all those people now who thought they knew him, like they somehow even owned him, not just Bobby but the club itself, the 'nation's team', so every newspaper, every broadcaster now said, a piece of public property, a piece of which, a piece of him, everybody seemed to want, want and expect. But not in here, within these wooden walls, sweating out all that nonsense, all that shit, cut off and set apart, all on his own.

Bolton had got the jump on United, they had booked the hotel nearest to Wembley Stadium, gone down to London early, planned to have a walk out on the Wembley pitch on Friday, get a feel for the ground, a touch of the turf.

Meanwhile, United were still checking out of the Norbreck Hydro, getting on a coach to Crewe, then the train down to London, sat in a blazing-hot dining car, exhausted before they even got on the coach out to their hotel in Weybridge, and all along the way, this long, hot journey north to south, Matt travelled with the team, in his sunglasses, with his stick, sat at the front, not saying much, if anything at all, and all along the way, people crowded in around their Blackpool coach, their London train, their Weybridge coach, whenever, wherever people glimpsed, they saw them, wishing them well, cheering them on, banging on windows, banging on doors, and so when they finally, finally reached their hotel out in Weybridge, all of the players, the staff alike, they went straight up to their rooms and collapsed on their beds, all except the lads who had not been picked, who would not play, they went back outside with Albert for a round or two of crazy golf, but the lads back inside, up in their rooms, exhausted on their beds, the lads who had been picked, who would walk out of that tunnel onto that Wembley pitch, shake hands with royalty and then play tomorrow in the FA Cup Final, watched by one hundred thousand people in that stadium, watched by millions on their television sets, millions who wanted them, expected them to win, those lads, most of those lads, they found it hard to sleep.

*

Hark, the voices of history gather, thought Geoff, listened to them say, Every side beaten at Wembley one year, who then returns the next, they win: Preston North End in 1938; Charlton Athletic in 1947; Manchester City twice, in fact, in 1934 and in 1956. Last May, the Manchester United of old were the hottest favourites for many years but were surprised, beaten, some would say robbed by Aston Villa. But if United were to continue this tradition, the strange trick of losing one year, winning then the next, then Geoff knew most of the world beyond Bolton, beyond football, too, would be delirious with joy. But under Matt Busby's old pal Bill Ridding, Geoff also knew Bolton Wanderers were a hard, solid side who would be only spurred to greater efforts by the nation's sentiment, its sympathy for Manchester, only for United. The Wanderers had the England goalkeeper Hopkinson, a sure-footed defence built around the craggy, granite rock of Higgins and, of course, up at centre-forward, the lion-hearted Lofthouse. But if Nat sat deep, brought Holden and Birch on the flanks into play, created space for the inside-forwards, Stevens and Parry, then they may very well be able to press home a Bolton victory. Geoff worried that United had won only one of their last fourteen League games, that they had a weakness on the wings in Dawson and in Webster, that Charlton may well be wasted as a centre-forward, that the famous Wembley turf, it drained and sapped the best of men, in the best of form, and could likely prove a pitch too far, a game too soon for the return of Dennis Viollet to this new United side. Oh, what rot, what utter rot, said the voice on Geoff's shoulder, in Geoff's ear again. Have faith, dear boy, have faith. Destiny will play its last card in a Manchester win, you watch, you'll see. It will be the greatest human story in the history of sport. Yes, yes, thought Geoff, for Geoff knew, even to have got to Wembley in itself was a remarkable achievement. Incredible, frankly.

*

452

Back in Munich, at the Rechts der Isar Hospital, up on its fourth floor, on the morning of the Cup Final, the doctor came to tell Frank that he would be able to listen to the game that afternoon, that there would be highlights on German television, too, later on that day, and Frank nodded, smiled and thanked the doctor, but that morning, all that morning, Frank could not stop thinking of the Wembley press box, his pals who would not be there that day, that afternoon, who should be there, they should be there that day, Henry and Donny, Alf and Tom, Archie and George, Eric and Big Frank Swift, our Frank thinking of all the days, the times they had been there, all the games, the great games they had seen, Frank pushing his food, his breakfast, then his lunch around the plate, not hungry, not today, and after lunch, his wife Peggy, she said, Why don't we go down into the garden, dear, sit out in the sun for a while? There's time before the match.

Yes, said Frank, yes, a bit of sun, that would be nice, that would be good, and the orderlies, they lifted Frank from his bed into his wheelchair, then wheeled Frank out of Room 406, took Frank down in the elevator, Frank with sunglasses in his hand in case the sun was too strong, Peggy with blankets in her arms in case it was not, out onto the ground floor they went, past the hospital shops, the barber and the hairdresser, then out into the garden, to sit amid its lush, lush green, under its trees, beside its lawn, its flowerbeds, the pond with its water lilies and its ducks, Frank sat in his wheelchair, gazing at the lilies, then the crocuses, yellow, blue and lilac, until Frank felt his eyes begin to smart, to water, pool with tears –

Hello there, Frank, said Father Angelo, the always cheerful, friendly young Australian Franciscan monk who had been so kind to Frank these past long weeks, who had visited, sat and talked of sport with Frank, but who today saw the concern on Peggy's face, the anguish across Frank's own, the tears in his eyes, and Father Angelo said, he asked, What's wrong, Frank?

Oh, I don't know, said Frank, sniffed Frank. I was just thinking about the other boys. How they never got to see the flowers, see the spring this year . . .

Father Angelo, he smiled, he looked at Frank, the kindness of his heart in the kindness of his eyes, he smiled again and said, Oh, don't you worry, Frank. They will be in a far, far better place than this.

*

It was always quiet in the towns, the cities on the afternoon of the Cup Final. Half the shops, they shut, what was the point in staying open, what with no one about, that quiet you could hear a pin drop, the towns, the cities, they were like ghost towns, they were that dead. But that was how most days felt for many of the families of the Dead, many of the survivors, their families, their loved ones, too, that the game was always already happening somewhere else, played by someone else.

There was no somewhere else, no someone else for them, it was only here, only him for the loved ones left behind. The stares in the street, the sudden silences in shops, the whispered chatter when they left the shop and walked on, You know her husband, he was Roger Byrne, Geoff Bent or Mark Jones, their son was Liam Whelan, Tommy Taylor, Eddie Colman, David Pegg or Duncan Edwards. No, not *the* Duncan Edwards? What, you know another one? Oh, the poor thing, you wonder how they cope, you really do, you can't imagine how.

The times they'd think, they'd swear they heard Tommy's or David's car coming up the road, Eddie through the door, and Liam shouting, Mammy, I'm home.

The double take, the corner of the eye, a trick of the light, if that's what it was, the coat on the peg, the foot on their stair, in the dusk, the twilight, here –

454

Gladstone liked to go out into the light, the air, knew Duncan loved the open air, the countryside, they both preferred to be outdoors, so come rain, come shine, every day Gladstone walked to Queen's Cross Cemetery, spent the day among the stones, the flowers and the grass, tending to the graves of his daughter and his son.

But Annie, she preferred to stay indoors, behind the doors, in their front room, with the photographs on the wall: young Duncan with a cheeky grin, a soldier in his uniform, one with Molly on his arm, one in his red United shirt. His shirts, his England caps, his medals and his plaques, Annie kept them all in a glass cabinet in the room, the souvenirs he'd brought back from his trips abroad, his fishing tackle, an old cricket bat, the solid rubber ball he'd kicked before he walked, even the five-pound note he'd given Annie that last time he came back, she kept them all, looked at and after them all, all day long, day in, day out, she sat among them all, these things he'd worn, he'd touched, these things he was. But each light tap upon the window, the branch of a tree, a drop of rain, a flake of snow, it always made her turn, still made her look, still made her hope –

*

Harry would not have been surprised had he turned around on that coach to Wembley and seen the lads sitting there. That was the feeling he still had about it, three months on. They should have been there. They were taken away that quickly and suddenly, it hadn't really sunk in, just didn't seem right, seem fair. They should be here.

Bill wished he wasn't here, was anywhere but here, on this hot and sweaty, silent bus, the Boss sat back down the front with Jimmy once again, the journey to Wembley taking so long, so bloody long, thought Bill, Why are we going the bloody long way round? But the whole week had seemed so long, those Blackpool hours, Blackpool days stretched out, with too much time to dwell, to think, to doubt and start to feel a sense, Bill felt a sense of gloom, impending gloom, only deepened, thickened by the presence of the Boss, hobbling on his stick, crooked, grey and old, trailing with him in his wake the Dead, the Dead, stirring the memories of all those friends Bill had lost on that field of snow that terrible Munich afternoon, those mates he'd never, never see again.

Before kick-off, some of the families, the loved ones of the Dead, they came into the dressing room to see the players, to wish them luck, the best of luck, and Bobby would remember Mister and Missus Pegg were there, and how he promised he would score a goal for David, and one for Eddie, Eddie's mam and dad, his girl Marjorie, they were all there, too, and Marjorie seemed so full of life, trying to gee everybody up she was, but then in came the Boss with Ted Dalton and his stick, looking pale, exhausted, worn out still, and the Boss, he said, Thank you for everything you have given the club, and just remember all the things that Jimmy's said, but that was all he said, then again, he never did say that much, If you weren't good enough, you wouldn't be here, or maybe, Up together, back together, pretty much all he ever said, and then the Boss was gone again, helped out by Ted Dalton to shake the hand of the Duke of Edinburgh, and then, to a great ovation, he took his seat behind the bench where Jimmy and Jack would soon be sat, as the strains of 'Abide with Me', sung by a choir of one hundred thousand voices, now began to echo round the dressing room, and quieter, more sombre than he ever usually was, had ever been before, Jimmy swallowed, coughed, then said, Now then, lads, the fact that you have got this far is a miracle. All I want to tell you is, thank you from the bottom of my heart for all you have done. This is the last hurdle now, but win, lose or draw, I am proud of you all.

After the Match, Before the Match

The next day, when Bolton Wanderers returned through Manchester and Salford, it was like Cheyenne country. Hooligans stoned the Happy Wanderers with clogs, tomatoes and bags of flour. But as United's train went north, thousands and thousands came out to every station on the line, all cheering and clapping, waving their red scarves, and when United finally reached London Road, seventy, eighty thousand lined the streets of the city, and in Albert Square, where a reception was to be held at the Town Hall, the crowd of twenty, thirty thousand chanted, WE WANT MATT! WE WANT MATT! WE WANT MATT! And Stan Crowther could not believe his eyes, and he shouted to Bill, Bloody hell, imagine if we'd fucking won, and Bill smiled, but then Bill turned away, caught Bobby's eye, and their eyes, they said, Imagine if we'd never crashed.

Author's Note

I am aware that 'Munichs' is sometimes used as a term of mockery or abuse against supporters of Manchester United, particularly by supporters of their Northern rivals. This, along with similarly abusive references to Heysel and Hillsborough, directed towards supporters of Liverpool Football Club, is one of the things that sickens me most about modern football. One of my intentions in calling the novel *Munichs* is to confront this head-on. I would defy anyone to read this novel and then ever use 'Munichs' as an insult again.

Many supporters of United may profoundly disagree with me, particularly given that I don't support the club, but I strongly believe the term should be reclaimed and worn as a badge of pride, a symbol that this football club did not go under, that they were not defeated by the terrible events of February 6, 1958, and that this, above all else, is what sets Manchester United apart from all other football clubs.

Sources and Acknowledgements

This book is a work of fiction, a novel. The following books all helped to inspire this novel, but, in chronological order, these particular books have been invaluable –

Matt . . . United . . . and Me by Jimmy Murphy, 1968.
The Charlton Brothers by Norman Harris, 1971.
The Munich Air Disaster by Stanley Williamson, 1972.
Soccer at the Top by Matt Busby, 1973.
The Team That Wouldn't Die by John Roberts, 1975.
The Day a Team Died by Frank Taylor, 1983.
Matt Busby by Harold Riley, 1987.
A Strange Kind of Glory by Eamon Dunphy, 1991.
Harry's Game by Harry Gregg, 2002.
Jack & Bobby by Leo McKinstry, 2002.
Starmaker by Brian Hughes, 2002.
Manchester United in Europe by Ken Ferris, 2004.
Best and Edwards by Gordon Burn, 2006.
The Lost Babes by Jeff Connor, 2006.
My Manchester United Years by Bobby Charlton, 2007.
Manchester's Finest by David Hall, 2008.
United in Triumph and Tragedy by Bill Foulkes, 2008.
When You Put on a Red Shirt by Keith Dewhurst, 2009.
Duncan Edwards by James Leighton, 2012.
The Men Who Were the Busby Babes by Tom Clare, 2012.
Manchester United 1958–68 by Iain McCartney, 2013.
Manchester United in Tears by J. Paul Harrison, 2017.
Sir Matt Busby by Patrick Barclay, 2017.

The Day Two Teams Died by Roy Cavanagh and Carl Abbot, 2018.
Jimmy Murphy by Wayne Barton, 2018.

And then, alphabetically –

After the Ball by Nobby Stiles, 2003.
Air Disasters by Stanley Stewart, 1986.
The Anatomy of Manchester United by Jonathan Wilson, 2017.
Building the Dynasty by Iain McCartney, 2015.
The Busby Babes by Max Arthur, 1998.
Busby's Last Crusade by Jeff Connor, 2020.
Cissie by Cissie Charlton with Vince Gledhill, 1988.
The Devil Casts His Net: The Winter Hill Air Disaster by Stephen
    R. Morrin, 2005.
Does Your Rabbi Know You're Here? by Anthony Clavane,
    2012.
Don Davies by Jack Cox, 1962.
Eternal: Duncan Edwards by Wayne Barton, 2023.
The Football Man by Arthur Hopcraft, 1968.
From Goal Line to Touchline by Jack Crompton, 2008.
Johnny, the Forgotten Babe by Neil Berry, 2007.
Life and Death in the Balkans by Bato Tomašević, 2008.
Manchester, a Football History by Gary James, 2008.
The Manchester Compendium by Ed Glinert, 2009.
Manchester United by Percy M. Young, 1960.
Manchester United, a Thematic Study edited by David L.
    Andrews, 2004.
Manchester United in Europe by David Meek and Tom Tyrrell,
    2002.
Manchester United, Man and Babe by Wilf McGuinness, 2008.
Manchester United, the Betrayal of a Legend by Michael Crick
    and David Smith, 1989.
Manchester United, the Biography by Jim White, 2008.

Manchester United, Thirty Memorable Games from the Fifties by
    Iain McCartney, 2010.
The Munich Air Disaster by Stephen R. Morrin, 2007.
My Autobiography by Tom Finney, 2003.
My England Years by Bobby Charlton, 2008.
My Father and Other Working-Class Football Heroes by Gary
    Imlach, 2005.
My Life in Football by Sir Bobby Charlton, 2009.
Pardon Me for Living by Geoffrey Green, 1985.
Parkinson on Football by Michael Parkinson, 2001.
Portrait of Manchester by Michael Kennedy, 1970.
Red Voices by Stephen F. Kelley, 1999.
Reliving the Dream by Derick Allsop, 1998.
Sir Walter Winterbottom by Graham Morse, 2016.
Soccer in the Fifties by Geoffrey Green, 1974.
There's Only One United by Geoffrey Green, 1978.
Tommy Taylor by Brian Hughes, 1996, 2020.
Two Brothers by Jonathan Wilson, 2022.
The United Tour of Manchester by Iain McCartney and Tom
    Clare, 2013.

The following documentaries, newspaper, journal and online articles were also a great help –

British Pathé newsreels, March to May 1958.
The Times, March to May 1958.
Manchester Evening News, March to May 1958.
'Great Sorrow – Grief at Loss of Mark Jones', *South Yorkshire
    Times*, 1958.
The Busby Babes: End of a Dream, ITV, 1998.
'Les Olive', obituary, David Meek, *Guardian*, 2006.
Munich Remembered, BBC, 2008.
Sir Bobby Remembers Munich, BBC, 2008.

'Memories of Doncaster's Very Own Busy Babe', Peter Whittell, *Doncaster Free Press*, 2008.

'Presses Stopped in Manchester', Richard Williams, *Guardian*, 2008.

'Donny Davies', Richard Williams, *Guardian*, 2008.

'"Personality and Color into Everything He Does": Henry Rose (1899–1958)', David Dee, *Journal of Sport History*, fall 2014.

'Unlucky Boys of Red: The Funeral of Liam Whelan, 1958', Donal, Come Here to Me!, comeheretome.com, 2018.

'Liam Whelan: Remembering the Irish Busby Babe', Anthony Pyne, RTÉ Sport, 2018.

'About Bert Whalley', Mark Metcalf, Gary James' Football Archive, gjfootballarchive.com, 2021.

'Tommy Taylor, the Greatest Center-Forward', Steve Todd, greatreddevils.com.

'The Blackest Day of All', England Football Online, englandfootballonline.com.

I would also like to thank Angus Cargill and Ruth O'Loughlin at Faber & Faber; Andrew Fitzsimons for his invaluable advice on Dublin and Dublinese; and all my family and friends, home and away, living and dead.